REGENERATION

Also by Stephanie Saulter

Gemsigns
Binary

REGENERATION
STEPHANIE SAULTER

ⓇEVOLUTION BOOK 3

Jo Fletcher
BOOKS

First published in Great Britain in 2015 by

Jo Fletcher Books
an imprint of
Quercus Publishing Ltd
Carmelite House
50 Victoria Embankment
London EC4Y 0DZ

An Hachette UK company

TPB ISBN 978 1 78206 022 2
EBOOK ISBN 978 1 78429 941 5

10 9 8 7 6 5 4 3 2 1

Typeset by CC Book Production
Printed and bound in Great Britain by Clays Ltd, St Ives plc

For the children of revolution,
who build in the ruins

'What is REAL?' asked the Rabbit one day, when they were lying side by side near the nursery fender, before Nana came to tidy the room. 'Does it mean having things that buzz inside you and a stick-out handle?'

'Real isn't how you are made,' said the Skin Horse. 'It's a thing that happens to you. When a child loves you for a long, long time, not just to play with, but REALLY loves you, then you become Real.'

'Does it hurt?' asked the Rabbit.

'Sometimes,' said the Skin Horse, for he was always truthful. 'When you are Real you don't mind being hurt.'

The Velveteen Rabbit, Margery Williams

SINKAT

1

It is a rare thing, to see change coming. Embracing it is rarer still. We cling to the past even as we dream of the future, fearing always that what might be gained cannot make up for what must be lost. Those few who have an instinct for metamorphosis know only too well how bitterly it can be resisted, how unlikely it is for evolution to occur without struggle. They know that transition is most often an ungentle business, and that many weapons can be employed against it.

They know there will be casualties.

Among those few are a man and a woman: friends, lovers, partners: pillars of strength and dispensers of wisdom, although the latter is in short supply at the moment. They have received unwelcome news, though it may shed light on much else that troubles them; and so they grapple with it, trying to understand what it means and how it fits.

The man knows the woman is better at this than he is. For all his scholarship and training and experience, for all that he has been proven right far more often than otherwise, she has a gestalt gift that he cannot match. As he watches her framed against the city's skyline he knows that she is sifting through the cacophony of pending events, looking for connections, parallels, patterns.

Her perch is precarious, for she has eschewed the comfort of a chair, sitting instead in a window open to the cold, blustery air. Only here, in her particular space, can the glass panels be thrown open to permit this. The resulting gap in the skin of the tower is a couple of hundred feet above the ground, yet she dangles there unconcerned. He watches the dappling of shade and sunshine across her features just as she watches the clouds chasing each other across the sky. He has seen inspiration strike her before, is accustomed to the swift confidence of her decisions, so he waits patiently for the quirk of a smile that will tell him she has a plan, and a part for him in it.

It surprises him, the weary way in which she turns her back into the wind that gusts around her. He has spent hours, days, years gazing at that face, mapping its moods and memorising every expression. Only now does he notice that the laughter lines around her eyes no longer disappear when she is solemn. He wonders at what precise moment that happened, and how he could have missed it, and is filled with relief when the downcast gaze flicks up to hold his and he sees that they remain the same deep delphinium blue as the autumn sky behind her. The sun sails clear of clouds, though only for a moment, and the great span of her wings opens wide against the exterior of the glass as though to soak up every iota of warmth. Their shadow falls towards him even as the light glancing off them throws a shimmering bronze-gold aureole against the glazing above her head. It looks for all the world like a halo.

He knows better.

'It might be no more than coincidence,' she says thoughtfully, distractedly, as though her mind is still out among the clouds. 'We knew this would happen eventually. It may just be chance that it's happening now.'

'That's more plausible than the alternative,' he replies, equally thoughtful. 'But then again . . .'

'We are dealing with someone who defies plausibility, I know.'

'Could she be aware of Gabriel's involvement?'

'It's possible – more possible than I like to think. But the main incentives there are wealth and power.'

'She's not one to miss an opportunity for either.'

He knows it is an unnecessary reminder. They are quiet for longer than he can bear.

'So,' he says finally, and thinks as he says it how many times over the years he has directed these same words to this same woman, but never before wondered whether she would have an answer, 'what are you going to do?'

She takes her time replying. She does this with him now: takes her time, lets him see her pondering. He can remember when she would have replied quickly, glibly if necessary, rather than risk any suspicion that she was less than certain of her next move. It is part of the legend of Aryel Morningstar that she is never in doubt.

And yet doubt is what he sees in the slump of her shoulders and the tired twitch of her wings in the sunlight; it is what he hears in her voice, when she finally speaks.

'Learn more,' she says. 'Trust that Mikal can manage his side of things. And warn those who need to be warned. Money matters, but it's not all she cares about.'

The same cold wind that gusted around Aryel, finding its way inside the skin of the Bel'Natur tower and sending a chill trickling down Eli Walker's spine, also tugged at a front door several miles away. The door opened onto a high street that sloped gently in the direction of the river and quayside. Behind it, a narrow corridor transected the ground floor of a building that, like its neighbours, had recently been renovated. It now housed a popular café that would be bustling come the lunch hour, and a small grocery that was already seeing a steady stream of shoppers. Stacked above were two storeys of living accommodation. A staircase at the far end of the corridor led up to a spacious flat; beside it, another door opened onto a walled back garden.

Gaela was clearing away the remains of a late breakfast. She knew that the back door must be ajar when she heard the front, which would normally have been closed gently, slam shut.

A voice floated up through the window overlooking the street. 'Sorry! Wind got it!'

The shout was followed by the sound of footsteps hurrying away. Gaela glanced out the back window, surveying the garden. At first she saw no one. She pushed the window open, leaned out and scanned the enclosed space. With most of the summer flowers finished the visual onslaught had lessened a bit, but there were enough roses left to blaze warm in her specialised sight, and the ultraviolet starburst patterns on the blossoms of a few wandering geranium clumps threatened to make her seasick if she stared at them too long. Not many bees would be following the invisible nectar trail today, and any that did venture out would struggle to settle on the wind-tossed blooms.

Gaela was looking for a different signature; it took only a second or two to spot the small figure, crouched in a far corner of the garden between the shrubs, no doubt investigating earthworms or beetles. There was a flicker of heat and a flash of human-shaped ultraviolet from the bright white jumper as the child wearing it looked towards the house and waved.

Gaela waved back, sighing ruefully at her daughter's ill-judged clothing choice as she straightened up and closed the window. The jumper would be patchily dirt-coloured by lunchtime.

I'm not going to be able to tell her what to wear for much longer anyway, Gaela thought. *She barely listens as it is.*

She must have slipped out, sliding past her bleary-eyed father as Bal went downstairs to open up. She was the only one in the family not moving slowly this morning. They'd all been so busy recently: first the flurry of preparation, then the party. Gaela yawned. The day intended for a little bit of cleanup and a lot of relaxation hadn't quite worked out the way she'd planned; there had been far less of the latter and far more of the former.

Gabriel deserved the celebration, though. Maybe it was only natural for the boy to be this focused; gems of his parents' generation had been bred and trained under the indenture system, which did not permit an idle adolescence. They'd had to work from the onset of puberty, or even earlier, if their gemtech masters had judged their bodies and brains robust enough. So while Bal and Gaela and others bringing up their children in freedom would never allow them to labour so hard or so young, they didn't share the norm presumption of juvenile ineptitude.

But they had not anticipated that their son would turn out to be quite so diligent, or so accomplished.

This morning he was off to college for a couple of hours – not to take a class, but to present his own work for Thames Tidal Power as a case study in media management. He had confessed matter-of-factly that the junior students selected to take part in the workshop would most likely be his age, or even older. He'd get senior academic credits for the presentation and background work; they'd earn standard ones for showing up and paying attention. Then he'd return to the project office at Sinkat, back to the serious business of quietly transforming the city, and keeping its citizens mostly happy about it.

She crossed the room, still musing, and poked her head out

the front window to look up the street. The wind whipped her flame-red, faintly glowing hair over her face and she scraped it back, fumbling for a clasp. Gabriel was long out of even her sight, but he'd messaged a link and she'd promised to review it before he got home that evening.

Habit made her scan the street before she pulled back inside, turning her head slowly, letting her enhanced visual cortex process the scene, alert for anything out of place, any hidden source of radiation that might hint at surveillance . . . or danger. She saw a delivery van pulling up outside, a few people walking past, the usual heat signatures and tablet flashes and the faintly organic warmth of quantum-storage panels on the new building down the street. The current fashion was for autumn coats in vivid colours with UV-reflective surfaces that no one else could see but whose brightness made her wince. There was a man on the corner in a blessedly dull old waterproof, his shoulders hunched. Another van . . .

Her attention swung back to the man. Why would he just be standing there in the teeth of this wind?

As if sensing her stare, he stepped off the kerb and strode smartly away, cutting sharply in towards the buildings and moving out of sight in a heartbeat. Maybe he'd paused to get his bearings; he must be as eager to get out of the wind as she was. She pulled the window shut and glanced into the back garden again. Eve had emerged from the shrubbery and was now sprawled along the low, lichen-covered branch of an ancient apple tree, nose buried in her tablet. The sight made her smile.

Nothing to worry about, Gaela.

She could hear Bal downstairs, heaving barrels into the cellar. She could offer to help, whereupon he would roll his eyes and remind her that they weighed at least as much as she did. Instead, she picked up her own tablet, sank into a chair with a view of the garden and swiped up Gabriel's assignment.

She had barely begun to read when the tablet hummed in her hands and her earset pinged an incoming call. Noting with surprise the comcode that flashed onscreen, she tapped to receive. Perhaps the caller had forgotten that Gabe would be in late today.

'Morning. If you're looking for the boy wonder—'

'No.' The man's voice in her ear sounded as worried as the face that was now on her screen. 'I was looking for you. Something strange is going on down here, Gaela. We need your help.'

Mikal Varsi stifled a sigh, almost reflexively converting it into a rueful, slightly knowing smile. This generally flummoxed troublesome interviewers into wondering whether his grasp of whatever subject they were grilling him about was in fact more comprehensive than their own. More often than not, their suspicions were correct. Given that finding ways to mildly assert one's competence was a core skill for any gem in public life, he usually felt entirely sanguine about it.

Today, though, he was painfully aware of his own uncertainties.

The man sitting across from him shifted and cleared his throat. Robert Trench was short by norm standards – which made him *very* short compared to Mikal – and comfortably rotund. His hairline had receded drastically over the past decade, but he obviously hadn't lost the tendency to go red in the face when he felt particularly strongly about something. The effect, Mikal reflected, was not unlike one of the glowing gillung marker buoys deployed in the waters of Sinkat.

He raised a hand to try and forestall the next volley of persuasion, idly flexing the thumbs on either side of his palm, but Rob was undeterred.

'The synergy would be perfect. You already have a history of working together. It would reinforce our mutual commitment to integration, cement the association with the UPP . . . The way things are going, we all need to, you know, consolidate our positions.' He looked pleadingly at Mikal.

'I understand your concerns, and I share a lot of them. But there are other considerations as well.'

'You're not seriously planning to form a new party, are you? Please say you're not. That's *such* a bad . . . I mean, it could really weaken us . . .'

'I doubt strengthening the UPP would be a priority for a rival group,' Mikal said drily.

'That's precisely my point: the United People's Party stands for inclusion, you know that. They supported emancipation, they won the argument on universal suffrage, they've encouraged gem entrepreneurship and technology – they're keeping the reactionary element at bay. Public opinion is generally moving in the right direction, but it's cost the UPP support, especially outside the cities, and the gem vote only partly offsets that loss. Diverting it to a minor party would be a gift to the Trads. Why would you do that?'

'It's not my proposal. I've been approached. I'm not sold on the idea, but I said I would give it some thought, and that's what I'm doing.'

'But what's the point? Why not just join us?'

Mikal shrugged. 'Because for all that it's the liberal wing of contemporary politics, the UPP is still a bastion of privileged norms who have a stake in things not being disrupted any more than they already have been.' He caught Rob's gaze and held it. 'You know this. It's true that they've been good to us, but there's a suspicion that not being able to take us for granted is what keeps them that way.'

'I . . . Okay, so let's say there's something to that. For the sake of argument.' Rob looked down, breaking eye contact, sucking air in through his teeth with a faint hiss. 'If the gem community throws its support behind some new group, one that's only going to be looking out for their interests . . .'

'It wouldn't. At least, not if I were involved.'

'You think norms will see it that way? Even with your involvement? They mostly like and respect you, Mik, but not *that* much. Not enough. And the UPP would have to respond to their concerns.'

'So.' Mikal steepled his three-fingered, double-thumbed hands under his chin and glared at Rob. 'My choices are to join the UPP and risk becoming ineffectual, or to back an alternative and be thought of as the enemy.'

'I'm not . . . That's a bit dramatic . . .' Rob appeared to wilt slightly. 'Look, you're worried about whether they'll continue to prioritise gem issues? Well, they'd *really* have no reason to then. Neither of us wants that to happen.'

'There's a third option. I could stay the hell out of it, stay independent. I've won two elections that way. The UPP never wanted me until there was something in it for them.'

'You know that's not true, Mik. You could have joined any time—'

'*Could have*, yes. There's a difference between not shutting the door in my face – probably – and sending a parade of ever-more-impressive delegates to try and talk me into it.' He appraised the other man thoughtfully. 'What are they scared of, Rob?'

He threw his hands up in exasperation. 'What do you think? They're afraid of losing the next election. What happened last time wasn't a fluke, Mik. The Trads are starting to gain ground. It's one thing to have you and a few other indies scattered here and there, but most gems end up voting UPP because the only other option is a Trad candidate. If another progressive party emerges and splits the vote, they could very well end up winning. Then where would you be?'

'Thirteen years is a long time,' Mikal mused. 'The UPP is in its third term in government, and if they did manage to get in again . . . Two decades of the same party in power isn't great for democracy, is it?'

'It's the reason we've been able to build the kind of society in which I can be sitting here now having this conversation with you. You think we'd be better off with the people who opposed the Declaration and voting rights, who still oppose funding for reproductive and educational support, back in charge?'

'Probably not, but me joining the UPP wouldn't prevent it. And a new party might happen anyway, no matter what I do. I told you, it's not my idea.' He drummed his fingers lightly on the tabletop, still thinking. 'Which begs the question, really. How much of this desperation to get me on board is because of Thames Tidal?'

'A lot.' Rob looked straight at him, and this time his gaze did not waver. 'A *lot*.'

2

A sharp, season-shifting breeze cut facets across the water's surface, turning it from tea-dark choppiness into a shimmering kaleidoscope of mirror-bright wavelets every time the sun sailed out from behind a cloud. Gabriel, scanning the normally flat pool of Sinkat Basin as he strode across a footbridge, winced at the glare and came to a halt, leaning against the railing. There were fewer boats than usual casting their shadows over the water, and even fewer people to be seen on the quays. He was used to arriving much earlier, when residents of the amphibious neighbourhood were still bustling to work themselves.

He knew the basin was likely to be as quiet as the quayside at this hour, but still he directed his gaze straight down. As his eyes adjusted he felt the pull, hypnotic, drawing him below the first few light-dappled feet. Shadows shifted and moved down there, tempting him to try and identify something recognisable in the murky depths. Almost without realising it, he tapped at the thin wire that encircled his head. The background hum of stream-feeds, a barely sensed white-noise growl – the sensation for him of the cranial band on standby – winked out.

For a moment there was nothing in its place but true silence. Then he felt his own talent assert itself, whispers of thought and emotion sliding across each other like the echoes of distant

13

conversation. He bent over the railing, squinting into the water, concentrating hard. Something flickered across his consciousness: a blur of red twenty feet deep, sinuous and moving fast. It was as much a texture in his mind as anything he could have been sure of using his eyes alone.

He tilted his head, following as the red flicker curved towards the underwater entrance to Thames Tidal Power. The ovoid building sat at the terminus of the quay, all shiny, pearl-white curves soaring high above the hard edges of recycled stone and reinforced concrete, plunging down into the waves that lapped against it. Twelve convex wedges of tough, translucent thermal membrane, like the segments of a gigantic, elongated orange, were supported on a dense biopolymer scaffold embedded with the nanoscale capacitors of the company's quantum-battery technology. Two-thirds of the structure gleamed solid in the sunshine topside; the rest appeared to waver and flex in the dappling brown water below. The energy efficiency and seductively organic design of the building had made it famous, and celebrated. Gabriel felt a familiar surge of pride in his revolutionary workplace.

Just that morning he had ended up having to explain, again, that it was indeed his as much as anyone else's: the class found the cooperative concept both attractive and perplexing. He wanted to talk to Agwé about some of the things the students had said, and hoped she was on her way to the office. She'd been too distorted by the water for him to get more than a fleeting sense of presence, though he had no business feeling for her mind anyway.

He reluctantly pulled his awareness back – and it snagged on another mind, disconcertingly close beside him and with a familiar bite to it, knife-sharp, chilli-sharp, but overlaid with something that felt like toffee and marshmallows: a sticky, pillowy sweetness. He looked down, wondering whether the mood of the moment would be moon-faced self-possession or madcap silliness, and found his sister regarding him gravely.

'Hey. Where'd *you* come from?'

'*You* should know. Your band's off. How come you didn't know I was there?'

Gabriel resisted the urge to reach up and tap it guiltily back on. 'What makes you think I didn't?'

She gave him a look of pure scorn and turned to peer through the safety barrier, her cheeks squashed between the bridge's narrow, close-set balusters, the top of her head pressing up against the underside of the rail on which he was still leaning.

'You didn't,' she said, with a certainty that brooked no dissent. 'You were reading someone. In the water. I saw. *And*' – he could hear the needling tone come into her voice, probing, searching for a soft spot to poke at and annoy – '*you* didn't know I was there. You didn't hear me.'

'I wasn't listening for you, Eve.'

'Who were you listening for, then?'

'No one.'

'Then you should've been able to hear me. You *couldn't*!'

'I couldn't be bothered.'

'I am immune to your power!' She had lost interest in the water and was gripping the balusters tightly, the better to lean back at a precarious angle and peer up at him. Her dark eyes were alive with mischief now, under a tangle of summer-bleached blonde hair.

'I wish.' Gabriel started towards the quay and the topside entrance to the Thames Tidal building. Eve swung away from the rail to skip along beside him.

'You cannot hear what's in my head,' she declared, with as much pomposity as an eight-year-old could manage.

'That's 'cos there's nothing *in* your head, squirt.'

15

'Liar, liar! I'm *thinking* bad *thoughts*.' Eve hopped from one foot to the other, solemnity abandoned in favour of gleeful torment. Gabriel sighed theatrically at her. Her mind was indeed often as still and unruffled as Sinkat Basin itself, a slightly scary blankness beneath which he could sense half-formed thoughts and unfocused emotions morph and shift. But she had popped out of that tabula-rasa state with typical suddenness and now there was a distinctly Eve-flavoured refrain running through his own mind. He was relieved to note that her moral rebellion amounted, pretty much, to mentally reciting *bad thoughts bad thoughts bad thoughts* over and over.

'That's all you've got? Evie, that's just boring.'

'It's not boring. It's *bad*.'

'Bo-*ring*,' he repeated, as *Gabe is a doo-doo head* rang clear in his skull. She repeated the thought, watching him for a reaction. He considered mouthing the words back to prove he'd registered them, but decided against it; that was just as likely to encourage her. Instead he fell back on a disappointed head-shake, an attempt at unsmiling big-brother admonishment that had no effect whatsoever.

'*Yoouu* can't *heeaar* me,' Eve sang. She was in front of him now, skipping backwards and smirking. He tapped the cranial band back on. The hum settled in immediately, blurring out the fragments of nearby minds that washed through his brain the rest of the time.

'Okay, now I *half* can't hear you. Which is a relief, believe me. You can shut up with the other half any time you like.'

'*Gabe is a—*' she began, and then stopped abruptly, pouting. Gabriel shot his own triumphant smirk at her. She knew very well that the rude things she could get away with thinking were absolutely not permitted to be spoken out loud.

'You never answered my question. What are you doing down here? I thought Papa was going to be in the café all day.'

'He is. I came with Mama.' Eve pointed as they came up to the entrance. 'She's with Pilan, looking at something.'

'What kind of looking?'

'Her kind.'

They clattered down the short ramp that sloped gently from the end of the quay to the gillung entrance. The main doorway, an airlock, was currently unpressurised and riding just above the water's surface. Gabriel pressed a finger to the identipad while Eve fidgeted impatiently beside him. She darted ahead as the outer door hissed open, through the unsealed pressure chamber and into the airwalk passage beyond. 'They're along here, in the room where you work. I bet they've been *watching* us,' she said, for the internal photofilters of the biopolymer membrane were mostly set to transparent, and what looked like pearly translucence on the outside was from the inside clear as glass.

Mama would never have let you go without her if she couldn't watch you all the way into my care, he thought. *You are smart, Eve, and you know that.*

What he said was, 'Don't run,' reaching out to hook a finger into the back of her jumper as she surged forward. 'Eve, seriously. People live here.'

'They work here.'

'They also live here. And kicking up a racket where people work isn't okay either.' He released her as she fell into sullen step beside him and frowned down at the top of her head. She had been like this more and more lately: cocksure, mouthy, careless of others. He told himself it was just another phase in the mercurial, messy business of growing up, but underneath he felt a tinge of worry. Eve was no more an ordinary child than he himself had been, and the truth was that no one knew quite what to expect of her either.

Gaela looked up as they came into the main project office, a huge room organised into clusters of workstations that took up most of the first topside level. Gabriel wondered, from the appraising expression on her face as she glanced at Eve before meeting his own gaze, whether she had been having the same thought. With the cranial band now powered on, he couldn't tell.

Eve skipped over to Gaela, triumphantly declaring, 'I found him!' as she threw her arms around their mother.

'He wasn't exactly hidden,' Gaela responded drily, cuddling her daughter back and trying, and failing, to run a hand through Eve's hair. 'Though I guess your hairbrush is? Hi, honey.' This to Gabriel. 'We saw you on the far side of the quay—'

'*You* saw him,' Eve corrected, and Gaela sighed.

'Yes, Evie, I saw your brother and said you could go meet him, since it looked like you might spontaneously combust if you didn't.'

Gaela's comment drew chuckles from the people with her: a man and a woman of almost identical height, both with the long torsos, webbed digits and luminescent green hair characteristic of the gillung subspecies. Beyond that, the similarity faded. Pilan was barrel-chested and powerful, his copper-coloured skin contrasting sharply with his short, lime-bright locks. Lapsa was slender and seal-dark; her glowing shoulder-length ringlets were the deep shade of sea-grass. Her pregnant belly pressed her bodysuit proudly outwards.

Eve gave the comment a moment's tilt-headed consideration before silently ducking away to scramble onto a chair and peer at a screen on which an infographic was slowly morphing in response to incoming telemetry.

Gabriel slung his satchel onto a worktop. 'Hi Mama. Lapsa, Pilan. What's up?'

'Not much. Just some vid files Pilan thought I should take a look at.' There was a deliberate casualness to his mother's voice as she tucked her tablet away, and an exchange of glances between the other two, that told Gabriel she had let Eve go so they could speak privately, as well as get a moment's peace. He said nothing.

Pilan shrugged one brawny arm into the meshed utility vest that kept his tools and other kit organised and within easy reach underwater, and then clapped Gabriel on the shoulder. 'So how does it feel to be seventeen? We heard it was quite a party.'

'A lot like sixteen so far. The party was great, though.'

'Agwé was there,' Eve announced, without looking around.

Gabriel could think of no response except to glare at his sister; his mother would probably disapprove of him strangling her.

'She had a great time,' said Lapsa, watching him with amusement. 'Ready to get back to work?'

'Very ready,' he replied. Then, to Pilan, with a sideways glance at Eve, 'Anything I need to know?'

'It can wait until we get back.'

Lapsa slid her tablet into a pocket. Through the clear wall they could see a shuttle-boat preparing to head out to the estuary, and Gabriel blinked in surprise at the sight of Agwé, wearing a cherry-red bodysuit, leaping lightly on board with her vidcam slung over one shoulder.

'Just keep us looking good on the streams,' Pilan went on, following his gaze. 'Topsider attention's going to spike in the next few days.'

They all knew this; Gabriel could not imagine why Pilan felt it necessary to remind him. The look on his boss's face was unreadable. 'Thanks, Gaela,' Pilan added as the flame-haired woman started chivvying a reluctant Eve away from the monitor. 'I'll message you if there's anything else.'

And then he and Lapsa and his mother and Eve were gone, leaving Gabriel with the impression that deep and unseen currents had washed through the conversation.

There were enough messages waiting for him that he was able, for an hour or so, to push aside his curiosity. With the switch from storage- to supply-phase less than a week away, there was a rush on to make sure everything was done and checked and double-checked. A few months earlier, when installation of the turbines and battery banks was in full swing and the carping from rival firms, Trad politicians and random trolls had become increasingly frequent and frantic, Gabriel had feared that their opponents might succeed in delaying the launch, if not derailing it completely. Now a quick glance at the infographic that had captured Eve's attention confirmed that every indicator was green or, at worst, tinged with amber. The project looked to be right on target.

And that meant that while the engineers and technicians could expect to settle into a routine as they moved from the varied tasks of developing the plant to the regular rhythms of operation, his own workload was likely to increase in both volume and unpredictability – another good reason to have taken a few days off before the launch.

As he pulled up feeds and opened the bespoke monitoring apps Herran had helped him write, he could see that the constant murmur of stream chatter about Thames Tidal Power was already picking up. It was no more than he'd expected. He remembered Agwé's surprise, when the plan to extend the tidal turbine arrays that powered Sinkat and the Squats had first begun to leak out onto news and socialstreams, that the prospect of a cheaper source of cleanly generated, easily stored and infinitely sustainable energy had not been universally welcomed. That led to his mother consulting on security, especially for the two quantum-battery banks where vast energies were stored on either shore of the estuary, and to him having a series of increasingly intense discussions, first with Agwé herself, and then with Lapsa and Pilan, about how to manage the streams and deal with blowback from the public.

A year later and here he was, responsible for monitoring the random, usually ill-informed, frequently conspiracy-laden and sometimes hilarious socialstream commentary on Thames Tidal Power, while a publicity service managed the more sedate platforms of professional news coverage and planning-committee infostreams. He relished his role, enjoying the camaraderie of the largely gillung team and the sense of significance to what they were doing, and had not been surprised to discover that he had a gift for constructing perfectly pitched responses to slightly hysterical objections, or for inserting the right tone to turn some misinformed debate around. The cranial band might block his telepathy, but it could not take away what telepathy had taught him about people.

Now he seeded a few reassuring links into streams where environmental impact was being discussed, read an anxious post about the economic consequences of tidal energy for biomass agriculture and tagged it for follow-up, and rolled his eyes at a rambling screed warning of a secret gillung plot for world domination before reposting with an ironic comment that cast the whole thing as an exercise in bad comedy.

Immediate matters dealt with, he stretched, looked around and let himself wonder what vid files could have been troubling enough to bring his mother down here on such short notice – and with Eve. Something Agwé had shot? But in that case, surely he'd have been the first to know?

It struck him that the project office, like the basin outside, was quieter than usual. Pilan was not the only engineer missing, and there was nothing in the schedule to explain their absence – could they all be out in the estuary? Why? Surely all the work out there was done?

He called the infographic up on his own screen and examined it in detail, frowning. The amber tint he had noticed earlier was for turbine efficiency, but he was certain it had been entirely green last week – in fact, for several weeks now. He scrolled back through the timeline, increasingly puzzled. Sure enough, there it was: a sharp drop in one array in the wee hours of the morning, only now starting to come back towards normal.

Something had happened overnight. His mother's visit was no coincidence. He briefly considered contacting her first, then pulled up message mode on the band and sent to Agwé.

Are you in the estuary? What's going on?

There was a delay of more than a minute, and the slight sense of distortion in the band response that told him she was underwater.

Can't talk. Below with repair team. Explain when I see you.

He stared at the message, baffled, and unable to leave it at that. The picture of Pilan in his utility vest was suddenly sharp in his mind.

What repair team? What's happened?

And then, suddenly fearful of the answer,

Is everybody all right?

The response came back more quickly this time.

Everyone OK. Turbines damaged, not sure how. Array shifted, blades warped.

A pause.

We'll head back soon.

A longer pause.

I don't think it was an accident.

'It definitely wasn't an accident,' Gaela said to Sharon Varsi as they kept an eye on their children playing on the quayside downriver from Sinkat. 'I'm sure of it. I saw the trace.'

Sharon chewed her lip thoughtfully. 'Walk me through it again. Could there have been a malfunction? Some program gremlin they haven't caught yet?'

'That's what they thought at first, because of the way the turbines shut down. The vids showed a whole row just turning aside to the current, one after the other after the other. There's a protective subroutine that can shut an array down and collapse the blades if the flow gets really turbulent, in a bad storm or something.'

'So either the shutdown was triggered accidentally, or there really was turbulence.'

'There was. They're running diagnostics on the system, just to be thorough, but we already know what happened; I could see it on the security vids. It shows up in ultraviolet.'

She paused and glanced around, checking on Eve, blinked into infrared for a moment and found her heat signature as she crouched behind a recycling bin. Sharon's elder son, Misha, two years younger than Eve but already more than a head taller, was creeping up from behind. 'It was a focused jet of water, very sudden and quite large.' Gaela spread her arms wide to demonstrate. 'It was strong enough for some of the blades to be damaged before the shutdown could be completed. There's no natural current that powerful, certainly not one that shoots across the estuary at ninety degrees to the direction of the tide, so something *created* it. It moved down the line of turbines whacking them out of position and then stopped.'

'Could you see anything else? Besides the water itself?'

'Not much. The cams are all focused on the turbines. We zoomed in and there are streaks of silt and algae on the blades. Pilan's getting Agwé to take some close-ups, record the scene ahead of repairs—'

'He should've waited if they suspect foul play. Let police forensics get in there.'

'He'd already mobilised everyone before I arrived. And anyway, you know what he's like. They're so close to joining the grid, they've fought off so many attempts to delay and obstruct. I think he's decided he'll be damned if he lets anything get in the way now.'

'I understand how he feels, but they still should've waited. Charging ahead might just give the other side ammunition.' She winced as Misha pounced on Eve and opened her mouth to shout a rebuke, then closed it as Eve reached up, grabbed the boy's ear and twisted. Misha fell off with a good-natured yell. Little Sural, who liked to pretend to be above the fray but never really was, piled in too.

The mothers looked at each other. 'Oh well,' Sharon concluded, 'what's done is done. So your guess is – what? Some kind of submersible?'

'I'd say so. It happened at high tide last night, just on the turn. Maximum depth in the water column, black as pitch, no one around.'

'A good time for sabotage.'

'Exactly. They would've been able to slip away without a trace – or so they thought – and without evidence of an external cause, the presumption would have been that it *had* to be a system error, which Thames Tidal Power would then have been unable to find.'

'Was that the point? To cast doubt on TTP's system integrity?' Sharon waved at the children leapfrogging each other halfway up the quay, beckoning them back: Misha was getting five feet further away with every jump. 'Because it doesn't sound like the damage is that bad, and the turbines are not intrinsically dangerous, not like the battery banks.'

'No, but the battery banks have many more layers of security. And it would be insane to try anything that might breach quantum-energy storage. You'd never get away in time.' She shivered.

Sharon felt the chill too, and was not entirely certain it was down to the breeze off the water, sharp though that was.

'If they thought that no one would ever find out it was sabotage, an inexplicable fault that shut down a tidemill array would lend weight to fears that the entire project is risky and that implementation should be delayed.' Sharon was thinking aloud now, and vaguely aware that she sounded like she was reading a case-file aloud. 'I've heard an emergency petition claiming exactly that is about to be filed with the city, which is an interesting coincidence. It suggests that we should take a very hard look at the group behind the petition. But here's what's bothering me, Gaela' – she could feel herself frowning as she worked through the implications – 'connection to the grid hasn't happened yet. Even if it had, this stunt last night wouldn't have affected supply. The turbines are meant to constantly recharge the battery banks, but the whole TTP venture is predicated on the capacity of quantum storage. Even if every turbine in the estuary was shut down for days, there'd still be enough stored energy for the company to meet its targets.' She signalled to the children again, more vigorously this time. 'To put it bluntly, if Pilan and company had decided to just stay quiet about this, would anyone even have known?'

'It would never happen. Whatever else you might say about him, Pilan isn't underhanded.'

'You and I know that, but would the saboteurs? If not, how would they expect to capitalise on the damage they caused?'

'They'd have a plan to reveal it somehow – leak it to the streams, maybe? Remain anonymous?'

'Or not reveal it and use the threat as blackmail?'

'How many possibilities have we got? Thames Tidal announces that something went wrong and everyone gets worried about the technology. Thames Tidal says nothing, someone else does and the public thinks the technology is flawed and that the company can't be trusted to be honest about it. Or Thames Tidal says nothing, and then someone else holds them over a barrel.' Gaela looked for Eve before focusing once again on Sharon. 'But the reality is that none of those things are going to happen, because Thames Tidal *do* know it was sabotage and *have* reported it to the police. They're going to repair the damage, put new safeguards in place and meet their launch date anyway. So what's the contingency plan for that?'

'With any luck there won't be one.' Sharon's frown deepened. 'If the plan was to reduce public confidence in an already contro-versial project, my guess is it's about to backfire, and that means whoever's behind this will either have to back off or up the ante.'

'You think they might try something else?'

'I don't know. But Mik says Thames Tidal are putting some very powerful noses out of joint, and a submersible isn't the kind of gear your average disgruntled citizen can easily lay their hands on.' Her voice was grim as she watched the three children, now scampering back towards them. 'I doubt this is over, Gaela. It may be just the start.'

3

Aryel Morningstar concentrated on the mnemonic, mentally holding the pattern of what she wanted to retrieve. Her clasped hands were still, but when a row of icons appeared on the desktop screen, she visibly relaxed.

The young man sitting next to her chuckled. 'You still don't entirely trust it, do you, Ari?'

'I'm getting better.' She poked at the thin wire of the cranial band, its dull platinum set off by her dark hair, with an irritation he knew she would not have shown in front of many others. 'It's important to stick with it, set an example.'

Rhys inclined his head in acknowledgement. His elder sister's silent endorsement was something most marketeers would kill for. His own band was tucked up beneath tight curls of ruby-red hair that shimmered faintly against his dark skin.

'Sales not as strong as you'd like?'

'Not yet. Industrial orders are growing, but individual consumers are slower to adopt – which is a problem, because it looks like Herran's profit-share in psionic interface equipment is going to have to prop up genmed reproductive assistance for a while yet.'

'You don't think we'll be getting more public funding?'

'I think it's going to be tight for some time. You know there's a lot of tension around special support for gems – they can't deny care to people who are already damaged, obviously, but the Opposition is using that to argue that future genetic engineering should be minimised, which to them means reducing gem characteristics in the next generation. Is that what we want?' She gestured at the screen.

'No, it isn't,' Rhys replied. 'Trends over the past few quarters show quite the opposite.'

He leaned forward, using his own band to take control of the display, moving seamlessly between mental commands and hand gestures as they reviewed expenditures from the charitable foundation to which Herran had endowed his earnings from Bel'Natur. As they'd come to expect, there was a small but steady demand for specialised genetic medicine to counter the unique illnesses that afflicted some gems and which were tending to become more problematic with age; corrective gene surgery, so that future generations would not suffer in the same way; and most controversial of all, engineering compatibility so that dissimilar gems could conceive and bear healthy children together.

'What about mixed couples?' Aryel asked. 'Are they also holding on to the gem inheritance?'

He gestured at the screen. 'According to this they're trying not to select against either parent if they can help it. The Sharon-and-Mikal model is pretty standard. I reckon much of that's down to them setting such a public example.'

Aryel pondered that. The Varsis' high-profile careers had meant many stream images of the happily blended family: sweet little double-thumbed Sural in his father's arms, gangly, gregarious Misha holding his mother's hand.

'They're not usually too much of a challenge,' Rhys added, 'but we are starting to see more of them.'

'Hence my wish for a spike in cranial-band sales. Is Callan using his for translation work now? He started to tell me something at Gabriel's party but Eve charged in and we never got back to it.'

'He is; he loves it. Herran helped him customise a couple of apps and Callan says it lets him work much faster.' Rhys smiled, midnight-blue eyes sparkling with tenderness. 'He's engaged in a pitched battle with some ancient mathematical texts in Sanskrit at the moment. I was so late getting home from the hospital the other night I thought I'd get done for negligence – instead I ended up having to drag him out of the clutches of some thousand-year-old Indian philosopher.' He pretended to pout.

As Aryel laughed he realised it was the first moment of light-heartedness he'd seen in her today.

'We have become a tribe of workaholics,' she agreed, 'and Gabriel not the least. I'd love to ask him how we might make the band appealing to more users, but he's so busy – not just Thames Tidal, but keeping up with his coursework – that I don't dare.'

'He's a pretty effective advert for the band himself. He told me that there are people at college who he's sure only got one because of him, and even one or two others at Sinkat. Even though they can see that he keeps his active or on standby so he can't possibly be reading them.'

Aryel looked serious again.

Too serious, he thought, *given the subject matter.*

'It isn't fair that he should have to do that, but it was even harder on him before. He's found it a lot easier to fit in now that people know the band blocks his telepathy. But releasing that information bumped his stream profile back up a little, which was unfortunate. There's Eve to consider, and—' She broke off, looking weary.

'What's going on, Ari?' he asked gently. 'Something's on your mind, I can tell. Is the funding situation really that bad?'

'It's not that – well, not entirely.' She nibbled at her lip, brushed a finger along the cranial band again, dropped her chin onto her hands.

Rhys didn't need his acute situational sense to know she was not just anxious, but considering how much of her anxiety to share.

'We've come such a long way, Rhys,' she said at last. 'We've done so well, so quickly. We beat the godgangs and outflanked the Reversionists – in fact, we've infiltrated the mainstream so much we've made *them* look like cranks and outsiders. When Gabriel was born you and I were gemtech refugees, running and hiding, terrified of what would happen if we were caught.' She waved an irritated hand at the room in which they sat. 'Now I have an office in bloody Bel'Natur and you're a doctor in the genmed service we forced them to help fund. And not just that: Mikal's practically an elder statesman of London politics, our sister's a global superstar, Pilan and his team are revolutionising the energy industry—'

'—and aquatech agriculture and textiles are booming. So what's the problem?'

'Our gains aren't universally admired, are they? Opposition is growing, and this time it's not just fundamentalists and fools. A lot of people are very scared of Thames Tidal – quantum storage has the potential to wipe out the biomass industry completely, and while political progressives might be okay with that, a lot of norms won't be. They're beginning to realise that huge numbers of jobs could just disappear. There'll be new ones created, of course – but they're not going to be available to *everyone*, are they?'

'No,' Rhys said thoughtfully, 'not if it means working under-water – the gillungs will definitely have the advantage there . . .'

'Quite. And who hardly ever shows up in your reports?' She gestured at the screen. 'Gillungs, who tend to partner with each other and thus have uncomplicated pregnancies – which means they can have more children, more quickly. The gem baby boom is getting increasing attention on the streams and it's clear to anyone who's looking that gillung babies are a big subset of that.'

'So you think there's going to be a backlash?'

'I think it's already started. The United People's Party lost a chunk of their majority at the last election, and a lot of that was down to voters being upset about how fast the world around them is changing. When change manifests as fewer business or job opportunities, it gives them a way of thinking and talking about it that they're able to convince themselves isn't bigoted. So they turn to the Traditional Democrats, who have the backing of big business and have always been more popular in the suburbs and rural areas—'

'—where biomass agriculture is a big employer,' Rhys finished. His elder sister's political instincts had always been far shrewder than his; he wondered how long she'd seen this coming. 'I get it. No wonder funding for procreation is an issue.'

'Exactly.'

'Is there anything we can do?' He smiled, though he no longer felt cheerful. 'Of course, by *we* I mean *you*.'

'You'd be better off meaning Mikal. He's well placed to influence the players, far more than I am – and anyway, I'm not sure how much I *should* do. It was an easier decision when we were disadvantaged and endangered, when things were so clearly unequal. Now I wonder whether the right course isn't just to sit back and let it play out. But things could so easily spiral out of control, especially if—'

She had been gazing into the distance as she spoke, musing almost, but now she broke off and glanced sharply at her brother.

He was accustomed to her piercing gaze; he was not accustomed to it being so troubled. 'If what, Ari?'

She hesitated for a long time before answering, as though to put off whatever further complication she was about to share with him, or regretting having to share it at all.

'Our significant other,' she said, 'is back in play.'

On the way home, Eve was full of questions. 'How come you and Aunty Sharon were talking so much?'

'What else should we have been doing?'

'Playing with us.'

'We did.'

'More.'

'We couldn't have managed much more, Evie. You and the boys wore us out.' Gaela affected a weary sigh. 'Aunty Sharon and I aren't as young as we used to be.'

'You mean when she was a police officer?'

'She still is.'

'She's a *superintendent*,' Eve said, as if this was as far away from regular policing as it was possible to get.

'Detective Superintendent,' Gaela corrected automatically. 'That's still a police officer, just a very senior one.'

'Can she still *arrest* people and stuff?' Eve threw the words out as though they were a challenge.

What's she got a bee in her bonnet about now? Gaela wondered. She said, 'She certainly can.'

'Were you talking about arresting people?'

'Not particularly.'

'Were you talking about us?'

'Us who?'

Eve rolled her eyes. 'Me and Mish and Suri.'

'Honestly, Eve. Do you think you three are the only interesting things there are?' She scrabbled her fingers across her daughter's head affectionately.

'I *guess* not,' Eve said, sounding doubtful. And then, hopping backwards and looking up at her mother, as she had earlier with her brother, 'Mama, how come Gabe is named Gabriel and I'm named Eve?'

'What?' Gaela was momentarily taken aback. Then she chuckled. 'Would you rather be Gabriel and him be Eve?'

'*No.*' Eve kicked at the ground in annoyance. 'I mean, how did you *decide*?'

'Oh.' Gaela thought. 'Well, things were different when we got Gabe. There weren't many gems with children back then, and none at all in the Squats . . .'

'Riveredge Village. We're not supposed to call it the Squats 'cos no one's squatting anymore.'

'Riveredge, yes, right,' Gaela said, knowing she would never be able to think of their neighbourhood as anything other than the Squats, no matter how many City Council declarations and branding campaigns tried to convince her otherwise. 'So anyway, he was the first child here . . .'

'So he's the oldest?'

'There were kids around the same age in crèche . . .'

'Like Agwé and Roland and Jolay and Delial and . . .' Eve rattled through the names of all the adolescent gems she knew while Gaela mentally counted to ten, and then to twenty.

'Yes, like them. But it was a few years before things were settled enough for them to be fostered or adopted, and anyway they already had names. Gabe came to us from long before that, without a name, and we wanted him to have one that sounded right. It needed to fit in with us and our friends. So we looked at lists and we played around with "Gaela" and "Bal" and we came up with Gabriel.' She looked down at her daughter. 'Why, don't you like it?'

'It's okay.' Gaela noted that Eve's gait had gone from light-hearted skipping to a grumpy trudge. 'But Eve doesn't sound like Gaela or – or Bal. At *all*.' She squinted up accusingly.

'Well . . .' Gaela's heart sank. She'd not been prepared for this, not now. 'By the time you came along, things had changed, Evie. We were able to adopt you in the normal way; we didn't have to try and prove to people that you were ours. We wanted you to have a name with history, one that meant something special. You know,' she said encouragingly, 'in the old stories from before the Syndrome, Eve is the name of the first human woman ever.'

'*I'm* not the first,' Eve snorted, and Gaela felt her breath catch. She caught hold of Eve's jumper and tugged so that the child came to a stop, puzzled, and turned to look up into her face.

'You are,' Gaela said, her voice a little unsteady. 'You're the first and only *you*. That's important, Eve: it's one of the most important things there is in the whole world. You must never, *ever* forget it.'

Mother and daughter stared at each other for a long moment. The little girl's smoke-dark eyes bored into her mother's pale green ones as Gaela ran gentle fingers down her child's soft, dirt-smudged cheek.

Finally Eve blinked and shrugged out of the grip on her shoulder. 'Okay, Mama.'

They walked most of the rest of the way in silence. Gaela managed to smile and wave distracted greetings to people she knew. Eve glanced around occasionally, but mostly she walked with her head down, subdued, not quite slogging along but no longer bouncing happily either. She held her mother's hand, a thing she rarely did any more, and Gaela gave the grubby fingers a squeeze. She could not remember Gabriel – despite the trauma of his infancy and the terrors of his childhood, despite all the adult knowledge he'd had to deal with from far too young an age – ever being this volatile.

The café and grocery at the top of the High Street were already in sight when Eve asked another question. 'Mama?'

'Yes, sweetie?'

'Am I a gem?'

'*What?* Of course you are!'

'Are you *sure*, Mama? 'Cos I don't think I'm ever going to get as strong as Papa, and I only have one thumb on each hand, and I can't jump as high as Misha, or hear people's thoughts like Gabe, or see things like you. My eyes are *boring*.'

'Oh, *Eve*.'

'And my hair doesn't glow.' Eve's lips were trembling and there were tears in her eyes as Gaela put a finger under her chin and tilted her face up. 'Maybe they made a mistake,' she whimpered, 'Maybe they gave you a norm baby.'

'Eve, honey . . .' Gaela felt herself caught between the desire to comfort and reassure her daughter and utter exasperation. *If anyone had told me, all the times I couldn't get food or work or walk safely down the street because of this red brand on my head, that I'd one day have a child who wished for it, I'd've laughed myself sick. Or killed them. Or both.*

She crouched down and wrapped her arms around her daughter. 'Evie, so what? You're perfect. You really, really are. You know how my eyes give me headaches sometimes? And how Gabe doesn't always like the things he hears in people's heads? And sometimes Uncle Mikal's hands hurt – that could happen to Suri, too, when he grows up. Powers aren't always fun to have, you know that. It doesn't matter that you don't have a gemsign. A lot of kids don't. It doesn't mean anything.'

But it does, she thought even as she rubbed Eve's back, dried her eyes and coaxed a hesitant half-smile out of her. *It means you can go wherever you like, among gems or norms, and never have to worry. As long as you're careful. As long as the thing you don't even know about yet doesn't become a danger to you or the people around you. As long as it doesn't set you apart the way my hair does me. If we can teach you to manage the truth of who you are, you'll be safe, and you'll be free.*

Eli Walker caught sight of Gaela and Eve as he pushed open the door of the café. They were too far away to hail from the entrance; Gaela was bending over Eve, her head turned away. He stepped back inside, knowing the odds of managing to disappear around a corner before she spotted him were slim.

Bal was at the back of the big room, his brush of close-cropped indigo hair flickering with the movement as he morosely wiped down the service counter. If he wiped much harder, Eli thought, he'd wear a hole right through it. He looked up in surprise as Eli came towards him through the rows of scrubbed trestle tables and sturdy low stools, bearing two empty coffee cups he'd retrieved along the way.

'Weren't you off? I'd've got those.'

'Gaela and Eve are just coming,' he explained. 'I thought I'd wait, say hello.'

Bal nodded. His broad brown face was grim. 'We won't say anything in front of her.'

'Of course not.'

'Can't keep it from Gabe, though.'

'No,' Eli said, then, thoughtfully, 'Would you want to?'

'Not unless I could protect him from everything else as well. And it's way too late for that.' He flicked at the gleaming counter in disgust, then tossed the cloth aside. 'Gabe will be okay. He'll want to know, and he's solid. Reliable.'

'And Eve?'

'Eve—' He hesitated, scowling as he leaned against the counter. 'I'm not sure, sometimes. When Gabe was her age, we could tell, you know? We could already see who he was going to be, how he was going to handle the madness of his life. It's harder to be certain with Eve.'

Sighing, he straightened up, meeting the other man's eyes. 'Don't get me wrong, Eli. I don't for a moment regret the decision we made when you and Aryel came to us all those years ago. I love my daughter, but she's a very different proposition.'

4

By the time Agwé finally got back, Gabriel was up to speed with what had happened out in the estuary. Now he was watching for any mention on the streams and discussing strategy with Pilan.

'You need to be ready,' Gabriel told him. 'Even if you don't want to be the first to put it out there. Once the rumours start—'

'You think they will?'

'I wouldn't bet against it.' Pilan was leaning against a workstation opposite Gabriel, legs planted and powerful arms folded, the vexation he had suppressed earlier now plain to see. His bodysuit still looked damp, and Gabriel did not need telepathy to know that the head of Thames Tidal Power was angry.

Agwé appeared behind his blocky shoulder. The curvy girl in her cherry-red bodysuit, her band almost invisible beneath a cascade of green curls, caught Gabriel's eye and scrunched up her face into a good-natured grimace. She threw a glance at Lapsa, sitting near Pilan, and then headed for a workstation as though she had not noticed them at all. The workstation was only a few places from Gabriel's, just far enough for her to pretend not to be listening.

Gabriel swallowed a grin and continued, 'Once the police report gets filed it's in the system, it's on their infostream. Plus there'll be the investigation – someone's bound to get wind of it. Also, you're having to do repairs and install more gear to improve security, and Qiyem here' – he gestured at the young gillung who'd come to sit next to Lapsa – 'says that's supposed to be reported to the planning department.'

Pilan twitched with irritation. 'Really?' he growled.

Qiyem nodded solemnly. 'Any incidents or phenomena which might affect the operation of the plant and any alterations to submitted schematics must be recorded and the application updated.'

He sounded like he was quoting from an official document, Gabriel thought. In fact, that was probably the case: Qiyem might well have memorised the entire thing. His meticulous organisation, along with calm in the face of often contradictory directives from a ridiculously large number of regulatory authorities, had won him the unenviable job of coordinating project submissions, making sure they covered every single requirement and request, no matter how mundane or obscure. It was tedious, frustrating and vitally important. Qiyem made up for an otherwise aloof disposition by doing it very well indeed, which was why Pilan generally managed to contain his annoyance at the level of bureaucracy it entailed.

Gabriel was not sure Pilan would be able to do so today; his face had darkened visibly. Lapsa intervened, as she always did when things got awkward.

'That just reinforces Gabriel's point,' she said. 'I don't see any value in pretending this didn't happen, even if we could. We knew there was opposition out there – well, now we know someone has stooped to sabotage, maybe because they haven't been able to stop us any other way. And they still haven't: most of the array is already back online and we're making the system even more robust than it was before, so it's to our advantage to demonstrate that, isn't it? Why downplay it? Qiyem' – she glanced over at him – 'should include a link to the police file. Don't let Planning have to ask us for it. Make it very clear that we're not the ones who have anything to hide here.'

Pilan nodded as Qiyem silently made a note on his tablet.

Honestly, Gabriel thought, *couldn't he at least* pretend *to actually use the band?* When he looked back at Pilan, he found his boss watching him expectantly.

'I agree with all of that,' Gabriel said. 'The question is, how do you want to play it on the streams? If we put out a statement ahead of any leaks, the inference will be, "Look at what someone tried to do to us! Aren't they terrible? And look how we've handled it! Aren't we great?" We'll be calling attention to it, giving it importance and congratulating ourselves at the same time. On the other hand, if we do all the things we're supposed to, with the police and Planning and so on, but don't mention it otherwise, then when the story breaks our reaction is more like, "Yes, there was a sabotage attempt, we reported it and we're cooperating with the authorities, but it really wasn't much of a problem!" – well, that's dismissive, implying it was too pathetic to be bothered about. There might be really good reasons to go either way, but you can't do both. You need to decide.'

Pilan and Lapsa were both smiling oddly at him. Qiyem, who never offered an opinion if he could help it, sat silent and impassive, but Gabriel heard a muffled snort from Agwé. He did not dare look round at her. Most of the time he didn't mind relinquishing his telepathy and the unpleasant things it often showed him, but now he found himself wishing that he could reach up and tap the band off, just for a moment.

'If you *do* want to put it out there,' he went on hastily, discomfited, 'that should happen right away. If you don't, well, just remember it could kick off in the next five minutes anyway. Although it would probably be better for the police investigation if it didn't,' he added, remembering any number of Sharon's grumpy rants about how publicity generally got in the way of good police work.

'I think that's another good argument for staying quiet,' Pilan said. 'And I don't want to give these arses, whoever they are, any more of our time and attention than we have to.' He gestured at the screen behind Gabriel. 'Talk to Agwé about what she recorded, read what Qiyem's putting in the file, draft something for the streams and send it to me. Beyond that, it's business as usual.'

'You are *such* a grown-up,' Agwé laughed, as soon as Lapsa and Pilan had gone and Qiyem had taken himself back to his usual spot at the furthest end of the room.

'What?'

'You should hear yourself! You rattle off all this stuff – "reports to Planning" and "cooperating with authorities" and how to spin the streams – you're so *professional*, Gabe. Honestly.'

'*Me?* Remind me who's documenting this project?'

'Mmm . . .'

'For a degree in underwater photojournalism, no less?'

'That's just being sensible.' She shrugged and moved over to sit on the worktop next to him. 'All the licensed journos are topsiders, even the gems. Every now and then someone drags on a divesuit, but the truth is they're pretty rubbish at covering what happens below. I'm filling a niche.'

'How very *professional* of you.'

She grinned down at him, her luminescent hair tumbling in an unruly mass around a mobile, mischievous face with wide cheekbones, huge brown eyes and a never-ending smile. She favoured bodysuits in warm, vivid colours as rich and deep as her own dark skin. Lapsa might have chosen to foster her in part because of how alike they looked, but if Lapsa was a gentle whisper, Agwé had grown into a joyous shout.

'Do you want to split hairs or look at pictures?'

'Pictures, please.'

As Agwé spun smoothly off the worktop and onto the seat Qiyem had vacated, Gabriel felt the request for control of his screen as she activated her band. He assented, and the first of the sequences she had recorded appeared. She dropped into a low and, he thought, very *professional* monologue as she described what they were looking at. They spent a little time on close-ups of the turbines, hit so violently by the sudden current that blades had twisted and bearings ruptured, then she showed him some odd furrows in the silt, perpendicular to the array.

'That would make sense if there was a strong current directly above,' she said. 'Speaking of which, if I put a filter on the security vids, we might see what your mum saw.'

'Let's do it.'

She played it the first time without alteration, and they watched as a row of turbines turned broadside to the current, apparently of their own volition. Then Agwé added the filter and some of the surfaces assumed an odd, too-shiny patina. This time they could see a faint, silvery turbulence roiling out of the side of the image and separate into little whirligigs of force as it hit the turbine blades.

'Wow.'

'Your mum's eyes,' Agwé declared, 'are the coolest thing *ever*.'

'I'll tell her you said so. You're packaging this up for the cops, right?'

'Yep, putting it together right now.' She flicked with her mind and her hands, coordinating seamlessly, and then leaned back in the chair. 'So, no one's talking about this?'

'Onstream? No.' He checked his monitor apps, though he knew they would have alerted him. 'Not yet.'

'That's weird, isn't it? I mean, isn't the point of this kind of crap to take credit, make a fuss?'

'Maybe they're embarrassed at how quickly it's being fixed.'

'But nobody except us knows that yet. Unless there's a hack into the main system, but then—'

'—why not bugger the array that way?' Gabriel finished. 'Not that anyone's been able to get past Herran's firewall, though we know they were trying hard until a few months ago. I don't know, Ag. Maybe they just wanted to mess things up for the launch?'

'But then you'd plan it for a night or two before, surely, not a week. They might not have realised we could fix it in five hours, but they *must* have known we could do it in five *days*.' She sounded personally offended.

'When Aunt Sharon nicks them, I'll ask her to let them know how annoyed you are that they underestimated the competence of Thames Tidal.'

Agwé roared with laughter. 'D'you think she's going to handle this herself? That's big-time.'

'I think she might. That's who Mama went to see after she left here. *We're* big-time, Ag. Thames Tidal is a big deal for the city, in more ways than one. We're a priority for both of the Varsis.'

Mikal flicked his tablet to standby, unfolded his eight-foot bulk and stood up, looking out and several storeys down to the broad esplanade that ran alongside the river. He was in his City Hall office, just a few hundred yards upstream and on the opposite bank from Sinkat. Were it not for the huge, ancient double-tiered bridge that spanned the channel, and the unbroken line of buildings along the embankment, he would have been staring across at the pale, segmented silhouette of Thames Tidal Power's head-quarters. Instead, his view was of the enormous girders and piers of the bridge, recently repaired and coated with a tough biopolymer shield through which the scars of its own great age still showed. Mikal had always thought it the most solid of structures, at once functional and ornate, and reassuringly immovable, but the unexpected effect of the restoration work was that it now appeared slightly fuzzy around the edges. The protective layer that was supposed to preserve it had, ironically, given it an aura of impermanence.

He shook his head at the paradox and flexed his hands, thinking it would be nice to feel a bit less huge, ancient and subject to the vagaries of time himself. The call from Sharon, combined with the earlier unscheduled visit from Robert Trench, had left him contemplating his next meeting with a deep sense of foreboding.

It can't be connected, he thought. *Standard BioSolutions is too big, too powerful, too much a bulwark of the Establishment to engage in anything as criminally stupid as sabotage. And if they did*, he reflected grimly, *they'd be a hell of a lot more effective at it.*

Unless it had been intended less to damage than to intimidate, to demonstrate the extent of the industrial intelligence and logistical capacity Thames Tidal Power was up against. If that was the point, the saboteurs had miscalculated badly.

He was still trying to judge the likelihood of coincidence over conspiracy when his guest arrived. She was a norm woman some years older than himself, sharp-eyed and sharp-voiced, dressed in the well-tailored, unimaginative style of corporate executives everywhere. He offered his hand and she took it, almost managing to mask her momentary surprise as the double thumbs wrapped around her own. She shook quickly and let go.

Not bad, he thought, *considering.*

'Councillor Varsi, I'm Moira Charles. Thank you for seeing me.'

'It's always good to meet the people who maintain the city's infrastructure.' Mikal gestured towards the window, and the excuse for the meeting. He was quite certain it was not the real reason, and that she would not fail to grasp the full meaning behind his words.

She stood for a moment, regarding the bridge with a satisfied smile. 'We were delighted to work on such an important monument, part of the nation's heritage. What a stunning view you have of it. Do you like the new look?'

'Its preservation adds to its story,' he said diplomatically, showing her to a chair.

She started by fishing for information about the city's ongoing building and restoration programmes. Mikal gave her nothing, and waited through a monologue on the various subsidiaries – horticultural products and high-yield agriculture, pharmaceuticals and processed foods, paints and sealers and solvents – that together made up the behemoth that was Standard. The largest division was conspicuous by its omission. He decided that if she didn't mention it soon, he would do so himself.

'We're really a collection of local businesses that have expanded through investment and collaboration,' she said finally, with the slight straightening of posture and change in tone that told him she was at last approaching the point of the meeting. 'Some of the founders were community leaders from this very area, much like yourself.'

Probably not that much like me, Mikal thought. 'Bankside BioMass,' he said. 'The first network of local waste-conversion plants. I'm aware of the history.'

'Indeed. Bankside still provides more than a third of London's energy needs. They've been a reliable, safe supplier for a very long time.'

And would like to maintain that reliable, safe income stream for even longer, no doubt. Aloud, he said, 'It's been almost a century since they ran entirely on waste, I believe. Most of the country's gross agricultural output now goes into the converters.'

'It's true that recycled biomass isn't sufficient, especially for large conurbations like London,' she replied smoothly. 'That's another way in which the energy industry supports a wide range of employment, from farming and haulage to organic chemistry and heavy construction. It's a well-established, robust infrastructure.'

'Hence your company's opposition to the Thames Tidal venture.' Might as well get it out in the open.

'*Opposition* isn't quite correct,' she said. 'We're not averse to the development of new technologies. But this one is proceeding very swiftly, with a great deal of secrecy and isolation. The industry has legitimate reservations about that.'

'You think the heart of London is secret and isolated?'

'I was referring to the company's refusal to engage with partners in the field. We can't know whether the quantum technology, in particular, is safe—'

'—and yet the planning and patent authorities seem convinced.'

'With respect, Councillor Varsi, the best minds in quantum engineering don't work for the government.'

No, he thought, *and they don't work for you either. They're members of Thames Tidal Power. How that must piss your people off.* Bankside had tried hard to get in with TTP, proposing a joint venture that would give the larger business access to TTP's nanoscale bioelectric storage: the secret to growing the layers of cellular substrate that could safely sequester vast amounts of energy. Pilan had told them to get stuffed. Mikal bit back a smile at the memory.

'So,' he said, 'what are your *legitimate reservations*, exactly?'

She managed to look both pleased that he had asked and pained at what his question obliged her to point out. 'Turning the estuary into an open industrial site, for one, on top of what they've already installed in the river and the city.' She gestured at the window, towards Sinkat. 'We can't know for certain what impact that will have on the marine environment. It's also vulnerable in a way that a closed and secured plant isn't.'

'Are you suggesting,' Mikal asked tersely, 'that the facilities might be *targeted*?' Sharon's account of the previous night's sabotage was vivid inside his head. He treated Moira Charles to a slow, loaded, double-lidded blink.

She glanced away. 'I hope no one would be so irresponsible. But desperate people do foolish things and it's much harder, with an open site, to protect against intrusion – or accident. It's also not clear how a company as unconventional as Thames Tidal would react if something were to go wrong.' The sharp gaze was back on him now.

'I see,' he said. He thought he did, now. 'So what would your recommendation be, Ms Charles, were something *unfortunate* to happen?'

'They should be transparent – accept assistance. Utilise the expertise of the wider industry. We really do think a more collegiate approach would be beneficial.'

'So you're hoping that in the event of some . . . how can I put this? . . . *threat* to the project, wiser heads would prevail?'

'I am, and I'm confident that you'd be one of them.'

That knocked him back. He didn't bother to hide his surprise. 'You have a great deal of faith in me, Ms Charles.'

'I believe it's merited. We pay attention to the politics of this city, Councillor Varsi, and we're impressed by how effective and even-handed you've been.' A soft chime sounded, the signal that their time had come to an end, and she got to her feet.

'I look forward to a long and cordial relationship, here, or in Westminster.'

He had risen also and now he stared down at her in consternation. 'I beg your pardon?'

Her laugh was high, and false. 'I'm sure you know there are rumours that you'll stand for Parliament at the next election.'

'I wouldn't win.'

'You might.'

He managed to keep the incredulity off his face, but only just. *Standard BioSolutions are in the pocket of the Traditional Democrats. Or vice versa. Either she's telling me they're switching sides, or this is a Trad play – but for me?* Both possibilities were equally implausible.

'Independents do better at local level,' he said. 'I'd have no chance without the support of a party.' He looked at her enquiringly.

'That wouldn't be difficult to get,' she replied. 'The question is, which one?'

'You think there's more than one option?'

'I know there are.'

'That's an interesting proposition, Ms Charles.' The floor beneath his feet felt like it had become the deck of a ship, tossing on an uncharted sea. 'I'll have to give it some thought.'

'Excellent.' She smiled, a smile so insincere that it might as well have been a frown, and shook his hand again, brisk and brief. 'I'll be in touch.'

5

Aryel Morningstar dropped out of a blustery sky, landing between a row of battered water tanks and a cooling tower and sending a few pigeons fluttering up in alarm. She stepped further into the tower's shadow and scanned the roofscape and grounds of the blocky, faceless complex of buildings. She would have been picked up by the security cams of course, but she was relieved not to see any actual people: an advantage of the early hour and inclement weather. She had planned for one and was thankful for the other, although the sky was grey and lowering, and the sharp bite to the wind told her that the inconstant lashing rain she had flown through could at any moment turn to sleet.

The fenced and gated yards were deserted, as was the wide strip of treeless, sodden lawn surrounding the compound. The perimeter wall with its rampart of barbed wire covered in bird droppings bordered an urban hinterland of cracked pavements and crumbling warehouses. Nothing moved in it save for a fox trotting purposefully towards the shelter of a clump of scrubby vegetation at the back of a damp car park, and a few rooks cawing at each other in the branches of a blasted tree.

Satisfied, Aryel turned her attention to the roof on which she stood. She'd spotted the entrance as she swept down: a door being pushed open and a figure just inside. She could hardly blame whoever it was for not coming out to meet her in these conditions. She advanced to the far end of the row of tanks, saw a uniformed guard peering out and beckoning to her and darted across the gravel-strewn surface.

The guard – norm, male, middle-aged – had thought to bring a towel, which she accepted gratefully, pushing back the hood of her bodysuit to wipe her face and a few sodden locks of hair. The rest of her was dry; the bodysuit, a variation on the gillung model, was adapted to repel water and keep her warm aloft. She shook her wings vigorously, leaving behind a trail of droplets as she followed the guard down several flights of concrete steps.

She was conducted first to the governor's office, then a senior custodial officer and staff psychologist led her down another corridor, unlocked a door and stood aside to let her in. The door hissed closed behind her and she heard the soft thump of the bolts sliding home.

The room was plainly furnished: drab carpet, light panel in the ceiling, a stand against the wall bearing a water bottle and cups, a table with an inset tablet screen and a few chairs.

The woman sitting in one of them looked up. 'Well,' she drawled, '*this* is an honour.'

Aryel moved to a chair opposite and sat down, hooding her wings a little to fit over the back. She rested her hands on the table before her. 'Hello, Zavcka,' she said. 'Is it?'

A flicker of sardonic amusement passed over the woman's face. She was classically beautiful, with sharply angled cheekbones and a strong, patrician jaw, but the lines were deeper now, and there was a rasp to her voice that she did not trouble to hide. 'Not really, no.'

'In that case, thank you for agreeing to see me.'

Zavcka Klist briefly drummed long, elegant fingers against the table before she folded her hands together in mocking imitation of Aryel's pose. 'I was curious,' she said. 'This isn't the kind of environment you're used to these days, is it?' She indicated the bare room with a tilt of her chin. 'I couldn't fathom why you would want to visit me here, after all this time.'

Aryel watched her quietly for several seconds before responding, 'Will I have the option of visiting you elsewhere?'

Zavcka stared at her for a heartbeat, then threw back her head and barked out a harsh laugh. 'You know, that *is* a consideration. When I'm back in my own home, will I be inclined to entertain requests for audience?' She chuckled again at the absurdity of the idea. Her fingers were trembling slightly. 'From you?'

'I don't know. Will you?'

'I suppose it depends on the reason for your visit.' She rapped her knuckles softly against the table, laced her fingers together, leaned forward. 'Why are you here, Aryel?'

'Why do you think I'm here?'

'I expect it concerns my impending departure from this *glorious* abode.' Her voice dripped scorn. 'I shouldn't be surprised that they told you. What do you want?'

'They told me,' Aryel replied evenly, 'because I represent those of your victims who remain alive. You have done damage, Zavcka. There are people out in the world whom you have hurt. You're about to regain a measure of freedom and we would like to know what you're planning to do with it.'

She was watching closely, and thought that for the first time Zavcka looked ever so slightly shaken. The lips thinned into a tight line, fingers rubbed at knuckles, then clenched into fists. She wondered if it was bravado she was hearing in the ragged timbre of Zavcka's voice.

'I'm planning,' Zavcka said, with an attempt at something like the old arrogance, 'to have a hot bath, dig out some decent clothes and eat a proper meal. I'm planning to enjoy *not* having to listen to any more *stupid* damned questions. What else do you *think* I could be planning?' Her voice was rising in spite of herself. 'I'm going to be tagged and monitored. I won't be allowed to leave the house except under guard. I can only receive visitors *they* approve. My stream access will be restricted, I won't be able to engage in business beyond the management of my own affairs, I can't even *talk* to any of the industry people I used to know. I am *not* going to be free. I'm not going to be able to do fucking *anything*!'

It was almost a shout.

Zavcka glared at Aryel, sitting quietly and regarding her gravely, and seemed to realise for the first time that she was leaning over the table in her fury, halfway out of her chair. She dropped back into the seat, flexed her fingers and placed her hands in her lap, out of sight. 'All that's changing is that I'll be a prisoner in my own home, with the dubious privilege of paying for my keep instead of being a guest of the State. And believe it or not, I'm *grateful*. So you and all these people you're worried about can fuck right off. There is absolutely *nothing* I can do to affect any of you. All I want is to be left alone.'

Aryel waited until Zavcka's breathing had calmed a bit, though there were still two spots of high colour in her cheeks and telltale twitches in her arms. She was genuinely angry and, Aryel reflected, no less dangerous for it.

She said, 'You might find that difficult.'

'Why?' Definite bravado now. 'Don't think it's enough of a punishment for my sins? You don't trust the authorities to keep me isolated?'

'We're not the only ones who take an interest. You're a popular figure in some circles.'

'Give me strength. If I have to talk to one more psychiatrist—'

'I'm sure they've found you fascinating, but that's not who I mean.'

'No? Who—? Oh.' Zavcka's smile was mirthless. 'You mean the – what should I call them? – *longevity enthusiasts*?'

'The police call them the Klist Cult.'

'Do they now.' Zavcka cleared her throat, brought one hand cautiously into view, picked up a cup of water from the table in front of her and took a sip. 'Well, charming as it is to have fans, I don't know why it would concern you. Or the police. They still won't be allowed to contact me, whether I want them to or not. And I don't.'

'You don't want to talk to the only people who believe you're innocent? Who hold you in esteem?'

'A fat lot of good that does me,' Zavcka snapped, though the question appeared to catch her off-guard. She turned the cup slowly in her fingers, looking at it as she spoke. 'There's nothing I can do for them either, no matter what they believe. They can't share in what I have. There's no point to them being obsessed by it.'

'Celebrity doesn't have much to do with logic,' Aryel pointed out.

Zavcka glanced up at that, dark eyes flashing with recollection, and again that hint of dry amusement. 'You never did like it, did you? Hasn't stopped you using it, though.' She focused on the cranial band, its thin line circumscribing Aryel's face beneath her damp hair. 'I understand you're more successful than ever these days. *Your* sins have all been forgiven—'

'Zavcka . . .'

'—and you're at the heart of Bel'Natur, taking advantage of everything *I* worked to build. Well' – she gestured dismissively, and both hands remained in sight now, resting on the tabletop –

'maybe those cultists are on to something after all. You can't count on being around indefinitely, can you? I may outlast you yet.'

'You might,' Aryel said without rancour, 'but given how hard you're trying to distract me from the fact that your hands keep shaking, I wouldn't bet on it. Are the meds not getting to you, are they not working, or are you not taking them?'

Zavcka stared, this time definitely taken aback. It looked like she was winding herself up for a riposte, but then decided against it. Her shoulders slumped and she chuckled bitterly.

'No hiding anything from you, is there? They get them to me all right, when I request them. I forgot to ask last night.' She pointed at the cup of water.

Aryel understood. 'You took them just before I arrived.'

'Mmm.' Zavcka sounded tired. 'Another thing to look forward to: not having to ask for permission to not be ill.' She regarded Aryel wearily. 'You never got it, I suppose.'

Aryel shook her head silently.

'Lucky bugger. Anyone else?'

'Once we knew what to look for, we could identify the people at risk among those who share your sequences. They've all received tailored epigenetic suppressants.'

'What about the one who had it badly – Rhys?'

'Rhys opted for a dermal implant so he gets his meds automatically. He hasn't had a seizure in years.'

'And the sister?'

'Gwen never developed symptoms.' Aryel looked at her appraisingly. 'Even in here, I'd've thought you'd have had news of her.'

Zavcka shrugged. 'They're keen for us to stay abreast of popular culture and she's hard to miss. But I can't say I've been terribly interested.' Her gaze turned penetrating. 'What about the other sister?'

Aryel felt a warning chill run up her spine, although she'd known from the start that the conversation would inevitably turn to this. The precise nature of Zavcka's interest was part of what she had come here to learn, but it was important not to make it easy, nor to trade away more than was absolutely necessary.

'Do you actually have the nerve to ask about Ellyn?' She drummed her own fingers on the table; Ellyn wasn't the person Zavcka wanted to know about. 'She's alive. She's healthy. She's as happy as it's possible for her to be.'

Zavcka stared down at her hands. They were no longer shaking, but they still seemed to require much of her attention. 'And the child?'

'What makes you think I know?'

'Oh, for *fuck's* sake, Aryel!' Another angry explosion, quickly contained this time. 'Please don't insult my intelligence. You will know exactly where she is and what she's up to for as long as you're both alive. It's what I would do.' It was no more than the truth, and they both knew it.

'Ellyn's daughter is also doing well,' Aryel said. 'She's happy and she's safe.'

'She *isn't*—' Zavcka drew a deep breath, visibly calming herself. 'Never mind. Call her Ellyn's child if it makes you feel better. Where is she?'

'Come now, Zavcka. You know you'll never be told that.'

'Surely you can tell me whether she's in England, or if they placed her abroad—?'

Aryel was slowly, deliberately, shaking her head.

Zavcka sighed. '*Fine.* But you're sure she's all right?'

'She's all right.'

'She doesn't know anything?'

'Not yet. Possibly not ever.'

'Or . . . need anything?'

'No. She's well taken care of.' Aryel looked her over, remembering, acutely aware of the room's bareness. 'The thought that she might have ended up poor really bothers you, doesn't it?'

'It would just be . . . *wrong*. Unnecessary.' Aryel's stare was so long and hard that eventually Zavcka twitched and snapped, 'What?'

'Wealth is no more necessary than poverty.' Aryel didn't try to keep the sting out of her voice. 'She has everything she needs. We would never allow her to suffer on your account.'

She'd expected a comeback and was surprised instead to see Zavcka deflate, slumping in her chair, silent and stubborn. She was still the haughty aristocrat, still refusing to yield an inch, but there was an edginess to her now, an inconsistency to her focus and her temper, an odd fragility that Aryel had never seen in her before. Maybe it was just the grinding-down of illness and the stark reality of age, the soul-crushing bitterness of defeat and incarceration, but perhaps there was something else as well.

She thought back through the conversation, replaying bits of it in her head, and something Zavcka had said at the beginning came back to her. '"After all this time",' she quoted. 'Does that bother you, Zavcka? I did ask to visit, when you were first sent here. You wouldn't allow it then.'

'I'd had enough of you at the trial. I couldn't imagine what else you wanted, except to gloat.'

'You know that's not my style.'

Zavcka shifted uncomfortably. 'Whatever. I didn't want to, and it's not like you kept on asking.'

'You'd made your feelings clear, and I had other things to deal with. But send a message if you ever want me to come again.'

'You're too kind.'

'Sneering really doesn't become you, you know. And I didn't say

57

it was a kindness. It is what it is.' Aryel pushed herself to her feet. 'Eli would also like to talk to you, by the way. When you get out.'

'Oh, *would* he?'

She ignored the sarcasm. 'He's mapping attitudinal changes in the post-Syndrome era and you've been alive for most of it. Your recollections would be very helpful for his research.' The corner of her mouth kinked up in a wry smile. 'He's not confident you'll say yes.'

'Very wise of him.'

'But he's going to put the request in anyway.' Aryel went to the door and rapped her knuckles against it sharply. 'Maybe you'll change your mind. It'd give you something to do, since you'll be so idle.'

Zavcka Klist sat for a time after Aryel left. A keen observer might have noticed that she began again to play with her hands: rubbing the fingers together, worrying at the nails, as if distractedly delaying for as long as possible the moment when she would have to get up and quit the bare little interview room for a space even less inviting. They would have thought no more of it than that.

In fact she was noticing the network of tiny lines that she was sure had not been there a few years ago: the topography of veins and tendons on once-smooth skin, a faint scattering of spots, knuckles that looked more prominent than before. Her hands, like her face, like her voice and every other part of her, were beginning to show their age.

This is happening. It's really happening, and there is nothing I can do.

Despair and fear washed over her, along with an old, worn-out anger. She thought of Ellyn and the hope that had once resided there; of the child she had never seen. She would have given anything for a picture – just a glimpse – to tell her whether the image in her mind's eye reflected reality. Her eyes were hot and swollen with unshed tears.

The need to know was so intense that she found herself paralysed by it, unable to catch her breath as though it were a physical pain. She'd anticipated this moment when the request for the meeting had come through; had almost refused it out of hand. She hadn't been sure she could bear the presence of Aryel Morningstar, ascendant, serene and self-possessed. The absence of spite, the lack of acrimony, was almost the most infuriating thing about her, second only to the resolve that Zavcka knew no threat, bribe or promise could shake.

Aryel was never going to tell her anything; she would never offer her a crumb of comfort. She would never understand, or pretend to sympathise – and yet Aryel had come to her, and had offered to come again.

What was the fucking point?

Zavcka's rage crested and broke on the thought, then receded, revealing a landscape that she had, in her anger and self-pity, failed to notice. She felt her own sharp intake of breath, an easing of the tightness in her chest as she began to pick out the shapes and shadows of a bigger picture.

Aryel Morningstar did not ask stupid questions, or make empty gestures. Nor did she act without purpose.

Have you forgotten with whom you're dealing, Zavcka? Foolish girl. It was never about what you *could learn from her.*

What did she *learn from* you?

6

In another meeting room, many miles from where Zavcka Klist sat in contemplation while Aryel Morningstar, equally troubled, launched herself from the roof of the prison into a storm-wracked sky, Detective Superintendent Sharon Varsi was picking through the details of a different skirmish. It was not going as well as she'd hoped.

'I understand that the technical specifications filed with Planning would have been enough for someone to work out how to damage the turbines with a water-jet,' she said to Pilan and the young compliance coordinator, Qiyem. 'And although access to the full application must be requested, there's no real barrier to anyone getting hold of that data. But the security setup for the power plant is *not* public information. And yet whoever sabotaged the turbines knew precisely how to pilot their vehicle to stay out of sight of the cams as well as how to avoid setting off proximity alarms. So who has access to that information?'

'The security plan was included in the submission,' Qiyem pointed out. 'It's redacted from the infostreams, but it is nevertheless held by the city's Planning Department and the Energy Regulatory Authority. It had to be approved by Environmental Management and the Home Office, as well as the police, in order for the submission as a whole to be successful.'

He nodded respectfully at her, and she felt her jaw tighten. She had at first been pleased to have his comprehensive knowledge of what information had flowed where, and when, placed at the service of the investigation, but his endless repetition of facts she already knew was becoming annoying.

'So at various points in the process it would have been reviewed by departmental specialists and signed off,' she snapped. 'I get that. But as I said *before*, none of those people would have been able to make copies. They could only have accessed the files at work, via a secure connection. And that's not just wishful thinking on my part – forensics have already confirmed there were no security breaches during the submissions process.'

She turned her attention to Pilan. 'So let me rephrase the question: Who *else* could have had access?'

'Just us,' Pilan shot back. 'And a detailed security schematic isn't available to everyone on our own infostream either: only a handful of us can see it.'

'Do you think,' Sharon said steadily, 'that there is anyone in Thames Tidal we should be taking a closer look at? Anyone who has that access, or might have been able to gain it?' She raised her hands for calm as Pilan's copper-brown face began to turn red. 'I know you're not going to take kindly to that idea; no employer ever does. But we need to be realistic, Pilan. If there's someone who might be disgruntled, for whatever reason, or could be persuaded to pirate a file in exchange for payment . . .'

Qiyem, she noted, was listening with a kind of placid disinterest; he appeared to be in no doubt about what the answer would be.

Pilan breathed deeply and flattened his webbed hands on the table. 'None of our people have anything to do with this,' he said. 'I'd stake my life on it. And remember, no one here is *employed* in the usual way. This is a cooperative – so *everyone* owns a share of the business. Everyone stands to win if it does well, and we all lose out if it doesn't.'

'The owners – that's us – will make a hell of a lot more money in the long run,' Qiyem interjected. 'Trading that for a bribe doesn't make any sense.'

Sharon and Pilan both looked at him in surprise; it was the first time he had spoken less than formally, or volunteered anything that sounded like a personal view. He shifted as though embarrassed by the attention and said, 'But it's not only us and the authorities who know the security setup. There've been a few outside specialists, including the consultant who identified the sabotage. She also helped design the system – a fact which is noted in the submission. So maybe she was hacked – she probably doesn't have the same level of protection . . .'

Oh yes she does, Sharon thought. *If only you knew.*

'No,' Pilan said. 'We constructed it based on Gaela's recommendations, but she doesn't have the final layout. And we've already had our own servers checked – by Herran.' His tone was heavy with the significance of that fact.

He turned back to Sharon. 'My money's on it being someone in one of those departments Qiyem mentioned: some disgruntled civil servant, taking a backhander from Bankside.'

Sharon sighed. 'Be careful, Pilan. I can't completely rule it out, but so far there's no sign of any unauthorised access or hack. And Bankside might be heavily involved with the Estuary Preservation Society, but that doesn't automatically make them suspects. You don't want to go throwing around accusations that you can't back up.'

'They've been hell-bent on stopping us from joining the grid tonight. Both Bankside and the EPS. And we know they requested the technical specs.'

'So did a great many other interested parties. Having the information and a motive doesn't mean they had the intent, or the means.' She swiped at her tablet in irritation. 'I can tell you that the key players all have rock-solid alibis for the night of the sabotage.'

'Suspiciously solid?'

'We're looking into it.' Sharon tucked the tablet away. 'In the meantime, we need to consider every other possibility, even if it's just to rule it out. That includes internal access to security information. I want to know who looked at what, from installation to the date of the sabotage.'

Pilan looked baleful, but he didn't argue. 'I'll tell the security director to run an analysis.'

'No. I know you trust her completely, but it can't be anyone who has responsibility in that area.'

'I can do it,' said Qiyem.

'You have access? Good. Send it via the secure link you used before.' She stood up. 'The answer is here somewhere, Pilan. We just have to find it.'

Gabriel caught a glimpse of Sharon hurrying along the quayside, wrapped in a wind-whipped waterproof. He doubted it was giving her much protection from the rain, which was washing down the transparent biopolymer membrane in rippling sheets. The interior of the Thames Tidal project office felt watery, cool and slightly grey; everything outside was refracted and distorted, as if seen in some strangely warped mirror. The first true storm of autumn appeared to be trying to submerge them entirely, drenching the topside levels of the amphibious building as thoroughly as those below the waterline. Standing at the window with a steaming cup of tea in his hands, Gabriel thought that perhaps this was what it was like to see and move and breathe and live underwater.

He glanced round, past colleagues clustered at workstations in intense, quiet discussion or working with heads bent and webbed fingers flying, to where Agwé was sitting. It was the kind of notion that she, with her eye for composition and documentarian's feeling for perspective, would appreciate – but she too was concentrating, earbuds in, hands dancing across screens, the activity light on her band pulsing softly. As he was the one who'd requested the last-minute edits, he could hardly interrupt her.

Qiyem walked by, head turning to watch Agwé as he did so. As always, his tablet was in hand, although his band was in place; as always, its light was a steady standby blue. Gabriel sighed inwardly and told himself not to mind. Qiyem was not the only person who used the band to guard against the risk of having his mind read, and he could guess at least one of the things the submissions coordinator did not want him, of all people, to know.

As though aware of the thought, Qiyem looked across at him and their eyes met. Gabriel nodded a greeting; Qiyem stared back, unsmiling. For the briefest of moments his expression was a mixture of the usual jealousy and, oddly, contempt. Dropping his gaze to the tablet, he began to tap away ostentatiously.

Gabriel turned back to the window and sipped his tea. *That's it*, he thought. *I'm done trying.* No one quite knew what Qiyem's problem was, why he was so remote and unsociable – he laboured as hard as any of them for Thames Tidal, though he never looked inspired or sounded passionate about the company. Agwé had once declared he was more *go-along* than gillung. Gabriel had laughed heartily, although he suspected there was more to his reserve than that. But Qiyem had rebuffed every attempt to get to know him better, anything that tended towards friendliness.

He wouldn't rebuff Agwé, though, and Gabriel was quite sure she knew it – but he hadn't appeared to grasp that his coolness towards the people she liked left her with no reason to like him back.

Whatever. Gabriel buried the sting of this latest snub in that knowledge, staring out at the rain-washed basin as Qiyem passed behind him. He wondered what would happen in the months to come when it became evident that there were no more submissions to coordinate, no need for an ongoing liaison with Planning; and that, in spite of his talents, no one wanted Qiyem in *their* team.

Don't be spiteful, Gabriel, he scolded himself. *Think about something else.* Resting a hand against the gently curving biopolymer, cool but not cold against his palm, he squinted at the material. It was latticed through with a silver-white honeycomb of fibres, a unique cellular geometry that gave the walls strength and rigidity, while keeping enormous energies in quantum stasis. He had struggled to grasp the sheer scale of what was stored there, until one of the engineers explained in terms morbid enough for any teenage imagination. Now he found himself contemplating the power beneath his palm: *Here in this hand's-breadth, this finger's-width, the curve of a nail, is enough to take my hand, my arm, my life. Right here against my skin, completely safe.* It was like stroking a tame dragon.

Agwé would like that notion too, though perhaps it wasn't the best metaphor with which to calm an anxious public. A new alert popped into his consciousness; he sent the feed to his workstation and closed his eyes as he formed another, less familiar command.

The background hum in his brain dimmed as the content flagged up by the monitor apps became intelligible. He suspected the new app would scare as many users as it enticed. No longer just a command-and-response interface between user and equipment, it turned the cranial band into a kind of translator: a conduit that converted stream chatter into mental conversation. It would be the closest thing to telepathy most people would ever know, if it could be perfected enough to work for someone who was not already a telepath. So far, Gabriel had his doubts.

He was pleased to see how quickly the input resolved into a coherent dialogue. He was less pleased with the discussion itself. It lacked the emotional resonance of human thought, but the meaning was clear enough.

> [City Council rejection of petition to delay TTP pure political gerrymandering. They have failed the people.]

> {Expected better? All in the pocket of the New-nited People!}

> [Quantum storage could be a catastrophe for Thames Estuary. Should never have been allowed. Next 'sabotage' target?!]

> (What about fishes crabs plants etc. Power radiation equipment, what will it do to them.)

> {What'll it do to US? Eat quantum-farmed lobster! Grow your own gills!}

> (Is that true!?)

> {Guess we'll find out!}

> [Police response inappropriate & unacceptable. Should have supported post-ponement until investigation complete.]

> {Better luck next time, hey? Can't get the staff.}

> (Another petition?)

> [Can't tell what might disrupt quantum containment. TTP denials not credible.]

> {We'll see if electricity & water mix after all! KABOOM!!!}

Gabriel slid into his chair, his tea unfinished and all but forgotten. He checked their IDs onscreen, making a mental note to let Herran know that while this latest version of the app could distinguish between different participants, it was rubbish at communicating their identities. The pompous complainant about the failed peti-tion turned out, predictably, to be the group that had sponsored it: @EstPresSoc, the Estuary Preservation Society. The credulous streamer ready to believe in mutant shellfish looked like a real person. Kaboom was obviously an avatar: a syntactically generated alphanumeric ID, a boilerplate profile and a timeline that went back all of ten minutes. They were randomly generated, existing only for the duration of a particular streamchat and then were never seen again – an increasingly common tactic among corporate rivals and lobbyists, despite breaching the Code of Practice they all claimed to abide by.

Gabriel tagged the feed for future reference, though he knew there was little point; whoever was composing the text would already be activating a new, equally temporary virtual mouthpiece, ready to spout more unfounded rumours and outright slander. The dishonesty grated at him – but Herran had shown him how to game the streamfeed algorithms so that they pulled his posts into any discussion tagged relevant to Thames Tidal. Maybe that wasn't particularly scrupulous either, but under the circumstances he felt it was justified. At least it meant anyone following the feed would get both sides of the story. He checked the posts already in queue, editing and reordering, dropping them onstream, steadily but not too quickly:

@ThamesTidal: **Tomorrow we power London.** Quantum-battery banks fully charged, ready to go.

@ThamesTidal: **New vids of dolphins** around estuary power plant! **Environmental Management** confirms healthy ecosystems, no damage to wildlife.

@ThamesTidal: TTP celebrates 10 years of tidal turbines, 5 of quantum storage, 0 casualties or serious accidents. **Best safety record** in the industry.

@ThamesTidal: We've been around for a while, folks. London launch expands on Sinkat/Riveredge service: **lowest bills in city** past 3 years.

@ThamesTidal: We're at the **TideFair** to answer your questions. Food, fun, facts. Tomorrow in Sinkat Basin, all welcome.

@ThamesTidal: What happens at midnight? Clean, cheap energy for all Londoners. Don't take our word for it, check out the **independent audits**.

It took Gabriel fifteen minutes, though Kaboom disappeared as soon as the first Thames Tidal post popped into the feed. He sipped cold tea and grimaced. Kaboom would be back under a new handle, insinuating danger, death or malfeasance in a tone variously jocular, conspiratorial or frightened. The jibes always skated close to, but never quite over the edge of what could usefully be reported to the police. He'd seen the pattern a lot over the past few days, ever since news of the sabotage attempt had surfaced. The dashboard panel in a corner of his screen registered a steady uptick in traffic along the links he'd laid down to the Thames Tidal infostream and he allowed himself a small smirk of satisfaction.

'What's funny?' Agwé had appeared at his elbow.

'Just another troll sent packing. For now. The fuss about turbine vulnerability has died down, but all of a sudden they're getting worked up about the battery banks. It's like they think when we join the grid they'll somehow become dangerous.'

'That doesn't make sense. The batteries are already charged, so releasing power to the grid would make them *less* dangerous.' She looked perplexed. 'That's if they were dangerous in the first place. Which they're not.'

'Welcome to my world, Ag.'

'I'm not going to have to make more changes, am I? We've already said as much about quantum tech as we can. Anything else and Pilan'll think we've joined the Bankside brigade.' She scrunched up her face at him. 'Besides, it was *perfect* before.'

'I'm sorry, Ag. Truly.'

'Don't worry. It's even better now. But I don't want to keep messing with it.'

It *was* even better: a beautifully composed vid sequence that conveyed the immense power of the tides, showed how that power was captured by the turbines and contained in the delicate cells of the quantum batteries, then followed it up out of the estuary into homes and streets and industry. She'd managed to make the entire narrative of energy generation at one with the teeming life of people and plants and animals, above and below the waves. Lapsa's calm voiceover was, Gabriel thought, almost unnecessary; the pictures told the story brilliantly. Agwé had embedded the links he'd asked for in a series of softly pulsing icons; anyone who wanted hard data would find it a tap away. But he knew, looking at it, that few would bother. They would not want to sully the vid's magic with mere facts.

'Ag, this is wonderful.'

'It's not bad, is it?' She looked over to the end of the room where Pilan now stood. Everyone else was drifting towards him. 'Come on, presentation time. Let's see what the others think.'

The others watched the vid in awestruck silence, as if they had not fully appreciated their own achievement until that moment. At the end there was raucous applause. Lapsa beamed, while Agwé ducked her head and looked embarrassed. Even Qiyem forgot himself enough to stare openly at her.

'Well done, both of you,' said Pilan. 'I can't see any way of making that better; anyone else?' The enquiry was directed to the room. There was more applause and whistles, and a general shaking of heads. Someone shouted, 'Stream it now!'

Pilan grinned. 'I think we'll stream it at 18.00 hours, as planned. That way it'll get maximum pickup on the evening feeds. Gabe, what's going on out there?'

Gabriel stepped forward. 'It's mostly positive, but there've been

69

some new conspiracy theories around the Estuary Preservation activists being questioned by the police and then their petition being rejected by the City Council. A lot of people have only started to pay attention because of the news over the past few days, so they need reassuring. Our strategy's the same: keep pushing information out, keep stressing our safety record and the independence of the reports, keep being friendly and open. What Agwé's done in the vid emphasises that we're just another part of London life, nothing to be scared of. So thanks for making my job easier, Ag.' Another ripple of laughter, as Agwé, obviously recovered, saluted with a flourish. 'We've got monitor bots running on all the main feeds plus a few of the fringes, but if you notice anything unpleasant please send me the link. And remember to stay on message in your own posts. You don't want to drop anything into a public feed that could be taken out of context.'

He glanced at Pilan. 'Um, one thing in particular. I know many of us are interested in politics, but the company has to remain neutral. So please make sure your personal views don't sound like they're being expressed on behalf of Thames Tidal, okay? It's really important. That's it. Thanks.' He stepped back, feeling a little nervous.

Pilan was nodding, his expression thoughtful rather than annoyed. 'That's a good point,' he said. 'We've been living and breathing this project for so long that it hasn't felt like personal stuff was over here' – he gestured broadly – 'and professional stuff was over there. That could be used against us if we're not careful, so let's not give the idiots who don't think we're up to this any ammunition. Okay?'

He surveyed the room. The euphoria of a few minutes ago had tempered a bit as the awareness settled in that the next stage was going to be less about bravura construction and clever engineering and more about public-approval ratings and reputation management.

Gabriel felt eyes on him and heard the mutters; they sounded terse, but approving. Everyone knew who his warning had been aimed at, and he was vastly relieved that Pilan had not taken exception. Instead his boss looked over at him and said, 'Thanks,' like he meant it. Then, to the others, he said, 'Right. Let's move on.'

It was another hour before every last detail was nailed down to Pilan's satisfaction. Much of that time was dedicated to Lapsa's final briefing on the TideFair.

'The weather's supposed to clear overnight, so we should have a good turnout,' she said. 'We've got a dozen activities and exhibits, maybe more, and we've been encouraging people to bring their families. If we keep the kids entertained, that's half the battle with the parents, right?' She waited for the laughter to die down. 'Now, one of the things that concerns people is whether quantum batteries are safe. We mustn't forget that they mostly haven't read the technical submissions, and even if they had, they probably wouldn't understand the science. So all they know for certain is that a breach will set off a reaction that will destroy the battery, and that the battery banks store a tremendous amount of power. Put those two things together and they sound like an accident waiting to happen. So, instead of us just telling them not to worry, we've come up with a game.'

She swiped a new image onto the screen and held up a disk-like membrane, translucent blue tinged with pink, about half the size of her palm. 'This is adapted from the single-watt samples we provided as part of the planning process. We've turned it into a pretty toy that demonstrates how the entire system works. The idea is to show it's so simple and safe that even a small child can understand and play with it.' She tapped the screen. 'We've set up a couple of tubs to act as tidal basins, with tiny turbines in them to charge the tiny jellyfish batteries – yes, that *is* what we're calling them, Agwé, don't laugh – and a table full of these dinky little filament-and-algae-paper dynamos.' She held one up. On the screen, a pair of webbed hands showed the charging of the battery and its attachment to the base of the toy. The pinwheel on the top whirled around, sparkling silver and gold and green.

Eve will love that, Gabriel thought. *The first thing she'll do is take it apart to try and see how it works.*

'That'll deplete the battery in a few seconds,' Lapsa went on. 'Whereupon the kids can run back and charge them up again. The dynamos come in various sizes, so they'll get to see how different devices draw different amounts of energy. It's all very educational – especially when we ask if anyone wants to see what happens when a battery is damaged, which we'll do regularly. The kids will all shout, "Yes!" and we'll let them have a go at trying to break the battery, stamp on it, twist it, that sort of thing.' She rolled and pulled the jelly-like membrane in her fingers. 'They won't be able to break it like that, of course, so we'll tell them the only way is like this.' Pilan ceremoniously handed her a pair of scissors and Lapsa snipped briskly into the disk. The gel began to collapse around the cutting blade, the blue washed out and the pale pink darkened until the whole thing fell apart into a gloopy, reddish-brown mess.

'You *killed* it!' Agwé whooped. 'That's *terrible!*'

'Dramatic licence. Jolay came up with the colour scheme.' Lapsa smiled at the youngest member of the bioelectrical engineering team. 'If it's a depleted battery, that's all there is to it. If it's charged, the gel will warm up as the energy dissipates, but not enough to burn. No explosions either way.' She wiped the slime off her fingers and into a lab dish. 'We'll dump a few of the ruptured batteries under a scanner, alongside some water samples. Everyone'll be able to see that everything the batteries are made of is already in the ocean anyway.'

She looked over at Gabriel. 'What do you think?'

'I think it's brilliant,' he said. 'If Agwé can get some vid of children playing with them, it'll be even better. That should shut a lot of people up.'

TideFair

7

The weather had cleared as predicted and those out early were treated to a bright, sharp morning. The air smelled like it had been freshly washed, thoroughly rinsed and buffeted clean. On the great bridge that spanned the river between City Hall and Sinkat, two people paused, leaning against the chest-high railings and looking out over the water on the downstream side as they talked quietly. They appeared to take a particular interest in the gleaming apex of Thames Tidal Power, just visible behind and between the buildings; there was an intensity to the conversation that was at odds with their apparent idleness. They fell silent as a small shuttle-boat emerged from the basin and watched as it swung into the main channel and picked up speed, heading downstream towards the estuary. The passengers sat in the stern, their wind-blown hair glinting green.

The boat was quickly out of sight and the conversation resumed, the speakers now looking down at the water flowing beneath the bridge. They strolled and stopped and strolled again, still looking; actions that had become commonplace on the bridges and quay-sides of London, though few would be willing to admit that they were engaged in gillung-spotting. This slow perambulation brought the pair eventually to the northern end of the bridge, where they descended from roadway to riverwalk via a flight of wide stone stairs. They emerged onto a wide piazza in the bridge's shadow, barely a couple of yards above the water's surface, and made their way once more to the safety barrier.

They paused by a public infostream screen as it progressed through descriptions of the landmarks that could be seen from this point; among them was the pale ellipse of Thames Tidal, accompanied by a banner announcement that the company's revolutionary energy technology, designed and executed from that very building just a few hundred yards away, was now helping to power the entire city. A live infographic showed how much had been captured since midnight, how much fed to the grid, how much held in reserve. All three metrics were in excess of target.

One of the pair tapped to hold so that they could finish reading. Their review was punctuated by sounds that might have been derision or dismay or perhaps just disbelief. When the screen was finally released, transitioning to a history of the bridge and its recent restoration, the lift in their mood was palpable.

They spoke for a few minutes more, looking upstream to where the water roiled around the massive piers, then they parted, one walking up the stairs to re-cross the bridge and go back the way they'd come, past the gleaming glass curve of City Hall. The other crossed the piazza, heading east, downstream, towards the riverwalk that led into Sinkat.

Even further downstream, in the newly christened Riveredge Village, Mikal Varsi was negotiating with his sons.

'We *have* to go now because I have to be there for the opening,' he explained again patiently. 'There'll be things to do, and lots of people—'

'What *kind* of people?' asked Misha, with an air of disdain.

'You know what kind: the kind who show up for the openings of things. Journalists and officials, mostly.'

'*They're* no fun.'

Mikal opened his mouth for a rebuttal and rebuke, then closed it again. Misha was dead right on that score.

'They won't be the only ones,' Sharon pointed out. 'There'll be people you know – Agwé and Delial and Jolay and Lapsa – and Gabriel's probably there already . . .'

'Well, will Gabriel take *Eve*?' Sural demanded. The urgency in his voice made it squeak.

'I don't think so, honey. He'll be working.'

'That's what I *mean*, Mum.' Misha's attempt at patient explanation was such an infant mirror of his father's that it was all Sharon could do not to dissolve into laughter. 'It's going to be all *grown-ups.*'

'What've you got against grown-ups?' Mikal asked, and then hastily, to forestall an answer, 'The fair's on for the whole day, Mish. We don't need to leave early—' He cast a look of desperation in Sharon's direction. 'We can stay for a bit once the speeches are over, can't we?'

'But everyone always wants to *talk* to you, Dad.'

'Talking to people is pretty much my job, Mish.'

'But it's *boring*. We can stay home with Mum and go later when—'

'No, you can't, because Mum has to go now too,' Sharon interjected.

'But *why*?'

'I'm one of those boring officials, remember?'

Four-year-old Sural stuck out his lower lip, stomped over to a large chair with oddly shortened legs that stood against the wall, hauled himself up onto it and sat with crossed ankles, folded arms and mutinous face, as though nothing in the world but a visit to the TideFair at a time of his choosing could ever make him move again.

For some reason his parents found this hilarious. Misha, who recognised an opportunity when he saw one, dived back in while they were struggling to compose themselves. 'But *why* can't we go with Eve?'

'Because you're going with us.'

'But she could come too!'

'She's going to go with her family.'

'But we *are*!' Sural piped up from the corner, unable to contain himself, immediately perplexed by what he had just said.

Misha threw him the exasperated look of one whose job has just been made even harder by the bungling of others. Sharon reined in her mirth before it could escape entirely. On the other side of the big kitchen, Mikal was similarly struggling.

'*Mum*,' Misha said in his most reasonable voice, having apparently decided that his mother was amused enough to be persuadable, 'Eve would have lots more *fun* with us. Don't you want us to have fun?' He heard himself, and swiftly corrected, 'I mean, *all* of us?'

'I think you can survive an hour or so without it,' was her disappointing reply, and Mikal said, 'You don't think your Uncle Bal and Aunt Gaela are fun?' with as much innocence as he could muster.

'Not as much as us,' Sural popped back with the certainty of one for whom this statement was too obvious to be contested. Mikal made a pleading face at Sharon. Sighing, she picked up her tablet and tapped out a message to Gaela.

We've got a rebellion on our hands over here. Boys refusing to move without their leader. When are you going?

'Mum,' said Misha, sensing weakness, 'are you *checking*? Are you *asking*?'

Sural scrambled off the chair and pelted over, standing up on tiptoe with his nose pressed to the countertop, little hands with their double thumbs gripping it hard in his effort to look over and onto the tablet screen. Sharon peeled one of them off and turned it over for examination.

'I am checking and I am asking. In the meantime, you two go and wash your hands.' She tilted Sural's face up to rub at a smear of egg on his cheek. 'And faces.'

'Mum—'

'And brush your teeth, and don't soak yourselves. Or the bathroom.'

'*Mum*—'

'Right now, please.'

There was that particular tone to their mother's voice that said further nagging would be fruitless; might indeed prove severely counterproductive. Both boys knew it well. They beat a tactical retreat. Mikal just could hear them over the sound of running water, soberly discussing the encounter and judging it a win.

'I feel outnumbered,' he said to his wife.

'There's only two of them. And they're tiny.'

'They're gaining on us.'

Sharon chortled. 'I reckon we can stay in front for a few more years.' The tablet pinged and she looked at the screen. 'Right – Gaela says they're planning to get there once the ceremony is over so they don't have to contend with the scrum of journalists. Sounds like Eve is giving them a hard time too.'

'No news there.'

'She's a good kid, Mik. Mostly. Wilful as hell, but then—' She gestured in the direction of their own children.

Mikal looked rueful. 'They aren't a gang anyone could've predicted, are they? Not that I'm complaining. Endless wrangles with small children is the perfect training for a life in politics.'

'Endless wrangles and the occasional ultimatum,' Sharon said quietly, poking her head into the hall to make sure the boys were out of earshot. 'Anything new since last night?'

'A chatty message from Rob Trench saying he's going to be there with his good friend the Energy Minister, who, he hastens to remind me, has always been a big gem-rights advocate, is delighted by the rapid progress of Thames Tidal, is looking forward to everything, and so on and so forth. Alongside a message from the office that Standard BioSolutions want to schedule a follow-up meeting. Naturally it doesn't mention what they want to follow up *on*.'

Sharon snorted. 'They have some nerve. A disclosure order was served on one of their divisions two days ago – rumour is they might have acquired a high-power submersible at some point.'

'Really? Good. I can use that to politely decline until the investigation's over. Anything else pointing their way?'

'Nothing useful. The whole damn thing's pretty much stalled. I got the internal audit yesterday and as Pilan predicted, no one inside the company looks like they could have had anything to do with it either.'

'That was never likely. They're a tight group, which is part of why the rest of the industry has such a problem with them. I wouldn't be surprised if Bankside sends someone along to poke around today, though with any luck they'll keep a low profile. So anyway, there's Standard, there's Rob, and Pilan wants to have a word with me, though I already knew that.' He looked resigned as he started gathering up tablets and jackets and the various accoutrements necessary for venturing forth with offspring in tow.

'You'll have to give him an answer eventually, honey.'

'I'd rather convince him it's a bad idea than refuse to be involved. It would be misguided if I did join; it might be disastrous if I don't and they go ahead anyway.'

'You do know that keeping people from making their own mistakes isn't your responsibility, right?'

'I know, but I have to try.' He poked his head around the corner, shouted, 'Boys! Time to go!' and turned back to her with a grimace. 'I suspect this morning is not going to be quite as boring as I'd like. Although I'm sure Mish would disagree.'

A few streets away, in the flat above the café, Eve was equally desperate to go. 'Why do we always have to be *late* for things?'

'We're never late,' Bal pointed out peaceably. 'We get where we're going exactly when we mean to.'

'But it's never when everyone *else* gets there.' She appealed to Aryel, who was perched on a stool at the kitchen counter, nursing a cup of coffee. 'Aunty Aryel, *tell* them.'

'Tell them what, Eve?'

'That we need to go now!'

Aryel shook her head. 'Now would be too early, sweetie.'

Eve looked angry enough to indulge in a bit of foot-stamping – until she caught her mother's eye and thought better of it. Gaela swiped to send the message she'd been tapping out. 'Mikal and Sharon are going to be at the opening and I've just arranged to meet up with them afterwards. So that's fine. You wouldn't be able to play with the boys until the ceremony's over anyway.'

Eve did not appear mollified. 'Mish and Suri always get to be *on* things.'

'What sorts of things?' asked Eli, from the depths of an armchair.

'Streams.'

She apparently felt further explanation was necessary, given the silence that followed. 'Uncle Mikal and Aunty Sharon always take them to things where Uncle Mikal has to make a speech or sometimes Aunty Sharon does, and the people put it on the streams and sometimes they talk to them after and put *that* on the streams too, and Mish and Suri are always there even though they're usually not talking 'cos Uncle Mikal and Aunty Sharon say to be quiet but one time one of the stream people asked Mish a *question*, and he *answered* it. And it was on the *streams*.'

It came out in a rush, with barely any punctuation or pause. She stopped for breath and looked around at the adults with an expression that said matters had been made so clear that they could not now fail to take action.

The adults exchanged glances and shifted uncomfortably.

'Do you really *want* to be on the streams, Evie?' Aryel asked finally, 'or is it just that you don't want Misha and Sural to do things without you?'

Eve's brow furrowed, as she tried to work that one out.

'In other words,' Gaela said, 'if Mish and Suri had never ever been on any streams, would you still want to be on them your-self?' She could feel the tension in the room as they waited for an answer, although Eve didn't appear to notice.

She shrugged hugely, as though this was too implausible a sce-nario to be worth considering. 'I just want to *go*.'

'Right.' There was a note of finality in Bal's voice. 'We all do, and we'll head down in about an hour.' Gaela nodded and he added, 'In the meantime, do you have schoolwork, Eve?'

'No.' She was pouting. 'I finished it.'

'Well then—'

'Can I go out in the garden?'

'Yes,' her parents replied in unison, and Gaela added, 'Put on your jumper. No' – as Eve turned to go up to her bedroom – 'this one.'

She handed over the freshly laundered white jumper with its UV-reflective finish. Eve took it and stomped downstairs, far too loudly. The door banged. Gaela looked out of the window and waved. Eve looked up at her, turned away without waving back, then glanced swiftly back over her shoulder at her mother and waggled her fingers half-heartedly. Unmitigated rudeness was presumably a step too far, even for her.

Gaela turned back to the others, feeling mildly relieved.

'Sorry,' Aryel said. She sounded troubled. 'I could've just messaged you, but even though Herran's got me covered with the heaviest encryption there is . . .'

'I think we're all happier if some things aren't trusted to the streams.' Bal refilled her cup. 'And don't apologise. Eve's going through a strange stage at the moment.' He returned the pot to the hob. 'At least, I hope it's just a moment.'

'I haven't seen her in a while – too long. After yesterday I wanted to catch up in person.'

Gaela swallowed past the constriction in her throat. 'So, catch us up. Although going there was beyond the call of duty, I think.'

Bal came to sit beside her by the window, glancing out himself as he did so, then wrapping a comforting arm around her shoulders. 'How was she? Not happy to see you, I'll bet.'

'No, but she had to agree to it. There was that awareness underlying the hostility. And you know what Zavcka's like: she could never allow herself *not* to be hostile.' Aryel also looked towards the row of windows facing the garden, although she couldn't have seen Eve from where she sat. Her gaze was on the breeze-blown branches of a chestnut tree, its leaves mostly brown now, and falling. 'She was arrogant and angry, but also a bit . . . sad. Diminished. I think the reality of having to play by the same rules as other people hasn't just pissed her off, it's shocked her. She doesn't quite know who she is in a world where something like a criminal conviction and prison can happen to her.'

'So she's having to deal with being the same as everybody else. It's about time.'

'I wouldn't go that far. She still sees herself as different. Better. Distinct from the rabble.'

'Which she is,' Eli said. 'Different, I mean, and by a number of objective measures, whether we like it or not. And now that wealth and status don't elevate her any more, what will she turn to?'

Bal's jaw tightened. Gaela said, 'You think she's going to be . . . looking for something?'

'I think she'll need to,' Aryel replied. 'She said she was planning to go home, ignore the world and wait out her sentence. I didn't believe it for a minute, and apparently the psych reports don't suggest that either. I gather they're troubling, but not definitive enough to keep her in high security.'

'What do we need to do?' Gaela could feel a buzzing behind her eyes; the stress would lead to a headache if she wasn't careful. She took a couple of deep, steadying breaths and leaned into Bal's solid bulk. 'Aryel, you need to tell us: should we leave again?' She felt Bal tense up.

'Absolutely not.' Aryel's response was reassuringly firm. 'She'll still be confined for many years, and I doubt she'd stroll around the Squats even if she could. You don't need to do anything other than continue to keep a low profile. You and your children, along with Rhys and Callan and a few others, are among the topics redacted from her stream access, but she doesn't have a list of what's forbidden. She knows it'll include victims and their families, and the trial established Gabriel as one of those victims, so even if she notices a Gaela-, Bal- and Gabriel-shaped hole, she won't put it down to anything more than that. Public figures like Mikal and Sharon can't be redacted, though, so you're right to keep Eve away from Misha and Sural when they're in the spotlight.'

She ruffled her wings slightly and walked over to look down at the garden. 'I'm not saying she won't use whatever means are at her disposal to search. She's already tried, even though she knows it's pointless – she'll never be allowed to reclaim the child Ellyn carried. I think she's had enough of feeling frustrated. My suspicion is that she'll focus her energies on something that gives her some gratification.' She turned away from the window. 'And maybe lets her believe that one day she'll be able to try again.'

'How?' Bal had relaxed a little as Aryel was speaking, but his voice was still tight around the question. 'She won't be able to deceive her way back into the kind of position she had before. Mind you, she's got a bunch of followers waiting for a leader – think she'll try to hook up with them?'

'I'm not sure. I pressed her on it, but it didn't sound like she takes the Klist Cult seriously. I know' – as Eli looked sceptical – 'she's perfectly capable of hiding them in her pocket while pretending they're beneath her notice, and I did get the impression she'd thought about them more than she was willing to let on. She changed the subject, which is odd for someone so narcissistic.' She perched again, this time on the arm of Eli's chair. 'There was also the fact that, apart from a couple of snide remarks, she didn't want to talk about Bel'Natur – she didn't try to get any information out of me, although she'd ranted about not being allowed to engage in business. That surprised me.'

'You think she's going to try and find a way back in?'

'I'll bet she's already working on it.'

'So she's not concerned any more with—?' Gaela looked towards the window. She could not bring herself to say her daughter's name.

'No, that's not what I'm saying at all.' Aryel looked down at her hands resting on her knee, as though an answer she preferred might be found there. 'The fact is, she's desperate to know. *Desperate*. It was the only thing she genuinely seemed to care about. Remember, she doesn't see herself as the villain in this – as far as she's concerned, we're the ones – no, *I* am the one who's done her wrong.' She gazed around the room, catching everyone's eye in turn. 'But even that's not straightforward, because in addition to everything else, I do think she is horribly, horribly lonely, though I suspect she'd rather die than admit it, even to herself. But although she was hostile and the conversation was fraught, although I know she reckons me an enemy, I couldn't shake the feeling that my going out there *meant* something to her. I think it gave her a sense of connection, talking to someone who has the measure of her. Someone she can match wits with.'

'Someone with whom,' Eli said quietly, 'she has so much in common.'

'She'd sooner give up her fortune than admit that.' Aryel sighed and stretched. 'And I'm not crazy about the comparison myself. But yes.'

Eve cast a swift glance up at the window. Aunty Aryel had only stood there for a moment and she was gone now, but Eve could see the flame-red and indigo shimmers of her parents' heads, side by side on the little couch where Mama often sat to read. You always had to assume Mama was about to turn her head and scan the garden, and take precautions accordingly.

Eve had no idea why her mother checked on her so much, even when they were at home. It was like she thought Eve might disappear if she wasn't looking. She was sure Aunty Sharon didn't watch Mish and Suri that hard when they were in their own house.

She hunkered down in her little cave under the shrubs, holding her battered tablet so it was covered by her jumper. She was fairly sure Mama couldn't see it, not as long as she held it like this. Not that there was anything *wrong* with having it out here, or anywhere else, as long as she was using it in the approved manner. She was restricted to the children's newstreams, so that meant stories and games and puzzles; and schoolwork, articles and vids on the school's firewalled pupil network, where she was also allowed to have streamchats with Mish and some of their classmates. Apart from that she was not allowed to post anything, or set up a profile, or have any onstream life at all. Many of her friends could do what they liked and she resented being excluded.

So when one of the older girls who'd left school last term sent her an invitation, a link to a private stream where the cool, clever kids could talk to each other without their parents butting in or harassing them, she'd jumped at the chance. She did wonder for a moment why Dorah's account was still active even though she'd gone to a different school, and why she hadn't said anything before she left. But by the time the explanation came back – that accounts were left open for a short time so that goodbyes could be exchanged, and that Dorah had really liked Eve, but had been too much in awe of her to reach out before – she no longer cared; the new socialstream was full of the kind of sarcastic, self-regarding chatter that she didn't normally encounter, nor was allowed to indulge in. Eve knew full well that even if she wasn't breaking the rules by being onstream there in the first place, her new stream-friends were not the kind of kids her parents would approve of.

They thought so too, and had given her lots of tips for avoiding attention.

Other than Dorah, now known as @dorok235, Eve had no idea who any of them were in real life, but that part didn't much matter: everyone was anonymous here. She'd got a real thrill out of coming up with her very first alphanumeric handle, and felt grown-up and important every time she ventured onstream under her new secret identity. And she wasn't an idiot, *everyone* knew how essential it was to keep that secret; *everyone* knew stream-friends weren't the same as *real* friends, and that even on children's streams you could never be sure that someone was telling the truth about who they were and that you must never *ever* say who *you* really were, nor *where* you were. Her secret friends might live across the street or on the other side of the planet, for all she knew. She didn't know their real names and except for Dorah, they didn't know hers.

But @dorok235 and a couple of the others were always there for her when she was angry or upset, and it always made her feel better when they told her how special she was, and how much they hoped to meet and become real friends one day. They got excited whenever she let slip the tiniest thing: that she was adopted, that she was blonde, that she was eight, that her parents never let her out of their sight. Her stream-friends asked lots of questions about that, agreeing that it was bitterly unfair, and Eve's sense of injustice swelled.

She didn't think it was at all surprising that they found her so interesting: they told her all the time how clever and important she was.

8

The festivities were well under way by the time Aryel Morningstar swept in, folded her wings and touched down on the quayside in front of Thames Tidal Power, landing between the stage and the airlock through which visitors were being escorted for tours of the power plant's control room. The dignitaries had not long concluded their speeches and the press corps, only just beginning to disperse, all swarmed back to cover her arrival, angling vidcams to catch her falling gracefully out of the sky, then rushing forward, microphones ready to capture whatever pithy comment she might have for them today.

Agwé, recording the proceedings from a vantage point near the Child's Play marquee, shook her head in admiration. 'Sink me, she's good – late enough not to interrupt, early enough to get lots of attention, casual enough for them all to feel it was pure luck they were still around when she got here.' She glanced down at Gabriel from her perch on the stepladder that enabled her to see over the heads of the crowd. 'She plans it all down to the last detail, doesn't she?'

'No – I mean, it's not quite that contrived, Ag.' He floundered, caught off-guard by Agwé's penetrating observation. 'Not usually, anyway. She has great timing, but it's more like an instinct than a plan.' Realising that he was in danger of batting away the question, he stopped himself. Agwé's own instincts had recognised a deeper truth about Aryel and he needed to try and explain his aunt's actions in a way that would neither puncture nor propagate her mystique. 'She's trying to *not* be the centre of attention so much any more, especially now that there are others like Pilan and Mikal who can represent us. She never wanted to be such a big deal in the first place. She didn't have a choice back then. But she can't just disappear, either. She's too famous.'

'So what you're saying is, she's pulling away slowly—'

'I guess so—'

'—letting herself become a footnote to the main story while the spotlight settles on other people. Passing the torch, so to speak.'

'That's about right, I think. I mean, I've never heard her say that in so many words, but yes.'

Agwé indulged in one of her voluminous eye-rolls and Gabriel conceded an embarrassed wince. They both knew that what he heard people actually *say* wasn't likely to be the full sum of his knowledge.

'So, to repeat my *earlier* point,' she said firmly, 'Aryel knows *exactly* what she's doing. And *damn*, is she good!'

He grinned up at her. 'I'm not going to argue with any of that.'

'You better not. I hope Pilan, Mikal and everybody else she's stepping back *for* are taking notes.' She clambered down the ladder. 'Nothing else to see from up there. I should go and be a proper journo, join the scrum.'

'Uncle Mik is pretty good at that stuff,' Gabriel observed, holding the ladder steady as she swung her equipment clear. 'He's got his own style, of course. Pilan . . .'

The eye-roll this time was mutual.

Agwé chuckled. '*Style* is one word for it. Coming?'

'Nope. Aunt Aryel and me in frame together is always an excuse for someone to bring up the story about how I was kidnapped and I'm not having that distract from Thames Tidal. Not today.'

'Fair enough.' Her expressive face was suddenly deeply thoughtful. 'You work these things out kind of the same way she does, you know that?'

'Who do you think I learned from?'

She thumped him companionably on the shoulder before making for the forest of bodies, in the thick of which could be glimpsed huge bronze-and-gold wings. Aryel would be shifting and moving there, the gestures apparently unconscious but in reality calibrated to maintain enough clear space around herself so as not to feel too unbearably hemmed in. The vidcams would love it.

Agwé would probably work out the nature of that compromise too.

Gabriel turned away, thinking that his famous aunt was better at this game than even Agwé could guess. He would talk to her later, when the furore had died down a bit; for now, he'd go and find his parents. Aryel's arrival on the main quay would have been their cue to slip unobtrusively into Sinkat.

They were by the food kiosks in the tented dining area; Bal had already deposited fresh provisions with Delial – who usually waited tables, but was on loan from the café today – and was grinning broadly as he reviewed the morning's takings. Horace, who normally worked in the grocery, was serving teas and hot chocolate to a norm family with two little girls who looked just a bit older than Eve. They were staring with fascination from Gaela, with her cascade of glowing red hair, to Bal's short indigo glimmer, to Eve's non-luminescent blonde curls. Gabriel decided the parents had noticed, but had chosen to ignore their children's naked curiosity; they had that slightly furtive, tense, nothing-to-see-here look about them, as though they were desperate to get their drinks and leave before one of their offspring asked an embarrassing question.

Luckily for them, Eve was paying the girls no mind whatsoever – if she'd appeared at all interested, Gabriel thought, the younger one, now squinting at some strands of her own straight black bob, would have taken the plunge. But Eve's studied indifference was like a damper field, a curb not just on sound but on the very impulse to communicate.

Eve looked up at her brother, expressionless, as he stepped close enough to ruffle her hair and give their mother a hug.

'Hi Mama, Papa, Evie,' he said, 'hey Horace, Del.' His voice was casual, but loud enough to carry. Hellos were returned. Bal reached a large hand over to touch his son's face in greeting, as he'd done ever since Gabriel was a small child.

Gabriel glanced at the customers. The older girl's mouth had dropped open and they were both staring at his hair now too, visibly trying to work out how sandy brown fitted in with blonde, and fiery red and indigo. The father hastily pressed a credit tab to the reader. Horace thanked him when it pinged acceptance. With a palpable air of relief the parents herded their children back onto the quayside, but Gabriel could see the questions starting to batter at them as they headed around the perimeter of the basin.

'Hey,' he said to Eve's upturned face.

'Hey,' she replied, still deadpan, but with a note of approval. They knocked fists together. The routine was too well worn to require further acknowledgment.

Gaela, watching, chuckled, then asked, 'How's everything going?'

'Really well. We've had even more coverage than we expected. I'm monitoring,' he tapped at the cranial band, 'so I might have to slide off if something needs taking care of, but so far it's fine. Aunty A just arrived; she's doing her thing.'

Gaela smiled, their eyes meeting in shared understanding.

'Did you see Misha and Suri and Aunty Sharon and Uncle Mik?' Eve demanded, pulling at his arm.

'Yep. Uncle Mik made a speech, and then I think he was going to do an interview with one of the newstreams. Aunty Sharon and the boys are probably still around there somewhere.'

He wondered why his mother looked slightly pained. Eve drew breath to say something, but Gaela stopped her with a look. 'We'll go and find them in a moment, Evie.'

Surprisingly, she stayed quiet.

'That's excellent,' Bal was saying to Horace. 'Looks like I'll need to send more supplies down for lunch. Any problems I should know about?'

'No, none at all.'

Delial, briskly replacing empty tubs with the full ones Bal had brought, snorted. 'Not unless you count Horace having to explain a *gazillion* times that actually, yes, you *can* have green hair and *not* be a gillung. Even if they'd overheard him telling someone else, the next person in the queue *still* found it necessary to say something.'

'I don't mind,' Horace said. He had a mournful face, and always managed to sound a little anxious, as if the subject at hand, no matter how mundane, might at any moment become fraught. 'They don't know. It's not their fault.'

They should, and it is. Gabriel knew as surely as if he'd sensed it that his parents shared the same thought; he saw the way his father's jaw twitched and his mother's eyes slipped off Horace as though needing something else to look at just then. Delial, who came from the same school of expressive eye-rolling as Agwé, shoved the last of the supplies into place with a particularly eloquent thump.

Eve was oblivious. She yelled, 'I *see* them!' and pulling away from Gaela, she ran out into the blustery sunshine and pointed. Sharon, Misha and Sural were heading their way, but there was no sign of Mikal.

Maybe he's still in that interview, Gabriel thought, *or another one, or he's been cornered by Pilan.*

Gaela sighed. 'Finally,' she said. 'If those kids didn't know what to make of her before, they'd be beyond confused if they saw her now.'

Mikal Varsi was being neither interviewed nor harangued just at that moment, though he suspected he had earlier been roundly, if silently, cursed. He'd been standing beside the stage, talking to a technology journalist from UrbanNews, when he'd seen Pilan pushing towards him through the throng, speaking too quickly – and probably too curtly – to the succession of reporters he was working his way past. On his other side he could see the Energy Minister, Jackson Radbo, concluding his own interview, while Rob Trench stood nearby, hands in pockets, beaming munificently.

Mikal had acknowledged Rob, shifting his stance to make it look as though he were just waiting to finish so that he could join the two men, but glanced across at Pilan to catch his eye as well. One benefit of being head and shoulders taller than everybody else was being able to see them all in a crowd, even when they could not see each other; it was one of the few advantages of his gem anatomy, and Mikal had no qualms about using it. So when Pilan arrived he came face to face with Rob and Radbo, approaching from the opposite direction.

Mikal clapped his double-thumbed hands together with, on reflection, perhaps just a bit too much relish. 'Isn't this excellent?

I haven't made it inside yet, Pilan, and I'm sure Mr Radbo is looking forward to a tour.'

'Jack, please,' said Radbo, as Pilan pasted on a smile and led the way. 'It's good to finally meet you, Councillor—'

'Oh, just Mikal. The pleasure's mine. I imagine' – raising his voice slightly – 'that you and Pilan are already acquainted?'

'We've met,' said Pilan, managing to sound gracious instead of grumpy. The head of Thames Tidal Power might not be much of a diplomat, but he was also not a fool.

'My office isn't allowed much contact during application and development – that's to ensure the process remains independent,' the minister explained with a politician's practised smoothness. 'Now that part's over, I'm looking forward to becoming *much* more engaged.'

Pilan glanced back at that. Radbo fell in next to him as he led the way towards the control room, Mikal following along with Rob, noting with satisfaction that a number of the journalists were now filling the corridor behind them.

The entire group ended up in the control room on the second level, with a polite and increasingly enthusiastic Pilan describing the system to a senior minister with newstream crews on hand to witness their easy rapport. Pilan's political instincts, Mikal thought, were not sharp enough for him to realise that he was publicly undermining his own argument about the need for a separate political party. He injected a comment or question from time to time to keep the conversation moving, and felt vindicated by the sight of them getting on famously.

'You're too clever by half, you are,' Rob grunted out the side of his mouth in the middle of an animated discussion about grid upgrade strategies. 'Get them in here and they're just a couple of energy geeks.'

'Nothing wrong with that,' Mikal muttered back. 'Work with me, Rob. This is your problem I'm trying to solve.'

'I get that. D'you think it'll be enough?'

Mikal leaned forward in an undignified slouch to bring his mouth closer to Rob's ear. 'If your guy can persuade him the UPP are really on board, that they'll support aquatic settlements and take the issues that matter to him seriously, then maybe. He's stubborn, but he's also practical.'

Rob nodded his understanding. 'Pilan's rubbed a lot of people the wrong way. But maybe now that they can actually *talk* to each other . . .'

'Exactly.' Mikal straightened up, his voice coming back to regular volume as Radbo turned towards them. 'Impressive, isn't it?'

'Very. I'd like to see—' He broke off, staring out through the clear biopolymer to the quayside below, where everyone's gaze had suddenly lifted skywards. Half a heartbeat later, Aryel Morningstar dropped lightly onto the bare space next to the stage where they had all been clustered just a few minutes before. There was a moment's stillness, and then the jostle of people and vidcams moving in towards her as though her presence was some sort of vortex. The journos who'd followed them inside all came to an instant and unspoken decision and headed for the exit, while other visitors piled up in front of the window. In a matter of seconds the politicians had gone from being the centre of attention to virtually ignored.

Mikal sighed inwardly. It was not – had never been – Aryel's fault.

'I wonder,' said Radbo softly, 'if we might speak in private?'

He was talking to Pilan, but his eyes flicked to take in Mikal and Rob as well. Mikal shot Pilan a look filled with as much meaning as he could fit into it. Pilan moved towards the doorway as though they too might be heading back outside, but instead he turned left, leading them through another door and into a small meeting room on the opposite side of the building, away from Aryel, Sinkat Basin and the TideFair.

'Thank you,' Radbo said. He was not speaking to Pilan this time, but to Mikal. 'Thanks for enabling us to meet this way.'

Pilan's eyes widened with comprehension and some degree of annoyance as Radbo turned to him. 'I meant everything I said down there, about how inspiring and exciting this project is, but I need you to know that we're also dealing with growing concerns from both industry and the public – I'm not sure you realise how big an issue the turbine sabotage last week is turning out to be. The physical damage might have been minor, but when we confirm that the power plant has met all safety and security requirements, it's pointed out that it was something the authorities didn't antic-ipate. I want to be able to deal with those objections in a way that is in all of our interests.'

'You expect me to act as if what happened was our fault?' Pilan asked, with an air of incredulity.

'No,' Mikal said, 'Jack's trying to be straight with you, so you can work out how to help each other.' He looked at Radbo. 'I assume that's the reason for this conversation?'

Radbo nodded. 'I have to respond to those concerns whether I believe they're justified or not. I don't, but right now reassurances that Thames Tidal Power has met all the regulations just makes people think they aren't strong enough.'

'What am I supposed to do about that?' Pilan growled. 'You think we don't know that there are bigots who would rather see us fail than accept that we know what we're doing? Who are convinced quantum storage is dangerous, no matter how many independent experts tell them it isn't? To hell with them. If they can't work out that being good at what we do is also the safest thing for *us*—'

'They can't,' Mikal interrupted. 'They can't see it from your perspective, only their own.'

'Right now the backlash is manageable,' Radbo said calmly, 'and I want it to stay that way. Most of what you're doing is exactly right. Your public-relations initiatives, this TideFair event, the live-stream updates – that's all excellent outreach work; it'll reinforce the support you've already got, and it'll go a long way towards persuading many who haven't yet formed an opinion. But those who are *already* convinced that this programme is dangerous and wrong and shouldn't happen?' He shook his head. 'Some minds aren't going to change very easily, Pilan.'

'You're talking about the people who stand to lose if Thames Tidal succeeds,' Mikal said. He was aware of Rob listening carefully. Pilan appeared to have got a lid on his temper, and was doing the same; Mikal sensed that his admonition had hit home. He also felt that the conversation had, in some way, become a test of his own mettle.

'Yes.' Radbo looked troubled. 'We – the government – know quantum storage is the future. It'll reduce our dependence on high-intensity biofuels – and we can't even begin to estimate how many other innovations the technology could lead to. That's all great in the long run, but in the short term it will be extremely disruptive. The infrastructure for biomass supports a big chunk of the economy, and the fact is, Pilan, that what you're doing represents a threat to a great many businesses, to say nothing of the people who work for them. We need to deal with that. We can't afford to ignore the folks who are afraid of you, even if we don't agree—'

'Who are *afraid* of us?' Pilan interrupted, disbelieving.

'Yes,' said Rob, finally breaking his silence. 'Jack, you need to speak as plainly as you can: our friends really need to hear this.'

For the first time, Radbo sounded nervous. 'Rob's right, you really do have to listen to what I'm saying,' he started, then swallowed. 'It's not just the fear of change,' he said. 'There's something else being whispered around – and it'll be out in the open soon enough. People are afraid that if this project succeeds, a large proportion of our energy supply will be dominated by a group with different priorities to the rest of the population.' He drew a deep breath. 'A group who might be motivated by the injustices of the past, as well as the opportunities of the present.'

'You mean,' Mikal said drily, 'who might behave the way they suspect *they* would, were the situation reversed.'

Rob looked appalled. Radbo was taken aback for a moment, then he looked at Mikal with an air of even greater interest.

Pilan, surprisingly, started to laugh. 'How the *fuck*,' he said, 'do you expect me to respond to that?' He waved his webbed hands at the room, the building, the window with its view of the city beyond Sinkat. 'So this isn't just a solid business based on high-quality science and engineering, it's a ridiculously elaborate revenge plot. Because that would make *so* much sense.' He looked at Mikal. 'Am I supposed to take this on? Seriously?'

'I'm not suggesting there's any truth in it,' said Radbo, 'but it's a rumour that suits our opponents and they're going to use it. They've got a strategy and whether we like it or not, we need a response.'

'You *could* say that such behaviour would be completely beneath you and your people,' Mikal observed to Pilan as though they were the only ones in the room, 'which would of course imply that we think we're better than the people who think they're our betters.'

'Just now, I don't have a problem with that.'

Mikal sighed. 'I understand how you feel, but you know it would be a counterproductive line to take.' He leaned back in his chair, steepled his fingers and regarded the others gravely. 'So, Jack: since we're dispensing with the usual doublespeak of our profession, let's have it. What do you want?'

Rob winced again, but Radbo registered the barb with equanimity. 'I understand the desire for independence,' he said, 'but there is safety in numbers.' Although he was speaking to them both, it was on Mikal that his eyes rested. 'It's best to negotiate when everyone's at the table.'

9

In long-distant days before the scourge of the Syndrome decimated the city's population and overturned many of its historic divisions, the area now known as Sinkat Basin had been a dock for the pleasure boats of the wealthy. Decades of abandonment saw richly appointed vessels sink down to oblivion, steel rust into nothing and once-stout wooden jetties crumble into jagged, rotting teeth that poked up out of increasingly stagnant water as the channel connecting the basin to the river silted up. The basin grew rank.

Some of the first gillung prototypes were put to work restoring the channel and clearing and expanding those old berths, a practical demonstration of the uses to which the hardy new water-breathing subspecies could be put. When emancipation came in the form of the Declaration, London's gillungs reclaimed the area as the fruits of their forebears' uncompensated labour, and expanded the dredging and reclamation even further.

Now gems and norms of every description mingled in a colourful, noisy flow of bright clothes and brighter hair: exploring the bridges and quays that crossed and knitted together this watery village, watching technology demonstrations and holographic displays, playing with interactive modules, investigating marquees selling everything from food and drink to scarves made of whisper-thin algae silk and vivid thermo-sensitive biopolymer bodysuits, to waterproof tablets and cranial bands.

A flurry of attention continued to follow Aryel as she strolled through the TideFair with Lapsa, but the media thicket had dissipated. Vessels came and went through the access channel to the Thames, manoeuvring within the designated lanes. Markers hung in the water to indicate the safe depth for anyone needing to cross paths with boat traffic, but in the rest of the basin gillungs swam just below the sun-dappled surface, their movements swift and graceful, and endlessly fascinating to the visitors swarming topside.

One of the most popular attractions was proving to be the Test-Dive, a ten-minute simulation of life in the gillungs' world. It was part of a larger exhibit on the complex biology of their oxygen exchange system, with delicate gill tissue simulacra and detailed anatomical projections meant to reflect the 'All Humans' theme in the current school curriculum. Eli thought it was a potent reminder of just how radical human gemtech had been, and of the irreversible legacy it had left behind.

He and Callan had walked around to where the basin met the Thames, taking in the sights with an anonymity that would have been impossible had he been with Aryel. Like Gaela, Callan's skin was pale and his hair glowed flame-red; unlike her, his eyes were untroubled by ultraviolet light, and he wore a fashionably flamboyant coat in radiant royal blue that had already made Gaela flinch when she'd greeted him earlier. Now they stood looking at the river, chatting and enjoying the sunshine for a few minutes before their lunchtime rendezvous with Aryel and Rhys.

A seagull soared off one of the buoys marking the channel entrance, arrowing past them as they turned to go, shrieking as though offended. Glancing down at the water, Eli saw the flickering shape of a swimmer turn in from the river; no doubt that was what had startled the bird. It might have ignored a seal, but nothing in its evolution could have prepared it for a fully aquatic primate. He grunted in satisfaction.

'Muttering to yourself,' said Callan, sauntering along with his hands in the pockets of the swirling coat and face tilted up to the sun, 'might not be considered an entirely healthy sign.'

'Sorry. Seagulls. Gillungs.'

Callan burst into laughter. 'That's too cryptic even for me.'

Eli grinned. 'I was thinking how much they've changed our sense of what's possible. Gillungs, not seagulls.'

They paused, watching a portly visitor in drysuit and divemask climb awkwardly down a ladder into the water while he explained his theory. Callan watched in appreciation as the norm's guide slipped in with barely a splash and stayed suspended in the water column, waiting for her charge to finish descending.

'I see your point,' said Callan as he and Eli resumed walking. 'It's scaring them though, isn't it? That's what Rhys says. It was hard enough for norms to accept us into society; they didn't bank on us *changing* it.' He gestured at the water. 'Us – gillungs – you know what I mean.'

'I know what you mean. And yes, there's going to be resistance, and some of it will no doubt get nasty. But societies don't run backwards, Callan. There's no way to unmake the last twelve, twenty, fifty years. The reality of gems – particularly gillungs – has transformed technology, literature, the arts, even the way we understand our own history. It's almost like a new mythology, weaving its way through the entire culture, becoming indelible: no matter what happens next, that reality will always *be* there.'

Not almost *like a mythology*, Eli thought; *it's* exactly *that*. He had grasped at a metaphor and hit on a truth. He could feel the revelation zinging around in his mind as it gathered up, sorted and reshaped his understanding. It made him want to laugh with the joy of discovery. He thought Callan must have noticed, but the younger man was leaning over the rail, calling out to someone below, 'You all right, friend?'

He was answered by coughing.

Eli stopped and leaned over too. A gillung man was standing on a narrow slipway, still calf-deep in the water, leaning against the embankment and spluttering. Eli recognised the bodysuit: it was the man who'd swum in from the river just a few minutes before. He was bent over, still coughing, and splashing water onto his face.

Callan had hurried to the head of the slipway and now he started down it. 'What's wrong?' he asked again. 'Do you need help?'

The man shook his head, blinking. Eli, at the top of the slipway himself now, did not recognise him; but then so many new gillungs had flooded in over the past few years as demand had grown for an estuary work force that it was no longer possible for everyone in the neighbouring communities of the Squats and Sinkat, much less the sprawling new settlements in Limedog further downstream, to know everyone else.

'I'm okay,' the man said, as Callan reached the water's edge and stopped. He sounded as though he was from Eastern Europe, maybe somewhere around the Baltic. 'Just couldn't get my breath. Was weird.' He shook himself, but the shake threatened to turn into a shudder.

'Maybe you're coming down with something?' Eli suggested, thinking how odd it would be if that were true. Gillungs, even more than most gems, had astonishingly robust immune systems.

'Don't know.' He squinted at the water, as though the sunlight was hurting his eyes. 'Everything went so strange. The river felt wrong.' He looked back at Callan and Eli, his gaze moving from

Callan's radiant hair to Eli's greying, and decidedly non-glowing pate. 'Is that what it's like? When you're ill?'

'Could be,' Eli replied, registering that the question had been directed at him. 'Depends what the illness is.'

'My husband's a doctor,' Callan said. 'He should be here by now; he's doing the afternoon shift at the medics' station. We'll take you there.' He was starting to shrug out of his coat. 'Put this on. Stay warm.'

'Hey, no, it's okay,' said the man, 'but thanks. It's not so bad now, and I'm almost home.' He pointed to a decidedly unglamorous amphibious building a little way along from Thames Tidal. 'I probably just need some rest.'

'You sure?'

'Yeah. Nice of you, though. Appreciate it.' He raised a webbed hand, stepping back down the slipway. 'Name's Tamin. Thanks, yeah?'

'I'm Callan,' said Callan. 'Don't mention it.'

'Eli,' said Eli. 'Look after yourself.' They watched as he dived beneath the boat lane and was gone.

Callan and Eli walked back to the marquees through crowds lively with holiday spirit. The tide was advancing out in the estuary, and as the water level rose, infostream displays tracked the amount of power generated turbine by turbine, minute by minute, inch by inch. Friends called each other to look, or tapped up panels that took them through the physics of energy capture, or simply stood and stared as though hypnotised by the slowly morphing infographics.

'It's so *clever*,' Eli overheard a young woman say, her voice slightly awestruck. 'All that energy from something that just happens *anyway*.' She was leaning in to her companion, hand in hand,

and the adoration with which she looked at the other girl was such that he doubted that TTP's telemetry was the sole source of her enchantment. But it was a sentiment he heard echoed again and again as they circled the basin.

Callan wore a thoughtful smile. 'It's what you were saying,' he remarked. 'This is transformative. Things may go well or they may go badly, but they can't go back.'

'Beautifully put. Can I steal that?'

He chuckled. 'Be my guest.'

Rhys was waiting for them. Eli got a quick handclasp before Callan wrapped an arm around Rhys' waist and kissed him, saying, 'Hello, sweetheart. Very canny of you, volunteering for this.'

'Wasn't it? I knew it would get even a workaholic like you out of the house. Don't even,' he added, as Callan affected a gasp of indignation.

'Fair cop,' Callan conceded. 'How long before you're on duty?'

'About an hour.'

'We almost brought you a patient,' said Eli, and described the encounter with Tamin.

'Strange. Is he coming in?'

'He said he was feeling better; he went home to lie down.' Eli looked around. 'Where's Ari?'

'Round the back, talking to Sharon. About you-know-who.' Callan's jaw tightened, and Rhys slipped a comforting hand into his.

'The boys are with Mikal?'

'No, with Gaela and Eve over by the kids' area. I haven't seen Mikal. Sharon said he was talking to reporters a couple of hours ago, then she lost track of him.' Rhys' nostrils flared slightly and he smiled. 'Here they are.'

Although Eli had had years to get used to Rhys' ability to tell, by smell and hearing and other barely understood cues, exactly where everyone within ten yards of him was, it still sometimes took him by surprise. It was another second before Aryel Morning-star appeared under the marquee, blinking away the sunlight. The rumble of conversation dropped as she threaded her way towards them. Sharon was a step or two behind, listening to messages with the tilted head and frown that they all recognised as Detective Superintendent Varsi in work mode.

Aryel looked as serene as a mountain lake, though even he could not always tell when she was really untroubled or just putting on the right face for the occasion. Sharon, for all her unflappable professionalism, had never been any good at pretending. She growled something into her earset and came off looking cranky.

'Don't ask,' she said to their enquiring faces. 'Police business. You don't want to know. *I* don't want to know.'

'So leave it,' said Rhys. 'It'll be better after lunch.'

'Thanks, but I really should reclaim my children. Maybe even find my husband while I'm at it.'

'How come he's not working the crowds and pressing the flesh?'

'Because he's the one being pressed and worked today. I got a message from somewhere in the bowels of Thames Tidal.'

'Pilan.' Aryel sighed.

'Not just Pilan.' Sharon's smile was tight. 'Apparently there are three different players, trying to back him into three different corners – it's like some overwritten vid drama, with extra scheming.'

Aryel's eyes widened in surprise. '*Three?*'

'Oh yes. I'll let him tell you all about it. He'll probably have some thoughts on our other looming challenge as well.'

Sharon shook her head in disgust as Eli claimed a table and Rhys and Callan joined the queue that Horace and Delial were briskly serving. 'There's a bit too much about to go wrong for my taste. I prefer my crises to be spaced out.'

'I wouldn't call it *that*,' Aryel objected. 'Just a number of sub-optimal events—'

'—possibly all occurring at the same time,' Eli offered.

'My love, you're not helping.'

Sharon snorted. 'I smell crisis, and so do you. Both of you. We've been here before.' She perused the list of offerings on the screen above Horace's head. 'They have fig cake? What the hell – get me some, would you, Rhys? I'll take it for the boys. Most of it.' She sat down. 'I could use five minutes off my feet. Gaela's got the kids corralled in the play tent. She won't mind.'

Gaela was in fact outside the Child's Play marquee, leaning against the safety rail with her eyes half closed, breathing deep and slow. The riot of light and colour, the spitting, sparkling whirligig dynamos and the strange subtle blur of radiation from the charged jellyfish batteries combined with the shouts and laughter of a dozen children at play, had brought her to the edge of a migraine and accompanying bout of synaesthesia. She'd left Lapsa, Agwé and Jolay to keep an eye on the kids and stepped away from the sensory overload. If she used it early enough, the breathing technique had a good chance of turning aside a headache that would otherwise batter her for hours in wave after wave of garishly coloured pain. She gave herself ten minutes, gazing at the water through slitted eyes as she slipped into the pattern that would help calm her misfiring synapses.

So she did not notice the man in the pleasantly dull brown waterproof who paused and watched her keenly before he stepped beneath the canvas. He moved quickly, putting as many bodies between them as possible.

When he emerged a couple of minutes later, she was straightening up and shaking back her hair as she worked through the last of the routine. Her body language was signalling an imminent return to the fray. The man dodged behind a clump of noisy teenagers camped on the quayside and cut in front of an elderly couple rambling arm in arm, moving with a swiftness at odds with the rest of the TideFair topsiders.

By the time she turned around, he was gone.

10

The TideFair was barely over before the first reports began to come in.

Gabriel knew that something was amiss the next morning when half the people who showed up to work at the Thames Tidal office were shivering and coughing and complaining of a strange, itchy ache in their lungs and gill tissue. Pilan, himself wrapped in a thick jumper and scowling with the effort to appear healthy, ordered them all to go home before they spread whatever it was even further, but by the afternoon many were arriving at the local hospital, aching and bewildered. By evening more than twenty gillungs had been admitted.

The onstream reaction was predictable, but Gabriel had half a day's head start. His monitor apps flagged the first, slightly quizzical socialstream posts commenting on the unusual phenomenon of gillungs seeking medical treatment. Those posts were quickly consolidated by newstream aggregators, and journalists began to file their own stories. By then he and Lapsa had conferred with Thames Tidal's publicity service and with the hospital, and were ready with a statement. It confirmed that company members were among a number of gillungs who had suddenly fallen ill, and that the health services were working to establish the precise nature of the ailment. Those affected were in a serious but stable condition. Anyone with similar flu-like symptoms was urged to seek medical attention, especially if they had been at the TideFair.

'Did it have to say that?' Agwé asked, sitting beside him in the big TTP project offices, watching as the reactions scrolled past. 'It makes it look like we think whatever it is started here.'

'We don't know it didn't, Ag. The TideFair is one thing everyone who's sick has in common – maybe we had an infected visitor wandering around, coughing on people.' He shrugged. 'There's no point putting out a Thames Tidal press release if we're going to pretend it doesn't have anything to do with us.'

'I don't remember anyone coughing on anyone. I don't remember any coughing at all. And if that's what happened, why aren't any norms ill?' Agwé looked at him accusingly. 'We're not supposed to be the ones who get sick.'

Gabriel made a face at her. She said, 'Sorry, I didn't mean it like that.'

'I know, but do me a favour and don't say it like that onstream, okay? That's why they're getting so worked up.' He flapped his hand at the screen. 'If there's some bug that can make even gil-lungs ill, what'll it do to the rest of us?'

'Probably nothing, seeing it's just us who *are* ill.'

'So far, Ag. So far.'

That fear was the focus of much of the stream commentary: there was sympathy for the sick and worry over what the sudden shortage of staff might mean for the power plant, but also bile from a vocal few who could barely contain their glee at the discovery of a weakness in the upstart water-breathers. Lacking concrete answers and cautious about trying to spin the story without them, Gabriel felt powerless to do much more than monitor the tide of opinion, which built as the day wound down, the news spread and the numbers in hospital increased. Vidcam crews gathered expectantly outside the Thames Tidal airlock, in the same spot where they had, the day before, assembled in the morning sunshine to salute the company's ingenuity and ambition. This time they were bathed in artificial light and a palpable air of Schadenfreude.

Gabriel groaned and dropped his head into his hands.

'What's the point of all this?' asked Agwé rhetorically. 'They already know everything we know.'

'They're not here for news. They're here to ask questions they know we don't have answers for in the hope that we'll be pushed into saying something they can take out of context. I thought you knew about journalism.'

'That's not my kind of journalism.'

Lapsa went out to talk to the press. 'Obviously, we're concerned,' she told them. 'Illness is very rare for us. The health service is working to identify—'

'How fast is it spreading?' someone called out.

'I couldn't say. We'll have a better idea once—'

'Can norms catch it?'

Gabriel, watching on a screen inside the office, saw Lapsa's normally serene features cloud over and knew that she must want to snap, *How the fuck should I know?* She didn't, of course, and he was immensely relieved that it was her and not Pilan out there. But there was a brittle edge to her voice as she said, 'I have no idea who can or cannot catch it, or how contagious it is, or how it's transmitted. I do know that most of us who don't have it spend a lot of time with people who do.' She spread her hands to indicate herself. The vidcam lights gleamed on the webbing between her fingers. 'That includes gillungs, other gems and norms. We're just getting on with—'

'Are you worried about your baby?'

There was a sharp intake of breath and Gabriel clenched his fists. He glanced sideways at Agwé, whose mouth had dropped open in outrage. Even Qiyem, also unaffected by the mystery illness and watching on his own workstation screen across the room, looked uneasy. Out on the quay, the noise of the media pack faded abruptly.

Lapsa's face had gone stone-quiet. She stared at the questioner, pinning him with the weight of her fury, before she said coldly, 'I have no reason to be worried.'

On the screen it looked like hesitation.

'So,' said another voice, sounding a little embarrassed, 'is it possible that not everyone is susceptible to this pathogen?'

'Or does it just take longer in some people?' came the voice that had asked about the baby.

'I suppose that's possible. By morning we hope to know more.'

By morning they knew it wasn't pestilential at all. Rhys, who had the triple advantage (or, as Callan observed, *dis*advantage, depending on your point of view) of having been duty medic at the TideFair, the doctor who had referred the first reported victim and one of the very few with a detailed knowledge of gillung physiology, had got himself seconded from Genetic Medicine to the closed ward where the sick of Sinkat were being treated. He had been grappling with the mystery ever since Tamin's housemate had come hurrying to find him and led him back to their semi-aquatic flat where Tamin lolled in an access pool in the floor, clinging weakly to its rim and unwilling to emerge.

'He says he feels better in the water,' said the housemate, 'but that's where he was when he got ill. So I'm not sure . . .'

Rhys had persuaded him out and into a hospital bed, where

he fell into a state of fitful unconsciousness overnight, failing to improve the next day. He was, Rhys was certain, Patient Zero in the unfolding crisis, and by some considerable margin the sickest of the lot. They'd still not managed to identify the pathogen, and none of the antivirals were having much effect. Rhys worked through that second night with the microbiologists and virologists, and by early the next morning they finally had some answers.

'It's not contagious,' Rhys told Aryel, Mikal and Sharon, crowded into a too-small office near the closed ward, along with Dr Budram, the hospital's senior pulmonary consultant; Dr Carvalho, a top clinical toxicologist, and Omana Dawny, the head of Physiotherapy. 'The symptoms are similar to a viral infection, so we assumed they must have contracted it from each other – but they didn't. We're certain now that it's not a virus. It's a toxin.'

Sharon, who had been as anxious as any of them but surprised that Rhys had asked her to attend a medical briefing, looked up sharply at that. Rhys took a sip of the coffee Aryel had brought him and met the detective superintendent's eyes over the rim of the cup. 'We think it must have been present in Sinkat Basin for two to three hours during the TideFair. Our estimate—'

'Hang on,' Sharon said, 'you mean this was *deliberate*? Something was released into the water?'

'Something was; whether it was deliberate or not I don't know. I thought you'd want to be aware of the possibility. Even if it does turn out to have been an accident, or a safety violation—'

'—we'd need to be involved either way. Good call, Rhys.'

'We'll be asking more questions today, but what's clear so far is that everyone who's ill, whether their symptoms are mild or severe, breathed in Sinkat water at some point during the afternoon. Lapsa and Agwé are a case in point. They're not ill, but Pilan is, even though they all live in the same house. He told us he went for a swim around lunchtime, said he needed to clear his head after a meeting—'

Mikal tutted under his breath.

Rhys waited politely for a moment, then continued, 'The other two were topside all day. Agwé swam over to a friend's house, but not until quite late in the evening and she's fine. Lapsa popped out through their access pool at dawn to supervise the setting-up and *she's* fine. Everyone we've interviewed fits that pattern. There are no reports of illness from people out in the estuary or elsewhere on the river. So our working hypothesis is that it was caused by a local aquatic contaminant, and we don't think the contamination is on-going, because it looks like people have stopped getting sick.' He squinted at the morning beginning to spread its canopy of sunlight against the window and said quietly, 'Of course, we don't know that it won't happen again.'

'There are water-quality monitors,' Aryel said, in the probing tone that meant she was going to poke at his theory to make sure there were no holes in it. 'All along the river, as well as in Sinkat and Limedog. They transmit to the Environmental Management datastream. A contaminant should have set off alarms, sent an emergency message to every gillung registered in the city to get out of the water.' She looked at Mikal.

'Indeed it should,' he said, 'and I will be having a very serious conversation with that department shortly. Do they know about the situation yet?'

'We've only just worked it out ourselves,' Rhys replied. 'Dr Carvalho has sent an urgent query, I think' – the toxicologist nodded confirmation – 'and I've had a look at the public infostream; there's nothing unusual that I can see, but we don't actually know what the contaminant is yet. Maybe it's a failure in the system, but it might also be something the monitors simply aren't programmed to pick up.'

Sharon was tapping notes into her tablet. 'Concerns have recently been expressed,' she said without looking up, 'about whether Environmental Management does enough to monitor the marine environment.'

'Noted,' Mikal replied drily, and returned his attention to Rhys. 'So this is essentially a case of poisoning, correct? Possibly accidental, and limited to a few hours a couple of days ago. But until we know precisely what caused it, we can't be certain it won't happen again. Have I got that right?'

'That about sums it up. We thought you ought to know as quickly as possible that whatever we're looking at, it extends well beyond the remit of the health services.'

'Thank you,' Aryel said to Rhys and the rest of the medical team. 'An excellent night's work. We can reassure the public that there isn't an epidemic in East London—'

'—unless more of this crap gets into the water before we find it,' Sharon muttered.

'Yes, but at least we know what we're looking for now. What about your patients? Can you cure them, now that you know what's wrong?'

'Well . . .' Rhys glanced around at the other doctors. Despite being the most junior in the hospital hierarchy, they looked content to let him be their spokesperson. As he rubbed a weary hand across his face and over the short ruby-shimmer of his hair, his finger brushed against the thin wire of the cranial band and he noted wryly that he and Aryel were the only ones wearing them. 'They all started feeling sick either in or shortly after coming out of the water, and they got progressively sicker as it worked its way through their systems. They've stopped getting worse, but they're not getting better either. My final hypothesis of the day is this: if we get them into clean oxygenated water, that might help to flush the toxin. It binds to the gills' receptor sites and we haven't been able to shift it. But Tamin, who's now dangerously ill, was conscious when I first got to him, and he was still mobile when Eli and Cal saw him earlier in the day – and he didn't want to come out of the water. Something about it was making him feel better, and that doesn't make sense if he was still breathing in the toxin. But if the concentration had dropped and clean water was starting to displace the poison, that might explain it.'

'That sounds like sense to me,' said Mikal, 'but it's still a risk, isn't it? Putting someone so sick back into the water?'

'It is – we'll test it first on one of the patients who's in better shape, and who can tell us how they're feeling. We'll need a volunteer—'

'Pilan will do it,' Aryel said before he'd finished. 'Bet you anything.'

Rhys chuckled. 'How right you are, Ari. Pilan was awake when I did my last round and I told him that we were hatching this idea – he said yes before I'd even finished getting the words out.' He looked at Ms Dawny. 'Assuming everyone approves, of course.'

'I've already cancelled today's bookings for the hydrotherapy pool,' the head physio replied. 'I'll get it set up.' She looked round at the other consultants for confirmation. Dr Carvalho was already nodding his agreement; he talked about various other antigens that behaved in a similar way, and why the suggestion was sensible.

Dr Budram agreed rather more succinctly, and said that she too had cleared her schedule. 'It's an experimental treatment, so all patients will need to be under my direct care,' she said to Rhys.

'But as it's your idea, Dr Morgan, and you've already recruited a volunteer . . .'

'I would very much like to be there,' he said with a smile. 'Thanks.'

The physio slipped out, followed shortly by the other doctors. Dr Carvalho, who had also been up all night, had begun to yawn hugely.

'Are you going home?' Aryel asked as she and Rhys walked arm in arm out to the hospital's main lobby, following Mikal, who had moved forward to take point and deal with the press pack who'd no doubt be waiting. Like Sharon, he was issuing a steady stream of instructions into his earset as he strode ahead.

'Not yet,' Rhys said. 'A lot needs to be confirmed in the next hour or so, and we'll probably get the answers quicker if I'm the one asking questions. Not that they don't trust norm doctors, but . . .' He nodded at the portraits of eminent physicians lining the walls of the lobby. 'You know.'

Aryel regarded the gallery of notables without expression. 'We need more gem doctors. I know.'

'So I think I need to stay close to this. They should be ready to try the treatment on Pilan pretty quickly, and if it looks like it's working, we'll get the others in too. I'm the only one here who really knows any gillungs – the only one who's ever been swimming with them, all that stuff. I might spot things the others won't.'

'I agree – but not just because it'll reassure the patients.' She looked up at him. 'With the best will in the world, Carvalho and the others wouldn't have figured this out so quickly without you. You're not just a good doctor, Rhys, important though that is, and I think we're going to need the full range of your talents. This feels too precise to have been an accident.'

He'd already thought the same himself. 'Thanks, Ari. Now I just need to persuade the department.'

'I'll have a word with your masters at GenMed, but given how serious this is I can't see them objecting to loaning you out for a while. Besides, I suspect Sharon would happily shoot anyone who tried to take you off this case.'

11

The medical team's conclusions, hinted at but expertly left hanging when Mikal spoke to the press outside the hospital, were confirmed by an official bulletin at noon. Lapsa, Agwé and Gabriel had been updated just before that by Pilan, speaking from the hydrotherapy pool where he was supposed to be staying quiet and immersed.

'It's a bloody miracle,' he said, via the tablet Rhys was holding for him. They could see he was lying on a gurney a couple of feet underwater, tilted to allow his face to break the surface while his body remained submerged. 'It's like I was never even sick.' There was an emphatic splash and a small wave lapped over the lower edge of the screen. Agwé chortled and Lapsa's drawn face went slack with relief.

'I wouldn't go that far,' Rhys said drily. 'You only get a couple of minutes topside to talk, so make the most of them.'

'But I'm better.'

'You're *feeling* better. There's a difference.' The image tilted a little.

Rhys must be crouched on the edge of the pool, Gabriel thought, *leaning over with the tablet.* The hospital wouldn't have had time, nor necessarily the inclination, to rig up a sub-aquatic communications system.

'Pilan's gill function is definitely improving,' Rhys said, speaking now to the listeners in Sinkat, 'but we don't yet know how long it'll take to flush all the toxin, or how quickly his other organ systems will recover. He definitely won't be going home today. We might start to think about it tomorrow, if things go exceptionally well.'

'But—' Pilan objected.

'But nothing, mate. Say your goodbyes before I tip you back under.'

'We need to work out how this stuff got into the basin,' Pilan said rapidly. 'Everything that came in for the TideFair needs to be checked. There were repairs to one of the wet buildings last week—'

'Pilan,' said Lapsa, while Agwé and Gabriel grinned at each other.

'One of their products might've become contaminated offsite—'

'*Pilan.*'

'Which is one way this poison could have been introduced deliberately. I know we don't want to say that yet, but—'

'Pilan!' Lapsa and Rhys shouted together, and Lapsa added firmly, 'Shut up.'

Pilan's face sank lower in the water as Rhys prodded threateningly at the gurney.

'We know all this,' Lapsa went on. 'Environmental Management teams are all over the basin and the river, taking samples and testing the monitors. Turns out they're months behind on their regular checks—'

'No surprise there,' muttered Agwé.

'But we now appear to have their undivided attention. The police are interviewing the repair teams and the vendors, testing everything they brought onsite, and searching the entire area including the canals, topside and below. We've spread the word to avoid going into the water until further notice. We're on top of it.'

Pilan still looked worried. 'What do people think is going on?'

'The toxin rumour's already out,' Gabriel said. 'We're just waiting for the hospital to confirm it.'

'That should happen in the next few minutes,' Rhys put in.

'Good,' Gabriel replied. 'That should send one set of scare-mongers packing. But we won't need to bring up the possibility of sabotage. It's in the air already.'

'Who's saying it?' asked Pilan.

'Who isn't?' said Agwé. 'Everyone here thinks that the point must have been to try and disrupt the TideFair – which it sort of has, because instead of talking about how great the fair was, the streams are full of this.'

'The police are going to issue an appeal for information,' Gabriel added. 'Aunt Sha— I mean, Detective Superintendent Varsi says that'll give every crackpot in London something to do for a couple of days, but it's worth it in case someone out there noticed something important.'

'The problem is, we don't know *what* might be important,' said Agwé. 'Do we? Do *you*?'

'We have some ideas,' Rhys replied. 'Remember, a toxin is a poison of biological origin. We know this one was produced by an engineered micro-organism—'

'That doesn't exactly narrow it down,' said Lapsa, and Agwé added, 'Half of everything is produced that way.'

'Yes, but everything that's a legitimate product or by-product is registered. Maybe some rogue microbe farmer decided to chuck an experiment down a storm drain rather than pay for proper disposal – that might explain why the toxin isn't on any of our databases. The point is, it's possible that the by-product of an industrial process got into the water without anyone knowing or intending it to cause harm.'

'Or,' said Agwé, 'they *did* know, they *did* intend, and this was specially planned to hurt us and no one else.'

'That can't be ruled out,' Rhys said grimly, 'but just remember, that's only one possibility.'

It turned out to be far from the only possibility the streams latched onto. Gabriel had thought himself impervious to even the nastiest of innuendoes, but as the afternoon wore on he became more and more appalled. Along with an outpouring of relief that there was no risk of contagion and speculation about terrorism came a wave of mostly anonymous assertions that the situation must, somehow, be the gillungs' own fault: who knew what they got up to in their secret laboratories and sub-aquatic dwellings? What illicit experiment of *theirs* had come back to bite them? And wasn't it just typical that they would try to blame *normal* people? In contrast to the public support that had followed the turbine sabotage – praise for the speed of the repair, delight at Agwé's vid, the huge turnout for the TideFair – it was as if those of a different disposition had finally found a hook upon which to hang their rage.

Gabriel found himself staring for far too long at what was becoming far too typical a comment:

If they're going to fall over every time something goes wrong, they can't be trusted with that power plant. How can it be safe when they're all lounging in hospital? How do we know the next thing they cook up won't put the rest of us there?

It was another avatar, one of the ephemeral battalion that Gabriel had collectively come to think of as Kaboom, although he could not tell whether it was a shadowy network with a central command or just disaffected individuals with a shared ideology. Either way, they were making great sport of a leaked image of patients on their submerged beds, detoxing in the hydrotherapy pool, and ridiculed the efforts of the police and EM officers crawling all over Sinkat and as yet finding nothing.

He did what he could to counter their scorn: wit and sarcasm here, updates from the hospital and the smoothly operating power plant there, links to newstream reports. He didn't need to add anything to the sober assessments of journalists who were openly discussing the likelihood of a targeted attack, and there was nothing he could do to counter the thread of anger and fear in the minds of his friends, his colleagues and himself. It showed in the unfamiliar emptiness of Sinkat Basin, where boats nosed in and out but people more used to swimming walked the quays and bridges instead; it flared in the tension between himself and Agwé when he made the mistake of musing aloud that some live shots of business as usual at the turbines, farms and factories of the estuary would be a useful counter-narrative. It had been wishful thinking rather than anything he wanted her to act on, but she hopped aboard the next shuttle-boat, chin tilted high and full of braggadocio.

'No way,' she said, when he wavered and tried to claw the idea back. 'We're *professionals*. No matter what these fuckers say, we get the job done. Right?'

'Right,' he'd replied weakly. 'That's us. Professional.'

He knew in that moment it would be their lifelong in-joke, a shared armour against every insecurity and slight, the tune they would whistle past the graveyard. They would work twice as hard to maintain that aura of impregnability, in the eyes of others as well as in their own.

He was on his way home, still monitoring despite having handed over to the night shift, mired in a swamp of unfairness and meanness. As he walked, the cranial band brought him the latest iteration of Kaboom, slipping into a streamchat with a group that had started off more sympathetic than suspicious; a few well-placed barbs later and they were talking conspiracy and cover-up. He noted that Kaboom had added nothing new for several exchanges now; in all probability had gone to seed doubt and distrust elsewhere. Something in him snapped.

He looked around, realising that he had passed unheeding from Sinkat into the Squats and was working his way home through the narrow streets on autopilot. He changed direction, messaging his mother as he did so.

Stopping off to see Herran. Won't be long.

That might prove to be very true, if Herran was not in the mood for visitors, but he responded immediately to Gabriel's next message and admitted him before he'd even rested his fingers on the identipad at the entrance to Maryam House. As the door slid sideways, Gabriel blinked in surprise.

He must have hacked the security vidcam. Waving at it, he stepped into the building that had once been his home.

Sadness lapped at him as he crossed the lobby. He had known death in this place, had felt the lights of other minds go out, and he still remembered the numbness that had descended on his own. The magnitude of the loss then had been so great that he, just a child, hadn't been able to comprehend it. He wondered if he would handle it any better now, and wondered too, as he mounted the steps and stopped outside Herran's door, how much of his willingness to wear the band was down to his wish to protect himself, not just from the fears of others but from his own fear of ever experiencing that sudden, gaping emptiness again.

He tapped out a familiar pattern on the door – of course Herran knew he was here, but it was a necessary part of the ritual. It slid open, and he stepped inside.

Herran had lived in the same small, tidy flat for as long as Gabriel could remember. He was a diminutive man, much shorter than Gabriel, with a mop of curls in the faintly glowing Bel'Natur red also borne by Gaela and Callan. As always he was sitting in front of his bank of screens, watching vid images, stream feeds and code scrolling across. The tiny pulsing light of his cranial band was almost lost against the riot of his hair; Gabriel's mind balked at the thought of how many channels he must be monitoring. He had pale grey eyes with long lashes and a scarred upper lip, in a face as imperturbable as glass.

Gabriel stopped just at arm's-length and held his hands forward, palms out. 'Hello, Herran,' he said. 'Are you well?'

The little man looked at him obliquely. His head and upper body were rocking slightly as he reached out and touched Gabriel's offered hands with his own. 'Gabe,' he said. 'Well. You?'

'Yes. Well, no, not exactly.' He pulled up a chair. 'I'm fine, but a lot of the people I work with are in hospital.'

'Bad water. Getting better.' He blinked. 'Rhys fix.'

He was still looking at Gabriel. It felt strange to be so much the focus of Herran's attention; before the band, he would most likely have been gazing at something completely unrelated on the screens while talking to a visitor. This new, more normal arrangement should be less disconcerting. Oddly, it was not.

Gabriel shook his head and focused on the problem at hand. 'Yes, they're getting better, and Rhys and the police are going to find out what made the water bad. But in the meantime there are streamers saying horrible things, trying to turn other people against them.'

'People stupid on streams.' Herran's voice was matter-of-fact. 'Always.'

'They aren't being stupid, Herran. They're actually really clever. Remember when you showed me how to monitor streamchats, when we talked about avatars? Well, they're using avatars for this: a *lot* of avatars.'

He paused, trying to organise his thoughts. His own sense of outrage would not simply sweep Herran along; the little gem's rigidly logical mind meant he had to explain things in a way that conveyed the precise nature of the problem.

'They're telling lies about Thames Tidal,' he started, 'saying things to make people think we're dangerous or careless. That would be okay if they stayed up long enough for us to respond, but they're like . . . like midges. They're everywhere, stinging and stinging, but you can't grab hold of them.' He mimicked flailing at a cloud of invisible insects. 'They pop onto the streams, into chats and forums, and they always sound like they belong so the regulars don't realise they're being infiltrated. They never post direct accusations, nothing that could be reported to administrators, or the police – it's always just suggestions, insinuations, the kind of thing that gets people thinking there really *must* be a problem. But there are no links to anything out in the real world, no evidence, nothing that could be followed up. They post maybe five or six times, then they dump the avatar and they're gone. The real users mostly don't even notice – they're too busy turning the slander into gossip. I've been seeing the same pattern for more than a week now, ever since the turbines were damaged. It's getting worse – it's become really nasty, and I don't think it's random. I want to know who's behind it.' He looked Herran in the eye. 'I want you to help me.'

Herran looked back at him, impassive. 'Bad people,' he agreed, 'but not against rules.'

'It might not be illegal, Herran, but it's *wrong*. They shouldn't do it. And everyone says they *don't* do it, which is why if I can find out who's breaking their *own* rules, I can make it fucking embarrassing for them.'

Herran sat and rocked for a full minute. 'Swearing,' he finally observed. 'New. Okay.' He turned back to his monitors. 'I find. Quick quick.'

'You *will*?'

'Yes. Need data.'

Gabriel felt the request to share his files as a tug through his band. Herran could have broken through with no more effort than it would have taken him to scratch his nose or shuffle his feet – no datastream that Gabriel knew of was secure enough to keep Herran out if he wanted in, and he had written the encryption code for the bands himself. But in his own strange, brusque way he was always scrupulously polite about personal digital space. Gabriel gave him access and he got to work.

As expected, it did not take long; barely long enough for Gabriel to have made them both tea.

He had drunk only a little of his when Herran announced, 'Five streamers.' He was studying the machine code scrolling across one of his screens. 'Many layers encryption. Good job.' He sounded faintly impressed.

'Are they working together?'

'Sequestered,' Herran said. 'Invisible. Different platforms, different streams. No sharing, no messages.' He checked something. 'Mostly different times.'

'You mean they've got nothing to do with each other?' That felt completely wrong; the pattern in the files he had shared was too consistent.

'Same apps, encryption, avatar generators,' Herran said. 'Special. Not seen before. Built for hiding and faking.'

'So they're all using the same set of tools and doing the same things with them,' Gabriel said slowly, 'but they've got different shift patterns and areas of responsibility? And they don't communicate with each other at all?'

'Same tools,' Herran confirmed, 'no communication.' He cocked his head as though a surprising thought had occurred to him, and added, 'Onstream.'

'Good point. Where are they, physically? Are they posting from the same location?'

'No.'

He thought about that for a moment. 'Are they all in London?'

'Yes.'

'Can you give me addresses? Do they move around?'

'No.' Herran's eyes unfocused as he parsed information through the band. 'Onstream from working places.'

'So we know where they work—'

'—work *from*,' Herran corrected. His face had gone vague, slightly confused, and he rapped the heel of one hand against his temple as if he might shake more useful words loose that way. 'Not work *for*.' A directory listing appeared on the screen and he moved aside so Gabriel could look at it.

'Oh! "Working place" . . . You mean a business hub. For freelancers.' Gabriel chewed at a fingernail in frustration. 'They can be used anonymously. Fake names . . .'

'Yes. Every time different.'

'But you can track the tablets, right, no matter what false ID they layer over them? Because they must go onstream from home too, or wherever they are the rest of the time – nobody's ever *not* onstream, even if they're not active.'

'Other tablets, maybe. These silent. No standby signal. No tracking.'

'So,' Gabriel said, 'we've got five people who have tablets and software that go dark when they're not onstream. And they're only ever used for one purpose, and only from locations where the users can remain anonymous. They have no contact with each other via these tablets. They could be using different ones to communicate, but since they're all in the city they could also be meeting up in person, getting their instructions that way.'

'Possible,' Herran agreed.

'For people who aren't doing anything illegal, Herran, they've gone to a great deal of trouble.'

Herran blinked at him. 'I watch,' he said after a bit. 'Maybe find more.'

'Thanks. Will you message me what you've got so far?'

'Yes. I make easy for you.' His fingers slipped over the input screen, organising the data into a form that someone other than himself could understand, while Gabriel sat back and tried to think through what to do with the information.

They had confirmed the existence of a conspiracy, one far more clandestine and well-resourced than he had anticipated when he'd asked Herran for help. They might not know who was behind it, but the sheer slickness of the operation eliminated several possibilities.

These are professionals. The word echoed in his mind, hollow and mocking.

They had no proof that the five anonymous streamers had broken the law, though he was far less confident about what he and Herran had done. And even if Herran did find out who the streamers were, it wouldn't be enough; they still had to find out for whom they were working.

Herran sent him the link, picked up his cup and sipped his own cooling tea. His grey eyes regarded Gabriel steadily over the rim. 'Aryel ask about Zavcka,' he said.

The change of subject was so abrupt that Gabriel felt momentarily disoriented. 'Because she's getting out of prison?'

'Yes. Worry for Eve.'

'But Zavcka Klist doesn't know about Eve.' He suddenly realised why Herran might have brought it up. 'She *doesn't*, does she?' he asked in alarm.

'No,' said Herran. 'Bad access from prison. Also, looking wrong places.'

'That's a relief. But when she gets out—'

'I watch.'

'Thank you, Herran. Thank you very, very much.'

12

Sharon Varsi paused just inside the door of the incident room assigned to the Thames toxin investigation, surveying the three people already gathered around the table. After a silent moment she sat down and looked expectantly across at DI Achebe. She'd felt a twinge of sympathy for him when she'd put him in charge of the case, knowing from experience how disagreeable it was to conduct an enquiry with a senior officer peering over your shoulder. Now, as his worried brown eyes met hers, her heart sank. Achebe was a competent officer and he'd worked on tricky cases before. Asking her to join a conference this early on was unlikely to be a good sign.

It comforted her somewhat that Rhys was there. Achebe introduced the other attendee, Fayole, a field supervisor from Environmental Management. She was a gem woman about Sharon's age with vivid blue hair braided and coiled on top of her head, casting a faint sapphire glow all around her face.

'We've met before, I think,' Sharon said, reaching across to shake hands. 'There was a recruitment drive a few years ago, about encouraging more diverse applicants to the public sector—'

'That's right,' the woman replied. 'And there was a reception at City Hall after the last election.' She dipped her head with a mixture of pride and resignation. 'They like sending me to things like that.'

Rhys snickered in amused recognition and Sharon's mouth quirked too, an acknowledgement of all that Fayole's remark implied. They were all members of the vanguard, and knew only too well the dubious honour of being forever trotted out as an example for others to follow. Sharon thought it unlikely that Fayole's normal area of responsibility included this part of the city; if it did, she suspected they'd have encountered each other more often. It was quite possible that her superiors, sensitive to criticism of the department and now under particular scrutiny from Mikal, had assigned her as liaison purely for public relations reasons.

Achebe looked perplexed, but apparently decided that whatever undercurrent was passing between the others was beside the point of his investigation. 'We've come to some conclusions,' he said. 'Unfortunately, they raise some new and disturbing questions.'

Rhys smiled wryly, and Sharon could see the strain. 'In other words, the mystery deepens.'

She glowered at him. 'That's possibly my least favourite phrase. Ever.'

'Sorry, but it does.' He turned politely back to Achebe.

'The incidence of toxicity in Sinkat Basin correlates with the presence of an algae,' the detective inspector said. 'As I understand it, that's not unusual – all sorts of micro-organisms live in the river, but they're in relatively low concentrations and in balance with each other.' He looked over at Fayole for confirmation. When she nodded, he continued, 'What's allowed as runoff from farms and so on is highly regulated, mostly to keep the Thames from being flooded with the kind of nutrients that can make things grow out of control and cause a bloom. But some variation is normal and expected, and within limits it doesn't trigger an alert from the monitoring system.'

'So was there enough of this algae to do that or not?' Sharon asked. There was value in Achebe's slow, methodical explanation, but knowing that didn't increase her patience.

'There wasn't,' said Fayole, 'because it's normally harmless. There was a spike that we can't explain, but the amount was still below the level that would generate an alarm.'

'Then why is it important?'

'Because it was altered,' Fayole said. 'This one was engineered. Our teams recovered samples from various spots along the river – to be honest, we didn't realise that there was anything different about them at first. The change is very subtle; it wasn't until they looked at this one particular sample, collected where Sinkat Basin joins the main channel, that they noticed it was secreting something . . .' She trailed off, looking at Rhys.

'It'd been hacked to produce the toxin,' he said bluntly, 'but it doesn't do it all the time, or at least, not at high enough levels to be a problem. The samples from further upstream are virtually dormant – they look and act just like the ordinary, unmodified organism. The samples from downstream are also dormant, but they are fewer, and they're degraded and dying: they look just the way the active sample Fayole's people sent to toxicology looked by the time we got it. The reaction had stopped. It was the concentration of toxin that allowed us to deduce what had happened. In the river it would've become so diluted I doubt we'd've been able to detect it.'

'You're telling me,' Sharon said, 'that not only has an ordinary river microbe been turned into a gillung poison factory, but that it doesn't start making said poison until it's in actually in the place where they *live*?' Her insides felt cold. 'And then it dies?'

'Basically, yes.'

She stared at Rhys, aghast, and then at the others. 'How is that even possible?'

'It reacts to something,' Rhys said. 'We don't know what, but it's the only explanation that makes sense. It travelled downriver, photosynthesising and reproducing and generally behaving the way a boring little brown algae is supposed to behave. It appears to have been quite efficient because it hadn't been too diluted by the larger volume of water, and that suggests that it was rapidly making more of itself – but as Fayole says, not enough to set off the monitors. By midday it started to arrive just where the river washes through Sinkat, and there it encountered something that acted as a catalyst. It triggered our innocent little algae to start pumping out toxin at an enormous rate, burning itself out in the process.'

Pausing for breath, Rhys met Sharon's eyes with a grimness she had not seen in him for years. 'If you think that's impressive, here's where it gets *really* clever: the other thing that happened when this algae arrived in Sinkat was that the tide was coming in. It peaked in the early afternoon. Do you remember when we met up for lunch? And all the visitors were clustered around watching the energy infographics? Well, at that point the water had essentially stopped flowing downstream. It pooled, and so did the algae, and so, of course, did the toxin.'

Sharon clenched her teeth to stop herself swearing. She looked down at the table for a moment, letting the full malevolence of what Rhys was describing wash over her. When she looked back up, she could see her own full-blown horror mirrored on everyone else's faces, as if to say now that she knew the truth, they no longer had to put on a brave show.

'And then?' she asked steadily.

'And then it all washed away on the ebbing tide, dying and becoming diluted as it went. A few people from the Limedog area have reported feeling poorly, and the timing of their symptoms matches up with when the toxin would have flowed past them. But there aren't many, and their symptoms are much milder: the toxin had become so diffused by then that it didn't have much impact.'

'I see.' Her own voice sounded alien to her, quiet and dangerously calm.

Rhys and Achebe knew what that meant; they shifted and glanced at each other as she turned to Fayole. 'You said there was a spike you can't explain.'

'Yes . . .'

'Try.'

Fayole met her gaze. Her eyes were, a little to Sharon's surprise, just as angry as her own.

'Can we put this back up?' Fayole asked Achebe as she swiped her tablet awake, but her gaze stayed on Sharon.

A map appeared on the screen on the back wall of the incident room: the Thames, centred on Sinkat and bracketed by City Hall and the bridge to the left and the long southern sweep of the river as it curved past Limedog on the right. Fayole flicked at the tablet and the map shifted with dizzying speed, scrolling sideways and upriver – but not far, Sharon realised. They were still in the city.

'These are the western suburbs,' Fayole said. 'There's a lot of green space, as you can see – some parts are quite densely populated, but there are many derelict neighbourhoods, especially south of the river.' She expanded a segment of the map marked out in different shades of green, crossed with meandering streams and the lines of drainage ditches. 'This whole area is wetland. Our monitoring station just upriver didn't detect any spike, and nor did most of those within the swamp itself. But there's one in this channel' – she tapped at a gently curving water-course, as blue as her hair, that led into the river – 'which did register a big increase in microflora count earlier that morning.'

Sharon studied the map. The white line of an access road ran near the channel, touching it at one point. 'So you knew there was a problem,' she said.

'No, we didn't,' Fayole replied. 'The system flagged it up, but there was no reason for the colleagues who received that alert to think there was anything wrong—'

'Why not?'

'Because it's a wetland,' Fayole said tiredly, 'and algal blooms are quite common in that environment. It's also common for readings to fluctuate after heavy rain when runoff goes into the catchment area – that's part of what it's for. And there had been storms the day before, if you remember. So yes, there was a spike, but it wasn't alarming, and resources were stretched really thin because of the rain: we have to prioritise alerts from areas of human habitation, places where there might be hazardous materials, sewage over-flows, that sort of thing. If the readings had *stayed* high, they would have known something strange was happening and someone would have gone out to take a look, but they dropped back to normal, which is exactly what you'd expect when you *don't* have a problem.' She looked Sharon in the eye again. 'I'm not trying to make excuses, Detective Superintendent. This was a major pub-lic-health threat that our systems failed to spot. But you need to understand that the *way* it was done . . .'

'They gamed the system,' said Achebe.

Sharon nodded, looking back at the map. 'Where does that lead?' She pointed at the access road.

Fayole moved the image again, following the line. 'Back out to the main arterial road through the area and from there to the southern ring road.'

'Do we have eyes on it?' Sharon asked Achebe, then, 'Do you?' She looked at Fayole.

The blue-haired woman shook her head. 'There's no reason to,' she said. 'At least we didn't think there was, and budgets are tight. There aren't any access restrictions – they close the road if there's a bad flood, but that's about it. I'm told people go out there, fishing, walking, kayaking and so on.'

Achebe was peering at his own tablet. 'We don't have eyes on it either,' he said. 'There're no cams in the immediate area – there's a few at the main junctions on the arterial, and of course on the ring road.'

She acknowledged the information with a nod; she didn't need to tell Achebe to pull the feeds from those distant cams anyway. They might get lucky, but she was not inclined to bet on it.

'You said you're *told* people visit the site?' she asked Fayole. 'This isn't your area, then.'

'I'm on the other side of the river,' she replied. 'The northwest quadrant of the city.' The map swept into motion again.

'Any idea why you've been assigned to work with us on this?'

'Probably because I'm a gem and they thought it would look good,' she replied tersely. 'It would've made more sense for it to be the district manager for the Sinkat area, but they told me they wanted someone with fresh eyes. Now that we know about this site, if you'd rather have someone from there—'

'No!' Sharon and Achebe said together. Their vehemence made Fayole start. Rhys' lips twitched.

'No,' Sharon repeated, more calmly, 'we absolutely wouldn't. What I'm getting at is: when did Environmental Management know or suspect that the algae in the wetland was connected to the Sinkat illness?'

'We've only just worked it out – it wasn't until last night that the hospital confirmed the algae as the source of the toxin, so then I started looking specifically at algae levels and noticed the wetland readings. Inspector Achebe, Dr Morgan and I correlated

that with the other data, calculated the river's flow rate and realised that the toxin would have washed down to Sinkat at precisely
the right time. And then Inspector Achebe called you.' She tapped
nervously at her tablet. 'I still need to let my managers know.
We've got to collect samples, but most of all we need to make
sure whatever's still in there doesn't proliferate and wash downstream again.'

'Understood.' Sharon rested her chin on her fists. Her eyes
flicked up at Rhys. 'Am I right in thinking there was no purpose
to the bioengineering of this algae other than to make it produce
the toxin?'

'Not as far as we can tell.'

'And the toxin itself isn't good for anything other than to poison
gillungs?'

'Not as far as we can tell,' Rhys repeated. 'Can I absolutely swear
to you that it was not developed for some legitimate industrial
process, that it isn't just an unhappy coincidence that it does what
it does to them? I can't, obviously, but the way it activates, and
the timing . . .'

'Is as solid as any evidence I've ever seen,' Sharon said. She
sat up straight, drumming her hands sharply on the table top, a
signal that decisions had been made and that action was about to
be taken.

'Fayole, I'm going to have to be part of that conversation with
your bosses. Securing the site is a priority, but it can't be done by
the local EM team. The area is a crime scene and at this stage we
can't assume that none of your colleagues are involved. Achebe,
you'll need to question the staff who normally manage it – which
is why I'm glad you're not one of them, Fayole. We'll be getting
forensics in too. I'm going to ask that you remain assigned to us,
if that's all right with you.'

Fayole looked profoundly shaken. 'Of course – I can't believe—But you have to eliminate people from suspicion, right?'

'Right. Achebe, I would like you out there with a team within the hour – Fayole and I will be breaking the news to Environmental Management. Rhys, what's the status of the victims?'

'Most will be released from hospital today or tomorrow. We think they'll make a full recovery, although they may be shaky for a while yet. We've got five or six who are still very ill, including Tamin, the first patient – he's in pretty bad shape.'

'You'll remain as our medical liaison.' It was not a question.

'I will.'

Again, she felt a moment's reassurance. But it was fleeting, and as she gazed at the faces turned towards her – shocked, solemn, quietly furious – she recalled the prediction she'd made at the TideFair. Not for the first time, she wished with all her heart that she had been wrong.

BANKSIDE

13

The news broke like a tidal wave over the city.

Sharon, Achebe and the rest of the Met had managed to keep it quiet long enough for the West London wetland to be secured and to complete the initial investigation of Fayole's colleagues. No one was arrested and, despite police requests for discretion, the interviewees were happy to add to the stream chatter springing up around the peculiarity of a police forensics unit descending on a soggy, uninhabited nature reserve. The waterway where a colony of the altered algae had been found was now blocked off from the river, but the danger was far from over.

'As long as we don't know what the catalyst is, we can't assume it isn't still in Sinkat,' Rhys told a briefing of the City Councillors. 'And until the police catch whoever's behind this, we also can't assume there aren't tanks of both algae and catalyst ready to be dumped into the river somewhere else – maybe in Limedog, or some other city with a gillung population – Bristol or Glasgow or Gateshead. Who knows?'

At least the estuary was safe; like most freshwater microflora, the algae did not long survive an encounter with the sea. But London's gillungs lived mostly in the city, in reclaimed and reconfigured neighbourhoods along the Thames' wide eastern reaches. It occurred to Mikal, gazing down at the river from his council office, that the toxin attack was likely to galvanise plans for new development further out, where it was salty and empty and safe.

Thames Tidal Power had already committed to investing a portion of its profits in the building of an estuary town. Mikal had understood the commercial logic, as well as the appeal of living in a place where gillungs' ability to inhabit dual environments was not an aberration for which accommodation might or might not be made but the standard to which everything would be designed. Even so, he had been unable to muster much enthusiasm for the prospect of a separate, homogenous, inevitably more insular outpost. But neither could he in conscience urge an angry, embattled community to remain where they could so easily be targeted. He wondered if that had been a part of the attackers' plan: to strike a blow against integration, driving the water-breathers away into enclaves not only separate, but apart.

He wanted to believe that the reaction to the joint bulletin issued by the Council and the Met – the timeline of events, warnings that the threat had not been eliminated and the label of terrorism now officially applied to the case – would be enough to reassure them. The public outpouring of concern was immediate, heartfelt and growing by the minute. There was a shared anxiety, an awareness of vulnerability to the hatreds of others; but among all the outrage and demands for the perpetrators to be brought to justice, a whispering dread of whether, and in what form, retaliation might come.

Mikal found himself wearily contemplating just how right Jack Radbo was turning out to be. There had been sound logic behind the strategy the Energy Minister had laid out in the Thames Tidal building – was it really just five days earlier? – while the TideFair carried on outside and poison built up in the water. Events had only strengthened the case Radbo had made for an alliance, and he was past due for an answer. Pilan was at home, returning rapidly to health, and Mikal knew that a decision could be put off no longer.

The ping of an incoming call interrupted his thoughts. As if timed to add to his sense of siege, Moira Charles, Standard BioSolutions came up onscreen. It pulsed there while Mikal considered whether to let it go to message.

She could simply have sent one herself without attempting to speak to him; she had already done so twice since their meeting. He'd replied to the first, politely referring her to the Met's enquiry into whether the submersible involved in the turbine damage could have come from a Standard subsidiary. She'd responded with a barrage of documentation showing that the suspect vehicle had been disposed of some time previously.

'We got that too,' Sharon had told him. 'Might be genuine, or they might just have been clever enough to shift it off the books. Whoever was behind the sabotage has done one of the best jobs of covering their tracks I've ever seen.'

He'd decided that the most agreeable tactic was to ignore Moira Charles, and had done so with alacrity, but she was failing to take the hint. At the last moment, almost on a whim, he swiped to receive and dropped into his chair.

She came up against the backdrop of an office that looked as blandly corporate as did the woman herself. She was leaning forward, fingers outstretched to tap at the screen – clearly she had given up hope that Mikal would answer. As before, she covered her discomfiture smoothly.

'Councillor Varsi! So glad I got you in person.'

'So sorry for the delay,' he said, with what he hoped was a sufficient expression of insincerity. 'It hasn't been the easiest of days. What can I do for you, Ms Charles?'

'I'm calling to offer our assistance to *you*, Councillor. Standard BioSolutions is deeply concerned . . .'

'What did you have in mind?'

'You'll recall that we have an extensive horticultural products division. As I understand it, the need is for some form of aquatic herbicide. We have considerable resources in that area.'

'That's very kind of you,' Mikal said, and did not add *you band-wagon-jumping opportunist.* 'I believe a similar offer has already been received. Of course, I'll pass yours on as well.'

Hard on the heels of the police bulletin, Bel'Natur's agricultural research division had volunteered to help engineer an organic inhibitor to deactivate the toxin-producing algae. The offer – prompted no doubt by Aryel – had been gratefully accepted by Environmental Management, but had not yet been made public. The industry grapevine must be working with its usual efficiency; and Standard must be after more than a share of public goodwill, to be making their offer through him. He waited for the rest of the pitch.

'Thank you,' she said. 'We do hope to be of service.' She straightened up, shoulders square, resting her forearms determinedly on the desk behind which she sat. 'Unfortunately, what we've learned today has reinforced our misgivings about the risks of working in an unsecured environment. We think an urgent safety review of marine workplaces is indicated—'

'Do you?'

'—before anything else happens to put people at risk.' She peered earnestly at Mikal. 'You must be concerned for your constituents as well, Councillor. I trust we can count on your support?'

He looked back at the screen for a long moment, reluctantly appreciating the cleverness of the manoeuvre. If he rejected a call for safety checks, he could be portrayed as indifferent to the welfare of the people he represented. If he endorsed it, he would be admitting that Thames Tidal Power might not be up to the job. Pilan would never forgive him.

'The Health and Safety Directorate has been diligent about extending regulations to cover all possible workplace contingencies,' he said finally. 'I fully support their efforts.'

Let her chew on that, though he disliked how easily the equivocation had rolled off his tongue. No gillung venture had yet fallen foul of HSD regs – unlike Standard itself, which, along with its monolithic terrestrial rivals, always appeared to be in breach of something or other. In contrast, Thames Tidal had won praise from the agency for its adherence to the rules – although cynics had been quick to point out that these were relatively few, since the directorate was at a disadvantage when it came to determining what was safe practice for a gillung worker.

'That's a very well-judged answer.' It sounded frighteningly like admiration. 'Have you given any thought to the other matter we discussed?'

Mikal had not, assuming that whatever strategy the Trads were pursuing would have been abandoned after his speech at the Tide-Fair and the inevitable rumours of the meeting with Radbo.

'To be frank, Ms Charles, I've been a bit preoccupied.'

'I've been tasked with arranging an initial discussion. Very discreetly, of course.'

Once again, he was astonished almost to speechlessness.

'Have you really?'

'Really.'

'I'm not exactly an obvious choice for them.'

'I think that's the point, Councillor. I'm not sure you appreciate just how much of an asset you could be.'

Damn right I don't.

He made a decision. *If you want the answer, you have to be prepared to ask the question.* 'Very well, Ms Charles. I make no promises, but I will admit to being curious. Let's set something up.'

That conversation was still looming large in Mikal's mind an hour later as he crossed the great bridge and descended the steps, heading towards the riverwalk and Sinkat. There were many, not least those he was going to see, for whom even a conversation with the Trads would smack of betrayal, and he wondered if the whole point might be to leak the news and damage him that way. But the risk had to be taken, and he had his own strategies for mitigating it.

He paused at the screen on the piazza below the bridge, noting with approval that the rotation still included a Thames Tidal banner with live data, and got drawn into conversation with a group of upcountry visitors, sightseeing for the day. They were treating the confirmation of terrorism as a mere *frisson*, part of their big-city adventure. He found them inordinately pleased with their own broad-mindedness, though they still gaped at him, and insisted on recording their encounter with the famous gem politician of London.

'I'm not famous,' he demurred, crowded into their midst and speaking to the tops of heads as one of the party backed up, tablet angled to try and capture the full length of him.

'You are!' they laughed back. '*We* knew who you were. Now we can show everyone at home that we met you!' Mikal smiled as though pleased, shook hands all round and left the group to revel in the peculiarly touristic satisfaction of having bagged an extra and unexpected souvenir.

But his annoyance was superseded as he turned in from the river and was confronted by the unlikely sight of Sinkat with no swimmers. A shuttle-boat had just arrived; normally its passengers would have slipped over the side and made their way home underwater. Instead, they were queuing to step onto the dock. The narrow footbridges and broad quaysides were filled with people wearing bone-dry bodysuits and frightened faces, taking the long way round rather than risk the usual swift swim. He felt anger building, alongside his determination.

Pilan was at his workstation in the big project office, hunched in front of a screen crowded with symbols and numbers that meant nothing to Mikal. He was muttering engineering jargon into his throat mic, ignoring the steaming cup at his elbow, the almost tangible solicitousness of the rest of his team and Lapsa's despairing glances.

Gabriel looked up as Mikal entered, glared pointedly at the back of his boss's glowing green head and then back at his titular uncle with an expression so eloquent it made Mikal chuckle.

Pilan jumped as a large, three-fingered, double-thumbed hand landed on his shoulder. 'Glad to see you're following doctor's orders *to the letter*,' Mikal said drily.

'I can't just lie around all day.' Pilan looked pleased to see him, though he made a show of scowling and shrugging the hand off. 'Had enough of that in hospital.' He failed to stifle a small cough.

'Which washed you out, dosed you up, sent you home—'

'Damn straight!'

'—and may be happy to do so all over again. Or maybe not.' Mikal dropped a kiss on Lapsa's cheek as she joined them. 'Rhys would probably come over and put him in a headlock for you,' he said to her conversationally. 'Or I could do it.'

'An interesting proposition. I'll consider it.'

'I don't have time to be a bloody invalid,' Pilan spluttered.

Mikal regarded him steadily. 'I'm afraid, my friend, that we don't have time for a lot of things. We've got urgent matters to sort out, so if you're well enough to be here instead of in bed, let's get them sorted.'

It was not, in the end, as hard as he'd feared: for all his bluster, Pilan was still weak, and more shaken than he was willing to let on. Back in the meeting room on the upper floor, with Lapsa asking intelligent questions and her bulging belly a silent reminder of all that was at stake, he listened to Mikal's advice with fewer objections than expected.

'There are no perfect options,' Mikal told them finally. 'There's no strategy that doesn't carry some risk. But we need to be building bridges, not pulling them down. I know it would mean having to live with things none of us wants, at least for a while longer. It's not as grand a gesture as you would like. It's not a bold statement. But it's safer.'

Lapsa said meditatively, 'I'm not sure that's true.'

Mikal's heart sank, but she caught the look and smiled, shaking her head. 'No, no – I'm saying it *is* bold. It's hard, what you're asking us to do; harder than what we had in mind.' She gave Pilan a long look, more loving than they usually were in front of others, and touched his hand where it lay on the table. 'The grand gesture is sort of easy. You say to hell with it, nail your colours to the mast, let the chips fall where they may. That approach eliminates a lot. This is more subtle. It means accepting a range of possibilities. It'll keep us close to the centre of things, and I think that's where we should be.'

'We'll be insiders,' Pilan said, 'playing by their rules. I'm not sure that suits me, personally. But in the longer term—' He waved a webbed hand to indicate their surroundings and Mikal remembered him doing so before, when they had been here with Jackson Radbo and Robert Trench. Then, the gesture had been defiant; now it was weary, the illustration of a point Pilan felt obliged to make. 'We don't need more enemies. There's too much to lose.'

He dropped his hand back onto the table, looking defeated, until Lapsa picked it up and rested it against her stomach.

Mikal closed his eyes, giving them a moment's privacy. He felt relieved, and immensely sad: if Pilan had not been a sick man with huge responsibilities and a pregnant partner, he would have been far harder to persuade. This outcome might well be the opposite of what the terrorists had been hoping for, but to have achieved it with so little resistance only stoked Mikal's fury at them.

They made the necessary calls, then Pilan, clearly exhausted, was persuaded to go home and rest. Once Lapsa had messaged the project team, the couple said goodbye and walked away slowly, arm in arm. Mikal watched them go, then headed in the opposite direction.

Opening the door to the stairwell, he was met by Gabriel, as solemn-faced as Mikal had ever seen him, the cranial band with its blue standby light on his head and a tablet clutched to his chest. It was a pose oddly reminiscent of Herran, on the rare occasions when the little savant could be persuaded to leave his lair.

'Uncle Mik?' Gabriel sounded as serious as he looked. 'Can I talk to you?'

'Of course. What—?'

But Gabriel shook his head and pointed, and in a minute they were back in the meeting room with the door firmly closed.

Gabriel drew a deep breath. For a moment he looked lost, as though, having got there, he did not know where to begin. 'I've found something out,' he said finally. 'It's part of my work for Thames Tidal, although I might have gone outside the lines a bit – but the thing is, I think it's a big deal, maybe really serious. But I'm not sure what to do about it.'

He looked anxious and tired, and suddenly much older than his seventeen years. Mikal, who had known Gabriel since he was Suri's age, was swept by another wave of sadness: the feeling that he was watching adulthood, with all of its grim truths and grimy compromises, settle like a shroud over the young man's shoulders.

'Tell me,' he said.

Less than a couple of miles away, Gabriel's mother was looking out at the walled back garden and worrying about her children.

The enormity of the situation her son was dealing with had crashed in on her when she'd heard the police bulletin, but she had already seen how weighed down he was when he'd arrived home from Herran's the night before. She and Bal had talked long into the night, wondering whether they had done the right thing in letting him take on so much when he was still so young. He had turned aside their concerns, and even with today's news he was so calm and steady, so insistent on remaining in post and doing an ever-more-necessary job, so certain that to pull out now would be to hand the terrorists a victory, that they'd relented and let him stay. She was still not sure it was the right decision.

And then there was Eve.

For days, even weeks now, she'd been growing increasingly convinced that something was different about Eve. Something was up. At first she had dismissed it as just the latest mood-swing; then she'd told herself that her little girl was picking up on the family's tension over Zavcka Klist's impending release. Then she decided that Eve was just reflecting the anxiety that had permeated the Squats since the TideFair. But she knew that her rationales contradicted each other, and that she was making excuses for not being able to put her finger on precisely what was wrong.

It was not Eve's cheek, because she had always been cheeky, but that precociousness was beginning to slide over into rudeness. It was not her boldness, because she had always been bold, but now her fearlessness was starting to feel like arrogance. Gaela knew too well where that could lead, and she also knew that whatever else was going on, she must act now to stop those occasional slips becoming habit.

One thing Eve had never been was secretive or withdrawn, but there was a new furtiveness about her, particularly when she did not have Mish or Suri or other playmates around. Gaela saw how she was always disappearing up to her room now, or vanishing to the end of the garden in response to the tiniest of rebukes; she saw that when Gabriel came home, his sister's first glance was for the blue light on his cranial band. Others did that, but never *them*, never family. Gaela saw it all, and she did not like it.

And then at other times, like now, Eve was completely normal. Shouts and childish laughter floated up from the garden below, where a rambunctious game of tag was being played around the shrubbery. Gaela smiled to herself as a small blonde figure peeled out from behind the apple tree, slapped the taller, dark-haired boy hard on the shoulder, dodged the flailing arm of the little one and pelted into the shadows behind the bushes; and thought that twilight was descending quickly and the children would soon find it far harder than she did to keep track of each other.

Turning away from the window, she eyed her daughter's satchel where it was lying with Mish's and Suri's in a higgledy-piggledy pile on the floor. The flap was loose; the corner of Eve's tablet poked out. Gaela, the memory of her own crèche childhood with its constant inquisitions and utter lack of privacy still strong, felt an almost physical revulsion at the thought of taking it out, tapping it awake and using her override command to examine the stream trails and school chatter of an eight-year-old. It went against everything she and Bal had taught their children about openness and honesty and not keeping secrets. But while she knew that Gabriel had absorbed those lessons, she was not at all sure the same was true for Eve.

She remembered with bitterness how adept she had once been at hiding from her custodians the thoughts, feelings and friendships she had desperately wanted to keep for herself. There was no reason to believe that Eve was not equally capable; no reason at all. And she knew, as she removed the tablet, that this was the reason she had come back upstairs. It had been growing in her from the moment she'd noticed that Eve had left it behind, and been struck by how unusual that was these days. It was what she had realised as she followed the riotous children down to the garden, when it had occurred to her that the mental picture accompanying her new unease was of her daughter tucked away with it in a corner.

It was why she had stopped dead halfway down the stairs, as they barrelled out through the back door and Eve called her to follow, laughing. This was where that moment of comprehension had been leading.

She looked swiftly out of the window again, marking the children's locations in the gathering gloom. Then she looked at the grubby tablet resting in her hands and swiped it awake.

14

Seven days after the last objections had been overturned and the estuary's new quantum-storage power plant had begun supplying the city; four days following the news of the toxin in the Thames; two days since the first terrorist attack against modified humans in more than a decade had been confirmed; the morning after a troubled mother had violated her principles for the sake of her child, on a bright, breezy noonday at the end of the most tumultuous week that London had known since she last walked its streets, Zavcka Klist came home.

She had not been there in more than eight years.

The palatial apartment looked much as she had left it – too much, in fact. She walked the high-ceilinged and intricately corniced, elegantly furnished rooms with a feeling of displacement, a prickling, atavistic sensation of having stepped backwards in time into a life that she remembered but that was no longer hers. Sunshine blazed through the sparkling-clean windows; fresh flowers glowed from a profusion of vases; the floors gleamed and smelled faintly of beeswax; the linens were as crisp and immaculate as the ruling of a high-court judge. It was too pristine, too desperately welcoming and, oddly, too warm – as though the staff had tried too hard to erase the dust and the chill, and the seasons of absence. She had instructed them to make the place ready and must now, she supposed, think kindly on their efforts; but she found herself wishing she had told them to leave things as they were, to let it be dank and unloved and empty. That would have given her something to be angry about on her return, to sink her teeth into, to grapple with and in the process to ground herself.

Standing at the window of her bedroom, she gazed out over the leafy square, rubbing her fingers together in the newly acquired habit she refused to think of as nervous, feeling the rough patches of skin and snagging nails but also noting that her hands were perfectly steady. She had taken her meds before leaving prison in anticipation of the aggravations the day would bring. Out in the hall she could hear the murmur of voices where the wardens who had transported her were laying down the law for some of those with whom she would now be permitted unscheduled and unsupervised contact.

Marcus, her housekeeper, would be unfazed; she had kept him on retainer these many years, recognising that he possessed a combination of diligence, loyalty and respect for protocol that was both increasingly rare and essential for her comfort. She was as certain as she could be that he would find it unthinkable to sell her to the streams, take on airs in response to her reduced state or otherwise forget his station. Marcus had on her orders hired two assistants, as they'd had in the old days, to clean and to cook. She trusted that he had chosen well and that the new members of the household would also be disinclined to try and leverage their positions. It was a grim irony that much of her confidence came from knowing that they had also been vetted by the domestic-security arm of Offender Management – the very agents of her confinement.

The fourth recipient of the wardens' lecture was neither friend nor employee but a financial consultant from the firm that handled the bulk of her business affairs. He had been assigned not only to her account but also, apparently, to her. 'Think of him as your assistant,' the firm's Executive Vice-President had urged during their supervised conference a couple of days before. 'Contact him as often as you like. We've arranged clearance so he can be available to work with you offstream.' The woman had made that sound particularly meaningful. 'We've been impressed by his performance and discretion, and he is of course covered by all our confidentiality clauses. We value your patronage, Ms Klist, and we want you to know you've got a dedicated professional on call.'

Zavcka had to admit that it showed a fine bit of anticipation for the kind of instructions she would be giving, although she was of the view that the dedicated professional should have been the Vice-President herself. But she had always found the woman too brash for her tastes; and she knew that someone clever enough to anticipate Zavcka Klist's needs would also be clever enough to stay clear of becoming directly responsible for fulfilling them. So she had agreed to the arrangement with the ill temper of one who is more accustomed to predicting and manipulating than being predictable or manipulated. Her impression of the 'assistant' when they'd met a few minutes earlier was that he was older, more diffident and better-looking than she'd expected, but she was still sufficiently miffed to dismiss him as a lightweight; she hadn't bothered with more than a cursory hello.

His boss was not present, although she, along with Zavcka's solicitor and physician, made up the rest of the paltry crew with whom the prisoner was now allowed unmonitored contact. *Seven people*, she thought, turning wearily away from the window. *The limits of my life, all that I'm allowed under this wonderfully humane system of ours. Seven people, none of them equals, none of them friends, and three of them not even here.*

She knew her isolation was largely a consequence of decisions made long ago, long before the crimes and machinations that had drawn the attention of Sharon Varsi and Rhys Morgan, before the discovery of Ellyn and the unborn infant, before Aryel Morningstar had uncovered the deepest of Zavcka's secrets and revealed it to the world. Throughout her protracted life, her circle had rarely been much larger than the seven to whom she was now limited. There had been no one to make friends with as a child, and the need to protect herself from scrutiny had kept her aloof as the years passed by. She had always been able to slip out of relationships as if shedding an unwanted coat, to walk away without hesitation from those she'd claimed to care for, or anyone foolish enough to care for her. But those disappearances had felt like a choice, a game, an exercise of power that she could wield differently if it suited her. Now she had no choice in the matter at all. Except, she thought wryly as she crossed to the bathroom, of the most petty kind: she could hide out here and avoid having to witness the details of her humiliation being imparted to her staff.

It was a small, hollow victory and she felt its meaninglessness as she straightened up from washing her hands and bathing her face, and caught sight of herself in the mirror. She saw herself framed there, without glamour or subterfuge, every line and seam cast in bold relief; but the thing that drew her gaze, the focal point of her reflection, was the finger-thick strip of shaped polymer and bonded metal like a pliable piece of flattened rope wrapped snugly around her neck, glinting malevolently, far too ugly to be mistaken for jewellery.

They had put it on her that morning. She sat still as a statue, refusing either to flinch or to speak as the ends were pressed together and the molecular locks activated, sealing into place and beginning at once to transmit her location and basic biodata. It would be many long years before she could hope to be free of it – long enough to be as good as forever for anyone else.

In her case it was just possible she might outlive the limits of her sentence, but until then she would be tagged and tracked, and alarms would be raised and armed response dispatched if she ventured beyond whatever bounds were currently approved for her. The review board might have agreed to let her come home, but *home* was as far as she could go. Even to step outside her own front door would revoke the release and return her to prison. 'You are prohibited from leaving for any reason,' they'd told her, 'save an imminent threat to your own life.' The technician who'd been fitting the collar had smiled weakly as though to soften the pronouncement. 'We don't expect you to stay in the building if it's on fire, for example.'

'We also don't expect you to set the building on fire so that you have an excuse to get out of it,' said the warden, one of those who would form her homecoming party. He appeared to have assigned himself the role of reminding her at every juncture that she was no less a criminal or a prisoner, and still subject to the sufferance of the state. 'Or for any other reason.'

The technician had ducked her head, tightened her lips and looked uneasy. Zavcka had raised her eyes fractionally to rake the warden with a cool, contemptuous gaze. After a moment he'd felt compelled to add, in a tone he must have hoped she would find daunting, 'It's been tried.'

Not by me, she'd wanted to retort. Not that she could foresee doing such a thing; she was equally ready to snap that she had owned the building for longer than either of them had been alive and valued its beauty and history in ways such tiny minds would fail to understand; moreover, that burning oneself out of one's own home was both crude and conspicuous. Only an idiot would try something that obvious.

She'd held her tongue as they'd checked the bond and calibrated the signal, recited the rules to her and made her acknowledge each one, then fidgeted impatiently while she'd silently read through the small print. She had finally scrawled her acceptance into a tablet, validated it with a finger ident and retinal scan, suffered through a brief farewell speech by the prison's governor and equally insipid assurances from the staff psychologist. She'd had to be reminded to take the bioplastic bag with her pitiful collection of what Offender Management had termed 'personal items'. It would not have been politic to refuse.

Now, walking back into the bedroom, she caught sight of the clear bag, dumped unceremoniously on the floor and kicked halfway under a chair, and thought if there was anything here she wished to burn, it was that.

There was a sound of quiet footsteps in the room beyond, a tap at the half-open door and Marcus' voice saying, 'Ma'am?'

'Yes?'

He stepped into view, just. 'Sorry to disturb you, ma'am, but they've finished with us. They say they need to see you before they leave.'

'Do they.' She sighed and strode to the door. As he stood back to let her pass, she said, 'Thank you, Marcus. And, ah . . .'

She must say something to this faithful servant, somehow reconfirm the essential dynamic of their relationship. She glanced back at him, for once in her life unsure how to proceed, and another strong wave of dislocation rocked her. She realised that she stood spotlighted in a puddle of sunshine. The plush and polish of her surroundings felt transient and unreal, like a stage on which she was now obliged to perform.

She resisted the urge to put a hand to her throat. What came out felt like a tiny triumph, as disingenuous as it was truthful. 'The place looks lovely. Well done.'

*

Some time later, she was interrupted by a hesitant throat-clearing as she sat, tablet in hand, on what had been her favourite sofa. She had chosen it deliberately, determined that its luxury would become familiar again, and her awareness of it had indeed begun to drift away as she read. Even with the redactions on her stream access so much more was available to her now than in prison, and the desire to catch up was an almost physical urge, a visceral need to become fully reoriented in the chatter and conflict and flow of events. She was immersed in an onstream argument about the new Thames Tidal Power facility and whether direct action was a legitimate form of protest when the noise made her look up. She was almost too surprised to be annoyed by the sight of the financial-services flunky she thought she had ignored out of existence an hour before.

He had approached silently and stood just inside the sitting room, hands clasped behind his back, head inclined in a posture of deep respect, while his eyes scanned her face and form with an avidity that suggested something else as well, though quite what that something else was, she did not know. The intensity of his attention did not feel sexual, exactly, or threatening, or anything else she could easily put a name to. It wasn't how he'd looked at her earlier, either, when others had been present. It felt unsettling, without being either dangerous or attractive.

Zavcka rested the tablet on her lap and raised an enquiring eyebrow.

'I beg your pardon, Ms Klist,' the man said. 'I wanted to introduce myself. Properly.'

'I think you already did,' she replied, puzzled. She reached for his name, struggling to recall it. Something nondescript, pedestrian. Thinking back through the conversation with his boss, she arrived at *Patrick Crawford*. It triggered a memory of him murmuring the name earlier, when he had been one of the strangers assembled in the hall to welcome her home.

'Mr Crawford, I believe?' she said, and his face lit up to an entirely unwarranted degree.

'Yes, madam. I am very pleased to be at your service.'

There was something strangely antiquated about his phrasing. Zavcka was known to prefer formal speech herself, and anyone assigned to her would be briefed accordingly, but this felt excessive, as though the requirement had been embraced with an unlikely degree of enthusiasm.

'Thank you,' she said. 'It may take me a day or two to settle in and examine the details of the portfolio.' She knew its details by heart, but one learned more about a subordinate's capabilities by concealing the full extent of one's own. 'I expect I'll be making some changes.'

'Very good, Ms Klist. I am at your disposal. You are no doubt aware that your current investments are performing exceptionally well, but I am ready to carry out any instructions you might have.'

So he wasn't here with a list of recommendations upon which he would make a tidy commission. But the quiet intensity of his voice and his gaze had not diminished.

She was baffled, and beginning to be suspicious. 'I'm glad to hear it,' she said. 'But to be frank, Mr Crawford, I'm surprised to find you so eager. I can hardly be a plum assignment.' She extended her arms along the back of the couch, displaying the collar and looking him full in the face. 'Many would argue that I shouldn't even be here, much less have someone like you available to me. Surely you'd prefer a client with a less . . . questionable reputation?'

He glanced back towards the hall and the kitchen before he replied, 'The only question I have is how they could have seen fit to imprison you in the first place.' He kept his voice low, speaking quickly. 'I'm not alone in that, Ms Klist. There are many of us who feel that your incarceration was entirely inappropriate.'

He stepped forward, holding something out to her; it looked like a small piece of cloth. Curious, she leaned towards him and took it, then settled back into the sofa. He resumed his deferential pose. The something turned out to be a tiny pouch, made of a fabric so sumptuous that her fingertips tingled with pleasure. There was something inside: hard, round, no bigger than a memtab or a pre-Syndrome coin. She slipped it out of its silken case and held it up to the light.

It was a flat disk made of a rich, deep gold that caught the autumn sunlight and glowed in her hand. The 'K' was dominant, the 'Z' smaller, superimposed to share the upper diagonal. The letters were contained within a smooth circle like a wedding band. There was a tiny bulge at the bottom where the gold swelled into something that resembled a flower, or a mouth, as though the band were swallowing itself. It was a beautiful object, heavy and pure, and full of meaning. It was also, Zavcka realised distantly as she turned it in her fingers, the first gift she had received from anyone other than herself in more decades than she cared to count.

'A small token,' Crawford said, 'of our esteem.' His voice was thick with emotion.

She found herself clearing her own throat. 'I don't think, Mr Crawford, that the people who brought me here earlier would be happy about this.'

'No, madam, I don't imagine they would. But we've examined the rules very carefully and there's nothing that says you can't receive it.'

'No,' she mused, still looking at the pretty thing in her hand. 'But there are lots of rules about whom I'm allowed contact with.'

She held the symbol up, glinting between thumb and forefinger. 'This should disqualify you.'

'I'm a senior consultant at an exclusive financial services firm in the City of London,' he said. 'My qualifications in that respect are beyond reproach.'

'So, just to be clear,' she said, wondering how on earth they had pulled this off, 'you really do work for Dhahab Investments, you really are part of my account team and they really have assigned you to me.'

'Yes, madam.'

'I presume they're not aware of your other interests? Or is there a Klist Club in the premier-client division?'

'No, madam.'

'You must have done a lot of finagling, Mr Crawford, to find yourself in precisely the right place at precisely the right time.'

Crawford ducked his head as though accepting a compliment. 'I've merely been diligent, madam. We knew you would be allowed home eventually. We wanted to be in a position to make contact.'

'Now that you have, what do you expect is going to happen?'

'That's up to you, madam. There are things that belong to you that you must want back. I can and will, of course, undertake whatever business matters you wish to pursue, but we believe we have located the most precious asset of all: the child who was taken from you.'

Zavcka's breath caught, sharp as a knife in her chest.

There was a tiny smile on Crawford's face, almost a smirk, that told her he had seen. She recognised the look in his eyes now. It was longing, a longing that was worshipful in its avarice.

'There are things we want as well, madam, that you have been wise enough to keep from the authorities. The secret of your longevity, the knowledge you have guarded for so long. We hope we can prove ourselves worthy of your confidence.'

So for all the apparent reverence, there it was: an offer to horse-trade: the hidden child for the deepest secret.

Except there is no secret, you moron. I'm a mutant. I didn't disappear every couple of decades to turn back the clock with black-lab gene surgery, I went so no one would notice me not ageing in the first place. If I'd known it would be you idiots who believed that story instead of the jury, I'd never have let the lawyer try it.

Were it not for what the man had offered her, Zavcka would have said it out loud and damned the consequences. As it was, she felt the blood roaring in her ears, anticipation pounding down her veins and the symbol of devotion in her clenched fist, sharp against her palm. She made herself breathe deeply and slowly. This was going to be a far more immediate and delicate negotiation than she had anticipated.

'Sit down, Mr Crawford,' she said. Her voice was strong, full of authority. 'I'm sure we can come to an understanding.'

15

The access road that had been a pristine white line on Fayole's map was in reality a narrow, deeply rutted trammel of rich, dark mud. Its verges were thigh-high with nettles ragged with age and dirt, the recent passage of too many vehicles and the ravages of autumn. The bright blue line of the drainage channel turned out to be a wash of turbid brown. Detective Superintendent Varsi stood close to where the road ended in a stony apron wide and solid enough underfoot for a vehicle to turn, rubbing her feet through slippery grass to try and dislodge the worst of the mire from her shoes and thinking that her children would love the place.

Detective Inspector Achebe trudged along the bank towards her, trousers safely tucked into waterproof boots; the sludge line came up well past the ankle. Behind him, an EM engineer in a pair of waders was cautiously inching into the water along a crumbling slipway. Stakes had been driven into the earth at its head and the ooze at its foot and a pair of ropes, one on either side, acted as makeshift handrails. The engineer was using the knots along their length to steady himself as he went. Sharon could see more suited figures in the water and on the opposite bank of the channel, and yet another pair further out where it would normally empty into the huge sweep of the Thames. They were manning a small vehicle with a lifting arm that listed dangerously towards the water. A flatbed lorry bearing the EM logo, upon which the vehicle had presumably been brought in, was parked at the side, along with another EM van and a couple of police transports.

'We're certain this was it?' she asked as Achebe came up, and also started wiping his boots against the grass.

He nodded. 'The highest concentrations are – were – in the channel, and forensics indicates it's where the algae slurry was released. The sterilisation is complete now; they're just testing to confirm no viable organisms. Then they'll remove the barrier and let the water flow into the river again.'

'So they've had to kill everything.'

'In the channel? Pretty much. Apparently it's going to stink to high heaven if they don't get it moving soon. You can smell it already.' His nose wrinkled in distaste at the whiff of organic decay in the air. 'But once they do, I'm told it should all come back into equilibrium fairly quickly.'

'Right, well, EM looks like they're on top of that part.' Sharon put away her mental image of Mish and Suri playing hide-and-seek out here; it was too cold now anyway, and the water was dead, and the reeds and rushes were starting to sag as the year wound down. Maybe next summer, if it was warm and bright and all was well again. 'Walk me through what we think we know.'

'They arrived shortly before dawn,' Achebe said, pointing to the muddy track. 'It's all churned up now, but when we got here a couple of days ago there were several distinct sets of tread marks. Given the strength of the storm, we know they had to've been laid down after the rain had stopped. The ones we're most interested in were made by a heavy vehicle, probably about the same size as the EM lorry over there. It was driven in, turned and backed up to the slipway. We've got tracks going right onto the concrete. We think there was most likely a tank of some sort mounted on the back.'

'So they would've run a hose into the water and opened the tap.'

'That's what it looks like, and when they were finished, they drove straight back out. The departing treads indicate that the vehicle was considerably lighter than when it arrived.'

'And the other marks?'

'Just cycle treads along the margins, created some time over the next day or so. There've been a few cyclists and walkers along since we cordoned the lane off – regular users, but none of them recall anything unusual happening before we showed up. One of them said he'd already been out here since the storm and we matched his treads. We've got appeals out on the tanker.'

'Anything promising from the road cams?'

'Not really, and we've already eliminated everything that's registered within the local area. That's important because the weight and volume of a tank that could've been brought on a vehicle of that size down a road of this size aren't enough to account for the amount of algae that went into the channel, not if it was being kept in a healthy suspension.' He slapped at a late mosquito. 'The EM microbiologists and our own people all agree that the only way the maximum volume we've calculated works is if it's highly concentrated, and the algae wouldn't have been able to live long under those conditions, so that means it can't have been trucked in from any great distance. They think it would've been in the tank for no more than an hour.'

'So, subtracting the time to load up, get underway, manoeuvre into position and unload at this end . . . about a forty-five minute drive?'

Achebe nodded. 'Fifty, tops.'

Sharon made a face. That was probably too long to be helpful. 'What's within fifty minutes of here?'

'At least a thousand different farms, factories, industrial estates and private properties with outbuildings and a good water supply for the growth tanks. Quite a lot of biomass agriculture.' He caught her look. 'We're prioritising anyone who objected to Thames Tidal during the consultation stage, or signed that Estuary Preservation petition to try and block the power plant coming online, but unfortunately, that doesn't narrow it down very much. At this point I have to assume we'll be searching all of them.'

'How's that going?'

'Slowly. Lots of indignant farmers and site managers who can't imagine *why* we want to talk to *them* – or look round their premises.' He frowned, scratching at the mosquito bite. 'They all maintain they know nothing about it, and so far we haven't found any evidence to the contrary. But it's conservative country out here, boss.' He gestured in the general direction of the lane, the surrounding suburbs and the vast swathes of domesticated countryside beyond the ring road that defined the city's limits. 'No one's come right out in support of the attack – they're not stupid – but there isn't the level of *disapproval* you'd expect, either. There's a lot of "us and them" language, along with a sort of . . . well, *appreciation*, really. A lot of remarks about how it shows gems aren't the only clever folk around these days, all said very jovially, and when pressed they swear they don't mean anything by it. That's probably true, but it's not the kind of thing you'd hear in East London, is it?'

Sharon's jaw tightened. 'No, it's not. Not any more, anyway.' She remembered too well the kinds of things that *had* been said in East London, and elsewhere, when she'd first met Mikal. 'So even if only a few individuals are in on it, this is a pretty sympathetic region for them to be based in.'

'Exactly. It could be a local plot, or someone might have allowed their premises to be used without being too concerned with what they were being used *for*.'

'A tanker could've been brought in well before it was needed,' Sharon said, thinking through it. 'That would've increased the risk of someone noticing it and asking questions. But if you know the natives are friendly, you might not worry about that too much.'

'You wouldn't,' Achebe replied. 'Also, people are less likely to connect something they noticed several days before with an event that they know happened on a specific date.'

'And still less when it takes the police several *more* days to even know what they're looking for, or where to look.' Sharon knew that, had it not been for the swift work of the medics and scientists, it could easily have taken much longer. 'This was old news before we even got here.'

'We're off to a late start,' Achebe agreed, 'but maybe not quite as late as they expected.'

Achebe's remark nagged at Sharon as she drove an indirect and unfamiliar route back towards what her brain stubbornly insisted on identifying as The City. She had wanted to travel some of the roads the algae might have been brought in on, get a feel for the neighbourhoods where its creators might be sheltering. The journey wouldn't take her out to the countryside, with its high-yield biomass farms and low levels of either wildlife or human habitation, but on a long, winding loop through the crumbling southern conurbations Fayole had spoken of. Still, the distance felt greater than it was, for the character of the world outside the windows of the car kept shifting.

What had once been affluent suburbia was now a hinterland, neither city nor country, neither modern nor properly ancient, neither tamed nor truly wild. Instead it was an uneasy amalgamation of undecided environments, where time was in some places accelerated and in others strangely suspended. Glancing down from an elevated roadway she saw what might almost have passed for parkland, had it not been studded with the crumbling ruins of terraced houses like strings of mislaid, misshapen pearls. The corpse of a commercial district flashed past next, entombed in concrete, and all the more desolate for it. But even here, trees had erupted through the tarmac. Thick ropes of ivy shrouded the remains of a collapsed shopping centre, its levels flattened into each other like a stack of unappealing pancakes. The land humans had abandoned was being reclaimed, slowly and untidily, but steadily nonetheless. *The people who live around here must feel besieged*, she thought.

As if in confirmation, she found herself within a few seconds passing through a tired town centre with a few offices, shops and cafés bounded by residential streets. The buildings looked in reasonably good repair, but almost all were pre-Syndrome and the place had a tatty, dishevelled look to it. There was a school on one corner, from which a crowd of rowdy pre-teens spilled onto a playing field, well used if the graffiti on the walls and damage to the institutional fencing were anything to go by. She wondered if the kids thought of themselves as Londoners, or if the city was to them a distant, foreign place: a strange land to be sampled on a day trip, for some to dream of and others to fear; for some to avoid and some, eventually, to escape to.

For mile after mile she could see the struggles of the present and the scars of the past, but very little that looked much like a future.

Finally the neighbourhoods became busier, newer and more crowded, until she was travelling between buildings gleaming with polished aggregate and biosynthetic finishes, surrounded by the constant low roar of traffic and trains, people shouting and sirens in the distance: the myriad sounds of urban life. The road swept around and up and as she drove onto a bridge that would take her across to the north bank of the Thames she looked out at the great grey-brown ribbon, thinking that few things could be at once so innocent and so ominous. The red buoys marking the most upstream of the river turbines winked in the distance.

What *had* they expected, these people who had suborned the lifeblood of a city and turned it against its own? How long had they counted on a fruitless search for some local spillage to divert attention away from the real source of the poison, in the upstream heartland of those who sensed their own obsolescence? When it was eventually discovered, as they must have known it would be, what reaction had they anticipated from the police, the politicians, the public?

She caught a glimpse of the gleaming curve of City Hall as she came off the bridge and turned right. As though it had been a trigger, her husband's tale of his meeting with Gabriel came flooding back, now full of significance; it felt as though something that had been lurking at the back of her mind was now stepping forward and demanding her full attention.

At the time she had been so focused on the political tightrope Mikal was about to walk, and so annoyed at Gabriel and Herran for their amateur investigating, that she had pushed it away until she was in a better frame of mind to consider its implications. But somewhere on the too-long drive back into London, as she pondered not only the resources but the thinking behind the Thames toxin attack, the likelihood of a connection became clear to her.

Though one plot involved snark and spin on public streams and the other was a case study in black-lab bioengineering and black-ops execution, they played to the same whispered fears and simmering resentments. More than that, they shared a subtlety of implementation that she felt in her bones could not be coincidental, not when both had the same community in their sights.

Her instincts, honed by a decade and more of detective work, told her that Gabriel had uncovered another front in a hidden war. With any luck, its perpetrators still had no idea they'd been rumbled. And he'd had the sense to take his discovery to his uncle, knowing Mikal could act as a bulwark against publicity. Gabriel was smart and careful, and she wished there was a way to keep him completely out of it from now on. Gaela and Bal would not be pleased.

She considered the problem for a few more seconds, then shook herself in irritation, flicked her earset to active and called her husband.

16

Since he'd told his uncle about the Kaboom conspiracy, Gabriel had been overtaken by a covert conflict of an entirely different nature. Sitting at his Thames Tidal workstation the next day, he felt as if he had achieved a kind of equilibrium in the public-relations battle: he knew how to spot and hit back at Kaboom's avatars the moment they appeared onstream, and he'd decided to treat them as just another part of his overall responsibility to monitor and tag and post and respond, at least for now. It was what Uncle Mik – in his City Councillor Varsi incarnation – had advised, along with staying quiet until instructed otherwise. Gabriel was happy to comply. Uncle Mik would think it all through and talk to Aunt Sharon, and he would either find himself in trouble with Detective Superintendent Varsi, or not. But until then, there was nothing more he could do, and anyway his concerns about Kaboom had almost been eclipsed by the turmoil at home.

He had been so preoccupied when he'd followed Mikal's towering figure into the flat the evening before that it had taken him a minute or two to realise something was amiss. Darkness had fallen as they'd walked over from Sinkat and the children were already inside, talking over the adults and each other, scrabbling through a tangle of jackets and satchels and unfinished sentences as Mikal corralled his boys to take them home. Gaela had sorted them out, chatting with her usual efficiency and good humour, and it was only when Eve had marched across the room, trailing a jumper in one fist and clutching her tablet in the other, loudly declaring her supremacy in whatever game they'd been playing, that he realised his mother had pulled normalcy on like a mask. It had slipped for the barest of moments, in the indrawn breath between telling Eve to pipe down and returning to whatever she'd been saying to Mikal. The strain he saw there, and the depth of its concealment, was enough to shock him into reaching up and flicking off his cranial band without a second thought.

A swirl of thought and emotion washed over him: there was Misha, reluctantly accepting that the day's play was over but already looking ahead to tomorrow. Sural was beginning to want his mother and ready to be peevish about the chilly walk back to Maryam House. Eve's triumph at winning the game was both noisy and fleeting, her dragonfly mind already hunting for the next thing to focus on. He felt the deep currents of his uncle's thoughts, overlaid by the prosaic need to get his children home, fed and to bed at a decent hour.

Gabriel tuned all of them out with the ease of long practise and focused on his mother, but he couldn't make any sense of what he felt from her save for the clear knowledge that Eve was at the centre of it. Gaela's mind was a welter of anxiety and guilt and unfocused fear – there was something about a tablet, and whether it meant anything; whether she had done the right thing; whether she even knew what the right thing was. Her distress roiled beneath the surface while she held on to the need to reveal nothing, to be regular Mama and Aunty Gaela, to get the Varsis packed up and out and tend to her own family as though nothing at all was wrong.

And maybe nothing is wrong. The thought floated into his mind from hers as she bid Mikal farewell at the door, tucking treats into the boys' hands to keep them distracted along the way. *Maybe you're making too much of it, Gaela. Maybe it's what all the kids do – maybe this is what it's like to grow up in the world. Perhaps I'm the one who doesn't know any better, maybe it's me.*

He could tell his mother was not remotely convinced.

She met his eyes as she came back into the room – of course she'd known the moment his band went off, she saw far more of its emanations than the tiny blue pinprick of the power indicator – and gave a swift, tiny shake of her head. He tilted his own head just as minutely. He couldn't ask her what was wrong while Eve was within earshot, and his sister had already bounced over to wheedle a treat of her own.

'Why do Mish and Suri get cookies and I don't?'

'Because Mish and Suri have a cold walk home, and longer to wait for their dinner when they get there. Yours is coming up in a few minutes, so go and finish your reading.'

The child pouted. 'Well, what if Gabe wants a cookie?'

'He doesn't,' said Gabriel. 'Don't be a baby, Eve.'

Eve looked daggers at him, knowing full well that trying to refute the accusation would only reinforce it. She chose to subject them all to the silent treatment instead, retreating to the furthest corner of the long living room and curling up with her tablet and an air of disdain.

He must really have hurt her feelings; she wasn't even insulting him inside her head. He shrugged and turned back to his mother, who said wearily, 'Not now.' Then she added quietly, 'Do you know—?'

'No,' he said, just as quietly. 'You're too upset to make sense of.'

She made a sound that might have been a snort of laughter or the beginning of a sob, though he couldn't tell which; she was making herself breathe deeply and steadily, consciously bringing her mental state under control, and he felt her growing calmer, pushing the source of her disquiet further away, out of his reach.

'I'll explain later,' she said. Her voice already sounded less ragged, more like herself, as did her mind. 'I've got to go downstairs and help – they've been slammed since lunchtime. People are sitting for *hours*.'

He heard the thought she did not say. 'It's because of Sinkat – knowing it was deliberate,' he said.

'Yes – it's only natural, I suppose. People are frightened, and there's nothing they can do except hope it doesn't get worse. It's like—' She caught herself, but he knew she had been about to say *the old days*.

'You mean the *bad* old days, surely, Mama.' He tried to sound light-hearted, but she shook her head at him reprovingly.

'You don't need to pretend it's less scary than it is, my darling. Not with me or your father. And you in the thick of it – if we'd had any *idea* this could happen—'

'Mama.'

'I'm just saying, there's no need for you to tough it out. I'm worried about you too, Gabe.'

'Mama, I'm fine. I've got it under control.' He hoped that was true. 'What can I do about this?' He looked meaningfully across at Eve's small blonde head.

'Stay with her; make sure she's done her schoolwork. I'll send up some dinner.' And leaning closer, whispering although the thought was loud in her head, 'If she complains that something's wrong with her tablet, you don't know anything about it – and don't mention it if she doesn't.'

He had done as he was asked, and just before Delial rapped on the door to deliver supper he registered a wave of bafflement, followed by the frantic sense of searching for something misplaced, until the noise of the door shutting reminded Eve that he was there. She dropped a blanket over her inner turbulence, shutting it down almost as completely as he had earlier shut down his band. She put the tablet aside without comment and came to eat without fuss. He gently insisted on reviewing her schoolwork with her, thinking she wouldn't be able to resist chattering about whatever had startled her, or at least thinking about it while they were both gazing at the smeared screen of her battered old tablet, but she stayed surly and mostly silent, allowing no stray thoughts to form. By the time his tired parents came upstairs, he had long since sent her to bed, and he was none the wiser.

Thinking about it the following afternoon, while feeds scrolled past and his monitor apps tagged and aggregated news items and idle chatter, Gabriel was still not sure what to make of the socialstream account his mother had found and blocked, or of the archived streamchats that had left her so upset. The way Eve had whinged about her family, him included, was really hurtful, and she had told her anonymous stream-friends far more about herself than was wise, but the exchanges were childish and he could easily see how she'd drifted – or been led – into them. But there was an *intrusiveness* about the questioning that made him uneasy, even though it was in keeping with the hectoring tone of the stream. They could all see how that kind of boasting and cattiness might stoke the less pleasant aspects of Eve's character.

More worrying was how she'd found her way there in the first place, for it was invitation-only, accessed via a clever link that managed to circumvent the parental blocks. His mother had no idea who among Eve's friends was responsible, but maybe Eve would tell when Mama confronted her today; maybe by the time he got home from work that mystery at least would be solved.

It might be completely innocent, of course, but it didn't *feel* innocent, and the more he thought about it, the more it troubled him; so much that he'd started wondering if he could persuade Herran to go in and look. Though he knew the answer would almost certainly be *no*, he'd begun composing a message when his earset pinged.

'Gabe?' Mikal's voice was sonorous, a bit nasal and very serious. 'The police would like to speak with you. And Herran.'

Herran didn't leave home lightly, or without preparation, and in any event Detective Superintendent Varsi hadn't wanted them to be seen together where they might be noticed and commented on. Fortunately, Maryam House was only half an hour's walk from Sinkat and barely fifteen minutes from the café, so just a couple of hours later Gabriel found himself seated at his aunt and uncle's big dining table with his father on one side of him and Herran on the other. Mikal sat next to Herran, and Sharon faced them all. Detective Inspector Achebe rounded out the group, coming in on a secure channel and listening intently as Gabriel took them step by step through what he and Herran had discovered about the avatar-disguised provocateurs he'd dubbed Kaboom.

'Why didn't you tell us about this?' his father had demanded tightly as they walked up the couple of flights from Herran's flat to the Varsis' much bigger apartment.

'I was afraid if we'd done something wrong by tracing them and I told you or Mama, I'd be getting you involved,' Gabriel had protested. 'Then I worked out that it would be okay as long as I told Uncle Mik first, and after that I *was* going to tell you, when I got home. But that was last night, and by the time we were done with everything else . . .'

He'd trailed off miserably, looking at Herran trotting on up the stairs, oblivious. Bal had reached over as they got to the landing, wrapped a powerful arm around his son, pulled him close and dropped an exasperated kiss on top of his head. 'Gabriel, we are your *parents*. We're *supposed* to get involved – it doesn't *matter* what else is going on.'

'Okay.' He'd shrugged out of the hug and tried to sound steadfast, but his heart felt much lighter. Bal *tsked* at him and tousled his hair, and by the time Mikal had opened the door to them a minute later, with an apologetic face for Bal and a reassuring one for his nephew, Gabriel's anxiety was greatly reduced.

It had jumped again when he saw Aunt Sharon – Superintendent Varsi, now – speaking swiftly and in clipped tones to her inspector via the tablet. She looked over and smiled at him, but her eyes were stern.

Now he was explaining what he had observed onstream, why he had gone to Herran and how they had followed the trail, while Herran sat beside him, clutching his tablet and rocking a little more noticeably than usual, interjecting monosyllabic confirmations whenever Sharon asked a question. The blue light on his cranial band pulsed softly; he was still onstream, maybe just trying to keep himself calm. Gabriel had set his own to standby, the better to concentrate fully on the matter at hand.

When he finished, he faced his aunt with an expression he hoped was equal parts enquiring and contrite. Her own face remained inscrutable.

'Reprehensible though they may be, you were right to conclude that the posts and streamchats you've identified do not in themselves justify police involvement,' she said. 'And we do not ever

recommend that private citizens – or corporations – conduct inves-
tigations of this nature on their own recognisance, as there is a
risk that they will not appreciate the boundary between legitimate
enquiry and invasions of privacy. Not to mention acts of espionage.'

His father shifted irritably, but to Gabriel's relief he held his
tongue. The meeting was on the record; Uncle Mik had warned
them that there would be a degree of officiousness in the language
Sharon would be obliged to use. Gabriel had taken that to mean he
could expect a telling-off, but he hadn't thought he would actually
find her so intimidating.

'I'm sorry,' he said to Sharon. Even to himself his voice sounded
small.

'No,' she replied matter-of-factly, 'you noticed an unusual pattern of onstream activity and in the course of consulting with
your app developer' – she nodded at Herran – 'you uncovered several facts which suggested a conspiracy to engage in libellous and
inflammatory discourse. With the aim of discrediting a minority
group,' she added, with a glance at the tablet screen; they could
see Achebe was now looking down and to the side and they could
hear the soft, swift tap of his fingers as he frantically took notes.

'You weren't sure whether this discourse constituted hate speech,
but were nevertheless deeply concerned about the implications
and you rightly relayed those concerns to your City Councillor,'
Sharon went on. She glared at Mikal, who was chuckling softly.
'That is correct, is it not?'

The glare shifted across the table to Gabriel and a visibly perplexed Herran. His father grunted appreciatively, and nudged him.

'I . . . ah . . . Yes, that's correct,' said Gabriel. 'That's exactly what
happened, right, Herran?' He turned and gave the little gem an
encouraging nod; he sensed rather than saw that behind him, his
father was doing the same.

'Okay,' said Herran, without his usual certainty.

'Okay,' said Sharon, sounding very certain indeed. 'Now, those concerns *are* sufficient to warrant our attention, especially given the current threat level in the city. I'm going to remind you all that everything we say here is to be kept in strict confidence. You're clear on what that means, aren't you, Herran?'

'Top secret,' said Herran.

'That's right.' She looked round at them, her expression grim. 'It may be that this consortium we're calling Kaboom are simply taking advantage of recent events, but we'll be looking into the possibility that their actions are not merely opportunistic. What you've identified suggests an organised group working against the gillung community in general and Thames Tidal Power in particular. Our primary objective right now is to track down whoever's behind the recent terrorist attack against that very community. We know they are also very well resourced, highly organised and extremely secretive, and that suggests that Kaboom and the terrorists might be part of the same group, or at any rate aligned with and aware of each other's activities.' She focused on Gabriel. 'You suspected this too, didn't you?'

'I didn't put it together exactly like that,' he said hesitantly. 'At first I thought they were just random trolls, because we get a lot of those. Then when I realised how many avatars were being used, I thought maybe we were being trolled by one of the groups that lobbied so hard against us – Estuary Preservation or Bankside BioMass, someone like that. I was going to expose them because however much they don't like us, everyone's signed up to a Code of Practice not to use avatars and not to troll. But when we worked out how complicated the whole thing was, and how much effort had gone into making the avatars untraceable, I thought . . . Well, I didn't know what to think; it just seemed like it was a whole lot bigger than anything I'd been imagining. And then you confirmed that the toxin wasn't an accident, that it was targeted . . . Yes,' he ended, his voice almost a whisper, 'yes, I realised that it might be connected.'

'"Might be" is the operative term,' Sharon replied. Her tone had turned unexpectedly gentle. 'Remember, these are only suspicions at this point. It's going to take some time to unpick them and see where we end up. And by "we" I mean "we the police". You should continue to respond to Kaboom's provocations exactly as you have been, and we would find it very helpful if you shared links to those threads with Inspector Achebe. But I don't want any escalation in your responses to them, and definitely no more investigating from you, Gabriel. You're a minor as well as a civilian, and I don't want you any more involved than you already are.' Her smile lit up her eyes this time. 'Having said that, I would like to add, on behalf of the Met, that your and Herran's diligence has given us an important lead we wouldn't have otherwise. So thank you, both of you. Well done.'

Gabriel's head was spinning. 'I . . . um . . . okay. Thank you.'

'Don't do it again.'

He felt a tiny surge of rebellion. Why, if they had done so much, was it unthinkable that they might do more? But his father and uncle were both nodding agreement and there was an edge to Herran's rocking that signalled that it could easily turn into distress. And despite the smile, Aunt Sharon's face wore a don't-argue-with-me look that he had no good reason to challenge.

'No, ma'am, I won't.'

She was gone a few minutes later, now in possession of a memtab with all the files and links to Kaboom and still in contact with Achebe via her earset even as she bade Herran goodbye, gave

Gabriel a brief, fierce hug, followed it with another for his father and went up on tiptoes to kiss Mikal goodbye. Then she was out the door, talking rapidly into her earset even as it slammed behind her.

Mikal turned back to the others with a rueful smile. 'You know she's not just saying that, right? She's really grateful you found this. Also really worried.'

'I guess.' Gabriel shuffled his feet.

'You and Herran did good, Gabriel: you really did. The way you handled things went right up to the edge, but not quite over. Achebe and the officers in data forensics will replicate the trace you ran so there can be no challenge to the evidence, and they'll be doing whatever they have to so the people behind this won't ever know you were involved.' He looked over the boy's head and met Bal's eyes, wondering if his oldest friend was angry with him. They had been so few, not all that long ago: so outcast and so desperate. Back then they'd been used to living on the brink, Bal and Gaela, himself and Aryel, a scant handful of others. They'd been used to bad options and huge uncertainties and the endless, instinctive calculations of risk. It had been the stuff of daily life. They had hardly dared to dream of the future, let alone imagine that they might one day be so much better off – with so much more at stake.

'Bal—' he began.

'It's fine,' Bal cut in quietly. 'We've always known he'd be safe with you, Mik. Both of you. You and Sharon have to play it straight, I get that. It's fine. We know who you are.'

Tears did not come easily to Mikal's split-lidded eyes, but he found himself blinking them clear, and not for effect.

'Right,' he said, clapping Bal's broad shoulder. Then he turned to the little savant. 'You okay, Herran? Want to talk anything over?'

'No,' Herran said firmly. 'Not talk. Home.'

Mikal escorted them all to the door and watched them walk

away. Gabriel ushered Herran into the stairwell as Bal looked back to raise a hand in farewell. There was some indefinable thing about the body language of father and son, a shared tension as they glanced at each other, and Mikal wondered what else was going on.

Whatever it was, it was none of his business – not yet, at least, and probably not ever. The splintering into little cells of self-contained family – himself, Sharon and their boys, Aryel and Eli, Bal and Gaela with Gabriel and Eve – was a token of the freedoms they'd won in those old, old battles that had never really ended. Another sortie was imminent, and once more there was ground to be gained, or lost.

We're never not on a precipice, he thought. *The scenery changes, but never the drop.*

17

The Traditional Democratic Party, as the Trads were officially known, was headquartered in an old, grand and somewhat fusty confection of concrete and glass in the heart of Whitehall. They also had a network of local offices throughout the city and suburbs, including a glossy first-floor suite at one of the most desirable addresses in the financial district, where large public screens streamed party news, policies and promises for the edification of passers-by. Corporate allies were abundant in that area, controlling multiple floors of buildings into which Mikal Varsi could have slipped on the pretext of other business. The Trad members on the City Council had private offices like his own, which he thought would have been simplest of all. But it was to none of these places that he had been invited.

Instead, he found himself turning off a thoroughfare noisy with evening traffic into a passage between glass-fronted towers favoured by brokers, bankers and other less definable providers of financial services; then into an alley where darkness had already fallen, the gloom settling early in a space so narrow that he could stand in the middle and press his hands flat against the walls on either side. It zigzagged and dog-legged until it finally delivered him to an unmarked door set into a wall of venerable London brick. There was neither handle nor lock on its exterior. He looked around. The alley continued for a few feet until it met another, wider passageway, from where came a glow of brighter light, the mingled smells of cooking and bins and the clash of pots and pans. He glanced round the corner and saw a larger door open and a brief stream of what looked like kitchen workers come out, joking amongst each other, shouting back at unseen colleagues.

Mikal stepped back into the shadows of the smaller alley and checked his tablet. It confirmed that he had indeed arrived at his destination. As he slid it away, considering whether to knock, wait or walk around the corner and surprise the kitchen staff, the door swung silently inwards and a young, powerfully built norm woman in a livery he recognised poked her head out.

'Mr Varsi? Come with me, please.'

He ducked through the door after her, past what looked like a security office on one side and what sounded like the kitchen on the other. He had dropped the route he'd been sent into a standard navigational app and he knew both where he was and that there were far more direct ways of getting here. Under other circumstances he would have found being snuck in through the back door thoroughly objectionable, but it had taken only a moment's stream-searching to realise that he would have had no chance whatever of entering from the front without generating vidsnaps and instant, breathless gossip on all the wrong streams. Even this far from the bar, the clamour was deafening. The establishment, which styled itself a club, was a favourite of the city's thrusting business élite: a place to see and be seen, talk and be talked about. There would be few of his constituents here, unless they had found work pouring drinks or waiting tables.

Ascending the narrow stair behind his guide, he caught a glimpse of the main floor through a series of long slitted windows which allowed a clear view while maintaining the privacy of those on their way to the upper sanctum. He could see that punters were stacked five-deep around the bar, and there were so many chattering knots of humanity that there was barely any room to move about. The entrance to the dining room was guarded by a maître d' with a tablet and an expression of such smug complacency that Mikal fantasised for a moment about going down there and insisting he had a reservation, just to see what would happen. Braying laughter and the tinkle of glassware washed up from the general tumult.

At the top of the stairs, the woman pressed her fingers to an identipad next to a door as solid and unmarked as the one below, although of a rather finer finish. She pushed it open, said, 'Welcome to the Karma Club,' and stood back to let him go through first.

He stepped into an oasis of calm and realised that he had misjudged the place; it really was a club, although he suspected most of the patrons downstairs would find that as much of a surprise as he did. The room was large and softly lit, with a small bar at one end from which smartly suited servers brought elegant drinks to a clientele who sat in comfortable chairs or stood at tall windows talking quietly as they gazed out at the darkening city. For all that this was clearly where a select few came to meet and mingle, it lacked the excessive opulence that Mikal normally associated with the idle rich. Though tasteful and artfully designed, there was a business-like aura about the place, a sense that membership was based on competence and perhaps ruthlessness rather than any accident of birth. Those admitted here had worked hard enough and been clever enough, and paid enough attention, to discover the stair and the door and another level of achievement. The strivers had been left downstairs. These people had already arrived: they knew the price of admission, and the expectations that came with it.

He was not surprised to see Moira Charles in conversation with a business-suited man enough like her in age, demeanour and general upmarket ordinariness for Mikal to think him as likely to be friend or colleague as brother or lover. She caught his eye and nodded, but did not approach. It would suit no one – Trads or Mikal or Standard BioSolutions – for her to be party to their meeting, but from the look of relief on her face he surmised that she'd been on hand to take the flak if he'd failed to turn up. No one else in the room appeared to have noticed that an eight-foot-tall man with double-thumbed hands and split-lidded eyes had arrived in their midst.

His guide crossed to another door with a briskness that suggested they should not tarry, knocked sharply and opened it. This time she did not follow him in; instead, the door closed silently, leaving him to contemplate the person who was waiting for him.

The man sat at a table in what was evidently a private dining room. Water had been poured, and a tumbler of amber liquor rested near his hand. He was still burly although he was no longer young, his face heavy about the jowls and small, sharp eyes buried deep in folds of flesh. The receding hair was more white than grey. He conveyed neither the desperate ambition of the crowd downstairs nor the self-satisfaction of the deal-makers on the other side of the door. He looked like a man for whom the fine linens and crystal on the table, the exclusivity of the setting and the summoning of the nominally powerful were entirely ordinary. Mikal had often wondered if rich norms knew how much easy presumption they projected, without ever needing to say a word.

'Mikal Varsi,' said the man in a tone that suggested he did not speak the name lightly.

'Abraham Mitford,' said Mikal, and noted the tiny glint of

surprise in the man's eyes. So he had not automatically assumed that Mikal would recognise him. 'I wondered who wanted to talk to me.'

'I wondered who you thought it would be. Sit.' He gestured towards the empty chair opposite. 'Drink?'

Mikal glanced at the glass Mitford was lifting and said, 'Whisky's fine. Whatever you're drinking.'

There was a slight pause in the motion, again just a hint that this was not what he'd anticipated, but he tapped the order into a small tablet by his elbow without comment before sitting back, glass in hand. 'So,' he said. 'Whom were you expecting?'

'You were a possibility,' Mikal replied evenly. 'I knew it wouldn't be a party spokesperson, or a sitting politician.'

Mitford was beginning to get used to surprises. 'Of course,' he said, as though the significance of the fact were just sinking in. 'You've been doing this a while.'

'I have.'

'I've had meetings where people are surprised not to be seeing the leader or chairperson or whatever. It's good that you aren't that naïve. Although—' He paused as the door opened to admit a server bearing Mikal's drink and watched, silent and flinty-eyed, as the tumbler was precisely placed and the man withdrew.

'Although?' Mikal prompted, taking a sip. It was, as he'd expected, a fine single malt, smoky and peaty, and pleasantly warm going down. He noticed with weary resignation that Mitford was staring at his hand: the way the two thumbs and three fingers gripped and tilted the glass. He rested it gently back on the table, watching the opposition grandee pull his attention away with an effort. Like Moira Charles, no actual distaste was allowed to show.

Mitford recollected his sentence. 'Although I'm curious to

know how you imagine the current situation in the city is going to develop.'

'I assume you mean politically.'

'Also commercially, economically.' He smiled without mirth. 'A man of your experience must realise how linked those factors are.'

'I think,' Mikal said carefully, 'that the level of resentment at the moment is the highest it's been in at least a decade. We've been in economic recovery for most of that time, but the benefits have not been evenly distributed and that's generated a lot of discontent in segments of the population who feel left behind, particularly suburban residents and workers in traditional industries. That, in turn, is fuelling a new factionalism: people no longer believe that a rising tide will lift all boats. It's making them angry – both at those they think have benefited more than they have and at anyone they feel sold them false promises. They're going to punish whomever they believe is responsible, commercially and politically.' He took another sip of his whisky and regarded Mitford over the rim of the glass.

The older man harrumphed his approval. 'That's exactly what we think.'

'We the Traditional Democrats, or we the board of directors of Standard BioSolutions?'

Mitford chuckled. 'I have very little to do with the running of Standard,' he said. 'I'm a non-executive director; I show up to a few meetings a year, advise on strategy. I know Moira, obviously, and I can tell you she is part of a very sharp team who understand their business. But this conversation is in the context of my interest in the party.'

'So in that context, what's your interest in me?'

'You're going to get caught in the backlash, Varsi. I understand that some of the people behind the Thames Tidal venture are trying to drum up support for a special-interest party, and so far they have failed to get you on board. To be frank, that's what caught our attention. Now, I don't care whether they go ahead or not, because the UPP is not going to win the next election. If the gems splinter the vote, all that means is they'll lose by a bigger margin. I'm guessing you've realised that being part of that won't be good for your political career, but I'm not sure you understand that you'll be seen as part of the problem either way, by the UPP as well as their supporters. That's just how it is.'

He paused for breath and took a small swallow of whisky. 'Plus this whole toxin business being labelled terrorism – not everybody buys that explanation. There's talk about it being a cover-up. I'm not saying that's true,' he added hastily, presumably recalling that Mikal's wife was in charge of the case. 'I'm saying it's beside the point. The resentment you talked about? We both know who you mean. Come the election, people will not vote for a party or a candidate they think has made them less safe, or enjoyed advantages that they haven't.'

If that last part were true, Mikal thought, *you wouldn't have a hope in hell.*

'What's your interest in me?' he repeated.

'Not everybody's going to be happy when we win. If we're to keep a lid on things, we need to have a full range of representation, and that includes gems. We haven't done so well on that score, but we know it's not going to work, us coming into power looking the way we did fifteen, twenty years ago. It wouldn't be good for you or your people either, but believe me, if you throw in with this gillung splinter group or hook up with the UPP, that's what will happen. If you stay independent, maybe you can hang on to your council seat – maybe. But that's not going to get you anywhere you haven't been for the past eight years.'

He took another slug and glanced in a not-quite-casual way round the dining room as though to remind his guest of how far his horizons were being expanded tonight. When his eyes came back to Mikal, they were hard, demanding.

'You have talent. That's something we appreciate. You understand the practicalities of the situation, and you're a good talker – you can explain things in a way that your people will accept. We're going to need someone who can do that, which is why I want you to join the Traditional Democrats as a parliamentary candidate. We'll see to it that you win. You'll have a voice on gem policy – more than that, you'll be the first gem elected to national office.' He drained the glass and smiled as though it hurt. 'Though possibly not the last.'

Twenty years ago, during the Trads' most recent term in office, Mikal had been indentured on the production line of a factory where his engineered hands were put to work assembling and adjusting complex components far more quickly and delicately than either machine or norm could manage. He had been the most expensive piece of equipment in the place, a major investment in maintaining the brand's reputation for innovations in manufacturing and high-quality end products. His line boss had frequently reminded him of those facts, as though they were things of which he should be proud.

He had learned, then, how to keep his feelings off his face.

'That's quite an offer,' he said evenly. 'Is the rest of the party on board with it?'

'The ones who need to sign off have signed off. There'll be some grumblings no doubt, but the rest will come round.'

Mikal nodded, as if to indicate that this was acceptable. 'There's something in particular you want me to help sell. What is it?'

Mitford, in the act of picking up his empty glass, stopped and eyed Mikal keenly. 'You are sharp,' he said. 'The Thames Tidal divestiture, for a start.'

'You expect that to happen?'

'It'll have to happen. Quantum-energy storage is going to revolutionise every industry there is. One small group cannot be allowed to control a technology that powerful – especially when they have so little in common with ordinary folk. The risks are too great. People won't stand for it.'

I doubt it's too much power if the small group is one that you're part of, but it's obviously unthinkable if it's anyone else. There was nothing to be gained by making such an observation out loud. He wondered how many of the senior figures in the Trads understood the degree to which Abraham Mitford, financier, party stalwart, major shareholder in Standard BioSolutions, was leveraging their brightening prospects to make himself an even greater fortune. Maybe they did know, considering how much of that fortune was spent on them. Maybe they had agreed, tacitly or otherwise, to this grand strategy; maybe they had helped cook it up.

Or maybe when he spun them a line, they believed it.

'So,' Mikal said, musingly, remembering his last conversation with Moira Charles, 'you're fairly certain this safety review that Bankside is lobbying for will go ahead?'

'I'm completely certain of it.'

'And will end up recommending major changes, which I would then help to push through? For the good of the company and its employees?'

'Thus cementing your own reputation as an honest broker who does the right thing, regardless of the consequences.'

My reputation with whom? Mikal thought acidly. *Certainly not the people who think well of me now.*

'The consequences in this case being that Thames Tidal will

end up having to accept significant outside investment,' he said. 'Amounting to a controlling interest? It's a cooperative. How are you planning to deal with that?'

Mitford waved a hand dismissively. 'The structure will have to be revised, but by the time that becomes an issue those in charge will be amenable. Following the restructuring, it's reasonable to assume the new owners will start to develop a wide range of quantum-tech applications.'

'Something I would need to make okay with the wider gillung and gem communities. Got it.' Mikal had been ignoring his glass. He picked it up and swirled the remaining liquor while looking Mitford in the face. 'I take it I can expect to get more out of this than an office in Whitehall and a parliamentarian's salary.'

'You can expect a lot more – including shares in the successor firm.' He tapped another order into the tablet, looking grimly pleased with himself. 'This has been a more straightforward conversation than I anticipated, Varsi. I'm glad you understand how these things work.'

'Oh, I do,' said Mikal. 'Believe me, I do.'

By the time Mikal got home, his children had been asleep for hours. He stood in their bedroom, in the dim glow of the starfish-shaped nightlight Lapsa had given them, looking down at the two little bodies in their little beds and listening to them breathe. Misha was a sprawler, arms and legs flung at all angles. He already looked too big for his bed; in another year his feet would be sticking off one end and his hands mashed against the wall at the other. Sural was curled up on his side like a plump, happy caterpillar, knees and elbows tucked tidily away under a neat little rumple of blankets. He might roll from left to right several times throughout the night, but the pose would never change.

Mikal might have stood there until morning, barely aware of the miserly tears leaking one by one down his face, had Sharon not come up quietly behind and put her arms around his waist. 'Don't wake them,' she whispered.

'I won't.'

Something in his voice made her twist around so she could look up at his face. He could feel the muscles in her arms tense at what she saw, and she tugged at him to come away. He did not want to leave that room with its gentle light and the peacefully sleeping children but he let her pull him into the living room, where he sank onto the sofa, dropped his face into his hands and rubbed as though he might rub it into oblivion. Sharon sat beside him, arm as far around his shoulders as she could reach, and stroked his head and kissed his neck, and after a while he pulled himself together and told her about his evening with Abraham Mitford.

'And here I was thinking I'd had the bad day today.'

'Bal said he knew who I was,' Mikal told her dully. 'After you left. He said it was okay, the way things had gone with Gabriel. He said he knew.'

'He does know you. So do I.'

'Do you, Shar? I'm glad, because I'm not sure I do right now.'

'You did the right thing, honey.'

'I can remember when the right thing didn't leave me feeling like I needed to take a shower. For the rest of my life.' He sat back wearily. 'There are so very many ways for this to go wrong.'

'My mother used to say that things only *go* wrong if you *do* wrong.'

'Is this the mother who hasn't spoken to you since you started going out with me?'

'She was wrong about that.' Sharon tucked herself into the curve of Mikal's arm. 'But not about everything.'

18

The next day brought the first of the breakthroughs Sharon and Achebe had been hoping for, although, as Sharon grumpily observed, every answer seemed to lead to more questions. The cyclist questioned by Achebe had gone on to describe the experience in a nearby pub where there had been much annoyed talk about the continuing police presence in their sleepy, soggy neck of the woods. Over what sounded to Achebe like more than a few pints, the cyclist had heard tell of a disused hydroponics facility recently taken over by a pair of bright young engineers who were trying to make a go of it. They'd brought in lab equipment and started on refurbishing the tanks before bothering with the rest of the place, but they had big plans to turn it around, put the district on the map.

How, demanded the locals, were they supposed to attract more of that sort – people with plans and ambition, people who would generate jobs and industry – if the police were giving the impression that they were a haven for terrorists? Didn't they understand the *damage* that could do? Were they *trying* to drive out new businesses, as well as undermine the old ones?

The cyclist, no doubt mindful of the opportunity for further tales to drink out on, had then contacted Achebe: he'd been told the researchers were decent, upstanding people – he certainly wasn't suggesting otherwise – but the Detective Inspector had said he was interested in any new activity in the area. He probably knew all about them already. But just in case . . .

The DI did not know all about them and was very interested indeed, since the property the engineers were allegedly occupying had been mothballed a decade earlier by the owners, a large agricultural business. A police drive-by confirmed that it looked just as padlocked as it should have been, and just as deserted . . . save for a familiar treadmark impressed in the soft earth by the gate. Leaving stakeouts in place for the *agents provocateurs* of Kaboom, Achebe descended on the place, warrant in hand and with a team of officers and technicians at his back.

As soon as they got inside it was obvious that the facility had only recently been abandoned: the lab had been stripped and the tanks drained, but the electricity and running water were still connected. And in the sump of one tank and the spillage tray beneath another, in the water-filled treads where a heavy vehicle had backed in and loaded up, there were traces of the toxin-producing algae, dead now, and decomposing.

'We found it,' Achebe told Sharon, earset to earset on a secure channel, 'but they've scarpered. Looks like they've been gone at least a week – probably cleared out once the payload was delivered. No fingerprints, no security system to interrogate, and the clean-up's so good I doubt we'll find anything we can pull DNA from. Our only hard evidence is the algae, and if we'd arrived a few days later I don't think we'd have got that.'

Sharon ground her teeth in frustration, but an hour later Achebe had another lead. Neighbours along the potholed road were scarce, but the police found a farmer guiding a massive motor-plough over fields half a mile away.

He was perplexed by their interest in the place. 'I don't get why you're bothering them,' he declared crossly. 'They're already tight with your lot – not police, the other ones. Those Environmental Management jobsworths. Don't you people talk to each other?'

Fayole quickly identified the EM field officer who had visited the site and found among her pending items the only apparent record of the operation: a standard impact appraisal, signed off, but not yet filed. The officer was by turns defensive and contrite.

'I didn't want to get them in trouble,' she said. 'They didn't know they were supposed to file an application before they started work. It happens. They were very apologetic. I was just holding off a bit so they could get it in. They didn't want it to look like they were doing anything out of order.'

'I questioned you three days ago,' Achebe pointed out. 'I asked *specifically* if anything unusual had happened recently, or if you were aware of any new activity in the area.'

'I didn't . . . You were talking about the reserve; this is ten miles away . . .'

'But still in your area, correct?'

'Well, yes . . .'

'Did they mention the reserve at all?'

'They wondered whether it was safe to visit. If we patrolled it or anything like that.'

'What else did they ask you?'

'Just about the river, tidal flows and things. They said maybe they'd go kayaking when they weren't so busy . . .'

'There are times,' Achebe said in his next conversation with Sharon, 'when I wish we could lock up people for stupidity.'

'You don't think she knew what was going on?'

'She didn't try to cover her tracks, and I suppose their questions wouldn't have sounded suspicious at the time. On the other hand, we've just turned up a couple of transfers from the same grey account that was used to pay the utility bills. It looks like she took a backhander to delay the filing, which she naturally didn't want to draw attention to when I interviewed her. But by then she must have realised that her nice new patrons fit the profile.'

'Collusion and obstruction. Arrest her,' said Sharon. 'I'll set up another press briefing. We'll say we've found the terrorists' operational base and have detained a suspect. If all that does is get a rise out of Kaboom, it'll be worth it. Who opened the water and electricity accounts?'

'The same fake company that's on the EM documentation that was never filed. The individuals named on the documents were the two who ran the site, but their identities are also false and we have no visuals. Our suspect is on her way into town in the back of a transport. I was planning to have her work up some images with one of our artists.'

'Good. Do that first, then arrest her. We'll include the images in the briefing. Are the property's owners still claiming to know nothing about any of this?'

'So they say, but there's no sign of forced entry – if our terrorists broke in, they'd've had to change the locks, but the ones we found on the gates and buildings don't look new at all. They look the age they should look.'

'So they were given access. Someone on the inside.'

'Given, or stolen – it might have been one of them on the inside. We're getting the owners' employment records, and the facilities manager is on his way here now with a full set of keys and combinations to help us determine precisely which areas have been compromised.' Achebe said it straight, but Sharon could hear the grin in his voice.

'Achebe, you are turning into a properly sneaky copper. Let me know what he says when you point out they must have had keys to his locks.'

'Thank you, boss. I only take lessons from the best.'

'So who does this bloke work for? You said the place is owned by an agribusiness?'

'Pure Fuel Farmers.'

'Sounds cosy. Are they private?'

'I don't think so.' There was a pause while Achebe checked. '*Oh! Oh my.*'

'What?'

'They're owned by Southern Warmth, which is a biofuel aggregator who are in turn owned by . . . Bankside BioMass.'

They were both silent for a long while.

'Well,' said Sharon finally. 'Isn't that interesting.'

'Bankside were behind that petition, weren't they?'

'They were. They fund the Estuary Preservation Society, who fronted it.'

'This operation had to have been in place for a fair old time,' Achebe pointed out. 'They were here for a couple of months, and engineering the algae would have started earlier than that.'

'Bankside were working against Thames Tidal from long before the petition gambit – ever since they weren't allowed to buy in.'

'Would they be doing all of that officially, trying to get shares and everything, while also running an operation like this?' Achebe wondered. 'I mean, big public companies don't generally go in for terrorism.'

'Maybe it's just a coincidence that the company belongs to Bankside. It's three tiers of possession and goodness knows how many layers of management away. Maybe the terrorists chose it because they knew the connection might throw us, if we managed to track them this far.' But Sharon was thinking that Bankside was a subsidiary of Standard BioSolutions, and that Standard was elbow-deep in political manoeuvring to take over Thames Tidal, and that there was a limit to how many coincidences she could bring herself to believe in. 'We still need to look into it.'

'I'm with you, boss, but my money's on these guys having a local connection.'

'My worry,' said Sharon, 'is that this whole business'll end up having a lot of connections.'

The bulletin from Detective Superintendent Varsi was succinct, and she declined to take questions from the press. 'You'll appreciate that this remains an active investigation,' she said tersely. 'There are things we cannot discuss for operational reasons. If anyone recognises either of the men in these images, please contact the police immediately. Neither man should be approached. If any member of the public has information that might be relevant, they should get in touch with us right away. Thank you.'

As always when the streams had little to go on, they made up the difference in backstory and conjecture. It took them no time at all to determine that the suspect in custody was an Environmental Management officer, and to discover her identity.

'I'm really sorry,' Achebe said to Fayole, and left her to run interference with her bosses. Public records relating to the hydroponics site were likewise picked over, and the connections between it and multiple players in the energy game were made almost before the press briefing had concluded. Could this, several journalists wondered aloud, be the reason for the Met's reluctance to elaborate? Was this the active line of enquiry to which Detective Superintendent Varsi had alluded? It was too juicy a prospect to ignore. They went off to lay siege to the press offices of Pure Fuel, Southern Warmth and Bankside BioMass itself.

Sharon, looking at streamfeeds a couple of hours later, was moved to even deeper levels of cynicism by how so little actual information could generate so much erroneous content. There was no immediate response from Kaboom, but the stakeout teams had done their job: the identities of four of the five streamers were now known and they were under constant surveillance. At some point they would receive new instructions, and when that happened Sharon would have both them and their handler. In the meantime, all the froth and friction on the streams would serve to confuse, occupy and misdirect. She awaited with interest the reaction of the Bankside corporate hierarchy, had a screaming row with her counterpart in Environmental Management and then a few more quiet words with Achebe.

Among the profusion of reports, commentary and 'New Developments!' that weren't, the evening newstreams carried a brief but tangentially related announcement. It was tagged 'politics' and was therefore of little interest to many subscribers, though it raised eyebrows and fed speculation in both the halls of power and humbler homes throughout the land. The managing director of Thames Tidal, a divisive figure closely associated with talk of a new political movement within the gem community, had comprehensively put those rumours to bed.

Released as a personal statement, Pilan candidly admitted that forming a new party to focus attention on gem issues had been much discussed. He, for one, was now stepping away from the idea, and he was urging others to do the same.

'Recent events have convinced me of two things,' his statement read. 'First: we're still in danger from people who don't think we have as much right to life and freedom as they do, but they'd sooner poison us in secret than stand up and say so. They know what the public reaction would be if they showed themselves. Second: withdrawing from the mainstream won't help us defend ourselves against these forces. It would do more for their cause than ours. I know the majority of people, both gems and norms, truly believe in equality and inclusion, and so do I. We mustn't become distracted by our differences. We're lucky enough to have institutions that are committed to protecting all of us, and we need to focus on strengthening them.'

Anyone who knew Pilan well – or at all – would have detected a more conciliatory mind at work in the crafting of this message. 'Nothing to do with me,' Mikal told a reporter when asked, which was more or less the truth: he had seen the post before it had gone onstream, and been unable to suggest improvements. He assumed Lapsa must have helped her partner write it, as did most others, but they were wrong: Pilan had gone straight to Gabriel.

'This isn't a Thames Tidal job, obviously,' he'd said, 'and you can tell me to go and jump in the basin if you want. It's just that you're the expert at finding the right way to say things onstream. I need this to sound like me, only not . . .' Pilan trailed off, groping for a way to explain.

'Not,' said Gabriel, hazarding a guess, 'to piss anybody off?'

'Exactly. Did you pick up that language from me? Your mum'll kill me.'

'I picked it up when people started poisoning my friends. Of course I'll help.'

He listened while Pilan outlined what he wanted to say, looked at what he'd already written, then said, 'I have some questions.'

'Okay.'

Gabriel pointed at the cranial band. 'Can I turn this off while I ask them?'

'Can you . . . oh.' He hesitated. 'Okay.'

It took Gabriel ten minutes of unfiltered conversation and half an hour of drafting to come up with the statement. He put in things that Pilan hadn't thought to say out loud but that he sensed were part of what the Thames Tidal boss wanted to communicate. Pilan read the text with visible amazement.

'Did I tell you all that?'

'Yep.'

'It does sound like me,' Pilan said. 'But only if I were—' He stopped, then started to laugh. 'Damn. I could never have done this.'

Gabriel, his band back on standby and unsure what was so funny, guessed again. 'What, be a politician?'

'Yes.'

'Good thing you've given it up.'

Pilan was shaking with mirth. 'That was a brief career: here and gone in one post.'

'Better be sure you got everything right, then.' He made Pilan go through the piece line by line, ticking off all the messages that were being sent or subtly rejected.

'What's this bit about institutions?' Pilan asked.

'You're going to back the UPP, right? And you want everyone who was getting excited at the idea of a new party to do the same, and you want this statement to lay the groundwork. But,' he added anxiously, 'it should only say that if it's what you actually mean. I thought that's what I picked up, but we'll take it out if I got it wrong.'

'You didn't,' Pilan replied thoughtfully. 'It's something Jack Radbo said. I guess it stuck in my head.'

'That's where I found it. Are you okay with it?'

Pilan read the whole thing over again, then walked round the room, gazed out the window, came back, read it once more.

It seemed to Gabriel that he was undergoing some kind of reconciliation.

'Yes,' he said finally, 'I'm okay with it. It's stronger than I'd intended, but there's no point being half-arsed about things.' He straightened up and stretched. He was, thought Gabriel, looking and sounding much healthier and stronger, much more himself.

'I've got to show it to a couple of people,' Pilan said, 'but I don't think I'm going to let anybody change anything. I like it. Let's drop it into the mix and see what happens.'

The first thing that happened, at least as far as Gabriel was concerned, was that he was hailed from all corners when he poked his head into the hum and chatter of the café. The long tables were crowded with regulars and Pilan's about-face was running level with the day's incendiary police bulletin as the major topic of discussion. He threaded his way between the tables, stopping to return greetings and assure the diners that the Thames Tidal boss was quite well and had most definitely not been abducted or brainwashed.

'He's fine, really,' he protested to Aster: bone-white, violet-eyed, imperious and disbelieving. 'I think he just realised it was time to make a decision one way or another. He's in good shape.'

'Too good to be true, if you ask me,' she said. 'If he'd sounded that impressive from the start, I might have backed the idea.' She sniffed. 'Too late now.'

Gabriel grinned and finally made it to the counter, where his mother was checking orders before Delial delivered them to the tables. Eve, standing next to Gaela, was diligently organising cutlery, although it wasn't the sort of job that would normally hold her attention for long. Their father was busy at the big cooking range, wreathed in steam, alongside his two assistants. He could see they were working flat out, but Gaela shooed him away when he offered to help.

'We're fine, honey,' she said, as Eve grumbled, '*I'm* helping,' *sotto voce* from her station with the spoons and forks. Gaela looked down at her with a smile that was slightly less troubled than it had been, if no less weary. Relations were apparently not quite as fraught as yesterday, but Gabriel suspected that might change if they were all crammed in behind the counter. 'You've had a long day,' Gaela went on. 'I'll get Horace in if I need him. Aryel's here; go and join her and the others. I'll send over some dinner.'

Aryel was at her favourite spot in the front corner, where she could sit with her back to the wall and not worry about her wings being in anyone's way. At least, that was the reason she always gave and he knew it was true; but he also knew she was well aware that a glimpse of her through the window was the best advertising the business could have. Eli was sitting with her, along with Callan and Rhys.

Gabriel worked his way across to her, glad to no longer be the centre of attention, overhearing snatches of conversation along the way: mostly about the police investigation and the likelihood of further attacks, some about Bankside, Pilan or politics, and, for blessed relief, occasionally something else entirely.

'Strange things happening with the share price,' he heard Aryel say as he reached her table. She looked up at him and smiled. 'So,' she murmured, leaning across as he slid into an empty seat, 'win a bet for me. Did you write this thing that Pilan wrote?'

'How'd you know?' he asked, alarmed. 'We tried not to make it obvious.'

'It isn't, don't worry. Process of elimination. I knew he must have had help, and I didn't think it was Lapsa – she's a good speaker but not a great writer. Mikal ruled himself out, and it's not his style anyway. So—' She inclined her head at him. 'Well done. Your next job will be speechwriting if you're not careful.'

'Not unless Pilan changes his mind,' he murmured back, to knowing chuckles from around the table. He would have liked to talk to his aunt about Kaboom, and Eve. It was unimaginable that any injunction to secrecy, either from the Varsis or his own family, was meant to include Aunt Aryel, but the café was too busy and noisy and public, and although Uncle Eli and Rhys and Callan were family too, he knew that bringing them in would be a step too far. So he sat back and let his mind wander, until he was brought back to alertness with a jolt.

'Only one still in hospital,' Rhys was saying. 'He's finally showing some improvement, but the damage—' He shook his head bitterly.

'Is that Tamin?' asked Gabriel. 'Isn't he going to get better, like the others?'

'I hope so, Gabe, but the scarring on his gill tissue is the worst we've seen. He might never be comfortable underwater again.' Rhys was speaking quietly, his face serious. 'Don't repeat that, obviously.'

'I won't – but why was it so much worse for him?'

'We're not sure. He might just have been more susceptible. I've been combing through his genetype looking for anomalies, but . . .'

He paused while Delial and Horace, who had been drafted in from the empty grocery next door, delivered five laden plates to the table. For a few minutes there was no sound except for the clinking of cutlery and chewing. Gabriel, enveloped in the aroma of seashore pie, discovered that he was ravenous. It was one of his father's specialities, and one of his favourites, made from fish and shellfish farmed out in the estuary. He tucked in with relish – and then remembered that Tamin had worked on one of those farms.

'If that's not it,' he said to Rhys, 'what else could it be?'

The young doctor examined a prawn on the end of his fork as though it might have the answer. 'Another possibility is that his exposure was greater. Cal and Eli saw him swim in from the river and he was immediately symptomatic, whereas it took a while for most patients to start feeling ill.' Eli and Callan both nodded, their mouths too full to speak. 'If he was the only one who swam through a cloud of algae as it was releasing the toxin, then he would've got more of a hit than anyone else.'

'That would mean it was being released in the river,' Gabriel pointed out, 'not actually inside Sinkat.'

'I'm leaning towards that view, especially since he then went back into the water and swam across the basin – that suggests the problem wasn't actually in the basin yet.'

'It makes sense,' Aryel said. 'They haven't found anything in Sinkat that could have acted as the catalyst, and it would've been easier to get whatever it was into the main channel without being noticed. Mind you, they haven't found anything there either.'

'The police liaison told Lapsa they think they're looking for some kind of bioplastic or polymer,' Gabriel added, keeping his voice low. 'I thought the whole point about those is that they're not reactive, but they took samples from all the wet buildings, buoys, lane markers, even the hulls of boats. Everything that's underwater.'

Rhys was shaking his head. 'The idea was that the catalytic compound might have been incorporated into some perfectly innocent material. Think of the way quantum-energy cells are embedded in the biopolymer structure of the Thames Tidal building – that's pretty sophisticated, but the basic technique has been around a long time. With all the new development in Sinkat recently, the police thought maybe the terrorists had snuck something in through the regular supply chain.' He shrugged and stabbed another prawn. 'But there's nothing, not there, or in the river. So I don't know how they did it.'

'We're missing something,' Aryel said. Her eyes, huge and bright in the bronze oval of her face, rested on Gabriel. 'There's more going on here than a protectionist energy market or a reactionary political movement or even plain old-fashioned prejudice. It has elements of all those things, but it's bigger than any one of them. And I can't shake the feeling that we're being so bombarded by events and information, we're failing to notice something obvious.'

QUANTUM

19

Mikal Varsi was delivering three noisy children to school early the next morning when his earset buzzed.

'Honey? Have you dropped the kids yet? Oh, you haven't – why are they making such a racket? I've got news.'

'They have decided to form a band,' Mikal told Sharon solemnly. 'It will be a global sensation. They are going to travel the world and be on every stream, everywhere, all of the time. Won't that be lovely? I've been treated to their first rehearsal.'

He ushered the children through the school gate, across the narrow front yard and up to the building's entrance, managing to keep a straight face as down the line Sharon dissolved into helpless laughter. The aide checking pupils in and dispatching them to their classrooms took in the dancing, prancing, screeching trio and planted herself in front of them with arms folded and a look of polite enquiry. The clamour died away with a speed that Mikal, who had suggested in vain that they lower the volume during the tramp through the misty, sleepy streets of Riveredge Village, found little short of miraculous. The woman, who moved with the solid grace of an athlete, had tattooed hands and glowing teal-coloured hair and an expression that said she'd seen it all before but would be happy to accept an explanation if one were to be forthcoming. Eve, Misha and Sural grinned up at her. She gazed down at them thoughtfully, as though they were a particularly interesting and knotty problem, before turning her querying expression on Mikal. He decided it would be wrong to deny her the joy of discovery and returned his most sympathetic look.

'Morning, Teri. Children?'

'Good morning Miss Teri,' they chorused raggedly.

'Good morning, Mikal,' she said, imperturbable. 'Good morning, Misha. Good morning, Eve. Good morning, Sural. In you go. We are *walking*, not running, and *talking*, not shouting, correct?'

They scampered past with a volley of 'Yes, misses,' and an added, '*Singing* isn't *shouting*,' from Eve.

Mikal called, 'Have a good day!' after them, thinking that in their case the encouragement was entirely unnecessary, waved at Teri and backed away, pointing at his earset. She flapped an understanding hand at him, and he made his escape.

'Sharon? You still there? I've handed them over to Terissa. Is it too late to go back to bed?'

'Not for you.'

'If it's just me, there's not much point.'

'I can't help you with that at the moment, Councillor,' she said sedately. 'Maybe later. I do have some other diversions that you might appreciate.'

'I'll take what I can get.'

'Our two terrorist suspects have been identified. They have a history of working together, even before this latest venture. I thought you'd like to know that both are recent ex-employees of Bankside BioMass.'

That bombshell stopped Mikal dead on the pavement, where other hurrying parents almost collided into him. He sidestepped, mumbling an apology, and strode swiftly out of their hearing. 'You don't say.'

'I do say. Several former colleagues got in touch overnight, all giving the same names. They were checked against the employment records, and the EM officer arrested yesterday has now looked at their file photos and confirmed that they are indeed the men she met. I'm about to update the bulletin.'

'Has Bankside responded?'

'Not exactly,' Sharon said drily. 'The press officer I just spoke to was dumbfounded. Given that no one in the chain of command has come up with a credible explanation for how a random pair of chancers gained access to their hydroponics farm, I can't imagine why. I expect someone rather more senior will be in touch any minute now.'

'Any leads on where the terrorists are?'

'Hmm . . .'

He sighed. 'Oh, right, you're not supposed to tell me that. Shall I just assume there's no sign of them at their last addresses, and known acquaintances have no knowledge of their current whereabouts?'

'I couldn't possibly comment, except to observe that you would have made an excellent detective.'

He laughed. 'Nice to know there might be a career for me to fall back on. Although that news should smooth my way today considerably.' He remembered that it was not the news he'd been expecting. 'Is this what they called you in at the crack of dawn for? I thought it was Kaboom-related.'

'It was. Are you in a secure location?'

He looked round the residential street, quiet now the kids were all safely delivered to school, and with no one in sight except for a dog-walker far ahead. 'Nobody's within a hundred feet of me.'

'Okay, so I figure I can tell you this because arrests are imminent and you brought us Kaboom in the first place, but I'm going to be keeping it quiet until we've had a chance to question them.' She hesitated, then said, 'There's another reason too, I'll get to that in a minute. Last night two of the four streamers we'd identified visited the same address, a couple of hours apart. It's a public venue with a lot of traffic, so the first one went in and came out without the officers being able to tell whom they were meeting. The second was spotted parting company with a man outside when the premises closed, and we added this man to the stakeout list. Just before dawn this morning, said man was seen meeting another unidentified person in a night-workers' café. We think she's going to turn out to be the fifth streamer, because shortly after she left, another of those we'd already identified showed up – that's when I got the call. We're just giving it a little longer to see if he'll be obliging enough to meet with all five before we nick the lot.'

'Detective Superintendent Varsi,' he said admiringly, 'very well played.'

'You haven't heard the rest.' She sounded reluctant.

'Which is?'

'The first two meetings took place in the financial district, in a fashionable restaurant . . . one with a private members' club upstairs.'

Once again Mikal was shocked into immobility. He looked around, found the nearest wall and leaned against it. In his ear she said, 'Mik? Are you there?'

'Sorry – I'm here. Just . . . *What?*'

'I know. Remember, it might be coincidence.' She used the overly firm voice that meant she too had reached the obvious conclusion, but was determined not to fall for it too easily. 'The Karma Club is busy; it's popular and there're a lot of comings and goings, which makes it the perfect place for this kind of rendezvous.'

'So they met in the restaurant? The bar?'

'We don't know. The officer trailing the first one circled through but couldn't spot him – and yes, that might be because he'd gone to the members' area upstairs, but it could also just mean he was hidden by the crowd. It's too soon to read anything conclusive into it.'

'If you say so.'

'Mik, if you repeat this and they use it and it doesn't stack up—'

'—then my new associates will be the ones who end up looking irresponsible, if not downright unscrupulous, whereupon they will deflect the blame onto me. Got it. Do you know anything about the person they were meeting? Not another old Banksider, by any chance?'

'No.' She sounded even more reluctant. 'He did work for Standard at one point – the parent company. But that was years ago. He's had several positions since then; now he runs his own consulting business.'

'How convenient.' Mikal pushed himself away from the wall.

'Honey, I *know*. *But.*'

'Don't worry, I'm not going to tell them any more than I need to. I haven't been married to a cop for ten years for nothing.'

By the time Mikal got to Westminster, public screens were regularly flashing up the names of the Thames terrorists. The artist's impressions from the day before had been replaced by photos from their Bankside employment files, with the special Met comcode for sightings or other information prominently featured, along with the words DO NOT APPROACH. He paused at the corner of Parliament Square as the feed shifted to a live shot of an UrbanNews reporter standing outside a monolithic office block. The legend BANKSIDE BioMASS was clearly in frame over her right shoulder.

Mikal adjusted his earset to pick up the sound and listened for a few seconds, until the image transitioned to aerial footage of the wetland from three days before, when it had been crowded with police and EM vehicles and boats had been clustered around the barricaded drainage channel. He flicked the earset back to standby and set off again, feeling grimly vindicated.

His destination was a large office building on one of the capital's busiest and most venerable streets. Unlike the Bankside complex, it was at least a century old: stolid, functional and architecturally undistinguished, with the slight shabbiness that comes not from disrepair or disuse but from unrelenting traffic and endless pressure for space. Though it had other tenants, it was primarily known as the headquarters of the United People's Party.

Mikal wondered if the entrance was being watched. He hoped so. As always, his height drew every eye on the street, and for once he did not mind. He took the steps two at a time, and walked in through the front door.

Back in his City Hall office a couple of hours later, Mikal was unsurprised when his tablet once more signalled an incoming call from Moira Charles. This time he swiped to receive immediately. She came up against a different backdrop than before: the wall behind her was a rich crimson, and the furniture was gleaming dark wood. The bland professionalism was also gone, replaced by a pinched tension around the mouth and eyes that he found immensely cheering. 'Ms Charles,' he said heartily. 'Barely a day goes by. To what do I owe the pleasure?'

'Councillor Varsi,' she replied, sounding strained. 'Good afternoon. Your appearance alongside the Energy Minister earlier was extremely . . . unexpected.'

'Was it? You surprise me, Ms Charles. Surely it's the business of government to take an interest when its citizens' lives are endangered?'

'That might be, but it's unacceptable for him to infer corporate involvement in a criminal enterprise . . .'

'In my experience, corporations are entirely capable of engaging in criminal enterprises,' Mikal interrupted, idly flexing his double-thumbed hands where she could see before lacing them together atop his cocked knee. 'Whether that has happened in this case is yet to be determined, but Mr Radbo isn't alone in noting connections and expressing concern.'

'Your comments give the impression that you share his opinion.'

'That's reassuring, since I do. The possibility that the terrorists have received support – illicitly or otherwise – from within Bankside BioMass should be investigated as a matter of extreme urgency. I trust you don't disagree with that?'

He trusted also that she would hear the echo of her own words thrown back at her. She grimaced, then drew herself up. 'Standard BioSolutions will cooperate fully with the authorities. We will also vigorously defend our subsidiaries from any suggestion of involvement in these matters. A company is not responsible for what employees do once they leave, nor for unauthorised actions taken against company policy by those still employed.'

'Duly noted.'

'Councillor Varsi, we anticipated a more measured response from you on these matters. I wish to convey our profound disappointment.'

'Consider it conveyed. Anything else?'

'I— You don't seem to—' She broke off and looked to one side, listening to something he could hear only as a muffled growl. Then she moved aside, out of the tablet's field of view, and said, 'Someone would like to speak with you.'

Abraham Mitford took her place. Mikal knew immediately that wherever they were, it was his space: she had been sitting too far forward, perched uncomfortably on the edge of the chair as though she was not certain she was really allowed to be there, while Mitford dropped into it with the carelessness of ownership. The colour in his face was high. He did not bother with a greeting.

'Varsi,' he said, 'what the hell do you think you're doing?'

'Rejecting your offer,' Mikal replied with equanimity. 'I should have thought that was obvious.'

'It'll never come again, do you understand? We can just about pull this back, but if you walk away now it's over.'

'I'm delighted to hear that. This is me, walking. I would hate to have to have this conversation again.'

'What do you think this stunt is going to accomplish?' Mitford asked, his voice rising. 'Where can you possibly imagine it's going to get you? You are *finished*, do you understand? That's what's *obvious*.'

'Are you threatening me, Mr Mitford?'

'*You?*' he spat. 'You think—? I don't make *threats*, Varsi. I told you what has to happen, and some damn-fool gem turning down the chance of a lifetime is not going to change that.'

'There are a great many chances in a lifetime,' Mikal observed peaceably. 'The chance to undermine a lawful and progressive business because you don't like the competition is not the kind I'm interested in. The chance to let a new technology develop and flourish under the stewardship of the people who invented it is the kind I like. I choose the chances I take, Mr Mitford.'

'This isn't over.'

'You just said it was.'

'No,' Mitford said. He had his voice back under control, but his face was beet-red and he spoke slowly, as though Mikal might otherwise fail to understand. '*You* are. And Thames Tidal won't be far behind.'

There were, Sharon Varsi thought, few satisfactions equal to having suspects in custody. She would have been even more pleased if the two fugitives from the hydroponics farm were also banged up in the cells, but for now the six members of the Kaboom propaganda operation – the streamers and their handler, one Conrad Fischer – would do nicely. Every property in southern England that was owned by, leased to or otherwise connected with Bankside BioMass or any of its subsidiaries was now subject to one of the broadest search warrants in the Met's illustrious history, and she had no doubt that Achebe's teams would eventually turn up something.

'The bottom line is this,' she had said to an aggrieved Deputy Chief Operating Officer who was trying in vain to persuade her that such exhaustive scrutiny was quite unreasonable. 'If you can't even hazard a guess how your ex-employees came to know about the Pure Fuel premises, much less gain access to it, you can't expect me to accept your assurance that it was a one-off. For all I know – for all *you* know – they might have found their way into *any* of your other properties by that same mysterious route. Surely you must want to ensure that Bankside BioMass and its affiliates are not unwittingly harbouring terrorists, Mr Han – *don't you?*'

Which had left Mr Han even more aggrieved, and thoroughly flummoxed. He'd muttered something about challenging the warrant, which had made Sharon smile.

'That's your prerogative, of course,' she'd said sweetly. 'Would you like to tell the press you'll be doing that, or shall I?'

Han had looked appropriately horrified and hurriedly ended the conversation, and Sharon was pleased to have heard nothing from the company since. She would have been happier still if her warrant had extended upstream as well as down, to allow her to dig deep into the bastions of Bankside's parent company, but the Met's legal team had blanched at the suggestion and advised her to stick to what could be credibly argued from existing evidence. She'd not mentioned Mikal's clandestine conversation with Abraham Mitford to them; the likelihood that the financier was pursuing a criminal strategy alongside a corporate one would be judged too small, the link too tenuous to pursue. She could barely credit it herself. Unless Kaboom gave her something that pointed at Standard as well as Bankside, they would have to proceed on the assumption that the plot, if it had a corporate sponsor at all, was being directed from one of the limbs, not the head.

If Kaboom did link the two, that would change everything.

The streamers were all freelancers, specialising in the kind of unethical publicity work forbidden under that Code of Practice that Gabriel had felt so strongly about. They reacted with varying degrees of indignation and bewilderment to their arrests, all of them insisting that nothing they had done was illegal. The request to 'Tell us about your last instructions from Conrad Fischer' knocked them back a bit, although a couple of them tried claiming they knew no one of that name. When vid evidence of their meetings made those denials impossible to maintain, the more seasoned clammed up and asked for lawyers, and the others started talking.

Fischer himself was a different story. Sharon had suspected as much from the moment she scanned the Met's dossier on him, with its long list of top-tier companies he had once worked for and who had since become his clients. As the hours went by, it became clear that her initial assessment of him had been correct. Though he had never been arrested before, Fischer obviously understood the basic rule: if you said nothing, nothing you said could be used against you. Moreover, he was disciplined enough to be able to stick to his silence through increasingly frustrating sessions with her and Achebe, both singly and together. Even after his solicitor showed up he refused either to confirm or to deny that he had ever known, met, spoken with or instructed anyone, on any matter, at any point in his life.

'You realise,' Sharon said wearily, as she went back in for the third time, 'that we have recorded evidence of your meetings with these people, and that they are currently relating to us the details of those meetings? If you don't speak, we will have only their side of the story.'

'My client has no comment to make at this time,' Ms Marcos, the lawyer, repeated for the umpteenth time.

Sharon ignored her and stared at Fischer until he looked up, his face expressionless, as it had been from the moment he was arrested. 'Let me make this clear to you: because of the nature of the crimes, because of the confessions and because of the evidence we already have against you, we have more than enough to hold you. We have located the account you used to pay for the streamers' services and it is only a matter of time before we trace the origin of those funds. It will go far better for you, Mr Fischer, if you tell us now on whose behalf you have been acting.'

'My client has no comment to make at this time.'

'I don't think you appreciate the serious nature of the crimes here, Mr Fischer. We are not talking about conspiracy to slander, unpleasant though that is. We are talking about terrorism, do you understand that? We're talking about aiding and abetting a terrorist attack. We're talking about attempted murder. Those are not charges that you – or your business – can just shrug off.'

'My client has no comment—'

Without another word, Sharon got up and left the interview room. Outside, she spoke to Achebe, then called Mikal.

'I've advised the investigation that you were at the Karma Club for a business meeting the evening before several suspects were tracked there,' she told her husband. 'It would be helpful if you could look at some photos, tell us whether you recognise anyone.' She stayed firmly in official-speak and he picked up his cues smoothly.

'Of course. Anything I can do to assist.'

'I'm handing you over to Constable Danladi, who will take you through the photographs.'

Sharon sat in the background, listening silently as the young PC asked a few questions to establish place, date and time. Then she piggybacked a file link onto the connection and took him through the line-up, one at a time.

'No,' he said apologetically, 'I'm afraid I don't recognise any of them. Although—' He stopped, frowning.

'We need you to be as certain as you can, Councillor. Would you like to see them again?'

'Just the last one, please.'

It was the handler, Conrad Fischer. Sharon waited with bated breath as Mikal studied the photograph, but at last he sighed and shook his head. 'No, that's definitely not the man I saw talking to Moira Charles; he was shorter, with darker hair and skin. It's just that this bloke looks like someone who'd fit in perfectly in the private area upstairs – there's something about his clothes, his expression; that kind of senior-executive look. I wondered if maybe I'd glimpsed him in the background.'

'Did you?'

'I don't think so – but I was whisked through pretty quickly so I wouldn't swear to it one way or the other.'

Sharon scowled as Constable Danladi broke the file link with Mikal's tablet. He caught sight of her expression over Danladi's shoulder as the photo disappeared from his screen and said, 'Sorry. That's not very helpful.'

'Don't be,' Sharon replied, adding, 'A false positive would be even less helpful. As Constable Danladi says, it's important to know that the information provided is completely reliable.'

'Under the circumstances,' said Mikal, 'I believe it would be advisable for me to make a full statement about my visit to the club – what I was doing there, and who I saw.' He blinked solemnly at her.

Sharon had been thinking exactly that, and trying to decide how to tell him so; now it struck her that his mention of Moira Charles' name had probably been intended to signal *her* that this was what he was about to do. She shot him a brilliant smile and in her best Detective-Superintendent voice said, 'Obviously I can't take your statement myself; Constable Danladi can take it from here.'

'Me?' the young woman said in surprise as her senior officer stood up to leave the room. She was a recent arrival and Sharon barely knew her; she trusted that after a moment's thought PC Danladi would realise why that made her a good choice.

'It might prove completely irrelevant,' Mikal was saying, looming large on the tablet as he leaned forward, 'but I'd like to put it on the record, just in case. Shall I come in—?'

Danladi turned back to him, and Sharon slipped out. She wondered if something had happened in the aftermath of Mikal's meeting with the UPP, and his subsequent press conference alongside a thunderous Jack Radbo. Maybe Mitford or the Trads had tried to turn the screw somehow? She didn't doubt that very public display of which alliance he had chosen must have ratcheted up the stakes considerably.

She met Achebe in the corridor, coming up from the interview rooms below. The normally phlegmatic detective was looking rumpled and tired, still peering at his tablet as he walked.

'Boss,' he said, 'good. I was just coming to find you.'

'Anything new?'

'Nothing from the search teams. Fischer's still silent, but the others are singing like the proverbial. It looks like his instructions to them were timed to capitalise on specific incidents: the turbine sabotage, the Estuary Preservation petition, the TideFair, the first stage of the illness when it was thought to be contagious, the second stage, when it was identified as a toxin, and so on. They all maintain he never *told* them that he knew what was going to happen next, but they're all pretty certain he did.'

'Great: informed conjecture from a bunch of two-bit chancers.' She sighed. 'I believe them, but I don't know if a jury will feel the same way. Do we have anything useful on him *at all*?'

'No. Well . . . no.'

'What?'

'I can't see how it could be useful – it's curious more than anything. It's just that he's got a very tenuous link with a very old case of ours.'

'Which one?'

'Zavcka Klist and the genestock theft – remember that whole crazy business from eight years ago?' Achebe saw her expression change, misunderstood and grinned. 'I know: our first. At least we don't have Rhys Morgan trying to get himself killed this time.'

Sharon worked to keep her voice steady. 'So what's Fischer's connection?'

'He doesn't have one, at least, not with the case. But you know this weird cult that's sprung up since then? Those pillocks who think Klist knows the secret to immortality? The ones who think she deserves all kinds of exemptions on account of it?' He shook his head at the foolishness of some humans. 'It looks like he's a member.'

20

Eli Walker gazed steadily into the tiny round aperture of a vidcam as he spoke his name. The security panel was discreetly set into the side wall of the grandly pillared entrance to the townhouse. Glancing back from the porch as he waited to be acknowledged, he thought that the building, like the elegant square within which it stood, must be at least three hundred years old. The heavy panelled wooden door with its round brass knob stood at the top of four broad granite steps that led up from the flagstoned pavement; across the street, a matching ribbon of pavement fronted an ornate wrought-iron fence, behind which trees as ancient and tall as the six-storey townhouses were shedding their leaves in silent red and brown drifts. Beneath the trees he glimpsed patches of lawn between evergreen shrubs, winding gravel paths punctuated by slatted wooden benches, a central fountain and the spiky tendrils of a rose garden. Were it not for the state-of-the-art entry panel and modern vehicles parked on the street he could almost have imagined that he'd stepped into a vid documentary from the pre-Syndrome era, or even before, into a sepia-tinted still from the dawn of photography, when horse-drawn carriages conveyed their wealthy owners along this very street and up to this very door.

A chime sounded from the panel and the blue rectangle of the scanner was softly illuminated as a polite male voice instructed Eli to confirm his identity. He rested the fingertips of his right hand inside the blue border; the light brightened, flashed, and the door unlocked with an almost imperceptible *thunk.*

'Take the lift up to the fifth floor, please, Dr Walker,' said the voice, and Eli pushed the door open and stepped through into a hallway with an ornate staircase, an unmanned reception desk and a small lift at the rear. Though it was no more than an empty entrance hall in which no one would ever spend more than a few seconds, there was none of the scruffiness or air of benign neglect that often clung to such places; every surface was bright and gleaming, the floors were spotless, the potted plants were as jungle-fresh as if they had just been delivered. He had spent years of his life in flats that were considerably less inviting.

The lift opened to reveal an equally well-appointed hallway on the top floor, with light flooding in through a window that faced onto the square. There was no grand staircase this time; instead a closed door presumably led to an enclosed stairwell. On the opposite wall another door was opening as he approached.

'Good morning, Dr Walker.' The man was in late middle age, bald save for a fuzz of grey hair across the back of his skull, and neatly dressed in the kind of sober, dark, nondescript garments that made Eli immediately think *uniform*, although they were of the best quality and there was no insignia of any kind. 'I am Marcus. Please come in.'

He stood aside as Eli entered, then silently closed the door behind him and just as silently took his coat and hung it in a closet in the hall. Eli surveyed the rich, polished wood of the floors and furniture, the bowl of fresh roses that gently scented the air, the paintings – not vidart, but genuine acrylics and watercolours and oils – hanging on the walls and tried to think if he had ever before been anywhere that evoked so clearly the tastes of a different era.

The place lacked the self-consciousness of an interactive museum diorama or the self-importance of eminent old university chambers he had known, or the impersonality of either. Nor did it have their sense of sacrosanct antiquity, for the modern world lived here too: in the earset Marcus wore, and the outline of a tablet in the slide-pocket of his shirt; in the photosensitive glass of the tall windows and the baskets of engineered aerial plants that reduced humidity and cleansed the air; in the small screens of the household-management system discreetly tucked away here and there, and the large one for stream-feeds that he glimpsed mounted on the wall of a luxurious sitting room as he was ushered past it and into Zavcka Klist's study.

She was seated in an upright chair upholstered in quilted leather. He suspected it had been made for her, so perfectly did it conform to the lines of her tall frame. In front of the chair was an elegant console of engineered wood with an angled reading screen, a separate input panel for more comfortable note-taking and a dock for her tablet. There were a few other leather-covered chairs, a couple of small tables and several strategically placed reading lights. The narrow window had a view into the thinning canopy of the trees across the street.

But what struck him most forcefully was not the vista, nor the expensive furniture: it was the shelves of printed books that lined the walls.

He knew at a glance that they were neither replicas nor some carefully contrived selection put together for appearance's sake; there was too much variety in their sizes and colours and bindings, and many had the cracked spines of volumes that have been read and reread. Nor were they in temperature-controlled cases, as they would have been if their monetary value were the collector's highest priority. They just sat on the packed shelves, in rows and in stacks, obviously there to be touched and taken down on a whim. It was a bibliophile's fantasy.

Tearing his eyes away, Eli focused on his host.

She had not bothered with the pretence of ignoring him when he was shown in, as she might have done in the old days; she had looked up from the screen at once, though she did not immediately move. For a moment she merely regarded him, chin propped on her bridged fingers, elbows on the console; then she pushed the unit aside, sliding it away noiselessly, and rose to her feet. She was wearing a crisp white shirt with an upright, open collar, and for the barest of moments, as her hands dropped and he caught sight of her throat, he thought that a snake was coiled around her neck.

'Dr Walker.'

'Ms Klist.' She had not offered her hand, and he did not extend his.

'I see you appreciate my library.'

'It's impressive,' he said. 'It's rare to see this many bound books outside of a museum or university.'

'I imagine so – I've had these a very long time. Most were new when I bought them, or when they were given to me.' She nodded to Marcus, still waiting silently by the door, and he bowed slightly and disappeared, leaving it slightly ajar. She turned to contemplate the shelves herself, her arms folded across her chest. Eli knew from experience that the key to maintaining a sense of equilibrium with Zavcka Klist was not to be intimidated by her haughtiness; he decided to treat the gesture as an invitation instead of a snub and he moved to stand next to her and surveyed the shelves himself, thinking that this was oddly both like and unlike the Zavcka he remembered, or the altered woman that Aryel had described. She had never pretended friendliness towards him any more than she was doing now, but neither had she ever before been conversational, or offered an insight into her own pleasures and influences. He had never known what she cared for, beside herself. Perhaps there was less to hide now, he thought, although it did not follow that she would be less fierce in the defence of what secrets remained.

Still, the initial moves were, if not warm, not openly hostile either. And when a subject this enigmatic provided an opportunity, one did not pass it up.

'Given to you,' he repeated. 'By your father?'

'Some were gifts from my father – this one, and that. Most of those up there.' She touched the top corner of one volume, lifted out another and handed it to him, indicated a row of similarly bound books on a top shelf. 'This one was a keepsake from my tutor.' She passed him another hardback volume. 'There were so few students then, because of the Syndrome, and consequently many subjects were taught one-on-one, or not at all. And this' – she bent and pulled out a badly battered paperback – 'was from one of my university classmates. I was supposed to return it, but she got ill and so—' She shrugged, leaving the sentence unfinished.

Eli studied the books in his hands. From her father she had received *(Un)Natural Selection: Beyond Evolution*, from her tutor *An Incomplete Education* and from her long-dead friend, *The Time Traveler's Wife*. There was, he thought, a world of meaning in those titles, as well as in her decision to show them to him. He doubted they had been selected randomly.

A sound at the door made him look up. Marcus was bearing a tray, which he placed on one of the low tables set between plush leather chairs. He straightened up with an enquiring expression.

'Thank you, Marcus.' Zavcka glanced at another book she had half-pulled out, shoved it back into place and strode past Eli. 'I take it you still prefer coffee, Dr Walker?'

'I do, thank you.' He wondered how she had known that – he had never before had coffee, or indeed, anything much besides harsh words with Zavcka Klist. But back then she would have made it her business to gather as many details as possible about the likes and dislikes of the people whom she expected to manipulate, blackmail or negotiate with. Some of those details would be petty and some less so; she would have forgotten none of them. This was, he assumed, a reminder that, however far she might have fallen, she still possessed a great deal of information and a modicum of power.

'Please, have a seat.' She gestured to the armchair opposite as, with confirmation that nothing else was needed, Marcus departed silently, this time closing the door behind him. Zavcka busied herself pouring. They made a companionable picture, Eli thought, sitting across from each other, chatting about books with the sleek stainless-steel coffee service between them. It occurred to him that she might be constructing the scenario for Marcus' benefit, although he could not imagine what domestic intrigue might underlie such a stratagem.

He sipped, savouring the rich, bitter warmth of the coffee; he'd've been willing to bet it was neither tank-grown nor tent-reared but imported from lush tropical mountains halfway around the world.

'Thank you for seeing me,' he said after a moment. 'I was pleasantly surprised.'

'Did Aryel tell you I was going to say no?'

'She didn't get the impression you were inclined to say yes.'

Zavcka looked slightly, cynically amused. 'I wasn't when she mentioned it, or when I first received the request. I thought you and I had seen quite enough of each other. But the abstract you attached was interesting; I found that I kept returning to it. So much of what happened . . . People today have no idea what things were actually *like*. And it's not as though *I* could write about it.' She waved a languid hand at the absurdity of the idea.

'You could, if you wanted to.'

'Not if I wanted to be taken seriously. And I'm not allowed *noms de plumes*, at least for the foreseeable future.' She held the cup between the tips of her fingers and sipped delicately, frowning. 'That's beside the point, really. No amount of time is going to turn me into a writer, or an academic, so unless I talk to someone like you, everything I know will remain inside my head.' She shook it, as though irritated by the baggage there. 'I've had a lot of requests for interviews over the years, Dr Walker. Most were from two-bit charlatans happy to write endless treatises on what I'm supposed to know or think or have done. I refused to speak to any of them then and I'm certainly not going to be speaking to them now.'

'They'd be stunned if they knew you were speaking to me.'

Again that hint of wry amusement. 'I hope so. With any luck it'll shut them up.' She looked him straight in the face. 'I want to be absolutely clear on this: the research you're doing isn't about me, correct? You are interested only in my perspective as a witness. Do I have that right?'

'You do.'

'Good. I've witnessed a great deal and I can tell it to you, because you and I have a history that means no one will assume either fear or favour. You have an unimpeachable reputation, and I have a lot of time on my hands.'

'I understand.'

He was not sure that he did, although she sounded sincere. The notion of a Zavcka with no agenda, merely looking to while away the long, lonely days reminiscing, was too preposterous to entertain; there must be a scheme afoot, and he was not naïve enough to imagine himself exempt from it. Maybe she hoped her confidences would lure him into letting slip something about the fate of the child she had created and then lost? Perhaps this was part of whatever Byzantine strategy lay behind the recent financial fluctuations Aryel had noted at Bel'Natur – or maybe it stretched even further than that.

It wasn't clear to him or Aryel how volatility in the company she had once led and still had huge shareholdings in could benefit Zavcka, unless she had some plan to destabilise it now and capitalise on the chaos later. Whether, or by what means, she might be behind a conspiracy against Thames Tidal Power was even more obscure, and as they talked, Eli became ever more dubious of that possibility. But he constantly reminded himself not to be lulled by her apparent quiescence: they did not operate on the same time-scale as Zavcka Klist, and if he had ever been inclined to forget that fact, the brief tour through her century-old book collection was a sharp reminder. She had been alive for a hundred and twenty-six years already and might live centuries longer. She could wait life-times for a single stratagem to bear fruit.

At least he knew where he stood with her. Even if she lied, he would learn something.

They talked for more than an hour, and when Eli went over his notes later, he realised that he didn't think she *had* lied – or at least, not much. Her memory was prodigious, and while she revealed almost nothing about her personal life, there was enough anec-dotal detail of people, places and events to lend credence to the recollections she did share. He'd quickly fallen into the rhythm of the interview, discovering to his surprise that Zavcka Klist was possessed of a sly wit and an acid-tinged sense of humour.

'If I didn't know who she was,' he said to Aryel later, 'if I hadn't witnessed for myself some of the things she'd done, I think I might almost have ended up *liking* her.'

'It's one of Zavcka's tragedies,' Aryel replied. 'She is so *almost* likeable. It wouldn't have taken much: a handful of different decisions when she was younger; a mother who lived; a father who loved but didn't worship her; friends to call her out on her arrogance.' A chill breeze gusted, scattering leaves and sending stray wisps of dark hair across her face. She shook her head and blew at the strands to clear them, hands too full of fruit to brush them away. The raised vegetable beds in the roof garden on the top of Maryam House were almost barren this late in the year, but the espaliered and cordoned fruit trees had not yet dropped the last of their bounty. Eli carefully placed his handfuls of pears into the basket at their feet, reached out and tucked the unruly tendrils behind Aryel's ear and relieved her of the remaining apples.

'I hate to say this, but so much about her makes me think of Eve. The expressions on her face when she's telling a story, the way she commandeers a line of enquiry. I wish I didn't, but—' He shrugged helplessly.

'I felt the same when I saw her. Did she ask?'

'About Eve? Not yet. I reckon that'll be for the next visit.'

It had been possibly the most astonishing moment of the interview: the discovery that Zavcka Klist was willing – keen, even – to repeat it. 'Believe it or not, I have another meeting,' she'd said almost sheepishly, when Marcus had tapped on the door to tell her that Mr Crawford had arrived. 'Old habit. I must remember to ration my visitors.'

'There's a great deal more I'd like to ask you, if you don't mind me coming back sometime.'

'I don't mind. Let me know when you want to come.' She'd shrugged, sardonic. 'I'll be here.'

They walked out to the hall together, where she bid him a crisp farewell and took delivery of a man of around Eli's age, although his clothes and grooming pegged him as some sort of executive rather than an itinerant professor. There was a peculiar disparity between the almost obsequious diffidence with which he greeted Zavcka and the naked curiosity in the look he threw back at Eli as she led him towards the study. Were it not for that odd moment of discordance, the man would have been entirely unmemorable; as it was, Eli's own curiosity was aroused.

'Mr Crawford?' he murmured as Marcus showed him to the door. He half expected the servant not to reply, and there was indeed a moment's pause before he did.

'Dhahab Investments,' Marcus murmured back. 'An advisor to Ms Klist.' He held the door open for Eli. 'Good afternoon, Dr Walker.'

'Good afternoon to you, Marcus.'

And then he was back on the quiet, expensive street in blustery autumn sunshine, tablet in hand, reviewing what the infostreams had thrown up on Dhahab Investments.

Aryel, of course, already knew all about them. 'Brokers and business managers to the super-rich,' she said when he got to that part of the story. 'Two of their people are on her list of unrestricted contacts. The head of department is a woman, so he must be the one who actually does the work. Interesting he's coming over instead of doing business via tablet. Zavcka never used to have much time for peons.'

'She's hungry for company, like you said. He didn't strike me as a particularly exciting type, but after eight years inside I imagine she's less choosy. Hell, if she's having me back she must be desperate.'

Aryel laughed at that, although what he'd said made her gaze sharpen. 'This Crawford person. He'd been there before?'

'I think so – though no one said so, it was just—' Eli paused, trying to work out why that had been his assumption. 'There was something about the way they interacted. He seemed familiar with the place.'

'It stands to reason,' Aryel said musingly, 'that there are instructions she'd prefer to give in person.'

'Her communications with those contacts are supposed to be private, aren't they?'

'They are. Anyone else has to go through Offender Management like you did. The authorities won't be monitoring her, but she'll assume Herran is.'

'Ah.' Eli looked at her askance. 'This would all be a lot easier to work out if that were true.'

'I talked to him about it again, but he won't intercept private communications any more, not unless it's to protect Eve. I did find out why, finally: it's because he's become friends with Gabriel and he's had to try and comprehend why Gabriel would want the band even though it blocks his telepathy. Herran understands now that for many people the idea of someone reading their thoughts is a violation. Gabriel's experience appears to have given him a new perspective on the whole concept of privacy.'

'So the thing he learned from the person who can read other people's thoughts mostly choosing not to is that it's wrong to read other people's messages?'

'That's about right. He'll keep an eye on Zavcka only insofar as she might be a threat to Eve. But Zavcka doesn't know that, so she'll be doing whatever she's doing through others, so even if Herran *were* to monitor her fully, I doubt it would help much.'

One strong beat of her wings lifted her high enough to grab a final apple from an upper bough. She dropped lightly back to the path and placed it in the basket, frowning. 'Remember how she ran searches from prison, trying to find out what had become of the baby?'

'I do,' said Eli, 'but after the first few months she more or less stopped trying, didn't she?'

'Yes, but I thought she'd start up again once she got home. Apart from the redactions she's got close to standard stream access, and it would make sense, her looking to see what she could turn up. She knows we'd expect it, and it might distract us from noticing whatever else she's up to. But Herran tells me she hasn't, so I'm thinking she must have outsourced the search.'

'To this Crawford person? I could believe she's using him for the Bel'Natur shenanigans, since they only started since she's been out. He'd probably consider things like manipulating the share price, trying to manoeuvre executives into bad decisions, maybe trying to gain her influence via a third party all just part of the job. But would he really break the law to hunt down a small child with whom she has been forbidden contact? Why would he take that risk, knowing the penalties if they got caught?'

'Maybe he wouldn't, but she's rich and he's in the money business. Who knows what she has that he wants?'

If she'd heard Aryel's question Zavcka would have laughed, and enjoyed a moment's satisfaction that her famously perspicacious adversary had for once got it at least partly wrong. It was Crawford who had what she wanted, and she had only smoke and mirrors with which to bargain.

And money, of course. She would have appreciated Aryel's acuity on that point. Her wealth made the deception not only possible but easy, for he and his associates in what he ostentatiously called 'The K Club' were the type for whom great riches indicated something beyond power and ease, something akin to wisdom, some deeper knowledge of the world and its works. She was finding that instructing him in the manipulation of her vast Bel'Natur shareholdings was a nicely subtle way of pursuing her original project, while simultaneously reinforcing his already well-developed sense of awe. She let him see enough of her other holdings and portfolios to deepen his faith: a range of property assets beyond anything even his obsessive group had uncovered, safety deposits in banks they'd never heard of, exotic investments and obscure foundations. The trick was to reassure them that she *could* have secret formulae and black-lab protocols for genetic surgery locked safely away somewhere, along with access to the kind of private genmed clinics that she could anonymously disappear into every generation or so.

She chose one of her most remote bolt holes, revealed during the trial as a place to which she had indeed periodically vanished, only to reappear some time later as a daughter, a niece, a cousin. There was enough verifiable history there to make the deception plausible, and it was distant enough from her now, both in time and in space, that she could reasonably decline any requests to prove it was truly the repository of her secret.

In fact, there were no requests for proof, which should have pleased her but instead made her irritable. His associates in The K Club, Crawford informed her, were very happy. He confided that some had been nervous at the prospect of making contact given her previous disregard; now they understood that she had been protecting herself – and them – from the scrutiny of those who failed to grasp the significance of who she was and what she represented. Their fears had been overturned, Crawford had said with a simper; now they knew she was everything they had always believed her to be, and more.

She found their gullibility tiresome and their reverence

distasteful, but she could not dismiss the usefulness of the other tale from the trial that they, unlike the jury, had believed: that the baby had never been intended to replace an ageing body increasingly afflicted by illness, but to be the beloved child of someone who was fit but barren. The inestimably wise, infinitely wealthy Zavcka Klist had made herself a daughter. Any harm that had come to lesser beings in the pursuit of that goal was unintended, but more fundamentally, unimportant.

Zavcka wondered what they would think if they knew how completely she had lied, how they would react when they discovered that it was the little people they looked down on who had understood the truth. She wondered what they would be able to justify then, and she thought of the child who was not her daughter, and she feared for them both.

21

Several hours into a work-day in which stream attention had shifted dramatically from Thames Tidal Power and its poisoned workforce to Bankside BioMass and agricultural technicians-turned-terrorists, Gabriel was surprised to discover that having fewer fires to put out was, if anything, leaving him even more weary and stressed. There had been no sign of Kaboom since the previous evening and he was finding the tension of waiting for them to emerge harder on his nerves than actually dealing with it when they did. He did not know whether they had gone quiet in preparation for some new onslaught, or if Aunt Sharon had taken steps to shut them down; the Met bulletins made no mention of any propaganda angle to the investigation, nor of any arrests beyond the Environmental Management officer who had been detained the day before.

He wondered if he should try to contact DI Achebe, and then decided against it; he had been diligent in sending Achebe the links to his onstream duels with Kaboom, so if he found it strange that they'd stopped, he'd get in touch. As he hadn't, Achebe most likely knew more about what was going on right now than Gabriel did.

Or maybe the inspector was just too busy; the streams were gleefully reporting how many offices, farms and factories he had to search. Maybe he just hadn't noticed that Kaboom's streaming had stopped – maybe he was relying on Gabriel to bring any changes in their behaviour to his attention. That wouldn't count as the 'amateur investigating' Sharon had told him not to do, would it . . . or would it? He rubbed his eyes and stifled a yawn.

'You,' declared a voice close to his ear, 'are knackered. Why are you here? You haven't taken a day off in more than a week. They're going to chuck you out of school at this rate.'

He looked blearily round at Agwé. 'They'll have to chuck us both, then,' he said. 'We've been in crisis-mode for more than a week and you haven't taken time off either.'

She hoisted herself gracefully up to sit on the worktop and looked down at him with arms folded and a grave expression on her face. Her bodysuit today was a rich orangey-gold, with emerald-green trim almost as bright as her hair. Both hair and suit looked slightly damp; many gillungs were venturing back into the water now that it appeared their attackers were on the run, and Agwé never had the patience to stay under the dryers any longer than it took for her to actually stop dripping.

'Ah, but I don't work twelve, fourteen hours a day like some people,' she said. 'Also, we're not in crisis any more, are we? Look.' She waved at the quietly humming office, where almost every workstation was occupied. 'Everyone's back. Everything's running smoothly. And you said yourself the streams aren't a problem today—'

'I didn't say that. It's bedlam.'

'It's bedlam for Bankside, and about bloody time too. Let them enjoy having the police and politicians on their case for a change.'

'Yeah, but they could be back on *our* case any minute, Ag – we don't know if Bankside is really involved, or whether the danger's actually over, do we?' He tapped her damp thigh. 'Are you sure you should be swimming?'

'No,' she said serenely, 'but I'm doing it anyway. Don't change the subject. Lapsa's already said you should hand over to the publicity service and go home. And Pilan's not going to argue, is he, not when he owes you for making him look all statesmanlike.'

Gabriel looked around cautiously. Pilan had been in earlier, but he wasn't anywhere to be seen now. 'Where's he gone? Is he still getting press calls?'

'Not so many, I don't think, or maybe he's dodging them. I passed him on the way in – he said he was catching a shuttle, heading out to poke round the battery banks.'

'There's a problem?' he asked quickly.

'No, there is *not*.' He knew the eye-roll was coming and she didn't disappoint. '*Honestly*, Gabe: everything's *fine*. It's just that he hasn't been out there for ten days now, since before the TideFair – and you know what he's like, Mr Micro-Manager. He might have all the telemetry in the world streaming into his tablet, but he never feels like he's on top of things unless he's on site himself.'

He thought he saw an opening. 'See, that's exactly how I feel—'

'Bad analogy,' she interrupted firmly. 'Pilan also spent three days flat on his back in hospital, and four more at home taking it easy – well, for him. Whereas I worked out that you've been in every single day since you came back from your birthday break, and if – no, *when* – Lapsa realises that, you, my friend, will be in deep silt.' She grinned as he groaned.

He tried and failed to think of a comeback. It would be so much simpler if he could just explain about Kaboom, but that information was embargoed; he couldn't even tell Pilan and Lapsa.

'Here's the thing,' he began, not knowing what he was going to say and feeling a bit desperate. As if in answer to a prayer, he felt the buzz of an incoming call through the cranial band. The com-code that came up on his tablet belonged to Uncle Mikal. 'Umm, sorry, Ag. I need to take this.'

She looked dubious but said, 'Fine. I'll be back,' and pushed herself off the worktop. He watched her for a moment as she sauntered away, then shook himself back to attention and swiped to receive.

'Hi, Uncle Mik.'

'Gabe? Is that you? Why do you sound like an avatar?'

He finished slipping his earset back into place and shifted over to regular transmission. 'Sorry. I was on the band. It doesn't translate to voice very convincingly yet.'

'Maybe one day you can teach me how to use mine,' Mikal said, sounding doubtful. 'Look, I have some news. It's confidential, so mostly just listen, okay?'

'Okay.'

'Six people have been arrested in connection with Kaboom. They've been in custody since this morning, so I'm guessing you won't have seen any activity today. Is that correct?'

He felt himself sag with relief. 'Yes. I've been wondering what was going on.'

'I thought you might be. I can't tell you very much, but I know the police are trying to keep it quiet, at least until they've confirmed a link between the people they've arrested and the Thames affair. Between you and me, I don't think the connection's in any doubt at this point. Anyway, I reckon the story will probably break tomorrow, because that's about as long as the police can go without making a statement.'

'What happens then?'

'My guess is that every journo worth their salt will start crawling all over TTP posts and stream-chatter for the past few weeks and asking questions. Better rest up.'

Yet another person telling him to take it easy, when there was so much work to be done.

'We'll need to be ready for that,' he said.

'You can't talk to anyone there about this yet, Gabe – and it shouldn't come from you anyway. We're trying to keep you out of it, remember?'

'Thanks, but you can't. I *work* here.'

'I know—' Mikal paused, and Gabriel could almost hear him thinking. 'Look, I'm at the station now – for something else – but I'm going to tell Sharon that she needs to inform TTP about Kaboom ahead of any announcement so they can be ready for the fallout. She'll probably give you an hour's advance warning; that's kind of her default.' He sounded very mildly apologetic. 'So that means you can start to think about how you want to respond, but you can't tell anyone or do anything until the company is advised officially, which I expect will be first thing tomorrow morning. Fair enough?'

'Fair enough.' Gabriel could not imagine how he'd be able to sit there, knowing this was coming and unable to start preparing. He made a decision. 'Listen, everyone's been telling me to take the rest of the day off, so if nothing's likely to happen before then, I will – I can think at home as well as here.'

'That sounds like a good idea, Gabe. You've been working much too hard, we've all said so. The only thing is,' he added ruefully, 'your sainted mother is once more collecting my children from school today. So you're not likely to get any peace at home, unless you chuck them all out in the garden.'

Gabriel snorted. 'We couldn't keep them in if we tried, and Eve makes more of a racket than Mish and Suri put together.' He looked over to where Agwé was sitting at her workstation, editing something from the looks of it. 'Thanks a lot, Uncle Mik. I'll get out of here now.'

*

Agwé was not usually overawed by her own powers of persuasion, but when Gabriel got up from his workstation, shrugged into his coat and tucked his tablet away in its slide pocket, she pantomimed falling off her chair in shock.

'I'm taking your advice,' he said airily.

'You *are*?'

'I know. Wonders never cease, right?'

'Is everything okay?'

'Now look who's asking.'

'Seriously, Gabe—'

'Seriously, everything's fine.'

She gave him the sternest look she could manage and was gratified when he wilted a little.

'There was something I was a bit worried about,' he explained, 'and now I'm not, so I've handed over, like you said. I'm going to relax with my mum and my sister and the Varsi boys.'

Agwé grinned at him. '*That's* your afternoon off? Those three are a riot that hasn't been declared yet.'

He spread his hands. 'It's that or stay here.'

'Nope, and no remote monitoring either – we should be able to stay out of trouble for half a day.'

'That's a relief.'

'Maybe even a day *and a half*.' She widened her eyes in mock horror. 'You could take tomorrow off too!'

'It'll never happen, Ag.' He sounded too determined to be prodded further, but at least she'd got him to laugh. 'I'll be in early.'

After Gabriel had gone, Agwé returned to her own task, editing clips from the week-old TideFair into a short highlights vid for the streams. She'd been meaning to do it for ages, but in all of the terror and turmoil, the task had been pushed aside. Since then TTP's public profile had been almost entirely negative: images of illness and fear, curt press releases and terse police bulletins, spats with Environmental Management, stream commentary that was either infuriating in its condescension or downright hostile. She was sure that the unrelenting nastiness of some of the trolls he had to deal with was part of what was weighing Gabriel down so much.

Now that they had a bit of a breather, she was determined to recapture some of the magic of that sparkling day, to channel into a vid some of the delight and optimism they'd all felt. Gabriel's mention of Eve, Misha and Sural had reminded her that just about the best footage she'd got was from the Child's Play exhibit and she found herself smiling as she reviewed it. There was some wonderful stuff here.

She would have shown it to Gabriel first, as she usually did, if he hadn't already left. But that was a habit, not a necessity, not when there wasn't any actual news involved. There was nothing here that hadn't already been covered on the streams. If she sent it to him now it might make him smile but perhaps he'd also feel like he hadn't really stopped working after all. He needed to learn that it was really, truly okay to take a break now and again.

And in her heart of hearts she knew that when she showed him things ahead of anyone else it was as much as anything for the pleasure of hearing him tell her how brilliant she was. *Grow up, Agwé*, she thought. *Stop looking for validation. Be more like Gabe.* She made her final edits and sent the vid off to the publicity service.

It would be a nice surprise for him.

Gabriel would later kick himself for the fact that he had switched his band to standby; although the din he was subjected to when he rendezvoused with his mother at the school to collect the three children was so loud that he'd never have been able to monitor the streams anyway. Eve was still giving him the cold shoulder, but he was pleased to see that she was being a bit less bossy than usual with Misha and Sural. The three were in different classes, and from the enthusiasm of their reunion anyone would have thought they hadn't seen each other for weeks instead of mere hours.

'Eve still believes it was me,' he murmured to Gaela as they walked behind the chattering trio. 'I don't even need to read her again to tell.'

'I've told her you had nothing to do with it, that I was the one who knew something was up. I'm not surprised she's holding a grudge; I just don't understand why it's against the wrong person.'

'She's convinced herself that you're covering for me.'

'But *why*?'

'Because it's a lot easier to stay mad at mean big brother than lovely cuddly Mama,' he said. 'Don't worry about it; I'll live. She can't keep it up forever. Any luck finding the kid who sent her the link?'

'No, the family has moved abroad. The school was very surprised – they said it wasn't a child they'd've expected such behaviour from.'

'I think Herran should trace the family, just to be safe. He will if we explain it's for Eve. I wanted to ask him yesterday, but he was really rattled by the police interview; it kind of made him shut down a bit.'

'He doesn't like it when people he knows behave in ways he's not used to. Let's give him a day or two to get his equilibrium back.'

They were walking arm in arm, and when she looked up at him it made him feel a little disoriented: it was preposterous that he could, in the last year, have grown so much taller than his mother. 'Is there news?' she asked.

'Yes – "Top Secret", as Herran would say.' He told her about the conversation with Mikal. 'So the rest of today should be fairly quiet, but tomorrow will be manic. The police will try to keep the press from finding out that it was me who tipped them off,' he added quickly.

'You shouldn't be there at all. Leave it to Pilan to sort out.'

'Mama, I can't. It's my job and I'm good at it, and he'd be rubbish. Besides, if I suddenly disappeared, it'd be pretty easy to put two and two together, wouldn't it?'

'I don't like this, Gabe.'

'I don't like it either, but I'd like it even less if I couldn't do anything about it.' He looked askance at her. 'You and Papa aren't going to make me stay away, are you? Please don't.'

Gaela sighed deeply. 'We've talked about it,' she said candidly, 'and so far we've decided that as long as you personally are not in danger and you want to keep going, we don't want to stop you. But we're going to have to talk about it some more now, I think.'

'Mama—'

'No, listen to me, Gabriel. Your father and I admire your commitment, we really do. You know how proud of you we are. But we have a job to do too, and if we decide you're not safe or it's getting too much for you to handle, you're out. Not least,' she said with a catch in her voice, 'because it would kill me if anything happened to you. Got it?'

He had to blink hard and clear his own throat before he could answer her. 'Got it.'

She patted his arm. 'Good. Now, those three delinquents are about to charge into the grocery, climb all over the tables in the café and attempt to breach the kitchen. Your father will pretend to be amused, but it drives him crazy, so if you can help me corral them in less time than it usually takes we'll both earn major points.'

'It's a deal.'

In the end all it took was a promise to play mind-reading games to entice the giggling boys and a grumbling Eve out of the café and into the garden, where Gabriel put them to work gathering up the overnight windfall of leaves and small branches. 'So, Mish is thinking he doesn't know why we're bothering to do this,' Gabriel announced, holding to his end of the bargain. 'He thinks it would be better to use the sticks to play swords or horses or throwing games.'

Misha, examining a boomerang-shaped specimen as he trudged over to dump it on the growing pile, stopped and stared with his mouth open. Gabriel grinned at him.

Then he looked at Misha's brother. 'Suri thinks we're doing it just to tidy up for Aunty Gaela, and he likes things tidy so he doesn't mind. Right, Suri?' The little boy nodded gravely over a tiny armful of lichen-covered twigs collected from beneath the apple tree. 'Whereas Eve knows *exactly* why, don't you, Eve? *She* thinks we're building special houses, and she's imagining all the creatures that might come and live in them this winter.'

Misha rounded on her. 'What creatures?'

Eve, caught between her determination not to accept any over-tures from her brother and her love of showing off, wavered and broke. 'Hedgehogs,' she said hopefully. 'An' worms and bugs and spiders and maybe even *snakes*—'

'Snakes?' squeaked Suri, dropping his twigs in alarm.

'They're not *dangerous* or anything.' And she was off, spinning stories about all the creeping, crawling things she claimed to remember from back when they lived in the mountains near Grandpa Reginald, illustrating her tall tales by poking at rotting logs to disturb centipedes and woodlice, turning damp leaves over for earthworms, rediscovering the hole at the base of the old brick wall from which a toad had emerged in the spring.

Gaela shook with silent laughter, and Gabriel felt waves of approval rolling his way. 'Very good,' she murmured to him as she headed inside. 'We might have a visitor, by the way. It appears you're not the only one taking the afternoon off.'

Don't say anything, she continued inside his head. *That way it can be a surprise if she comes, and no disappointment if she doesn't.*

But she did come, of course. He had just about managed to get the drifts of fallen leaves raked up against the back wall despite the scattering charges of the children, when a shadow flashed across the sunlit garden: sharp-edged, bird-shaped and banking, far larger than any bird.

'Aunt Aryel!' Eve shrieked in delight as she curved round the treetops at the back of the garden.

'Aunty Aryel!' echoed Misha, hopping from one long leg to the other with excitement. Sural shaded his eyes with his odd little hands, lost his balance as he spun with face upturned to follow Aryel's movement and tumbled onto the damp grass, still looking up, barely noticing that he had fallen.

It was funny, Gabriel thought, that no matter how many times they had seen her in the air it was never any less of a thrill. The children scattered to give her room, though the idea that she needed much was an illusion born of the massive span of her wings; she swept them up to spill the air and dropped feet-first onto a small patch of lawn between a rose bush and Bal's herb beds. She carried a large, lumpy bag in her arms, and was immediately mobbed.

'What did you bring us?' Eve demanded as Aryel crouched to greet them.

'What makes you think I brought you anything?' Aryel returned, trying to hang on to the bag and hug three squirming children at the same time. 'Maybe it's for— Oh well.' Their enthusiastic hugs had knocked it loose and several small golden apples tumbled out.

As the boys scrambled after them Aryel scooped one up and tossed it to Eve. 'There you go. A present from Maryam House, since your old tree doesn't fruit any more.'

'Shonk'ou,' Eve said, around a massive mouthful of apple. Misha held his firmly clamped in his jaws as he returned two more to the bag, nodding solemnly in agreement. Sural considered the samples he held in either hand, made his selection and dropped the other back as Gabriel gathered the bag up.

'Aunty A, why are you flying with these?' he scolded. 'They're heavy. I could have come over.'

'They weigh slightly less than a small boy,' she said, smiling. 'And then I wouldn't have had the pleasure of a visit.'

'Are they for us or the café?'

'You,' she replied, and followed him inside as he took them upstairs to the flat. He glanced back over his shoulder at her.

'Your band is off. You want to talk to me about Kaboom? Who told you? Papa . . . and *Herran*?' He looked back again, this time in surprise.

'I'm having a break from the band,' she said guiltily. 'I dropped by to see Herran yesterday. He was a bit distressed, but I couldn't get him to explain why. He told me about the meeting, but not what it was actually *about* – just who was there. So I got hold of your father and he explained very briefly. I haven't said anything to anyone except Eli. But I wanted to ask you, because it— Hi, Gaela.'

'Hi – Wow, that's more than I expected—'

'Three less than there were.' She looked at the tray of sandwiches and drinks in Gaela's hands. 'They might not have any room left.'

'Are you joking? They're like locusts. If we're lucky, maybe they'll leave a couple for the rest of us. Make yourselves some tea.' And she was gone down the stairs.

Gabriel unloaded the bag thoughtfully.

'Because it reminded you and Papa of something,' he murmured, finishing Aryel's thought. 'Mama too.' He pointed at his own band. 'Sorry. I turned mine off to play games with the kids.'

'Gabriel, you've been poking around in my head since you were Suri's age. I don't mind. Tell me about Kaboom: how does it work?'

'How *did* it work – they've been arrested and the story's going to break tomorrow.' He explained how the streamers had operated, reading her thoughts as she processed the information. 'Blimey, are you serious? *Zavcka Klist* did the same thing?'

'Something very like it. She was lobbying for limits to be placed on the rights that were being extended to gems, and it was part of trying to stoke the kind of fear and distrust that politicians would have to respond to. And that led to the godgang attacks, the assault on Maryam House—'

'—when Mama and I were kidnapped and you rescued us,' he said matter-of-factly. 'They call it the "Maryam House Massacre" in college.'

Aryel's expression was bleak. 'It might have gone beyond what Zavcka intended, but she helped create the conditions that made it possible. That was several years before the crimes that sent her to prison, though – the theft of the Phoenix genestock, and Ellyn and . . .' She nodded at the window, which was open a crack, letting in the cool autumn air and the sound of Eve's laughter from the garden below. 'Her part in those earlier events was entered into evidence, but since it wasn't what she was actually charged with, it ended up being kind of a footnote.'

'And now you think – what? I can't tell.'

'That's because I don't know what to think. The similar methodology could be a coincidence, or it could be someone who knew about what she did then is part of this conspiracy now.'

'Maybe the someone is *her*?'

'I can certainly believe it of her, Gabriel, but I haven't been able to work out *how*. Kaboom's been active for weeks, and the toxin operation for months, but she's only been out of prison a few days. She was allowed very few visitors, all of whom were thoroughly vetted, and she had virtually no private communication. And apart from all of that, it's not obvious what she'd stand to gain from damaging Thames Tidal.'

'I don't want to sound like I think I'm important,' Gabriel said, 'but I work there. And Eve is my sister.'

'I don't think she knows anything about Eve, but she might know about you, and you *are* important.'

'This is what you were thinking last night: that the thing that connects everything might be Zavcka Klist.'

'It was.' Aryel sighed and rubbed a hand across her face. For a moment she looked tired, and older than he was used to. 'I've known for some time that there's a deep strategy against Thames Tidal, but not who's behind it – and I still don't, Gabe. Zavcka does have the kind of mind for this, but that doesn't prove it's her. It might just be sheer coincidence that she was released right into the middle of things.' She picked up the cup of tea Gabriel had placed in front of her. 'She's been our bogeyman for so long, and with good reason, but there's a huge risk that if we decide this is her work we might miss what's really going on.'

'What's really going on is that she might have found a way to do it even from inside prison – she's smart enough. She might be doing it because of you, because of me, because it's gems. This might be her revenge.'

Aryel blew on her tea. He felt the thought take form a moment before she spoke, in the moment that she gave up fighting it.

'I can't be sure it isn't,' she said. 'And it would explain a lot.'

22

For the third time that afternoon, Patrick Crawford apologised profusely and excused himself to take an incoming call, and for the third time, Zavcka Klist smiled graciously as he departed, although by now she was seething with anger. Had it not been for his other roles – sycophant, acolyte and potential threat – she would have been on the line to Dhahab Investments herself, insisting that he be replaced immediately. He was useful in the prosecution of her own business, but by no means irreplaceable; anyone from the premier-client division would be able to provide what she needed. It was only her knowledge of his other alliances that could compel her to put up with this behaviour, and he knew it: she could hear it in his tone when he begged to be excused; she could see in his eyes that he knew the answer could only be yes. His mask of respect hadn't slipped but he had become presumptuous with her time and her space. There was no need for him to have been there for so many hours but he was confident now that come what may, she wouldn't throw him out. He was taking advantage. Her blood boiled at the gall of the man.

She walked over to the window, idly noticing that the books she'd handed to Eli Walker were still resting on the table where he had left them. She found it ludicrous that their conversation was by far the best she'd had since she'd been released.

I'd rather spend another hour talking to Eli Walker than ten minutes more with this prat – even Aryel would be preferable.

Dear god, what is wrong with me?

Outside, evening was closing in, and she realised that she was doing exactly as she had on countless other evenings, staring out through the bars of the grimy little window of her cell: watching another day die. At least the view was better here, but the study was no larger than the cell had been, and she had spent the entire day in it.

Well, there was no need for that any more. Perhaps if she went to the living room and powered up the wall screen Crawford would get the message that it was time for him to take his leave. But that hope was dashed as she approached, and heard his voice issuing from within. So that was where he had gone, the bumptious bastard: not out to the hall, as he should have done, but into yet another of her precious – *personal* – spaces. Glancing in, she saw that his back was turned and he was pacing across the room. *Pacing.* What did he have to pace about?

'No, of course I haven't heard from Fischer,' she heard him say angrily.

He sounded as thoroughly irritated with whoever he was speaking to as she was with him, which was some comfort, although his next words put the lie to his obsequiousness of the past few days.

'Look, I'm having trouble on this end too. She wants me to— No, I *know* you think I should just do as I'm told . . .'

Damn right. She stepped silently back out of sight and headed for her bedroom, considering her options as she swallowed a dose of her meds. He could hardly follow her if she stayed there, but that would leave him free to roam the rest of the place until she emerged. And if she went to find Marcus in the kitchen the weasel

259

might take it as an invitation to stay for dinner. She grudgingly returned to the study, wondering whether he was speaking to his boss at Dhahab or his associates in the K Club. She was not impressed with his tone of voice either way.

Back in her chair, she angrily swiped away the price curves and market positions from her tablet screen and called up a newstream feed; she might as well see if there had been any new developments in the Thames Tidal business, and whether those idiots at Bankside had got any better at damage control since the morning. She would soon need to decide which of her holdings to liquidate, in order to scoop up more Bel'Natur shares at the new, lower price she had spent the last few days engineering. If the energy giant persisted in mismanaging this affair they would be prime candidates for a dumping.

She found little to distract her. The police investigation appeared not to have advanced much; the names and faces of the two fugitives were still being flashed as *WANTED* and their former employers had progressed from incoherent to indignant, but their response was still a long way from commanding. One reporter snidely observed that even Standard BioSolutions' attempt to get on the right side of the story had ended up looking po-faced next to the swift and unconditional intervention of Bel'Natur.

Zavcka followed that link with interest and learned that Bel'Natur had worked round the clock to develop an organic inhibitor that could be deployed against the algae. Test data indicated that the product was close to a hundred per cent effective and the company would make it available to endangered communities free of charge.

That's your work, isn't it, Aryel? So clever! A safeguard against future attack for your own people, at the cost of a few tens of thousands of credits in research time and materials. The company will gain millions in

public-relations value, possibly billions in future contracts. I wonder when
the current management realised how much of an asset you are.

She knew the answer to that one, of course: they would have
realised it when Zavcka Klist, major shareholder and Chief Executive *par excellence*, was hauled off to gaol, the reputation of the
company she had led once more in tatters, its only hope of salva-
tion to make good on her false promise of reform and throw itself
on the mercy of the Morningstar.

Zavcka mused on how well that strategy had worked, and considered how she might turn it to her advantage, barely seeing
the Thames Tidal streamfeed scroll by until a thumbnail of Aryel
fluttering down into a crowd on a quayside caught her attention.

You, again? She tapped it up, and watched clips of a bullish gillung man and a slender, pregnant woman looking self-consciously
pleased as they were complimented by some politician or other;
Mikal Varsi propping himself amusingly against a much-too-short
lectern while he said something funny and true about the Thames
always having been the source of the city's power; Sharon Varsi –
with superintendent's bars on her shoulder – chuckling along
with the rest and holding firmly onto the hands of two small,
bored-looking boys; Aryel sweeping low over the water and into
a graceful landing, close-up on the blue eyes and the smile and
the crush of the press around her; here was a norm man with a
delighted expression being helped out of a divesuit, and there two
young women strolling through the crowd with their arms round
each other; now a crowd of raucous children pelting back and
forth between a large, low pool of water and a table full of whiz-
zing, fizzing toys; everywhere were laughing faces and sunshine
on water, a carnival atmosphere, a sense of—

Zavcka's heart caught in her chest. She felt it spasm, like a
missed beat or a last chance . . . or a lost life.

She stabbed at the screen so hard that she would not have been surprised if it, or her hand, had shivered into a thousand pieces. She would hardly have cared. The vid rolled back under her scrabbling fingers: and there on the screen, a child with tangled blonde curls, dark, clever eyes and a lively, laughing face spun away from the pool, shouting gleefully at two other children, some pale-blue jelly-like thing clutched in her fist. She ran across to the table and shoved the jelly-thing into the base of a dormant toy. It fizzed and whizzed and threw purple sparks in the air. The little girl was jumping up and down in her excitement.

Zavcka froze the picture, froze the moment; was herself frozen in the moment as she stared at the leaping child. The child who was her. Herself at eight. In a place she had never been, with friends she had never had, in a time when she had never been a child.

She was never sure afterwards how long she'd sat and stared, a stone woman and a graven image. The tablet's timer suggested no more than a few seconds. But she had spent them elsewhere, in the universe between heartbeats, a silent, stretched-out place where aeons are reckoned differently. All of the years of her long, long life slipped by her in that space, and more of them, and more.

Then she moved, and when she moved she felt a rushing like a great wave, like a river roaring down, like the tide coming in, filling her with the speed and decision and power of the old self she remembered. She felt the heat and the cold and the fear and the joy of it, like worlds ending and beginning, and she moved like a new self she had never known.

When Crawford returned a few minutes later, as time is reckoned in this place, he found her standing at the window, hands clasped behind her back, gazing sorrowfully into the evening as it rapidly drew in. The tablet screen on her console was blank; it might not have been touched since he'd left the room. She knew that she looked lonely, and a little sad; needy, and vulnerable. Inside she felt light, as though some nameless thing that had filled her up and weighed her down had been jettisoned in that other place. In its absence there was a clarity that sought out and filled up every gap and crack and hollow. She stared into it, unflinching, and gathered the shadows around her on the outside.

Crawford launched into another round of apologies for how long his call had taken, spiced with the innuendo of one who knows better than to blame others directly, but is well-practised in the art of deflection. Zavcka, listening with the acuity that had replaced her annoyance, detected a note of genuine unease: things elsewhere were not as they should be, and he was distracted and resentful. Good. It would make him that much more malleable. They were playing charades for real now, though he did not know it. She readied herself for confirmation, and the forging of new tools.

'You must find it very difficult,' she interjected when he paused to draw breath, 'to focus on other matters instead of the thing that concerns you most. I know I do.' She gestured a weary dismissal: of the work they had been doing, the conversations that had called him away, the world itself perhaps. The gesture said, *We both know this is trivial and that we are merely passing time.*

'Madam?'

But she had turned away and was looking out the window again. A gust of wind blew another thousand leaves from the trees and she shivered as though the chill of it had rippled through her too.

'I beg your pardon, madam,' Crawford said hesitantly, 'but are you all right?'

She let a few seconds drip down before she answered, sadly,

'I'm thinking of my little girl, out there somewhere. It's cold this evening. I hope she's warm enough. I worry about her so much. Do you have children, Mr Crawford?'

'I . . . ah . . . No, madam, I don't.'

'That's a pity. I left it so late.' Zavcka shook her head, staring at the window as if into the darkness falling outside, watching his reflection keenly in the glass. 'I know you can't tell me very much, but— Do you think she's warm enough?' She injected a catch in her voice.

'I'm certain she is, madam. We believe she's well cared for.'

Almost exactly the words Aryel had used. *I need more, Crawford. I need to be sure the child I saw is the one you've identified. I'm almost certain, but almost isn't enough.*

'I envy you, knowing that. What I wouldn't give for just a glimpse of her. It's so difficult to believe in anything when you can't see it for yourself.' She bowed her head, tightening her jaw as though fighting back a greater emotion. 'I'm not blaming you, Mr Crawford. I know that you are . . . constrained. I'd never wish to get you in trouble.'

'I . . . um . . . Thank you, madam. I wish I could help—'

'I'm just finding it difficult to . . . *focus* at the moment.'

She heard him reaching into his slide-pocket, and in the shifting, fracturing window-image she could see him take hold of his tablet. As he hesitated she said softly, 'If there is anything that you could share . . . anything at all . . . I would be so very grateful.'

The sound of the tablet sliding free. In the glass he swiped and tapped and then scribbled a pattern password. *Encrypted file.* She did not react to the reflected tablet, looming larger as he held it out; only when it appeared beside her did she look round.

The face filled the screen, glancing up and to the side, mouth opening as if about to speak. The child's expression was quizzical, and a bit mischievous, as though she was asking a question to which she knew the answer would be difficult. The hair and clothes were tidier than they had been in the TideFair clip; Zavcka had a sudden memory of sliding in her chauffeured car past children on their way to school, and thinking how much more presentable they were than the noisy brats who filled the streets in the afternoon. There was an early-morning light to the image that convinced her this was that exact scenario: a child on her way to school. In a few hours' time this pretty imp would become the joyous harpy from the Child's Play exhibit. The eyes were the same, clever as sin and dark as smoke. Nothing of her surroundings or companions could be made out.

Zavcka put a hand to her mouth and gasped, bending towards the tablet, her other hand outstretched for it as though in the shock of the moment she had forgotten herself. She pulled back with visible effort, let her breath sob, once, twice, then dropped the hand from her mouth to her throat. She felt the tracker necklace under her fingers and kept them pressed against it. That was a problem that would have to be solved very soon. Her face worked as she visibly struggled to control herself.

'We believe this is your daughter,' said Crawford. There was a note of surprise in his voice, a hint of almost vindictive pleasure at his awareness of the power he believed he now held. As he began to withdraw the tablet, Zavcka grabbed not it but his wrist, holding it still for another moment, letting her fingers grind into him through the layers of clothing.

'My daughter,' she said with trembling breath, her head tilted as though to examine the image more closely. 'Yes . . . I think . . .' Then, 'Are you certain she's old enough?'

'She's the exact age, madam. Her recorded birth date is within a couple of weeks of when your daughter was expected to be born.'

Zavcka nodded and let go, slowly.

He blanked the screen and tucked it away. 'I can't copy that over to you,' he said uneasily. 'I'm sorry, madam – it's for your own protection, you do understand?'

'Of . . . of course I do. Thank you, Mr Crawford. Thank you so much.' She heard the break in her own voice, and knew she had not manufactured it this time. Brushing at her eyes for further effect, she crossed swiftly from the window to her chair, as though embarrassed to be seen in such a state. 'You've already done more than I dared hope.'

Agwé was dawdling, wishing she could manage to look busier, aware of the silent, watchful presence of Qiyem across the project room. They were almost the only members of the day team left and he had finally shut down his workstation for the evening. He'd seen her about to do the same a few minutes earlier, and had come over to ask if she wanted to grab some refreshment on the way home: a drink, maybe a bite to eat. She had muttered something noncommittal about not being quite done yet and sensed that he had now delayed his own departure in response. Now she was both kicking herself for having left him an opening, and feeling guilty at her own reluctance. She knew it must be wrong to rebuff someone who was so solitary, whose reserve was most likely a cover for shyness and loneliness. It was clear that he liked her but he'd always been uneasy about showing it; he'd probably spent *ages* plucking up the courage for this latest attempt to become friends. She suspected that he actually hoped they could be something more, and even though she wasn't remotely interested, she thought she should at least be kinder to him, let him down gently.

But there was just something about him – maybe he was too

studied in the way he went about it, too contrived? His line about 'on the way home' had annoyed her. He lived downriver in Limedog, while her home was a subaquatic flat in this very building. Why pretend they were both leaving anyway, when he knew all she had to do to get to hers was turn left instead of right, traverse a few corridors and a flight of stairs? It would be easier to take him seriously, she thought, if he didn't always try so hard. There was an undercurrent of manipulation in his advances that she disliked – but maybe that was the only way shy, awkward people knew to go about things. *I should be nicer,* she thought again.

He'd tucked his tablet away and had put on his coat: dutiful Qiyem, diligently following the official advice to stay out of the river until the authorities issued the all-clear, would be walking home instead of swimming. She sighed inwardly as she watched him crossing the room towards her again, and undocked her own tablet. There was no way to back out, not without looking like a complete hypocrite. Might as well go and have a cup of tea with him; she could try cracking a few jokes, see if he could be unwound sufficiently to laugh at them. Maybe it wouldn't be too bad. He stopped beside her workstation and looked at her with an expression that she thought was meant to be enquiring but instead just seemed uncertain. Her heart sank.

'Are you—?'

'Yep.' She made it sound as sunny as she could manage, shoved back her chair and powered down the main screen. 'Almost there . . .'

The tablet vibrated in her hand and she felt the buzz of her earset. She glanced down at the screen to see Gabriel's comcode flashing on it – flashing red, which meant *urgent.* Her surprise was tinged with a faint relief; maybe something really had come up that would save her from a difficult evening.

'Hang on, Qiyem, just let me see what this is.' She flicked to receive. 'Hey. What's urgent?'

'Agwé, what have you done?'

'Sorry?' He sounded frantic and angry and – was he *frightened*? She sank back into her chair, feeling alarmed. 'What have I done about what?'

'This— You— This vid that's gone up on the TTP stream, you did it, right? You must have, it's from when—'

'The TideFair? Yes, of course I did it. What's the matter?'

'You need to pull it, or change it or . . . or something. Ag, you need to fix it, *now*.'

'Fix what? Don't you like it? I thought you'd be pleased.' She ran through the clips in her head, trying to work out what could possibly need fixing, growing more puzzled by the second. 'There's a great shot of Eve in there.'

'Ag, how could you *do* that?' He was almost shouting at her. She had never heard him sound so upset. 'You need *permission*, you can't just—'

'I *what*? Hang on – hang *on*, Gabriel.' She looked up at Qiyem. 'I'm sorry, something's happened.' She could hear her own voice shaking; the shock of Gabriel's anger had brought her close to tears.

'What's wrong?' His uncertainty was genuine now, and mirrored her own.

'I don't know . . . There's a problem with a vid I made . . .' Gabriel was ranting in her ear, something about Eve. 'I . . . I think I've screwed something up. I need to work out what it is. I'm sorry.' She was already sliding her tablet back into the dock, fumbling in her haste. When she glanced up again, Qiyem was still standing there, looking worried now, and a bit lost.

'Should I stay?' he asked.

She shook her head, feeling her lips tremble, not trusting herself to speak. He watched her for another moment, then turned on his heel.

In her earset Gabriel was still going on about his sister, how his sister could not *be* on a public stream, how she had to take the vid down, take it down, *take it down now*! Bewilderment wrapped round her like an old fishing net, and the sound of Qiyem's footsteps walking away no longer felt like an ordeal she had dodged but a refuge she would gladly, *gladly* have escaped to.

23

The morning came up choking, drenched in a fog so thick it was as though the sun itself were drowning. Gabriel, watching through the windows overlooking the back garden, saw the weak silver-gold radiance of dawn on the horizon fade into a pale grey glimmer that settled on things without illuminating them. It seemed to him that as the minutes went by it grew darker outside instead of lighter – or maybe that was just his mood. He hadn't slept, and he felt cold and tired and upset with himself. His head was as thick and muddled as the air outside. The cranial band was already in place and on standby; he didn't think he could deal with any thoughts but his own at the moment.

'It's fine,' his father said as he came up beside him, one big hand heavy on his shoulder, a mug of coffee in the other, still gruff with sleep. He yawned. 'Don't be so hard on yourself. It was only onstream for – what? A couple of hours? It's unlikely any harm's been done. Just be glad' – with a glance over his shoulder to make sure Eve was still safely upstairs with Gaela, getting ready for school – '*she* didn't see it. Then there'd be hell to pay.'

'There will anyway. Her friends or teachers might have seen it, it'll come up . . .'

He stared into his empty mug, unseeing. 'It's not just that – I messed up, Papa. I really . . . I went overboard with Agwé. I flipped out, I was shouting at her . . . and it's not her fault. She couldn't have known. She must think I'm a complete lunatic.'

'Ah.' Bal nodded his understanding, and sipped. 'So that's what's grinding at you. I thought there was something else.' He grimaced at the first bitter hit of coffee. 'Listen, I like Agwé. She's sharp. She did a good job on the edit too – most people probably won't even notice the change.'

'She did a great job, especially considering how upset she was. She's my best . . . We're really close, but of course she doesn't know about Eve so she thought it would be fun, something we'd all like. She did it to be *nice*, and I went nuclear on her.' He drew a deep breath. 'I need to apologise today, try to explain, but I don't know what to say.'

Bal was gazing thoughtfully out the window himself now, the steam from his mug rising into the air as though the mist from the garden had snuck inside to warm itself up.

'You want to tell her.'

'Yes . . . well, I mean, I wish I could. But I don't want to make things worse – I don't ever want to do anything that . . . that compromises Eve. I know we have good reasons for not telling anyone other than those who've known from the beginning. I just – I wish I didn't have to go in there now and lie to Agwé, not on top of being so horrible to her yesterday.'

'I wish you didn't either, Gabe, but that doesn't mean we can make an exception.' His father's face was impassive, but there was speculation in his tone and Gabriel realised that he was considering doing exactly that. 'Do you trust her?'

'Yes.' He did, absolutely, but that conviction just made him feel worse. 'I don't know whether she trusts me any more, though.'

'Let me have a word with your mother when you and Eve are both gone, okay? We'll message you.' An affectionate touch on

his cheek, an amused, understanding glint in his father's eyes.
'No promises.'

It was shockingly cold, as though autumn had decided to skip
ahead a few months and sample the full, stinging bitterness of mid-
winter. The temperature and the clinging, cough-inducing murk
subdued even Eve, although by the time they met up with Uncle
Mik and his boys at the school gate she was back in full chattering
flow. Apparently it had needed no more than an afternoon's play
and pandering to return him to her good graces, but Gabriel was
weighed down by the irony that while he was being a good brother
and mending fences with her at home, he had failed in his greater
duty to protect her from the world.

But he didn't have time to dwell on it much, for they had to hand
the children over to Terissa and make haste to Sinkat; as predicted,
Sharon had scheduled a conference for first thing.

'We think the best chance of keeping you out of it in public is
to make sure Pilan and the rest of the senior team are told about
your role in private,' Mikal told Gabriel as they walked. 'Otherwise
I suspect they'll start poking around and asking lots of questions –
asking *you* lots of questions, about what you did or didn't notice.'

Gabriel winced. 'They'll do that anyway.'

'Maybe, but this way it won't be in front of others, which is what'll
probably happen if they aren't told. If I'm there in the room while
Sharon's onscreen, and we're both saying that we think you handled
your discovery in an appropriate manner – which you did – and we
ask them to cooperate in keeping Herran's and your involvement
quiet, it makes it a lot harder for anyone either to give you a hard
time or to go gossiping indiscriminately.' Mikal grinned. 'Besides,
Pilan already owes you, doesn't he? Here's where you get to collect.'

*

Pilan, Lapsa and the rest of the executive team were suitably stunned to learn that they had been the target not only of a biological attack but of a coordinated propaganda assault as well. They were even more shocked to discover that they were only now finding out about it.

'I don't understand,' Lapsa said, perplexed. 'How could we not have known this was happening?'

'We did,' Gabriel told her. 'We've all known how much negative commentary and innuendo and scaremongering there's been on the streams. People have been talking about it and messaging me and coming over to my workstation to complain for *weeks*, it's just that we all thought the chatter was being generated by lots of random streamers. Now we know that was part of their plan. I think,' he amended hastily, catching sight of Sharon's face on the screen and realising that this would probably count as *amateur sleuthing* in her book, 'it was organised to look *dis*organised.'

'That does appear to have been the case,' she confirmed, deadpan.

'And when did *you* realise it wasn't random?' Pilan growled.

'While you were in hospital,' Gabriel replied promptly. He had been rehearsing this one. 'You and almost everyone else here. Before that, I'd assumed it was just what it looked like: a bunch of unconnected bigots saying nasty things about gems – you know, the usual. Then, when I noticed how many avatars were being used, I thought maybe a few trolls had got together, or maybe they'd been put up to it by one of the pressure groups. I had no idea it was going to turn out to be this big.'

'When Gabriel shared his concerns with me, neither of us had any way of knowing these activities were connected with the toxin, or the earlier sabotage attempt,' Mikal interjected smoothly. 'If we had, it would clearly have been an urgent matter for the police. I found it very disturbing, but on its own it didn't sound like it'd be something for which you'd divert resources away from hunting down terrorists. I discussed it privately with Sharon to get her advice, and you initially felt the same too, didn't you, dear?' Sharon raised her eyebrows at him. 'It was only as the police investigation progressed that she realised there might be a connection between the terrorists and the situation Gabriel was dealing with.'

'That's correct,' said Sharon briskly. 'And I must stress that it was still just a suspicion at that point; it's what we've learned over the last twenty-four hours that makes us certain the smear campaign and the terrorist activities are linked. It also indicates an even more sophisticated conspiracy than we'd expected – a fact the press will no doubt jump on immediately.'

She leaned forward and stared directly out of the screen at them, mouth set in a firm line, her manner grimly serious. 'It also raises concerns for Gabriel and Herran, if they become associated with the discovery. I don't know how these people – or their supporters, if they have any – would react if they knew who was responsible for the police closing down this side of the operation. I'd like to think they've got bigger problems at the moment, but we can't be certain, and so I must ask you *all* to help us maintain confidentiality. For Gabriel and Herran's safety.'

Murmurs ran around the table as the significance of Sharon's words sank in. The half-dozen pairs of eyes focused on Gabriel went from some combination of surprised, impressed and mildly reproachful to overwhelmingly protective, and he squirmed in his chair, embarrassed.

'Surely you shouldn't be here at all?' said Lapsa anxiously. 'You should take some time off – come back when it's all over.'

You are going to be such a good mother, Gabriel thought. *You sound just like mine.* Aloud he said, 'Thanks, but we think that would probably just attract attention.'

'Gabriel is right,' said Sharon. 'It's been almost a full day since the arrests, I'm required to make an announcement. Plus, the news that we've got more people in custody is already leaking and I don't want anyone thinking the primary targets have been apprehended. We still need the public to remain on the lookout. So the attention of every news and socialstream is about to focus on this story and they'll be jumping at anything that strikes them as unusual. Believe me, I don't like to leave civilians – let alone minors – potentially in harm's way, but pulling Gabriel out might make him *less* safe, not more.'

And that was all it took to deputise the entire executive committee of Thames Tidal Power into feeling responsible for him.

Mikal laughed softly at the look on his face as the others came up afterwards to offer praise and reassurance and advice. Gabriel felt less like the efficient, talented and valuable press officer he knew himself to be and more like everybody's slightly delicate and overly doted-upon young nephew.

'You two *planned* this,' he managed to whisper accusingly in a momentary interlude.

'After a word with your parents,' Mikal whispered back sagely. 'Detective Superintendent Varsi is also your Aunt Sharon, and if she can't keep you where she or they can guard you personally, she's going to make damn sure everybody else is on point.'

So that was why they had decided to let him come in today. He supposed he should be grateful.

'If anything happens and you feel like you need to get out of the office,' said Pilan, his attention back with them as others departed, 'head for our flat. It's air-full, and I'll add your finger ident to the entry panel. Doesn't matter whether we or Agwé are there or not; if you need to go just go. Okay?'

'Okay,' he said, feeling wretched but determined not to show it. 'Umm . . . Is she around?' Under normal circumstances there would be a slew of messages demanding to know what was going on, but he'd heard nothing from her, nor yet from his parents; he still had no idea what he would, or could, say to her. His own abject apologies had been going out since the middle of the night.

'She went up to college early,' Lapsa told him. 'She left just before you arrived. She said there were some assignments she needed to discuss, some professor she had to see. She'll be back by afternoon, I suppose.'

Mikal stayed until after the news broke, more concerned about the fallout than he was willing to admit, and he took the time to catch Pilan up on political developments.

'Sharon couldn't be here in person because she also has to brief the government so they can be ready to respond,' he explained. 'Normally it would be the ministers for internal security and communications and their staff, but Jack Radbo's asked to be included. My guess is that this latest turn of events, on top of my backing yesterday and your statement the day before, will have given them all the political cover they need: as long as energy capture in the estuary stays on track, and barring any major incident, Thames Tidal shouldn't have to worry about outside interference.' Mikal chuckled softly. 'Jack liked your piece, by the way. I mean, he *really* liked it.'

'Gabriel helped write it,' said Pilan meditatively, then laughed. 'No, scratch that; he didn't just *help*, he worked out *exactly* what I needed, and that's what he produced. When he gave it back to me, it was precisely what I'd've said if I was a hell of a lot better at saying things than I am. And all the time he was doing his regular job and dealing with this too and never letting on.'

'By that point, Sharon had told him he couldn't discuss it.'

'I get that; I'm just blown away by how bloody competent the boy is. Were we that sorted out when we were his age, Mikal? I don't think *I* was.'

'We knew different things,' Mikal told him. 'Gabriel has been trawling through adult minds almost since he could speak. I'm glad my children aren't getting the education he did, but he's certainly learned from it – he's had to. We're just lucky he's so steady and decent.'

But Mikal was conscious that for all Gabriel's calm demeanour and whip-smart handling of the Kaboom situation, the boy was being stretched to the limit. He sounded strained and he looked exhausted. Part of that was doubtless down to the unfortunate business of the TideFair vid; Gaela had called them about that last night, but by the time Misha and Sural saw it, it showed only an abbreviated glimpse of them laughing with an unseen friend. Eve had been swiftly and neatly excised, and the chance that harm would come from her brief, anonymous exposure was vanishingly small. It was the kind of risk that Bal and Gaela always knew they were running; it was that, or hide themselves and their children away from the world. They were sanguine about it, but they said Gabriel was being very hard on himself.

Mikal was not at all surprised; he remembered the promise the solemn-faced little boy had made, to protect the newborn infant cradled in his mother's arms. Gabriel had looked around at them all – Bal and Gaela, Aryel and Eli, him and Sharon – and known the fear in their minds: of what that baby might become, what others would make of her if they could. He was just eight years old himself then, but he'd have felt the full weight of adult responsibility, and he would not have forgotten.

He looked just as solemn now, sitting silent and focused at his workstation, stream-feeds scrolling, cranial band pulsing, fingers flying. Mikal commandeered an empty chair and waited until Gabriel finished pushing out whatever it was and turned towards him.

'So what's the reaction?'

'*Gobsmacked* would be a good word,' Gabriel said. 'It doesn't look like any of the streams saw this one coming. The reporters are scrambling to find a way to talk about it without the kind of speculation that could get them in trouble. The socialstreams don't care about that, of course; they're already buzzing.'

'And the buzz is?'

'*Of course* Bankside have the resources to pull something like this off, and *isn't it interesting* that this guy Fischer used to work for head office. Also *it makes you wonder* what else they might be up to.' Gabriel smiled without humour. 'I'm guessing Bankside didn't get the advance notice that we did, since they haven't responded yet.'

'I expect not,' said Mikal noncommittally. 'Are you engaging?'

'Not much. There are loads of requests for comment, and for interviews with Pilan, of course, but the publicity service can deal with those; they're to direct everyone to the statement we posted. I expect a few news crews will show up here at some point, but we'll deal with that when it happens.' He glanced at the screen, checked something and turned back to Mikal. 'The commentators who might generate the kinds of conversations we need to respond to haven't had time to push much out yet; so far it's just snarky one-liners to reassure their followers that they really are themselves.'

'Think it'll put the frighteners on the regular trolls?'

'I think it might.' He pulled a face at his uncle. 'We can but hope.'

Mikal laughed out loud; that was one of his standard lines. 'Well, that's me told. How are *you* doing?' He looked around meaningfully, and dropped his voice. 'Anyone I need to head off for you?'

'Nope.' It looked to Mikal like Gabriel's gaze lingered on an empty workstation nearby, but he shook his head firmly. 'Lapsa's got it covered. I don't think there'll be a problem – well, not unless you all keep fussing, in which case everybody *will* start to wonder what's going on.'

Mikal chuckled and shoved himself out of the chair. 'Since you put it like that, I shall take myself off and go and represent the public. Call me if you need me.' He peered around the big room. 'Where is Lapsa, anyway?'

'Outside, I think. Some people from Environmental Management showed up and she went to deal with them.'

Lapsa was on the quayside, hands on hips, talking to two dive-suited persons in a small launch standing off the quay. They wore EM logos on their shoulders, the full head-and-body kit that was standard for underwater work, and the attitude of people who are already hard-pressed and put-upon and would like very much to get on with their job if only the nice lady in the aubergine bodysuit would leave them alone.

'Please, ma'am, don't come in the water yet,' said one, peering through his mask, his voice distorted by the breathing apparatus. 'We don't need any help, and the safety warnings for you folks haven't been lifted yet. Once we get these units in place and they've synced with the rest of the system, you can start getting back to normal.'

'But why weren't we told you were coming today?'

The two men looked at each other and shrugged.

'Beats me,' said the one who had been talking.

'We don't work for the most efficient department in the city,' said the other. 'You might have noticed.'

'My guess is someone decided they needed to speed things up, only they didn't think to tell you.'

'Typical,' grunted the other.

'Oh, all right,' said Lapsa crossly. 'It isn't your fault, and we're desperate to be back in the water. It's just that I didn't know, and we've got a lot on at the moment.'

'We'll be no trouble at all. Should be done within an hour.'

'Right. Well, come inside and have a cup of tea when you are.'

She waved to them and turned to Mikal as the boat nosed along the quayside towards the far end of the Thames Tidal building. 'They go from one extreme to the other, these people.'

'Environmental Management?'

'Yes. They were supposed to install new monitors around the basin next week, only they've showed up today instead.' She made an exasperated gesture at the boat. 'I don't know why I'm complaining. We wanted it done sooner, but they said it was impossible.'

'They don't excel at communications,' Mikal observed. 'Sharon tells me the liaison they appointed is good, though.'

'Fayole? She's been great. That's why I'm so annoyed.'

'You'll probably find that she couldn't tell you because whoever is responsible didn't tell her. I might push for a review of their management procedures when this is over.'

'I'll sign that petition. Thank you for coming. Are you off?'

'I am. You'll keep an eye on Gabriel?'

'I'll keep an eye on Gabriel.'

24

When Mikal looked back from the far side of the basin, the EM launch was moored in a distant corner, and neither diver was on board. Environmental Management appeared for once to have taken the initiative on something, even if they were still failing the finer points of coordination. Aryel had told him that their work with Bel'Natur on the inhibitor had mostly amounted to them staying out of the way. Thinking about that as he headed along the riverwalk towards the piazza and the steps up the side of the great bridge, Mikal was grateful beyond expression that Bel'Natur had moved fast enough to render Standard BioSolutions' offer redundant. Given what he now knew, the prospect of Standard being involved on the recovery side of this mess made him feel queasy.

The evidence was, as Sharon kept reminding him, circumstantial – but how many coincidences could there possibly be before it was impossible for them to *really* be coincidental? She didn't yet know the latest snippet of connection, innocently vouchsafed to him by Gabriel just this morning during their cold walk to Sinkat: Aryel's observation of the similarity between Kaboom's methods and the strategy that Zavcka Klist had once pursued. It felt satisfyingly like another piece of the puzzle sliding into place, and with any luck it would leave Sharon just as stunned as her news had left him last night.

*

She'd waited until long after the kids were asleep and the grownups had found better things to do than talk; they were lying together in lazy bliss afterwards and he was just about ready to drift off himself when she nudged him and said, 'Guess what?'

She sat up in bed. 'It's time for tonight's round of Improperly Shared Information. I know something about your mate Moira Charles.'

'Not funny,' he yawned, 'unless you happen to know that she's involved in the Bankside business up to her eyeballs and you've got a nice cold cell waiting for her. That would be very funny indeed.'

'Not quite, though I do know that she knows our man Fischer from when he was at Standard and that she continues to share an extracurricular interest with him.'

Mikal made a comic-shocked face at her and she batted playfully at his blanketed body. 'No, not this one, silly. Less fun, but possibly significant. Achebe turned it up this evening when he was working through Mr Fischer's extensive – and I do mean *extensive* – list of contacts. So, it transpires that a lot of the people Fischer's worked for are also founding members of the exclusive Karma Club – where you were recently wined, dined and unsuccessfully bribed? Mitford isn't on the books, so it was probably Charles who arranged for him to meet you there: she *is* a member, along with Fischer. Achebe discovered that mostly by accident, while chasing down *another* exclusive network that Fischer is part of. Turns out Ms Charles is part of that one too. It turns out that a *lot* of the members are.' She explained.

'The Karma Club is the secret headquarters of the Klist Cult?' He stared at her in open-mouthed disbelief. 'You *cannot* be serious. This is turning into a really bad vid drama.' He pulled the sheet over his head.

'Don't blame me, I just work here.' Sharon pulled the sheet back down. '*Headquarters* is probably overstating it, but there's a lot of overlap between the people who pay their dues at the Karma Club and some of the more active members of the Klist movement.'

'But how – who – *why*?'

'How should I know? Maybe the kind of self-important snob who's inclined to hand over ridiculous membership fees for the privilege of drinking the same wine in more expensive glasses is also the type to buy into a secret society dedicated to pursuing the Zavcka Klist model of eternal life.'

'You don't have strong views about this at all, I can tell.'

'It's the *arrogance* of it that makes me crazy. They don't seem to realise that they've just *invented* a reason to feel important. You should have seen Fischer when we went back in and asked him about the Klist thing – it was the closest to a reaction we'd got all day, but it wasn't embarrassment or defensiveness, oh no. He just had this superior little smile on his face, as if he expected us to be impressed.'

'You should've told him it was you who arrested her. That might have knocked him back.'

She laughed and snuggled under the blankets beside him. 'I was tempted, believe me.'

'Could she be involved? Directing them, somehow?'

'That was my first thought, but there's no sign that she's ever had any communication with them, or even wanted to. The prison governor says she was disdainful whenever they were mentioned, and Offender Management is certain there's never been any contact. But it's significant in that it's another point of connection between Fischer and Charles: they used to work together, they're both members of the club, they're both members of the cult . . . and one of the things we always look for in cases like this is: how do the various players find each other? As a rule, new networks form from within existing ones; people already know who they can trust, and who has the resources they need.'

'The Karma Club membership would be a hell of a network—'

'Exactly. And the Klisters would be people with whom you'd already share a somewhat clandestine interest. You'd know who you could go to with something really dodgy.' Sharon was the one yawning hugely now. 'This is all speculation though, honey, so don't look for us to be arresting Moira Charles tomorrow. At this point it wouldn't surprise me if she were running black ops against Thames Tidal on behalf of Mitford, alongside the upfront corporate strategy and the politicking, but I've got no proof. So far these are all coincidences.'

Then she had fallen asleep, instantly in the way she did, leaving him to lie awake wondering how long it would take for someone to find something tangible enough to act on.

That night-time conversation had loomed large in Mikal's mind as he listened to Gabriel's account of his conversation with Aryel, although he had said little; he could tell the young man nothing about the Klist Cult affiliations that had already been uncovered. That line of enquiry was being kept quiet, the better to be pursued without hindrance and dropped without fanfare if it proved a dead end. *But it won't*, he thought. *It makes perfect sense.* The Klist Cult's precise objectives and degree of organisation varied depending on whom you talked to, which streams you followed; but a common thread was the obsession with unearthing the mechanism for Zavcka's preternaturally long life. He had heard it said that they wished not only to reproduce the phenomenon for themselves but to understand how she had used it to amass vast wealth and influence. Any devotee of her methods would know about the propaganda campaign she had masterminded twelve years ago, and wouldn't be averse to emulating it.

Mikal strode across the piazza to the foot of the steps, idly glancing beneath the bridge as usual – and stopped. The heavy fog of the morning had lifted, although it was still bitterly cold; but there under the bridge, along the piers and up against the arches, shreds of mist appeared to be lingering. When he peered closer he could see that it was not fog but wisps of a translucent *something*, pulling away from the stone and concrete, clouded with condensation. It made the lines of the structure look even fuzzier than usual. He leaned over and squinted, then reached his long arm out and just managed to touch it with his fingertips. His fingers came away not just damp but tacky, as though he had touched paint that was not quite dry.

He stared for a moment, puzzled, then took the steps two at a time, hands clenched in aggravation. Here was another, more mundane reason to be relieved that Standard had no role in protecting gillung communities from future attacks: only a few months since the bridge work had been completed and the sealant on the underside was already washing away in the river. It was an *appalling* failure. He would have to get on to the Council's contract managers, get them to—

He was halfway across the bridge when it hit him.

—*washing away in the river.*

He stopped as suddenly as if he had walked into a wall, or a revelation, then swung round to lean over the rail, peering down into the water far below. The barrier that was chest-high for everyone else reached only to his waist, prompting cries of alarm from passers-by. Mikal didn't hear, not until a man tugged at his coat, urging him back, and he saw anxious faces staring at him and heard their remonstrations.

'It's fine – sorry – I'm fine! Nothing to worry about, thank you,' he gabbled at them, and ran back the way he had come, his long legs eating up the ground at a tremendous rate, almost pitching headlong down the stairs as he scrambled back to the piazza below the bridge, back to the point where he could see and touch the dissolving sealant. He had stood almost exactly here, he remembered, on the day he had come to see Pilan, newly home from the hospital, the day Moira Charles had offered Standard's help against the mystery microflora as well as the meeting with Mitford; the day Sharon had declared the Thames toxin a terrorist attack. He had stood here that day and he had not noticed . . . But it had been sunny then, and far warmer than today.

He fumbled up Sharon's Met comcode, rejected the message option and was routed to Danladi; he ordered her to get Detective Superintendent Varsi out of whatever meeting, interrogation, press briefing or other important matter she might be attending to, *now*. He was breathing hard and sounding desperate, and Constable Danladi did not argue. By the time Sharon's voice came in over his earset half a minute later, he had more or less got his breath back, but he knew that his voice was cracking as he stared at the piers that supported the bridge, and their fading, fragmenting armour.

'Sharon—'

'What's—?'

'Secure this channel.'

Silence, then a soft tone as the encryption was activated.

'What's happened?' The tension in her voice had ratcheted up several notches, mirroring his own. He glanced round again to make sure that he was alone on the piazza, then once more leaned over the rail that kept him from falling into the Thames. This one was no higher than his hips and he held on with one hand to anchor himself as he peered beneath the bridge and told her where he was and what he was seeing.

'The paint is peeling?' she said, puzzled.

'The paint, the sealant, on the underside of the bridge. Where the river washes past it, where all of the water from upstream washes past. Standard underbid everyone to win the contract, and then rushed to get the work done before the end of the summer. And it's not peeling, it's kind of gone soft; you can see through it, it's almost disintegrating. Sharon, you and Rhys and Environmental Management, you never worked out what the catalyst was: the thing that activated the algae so it was at its deadliest just downstream from here, just as it hit Sinkat. You were looking for something released into the water on the day, or maybe placed there a few days before, maybe a week or two. That's why you couldn't find anything. It's been here for months, just waiting. Sharon, *they painted it onto the bridge.*'

In her warm, bright, book-lined study, with a steaming cup of coffee at her elbow and a sense of slowly building rage, Zavcka Klist pored over every detail of the newly disclosed Kaboom operation. She too recognised her own traces in the way the group had gone about their work; unlike Aryel, she was in no doubt about the connection.

Someone had called Patrick Crawford while he'd been at her house the previous day; called repeatedly, perhaps desperately. Someone who was trying to find a person named Fischer, and had an interest in her too. Well, here was *Fischer*, caught in an act she had once perfected. And here was she, the originator of his methods, playing host for hours every day to one of his associates, ideally positioned to be incriminated herself. The prospect outraged her. It was one thing to be sent down for something she had actually *done*, to be outflanked and outfought by Mikal and Sharon Varsi, Rhys Morgan and his sister Gwen, Herran and Callan, Eli Walker and, most of all, Aryel Morningstar: it had taken *all* of them to find her out, corner her, strip her of liberty and dignity and power. Though she might rage at the defeat, she knew their victory had been fairly won. But to be dragged into some Byzantine scheme that was not of her making, to have her own plans put at risk because of it – *that* was intolerable.

Presumably Fischer had not yet implicated Crawford and his associate – or associates – since they were still at large. Or were they? Had Crawford been picked up overnight? Was he free, but under surveillance? If the latter, she would already be in the frame. She glanced out of her window for the dozenth time that morning, scanning the elegant square with its trees and grand houses finally emerging from the morning fog, expecting at any moment to see a police transport cruise to a stop outside her front door. But no, all was quiet. Turning back to her tablet, she went through the announcement again.

The language of the bulletin was typically terse, but there were links to much of Kaboom's false-flag commentary. That would give the streams a great deal to chew on, and one of the journalists at the briefing had had enough presence of mind to ask why evidence in the case was being released.

'This evidence is already in the public domain,' Superintendent Varsi had replied crisply. 'In light of our investigation, we feel it is in the public interest to release these details.'

So: damage control. Someone was worried enough to insist on swiftly discrediting the message as well as rounding up the messengers. This strengthened her conviction that there was far more going on than was being revealed. There were subtler cues as well, and again she was not alone in spotting them. Someone else observed that the code name 'Kaboom' was an unusually evocative choice for the Met; Varsi's curt explanation, that it had been the use of a peculiarly threatening word in an apparently innocuous context that had first caught the attention of investigators, struck Zavcka as oddly specific.

There are depths to this affair that you're being careful not to reveal, Detective Superintendent. It'll end up being another coup for you, I imagine. Two promotions since last we met, along with two children! I suppose I should be impressed.

She had already learned as much as the streams could offer about the Varsis' children – their names, their ages, where they went to school – and in so doing, she had caught up on the parents as well, following every link she could find. Their career trajectories were easy to map, with achievements and controversies well covered, but no trail that she followed led to a small blonde girl who was friends with their boys. Not only that: the child had disappeared from the TideFair vid, as completely as if she had never even been there.

Are you surprised, Zavcka? You did the same thing once. Control information and you control perception. If anything slips out that shouldn't, fix it, quick.

But they didn't lock it down tightly enough. Someone in the K Club spotted her; someone realised the authorities hadn't sent her away, that they'd kept her close to the gems. I didn't guess that. I'd wager my fortune it wasn't Crawford who worked it out, but he knows more than he pretends. So who's her guardian? It isn't the Morningstar, or Walker, or the Varsis; they're all too public. They'd never be able to keep her offstream like this. But I know where to look now, and I will find out. And, once Crawford and his cult are out of the way, I won't have to worry about her safety, or my own.

As long as the fools don't drag me down with them.

*

The question of Crawford's whereabouts was soon answered, and not in the way that Zavcka had hoped. It was not the police who appeared at her door but the man himself, unannounced and visibly anxious, barely an hour after the Kaboom news had broken. Marcus showed him to the sitting room with an unmistakable air of disapproval. Zavcka was already there, sorting through the possible reasons for this visit in her head as she scrolled through streamfeeds on the wall screen.

'I wasn't looking for you at this hour, Mr Crawford.'

'I apologise, madam. It's become necessary for me to . . . ah . . . to go away for a while.'

That much I had assumed. You're going to try to run – but why have you come here first? 'That's most inconvenient.'

'I'm afraid it's unavoidable.'

'Where will you go?' she asked, thinking that if he was foolish enough to tell her it might be information she could bargain with later.

'South Africa.'

She stared at him in amazement, although part of her was already thinking, *Of course that's what they'd do. Silly of me not to have guessed.*

'South Africa?'

'Indeed, madam. An associate and I have been planning a journey there to pursue the – um – guidance you've so generously provided. Circumstances have arisen that require us to travel sooner than intended.'

'How much sooner?'

'Today. As soon as I leave you. There is something I must collect, and then—' He glanced at the clock on the wall screen, which appeared to spur him to swifter action. Once more he was bowing, and holding something out to her, but the deference with which he had presented his first gift was now tinged with desperation.

She took whatever it was without looking, and felt the hard curves of bioplastic and cold metal studs.

'And what do you hope to achieve, Mr Crawford, when you arrive in South Africa?'

'We . . . What we talked about, madam, the epigenetic manipulation, the gene surgery . . . I believe,' he said, drawing himself up, 'that my associates and I have done enough . . . more than enough . . . to have earned your indulgence in this matter. Time is pressing.' He enunciated the last words heavily, leaning on the symbolism, but beneath the portentousness she sensed real fear.

'For some of us, perhaps,' she replied brusquely, and held up the memtab. 'What is this?'

'A means for us to communicate. Attach it to your tablet. It'll bypass the restrictions on your contacts. No one will know that we've spoken.'

'But I am already quite legitimately allowed to communicate with you,' she pointed out. 'Are you saying that will no longer be the case?'

'I suspect it won't, madam.'

'Then why should I accept this? You're obviously in some sort of trouble, and I have no desire to be caught up in it. If you're being investigated, questions will be asked of me too. I'm not about to risk a return to prison over a piece of illicit tech.'

'I'm sure you can hide that where no one will ever find it. Until it's attached, it's inactive. There's no signal, no trace.' Crawford was backing away as he spoke, glancing at the door, desperate to go. 'We'll need to be in touch so you can tell us how to access the gemtech protocols – and the genestock. I don't have the time to get that information from you now.'

'You don't have the time, Mr Crawford, and I don't have the inclination. You shouldn't have come here.'

He stopped, staring at her with a kind of wounded comprehension, as it finally dawned on him that she was being neither sympathetic nor amenable.

She sighed inwardly at the delay, but surely it would only be a few more seconds and he would be gone. She kept her face still and implacable.

'I had hoped that this would be a surprise for you madam, once we arrived at our destination,' the man said slowly, reluctantly. 'It appears I do need to let you know after all . . . I should tell you now . . . You'll want to be in contact with us.' He hesitated. 'So you can speak with your daughter.'

'My . . . *what?*' Zavcka felt the shock run through her like electricity, felt the tingling and the first uncontrollable twitches in her hands, felt all her carefully calculated plans and contingencies shatter around her like glass. 'You're *taking* her?'

'We are. We have to.'

'Why?' she asked viciously. 'So you can make me give you what you want?'

'I . . . I would *never* put it like that . . .'

No, she thought, forcing herself to reason through her fury, to contain it, bank it, let it grow white-hot. The cold, clear part of her mind was already telling her that it was a weapon she could use, but only if she kept it under control. *No, you wouldn't. But somebody else did; somebody told you to tell me this, told you to make it clear that my cooperation was required, not requested. But you didn't want to. You don't want me to be angry with you.*

'Then you have to take me too.' The words were out before she had properly grasped her own strategy, but she felt the rightness of it and ploughed on, improvising. 'What you want is secured behind a five-point system. Finger and retinal scans, DNA match, voice recognition and an alphanumeric code. I can give you the code, you can record my voice, and I suppose' – she injected a contemptuous sneer into her voice – 'I *suppose* you wouldn't balk at taking DNA from a *child*. But it won't be enough, no matter what you do. You can't get to it without me.'

'You never said any of this before,' Crawford replied, looking horrified.

'I told you the longevity gemtech had impregnable security. I didn't think it was necessary to provide specifics. I didn't think,' Zavcka said, dripping bitterness, 'that *this* was the nature of our relationship.'

'It isn't! Madam, I wish you could come with us, I wish I could escort you to our rendezvous point right now. But it's impossible.' He was pleading, pointing at her with a shaking finger, pointing at her throat. 'You can't leave this apartment, remember? There'd be alarms the moment you stepped outside, you'd be tracked wherever you went . . .'

She touched the slender polymer and metal rope around her neck. The thought floated through her mind, in the odd, abstract way that unnecessary thoughts did when there were more pressing matters at hand, that she had grown quite accustomed to it.

She raised an eyebrow at Crawford: superior, knowing.

'I can deactivate it.'

'Deactivate . . . How?'

'I bribed one of the technicians to provide me with a means of blocking its transmissions. You paid the bribe yourself, in fact – one of those transfers I had you make? The Prague portfolio?' She spread her hands. 'Now you know what it was for.'

'But . . . I beg your pardon, madam, but if you were able to do that and get out of here, surely you would have done so already?'

'Would I? Think about it, Mr Crawford. Once the signal goes dead and they discover that I am not in this apartment, every train station, airport and helipad will be on alert. Every security cam on every road in the city – not to mention those leading out of it – will be scanning for me. If I'm already out of London, that won't matter, but I no longer have travel documents or access to personal transportation. I might be worth billions, but I don't have access to money that I can easily spend. None of those problems are insurmountable, of course; I wonder whether you realise how much of the work you've been doing for me has been aimed at solving them.'

It was Crawford's turn to look stunned.

Zavcka smiled coldly. 'However, the necessary arrangements are not yet in place and you are departing. As things stand, I'm unlikely to be able to find my own way out before all routes are blocked. Unless, of course, I go with you.'

'I don't . . . I can't . . . How long will it take?'

'The tracker? Not long. The device in my possession corrupts the circuitry. No more than half an hour.'

'What if it doesn't work? I'm sorry, madam, I can't risk it – I can't wait that long.'

'I'll meet you. You won't be taking a commercial flight or a train, not with the child. Private car or helicopter? Tell me where.'

'No, we're using the . . . None of the things you said. Madam, I can't. We don't have travel documents for you. You're too recognisable.'

'Mr Crawford, you and your companion and the child you intend to kidnap are about to become equally *recognisable*. Clearly you have a plan to avoid detection.' Zavcka was watching him narrowly and decided to gamble. 'If it's the same one you've been using to keep the police from catching up with these two, it must be good.' She gestured at the screen, where the WANTED banners for the Thames terrorists were once more interminably flashing. 'Just include me in it.'

He went white with shock and his knees sagged. Stumbling, he sank onto the arm of a chair as though all his strings had been cut. Zavcka smiled again, her lips thin, amused, as though she had only stated the most obvious thing in the world.

'Oh yes, I know what you're running from. Your friend Mr Fischer must be of great concern to you at the moment, and with good reason. We had better stop wasting time.'

Crawford's eyes were flicking from side to side. He looked like a trapped animal. 'We . . . we only have room for the three of us . . .'

'Perfect. Take *me*. I'm the one who knows what you're involved in; I'm the one who can give you what you want. Leave my daughter out of it.'

'Madam, I *can't*.' It was a wail, lost and desperate. 'It's not up to me. Events are already in motion.' He was scrambling for the door, frantic now, chest heaving.

'Mr Crawford!'

He stopped in his tracks. He turned.

'I am going to call you,' she said. 'In half an hour or less I am going to use this device to call you. I will confirm that the tracker is deactivated, and that I am safely out of this apartment. You are going to tell me where to come. I will sort things out with your companion when I get there. You will leave it to me. Is that clear?'

He stared as though she were a witch or a vision, some monstrous thing he had never seen before. Then he nodded sharply, silent and frightened, and was gone.

GENERATION

25

They had turned the heat up in the classrooms of Riveredge Primary to ward off the freezing fog of the morning and, as always seemed to be the way of things, it had gone from so cold you had to keep your coat on and could see your breath indoors to so hot that children were shedding layers of clothing as though they were snake skins and drowsing at their desks. Eve, like most of her classmates, was down to a thin pullover. She worked through the list of problems on her tablet – easy, these were all so *easy* – squinted suspiciously at the example on the wall screen just to make sure there wasn't a trick lurking somewhere to catch her out, and swiped to send the answers to the teacher. Then she slouched, chin on fist, and gazed longingly at the window. There was something that might almost be sky out there now, instead of the grey-white cloud that had earlier pressed up against the glass and condensed, first into fine dots, then into big drops, and then run down in fat streaks like rain. She knew from experience that the more often she checked the time, the longer it would take to get to lunch, but she could tell from where they were in the lesson and the first rumbles of hunger in her stomach, that it *had* to be soon.

Her tablet pinged softly. All of her answers were correct and she'd been sent another three problems to solve. These looked a little trickier. She glanced over at the teacher, Mr Yucel, who smiled at her approvingly. Eve sent a tiny smile back, although for once she would have preferred to daydream the remaining minutes away with nothing to do until everyone else had completed the set. But this was the price for being at the top of the class: you got more – and more difficult – problems than the others. You got to be the one who explained things to the kids who weren't as clever. You got away with a little more cheekiness, a little more rowdiness, a little more independence of mind. You got approval, and indulgence. She bent to the task.

She did the first problem quickly, spotted the trap in the second and reworked it and was deep in contemplation of the third when a sound intruded: a high, wavering electronic screech that resonated unpleasantly up and down her spine. She looked up. All around her, chairs were being pushed back. The sample problem on the wall screen had been replaced by the words EVACUATE IMMEDI-ATELY, pulsing ominously in time to the screeching. Mr Yucel was on his feet, frowning at it as he tucked his own tablet away, then frowning worriedly around at his class.

'Right, children,' he said, calmly, but Eve could hear an anxious note to his voice, 'you all know what to do when there's a fire alarm. Don't worry about your tablets or fetching your coats. Just move outside quickly and in an orderly manner like we've prac-tised. This isn't a drill, so no mucking about, please. Yes, Tufiq, that means you too. Come along, Darla, quickly, now. Eve, Perce, hurry up both of you.'

Eve grabbed her discarded jumper in one hand and her tablet in the other and joined her classmates heading for the exit. Contrary to instructions but true to form, Tuffy was clowning up at the front. She could hear Mr Yucel at the back, making sure that no one had been left behind, urging Darla to move more quickly. The corridors were crowded with everyone from the very little kids – Suri's age, though she didn't see him – up to the ten- and eleven-year-olds with whom Eve was at constant war on the playground. But even they looked subdued by the unscheduled scramble and rush and the high, worried voices of the teachers. Eve looked for Mish and thought she spotted his gangly frame up ahead. But it was just a silhouette glimpsed against the wide gap of the open doors and whoever she'd seen was lost in the crush. Fumbling a little, she slid her tablet away in the pocket of her jumper as she shuffled along towards the rectangle of daylight. It was too packed to try and pull it on in here, and anyway, it was much too hot – maybe there really *was* a fire somewhere, underneath their feet perhaps. Maybe turning the heat up so high had made the building start to burn? She imagined flames licking up from the basement, red fingers painting the underside of the floor beneath her feet, and she shuddered with fear and curiosity as she wondered what the school on fire would look like.

She was at the door now, tumbling down the steps into the yard, turning round immediately to look up at the building as she backed away. There was no sign of any fire or smoke and she felt a twinge of disappointment; then the cold hit her like a slap and she scrambled to pull on her jumper over her head. Through the openings of neck and sleeve she caught flashes of others all around her doing the same, while the teachers anxiously tried to herd them towards the playground. Children were still continuing to pour out of the door, an endless wave of them, all crowding into the space, and Eve hopped backwards to avoid being knocked over as she struggled with the jumper.

We assemble on the playground, to the side and out of the way, Eve thought. *I know that.* She popped her head through the neck opening in time to catch a glimpse of Tuffy staggering away in the distance, gurning, with his coat half on and backwards. *Twit.* At least he was going in the right direction. She got her arms out through the sleeves, straightened the jumper and made to follow.

'Eve?' said a voice she did not recognise. It came from above, behind and a little to one side. She turned.

It was a norm man, one she'd seen a couple of times before, once in the morning as she was arriving at school and another time when she'd run out to meet Mama in the afternoon. Those times he had been out on the street, but now he was standing just inside the gate, as though he had stepped in to see what was causing all the commotion. She wondered why it was unlocked at this hour, then realised, *Of course, it must be because of the fire.* The man had a deeply lined face and a lumpy, purplish nose; he was wearing a dull brown waterproof. She didn't know which child was his, or how he knew her name.

'Evening8,' said the man, 'have you seen dorok235?'

'What?' said Eve, so perplexed by the question that she forgot to be suspicious of the questioner. Those weren't *real* names, but she knew them.

'You're friends with her onstream,' said the man. 'See?' He held out a tablet, bending a little to bring the screen level with her eyes, and when she looked at it she saw her last chat with @dorok235 and the rest of the banished gang. The man's other hand was coming down beside the one that held the tablet, holding something, a small dark something, and her attention shifted to it, trying to make out what it was. A puff of white mist blew into her face, cold and chemical-smelling, and she coughed, then gasped. She looked up at the man, blinking, and suddenly deeply confused. There was clamour and shouting behind her, but she could not remember what it was about. There was a man she did not know in front of her, talking to her, telling her to come with him. She recalled vaguely that there was something you were supposed to do if that happened, but she could not think what.

'Come this way, Eve,' said the man. He sounded far, far away, but he had a kind voice. Kind man. 'Quickly now.'

She felt someone take a hand that might have been hers. She felt feet somewhere lift and move in a slow, dreamlike motion that was almost like walking. She did not know who the feet belonged to or where they were going, and she didn't care. It didn't seem important. The man led her out of the gate, past the passers-by who were gathering to peer curiously into the teeming, screeching schoolyard, along the pavement, swiftly round the corner and out of sight.

Gaela was in her kitchen, eyeing the bounty of apples Aryel had brought and thinking that she really should make something with some of them, if only to remove them as a task for Bal. The trouble was, they both knew that he would do a far better job than she could, no matter what she tried. In the fifteen years of their relationship she had yet to achieve more than basic competence in cookery, while he was able to generate an endless variety of delectable dishes from the most mundane of ingredients. She tried every now and then, but it was more about showing willing than expecting much in the way of results and the whole family knew it.

Still, it had been a while since the last attempt and she had just about decided to go for it when her tablet pinged: probably Gabriel, replying to the message she'd sent a few minutes before. She glanced at the screen, expecting his comcode along with an acknowledgement, maybe a question. What she saw instead made her snatch up the tablet and leap for the door, grabbing the coats hanging beside it as she went.

Bal met her halfway, charging up the stairs as she was charging down. 'Did you get—?'

She answered by tossing his coat at him; he pivoted and led the way, hauling it on as he went, saying, 'It's probably nothing. False alarm—'

'I know. I can go on my own—'

'Don't be ridiculous.' He stuck his head round the door of the grocery, yelled to Horace to hold down the fort and ran to catch up with her.

It had taken Agwé only a few minutes to work out that some big new thing must have happened during the few hours she'd been gone. Her route back from college was topside all the way and as she zigzagged through the narrow streets, then onto the quayside and across the footbridges to the Thames Tidal Power building she noted a newstream van pulling up in one of the side roads that dead-ended at Sinkat, an unknown launch moored in a corner of the basin with an EM tech pulling himself onboard and a flutter of voices and tension as she stepped into the big project office. Gabriel was at his workstation with his back to the door, focused on his screen or his band, or both. At the far end, Qiyem, who would normally be sitting just as quiet and focused, looked like he was about to leave; he had coat and satchel to hand, and seemed weirdly *twitchy*. For once, his band was pulsing, as if he might actually be using it. He saw Agwé immediately and half rose, as though he'd been waiting for her. She nodded an acknowledgement in his direction, but headed straight for Lapsa, who was finishing a conversation with someone.

'—unbelievable. No, I know it's not your fault, Fayole; I'm not trying to drop you in it. Just . . . You will? Thanks. I'll ask them. Okay, bye.' She flicked off and looked up at Agwé.

'There's a bloke from Environmental Management in a boat outside—'

'Tell me about it.'

'—and I just passed an UrbanNews van on Star Mews. What's going on?'

'You haven't heard?' Lapsa sounded surprised, then added, 'No, I suppose you wouldn't have done. I'm sorry, I haven't had time to message, and I guess Gabriel didn't either.'

They both glanced over at him. He had seen her now and his expression was so woebegone that she almost melted. He didn't appear to have slept any more than she had.

Lapsa said, 'He's working too hard already and I'm afraid today isn't going to be a quiet one.' She explained about the Kaboom operation.

'Are you *joking*?' Agwé was shocked rigid. 'So all those trolls, the horrible things they've been saying – they were the terrorists too?'

'Not all, but a lot of them. Gabriel,' she said significantly, 'has been very busy.'

'Bloody hell. I'd better go and talk to him.'

But she had made it far enough only to notice that his face had managed both to brighten and to look more anxious when she was intercepted by Qiyem.

'Agwé.'

'Hi,' she said, 'sorry about yesterday. I still have to sort a couple of things out.' She gestured vaguely towards Gabriel.

'I was wondering where you were,' Qiyem said, sounding desperate.

Honestly, give the man a hint of a chance and whatever coolness he had washed out like the tide.

'I need you to . . . come and have lunch with me.'

'Already?' she said in surprise. 'It's too early – I had breakfast at college not that long ago. Anyway, I've only just got back.' She made to move past him. 'How about tomorrow?'

He stood his ground. 'Tomorrow isn't going to work.'

'The day after, then – or next week.' He was still standing there. 'Qiyem, I've got things to do.'

He stepped aside, reluctantly. 'I'll wait. As long as I . . . can.'

That was so bizarre that she didn't even attempt an answer. So much for listening to her guilty conscience; she'd been right to think there was something weird about him.

Gabriel had been watching the exchange with that strange mixture of eagerness and hesitation. As she finally got to his workstation he stood up and plucked his tablet off the dock, his face looking tired and solemn.

'I need to talk to you,' he said without preamble.

'No – *really?*'

'Really really, but not here.'

There was something about the seriousness with which he spoke that made her bite back a snarky retort, and she followed him out and upstairs to an empty meeting room.

'We need a conference for this?'

'We need privacy.'

'Lapsa just told me about this troll team?' she said conversationally. 'Operation Kaboom, the ones that got arrested yesterday? And you've been having a hard time with the trolls, and I *guess* if you already knew about them you'd be on a short fuse.'

'Oh, that,' he said distractedly, 'that's a whole other story. Yes I did, but no one's supposed to know I did, and anyway, that wasn't the reason.'

She had no comeback for that, and the quiet gravity of his manner made her uncertain, almost afraid. Without their usual banter, she felt adrift. As he was closing the door behind them, she said, 'Look, I should've messaged you back; I just didn't know what to say, or what to think . . .'

'I don't blame you.'

'I know Sharon and Mikal are okay with Misha and Sural showing up in clips, because I'd checked with them when I'd done it before, but it never occurred to me I'd have to check with *you* – and I know I shouldn't have assumed, and I'm *really* sorry about that, but it's not like I did anything *bad* to Eve.' She dropped into a chair. 'I just don't understand why you would react like that. I felt like I didn't even know who you *were* all of a sudden.'

He sat down heavily, his face twisting in distress, and it struck her that if they'd both been just a little bit younger they'd probably have been in tears by now.

'I'm sorry,' she said quickly, appalled at herself. 'That's really harsh. I didn't mean . . .'

'No,' he interrupted. He had his tablet in his hands and was flipping it end to end, looking at it and not at her, 'that's probably about right. I know you don't understand; how could you?' He met her eyes, finally. 'I need to explain, but before I can, I need to ask you to do something that's going to make you even more pissed off with me. I'm sorry, Ag, I am so, *so* sorry, but this part isn't up to me.'

He swiped his tablet awake and turned it so she could read the screen. There was a message there, from his mother.

Papa & I have decided OK, but only if you're SURE. Check first. After that, we trust your judgement.

'Sure of what?' she said, deeply puzzled. A chill ran down her spine, a sense of foreboding. '"Check first"? What does that mean?'

'It means I have to turn this off.' He touched his band. 'And I have to ask you to turn yours off.' He pointed at her head.

'You . . . *what*?' Agwé stared at him, aghast. 'You want to *read* me before you explain yourself?'

'If I'm going to tell you the whole truth then I have to, Ag. I'm sorry. I could make up an excuse that would be sort-of-true, but I don't want to do that. I don't want you to be someone I have to hide things from. My parents like you a lot, otherwise it wouldn't even be an option, and *I* already know I can trust you with anything, but this is—' He gestured helplessly at the tablet. 'It's *this* important.'

'It'd *better* be.' She reached up, found the power stud on the band and tapped it off. Across from her Gabriel did the same. His eyes went a little unfocused, as though the Agwé he was now looking at occupied some other, more liminal space.

After a few seconds she snapped, 'Well? What are you waiting for?'

'For you to be less angry – that's all I'm getting right now.'

She dropped her head into her hands, took several deep breaths and thought, *This is Gabriel, and Bal and Gaela are good people, and they wouldn't be doing this just to make me feel like a shit.*

Across from her he chuckled softly and with relief. 'No, we definitely wouldn't.'

She looked back up at him.

'My sister Eve,' he said, 'is adopted.'

'I know that. You both are.'

'Yes, and everyone knows my back story. But hers is secret. The cover story is mostly a lie, and very, *very* few people know the whole truth. Lapsa doesn't, Pilan doesn't. Eve doesn't, for her own safety. We have to keep her from being widely seen, from being . . . *publicised*. When you meet her, you think she's just a regular kid living a regular life, and my parents are doing everything they can to make sure it feels like that for her too, just like they did with me. But what you *don't* see – and this is *very* different from what happened with me – is that she is being prevented from having any kind of profile, any *visibility* outside her immediate circle of school, friends, family. That's why her image can't appear on any streams, because someone might recognise her, and if they did—'

He broke off, rubbing his hands over his drawn face and through his hair, pulling the band off and chucking it onto the table. 'Well, maybe nothing would happen, but it's not a risk we can ever take, not while she's little.'

'What do you mean, "recognise her"? Recognise her from where?'

'From her original: the person who made her, who she's made *from*.' He took a deep breath and looked her straight in the eye. 'Eve,' he said, 'my sister Eve is Zavcka Klist's clone.'

26

Mikal was still waiting beneath the bridge when the message came through from Riveredge Primary. Sharon had told him to stay there until a forensics unit arrived, along with a police river patrol so they could get alongside the piers and take samples. He'd told her about the Environmental Management technicians now at work in Sinkat and suggested they be redirected to support the forensics team; they had a boat and they could examine the state of the sealant below the waterline as well. That had been half an hour ago.

'Poor Fayole,' she was saying in his ear, her frustration at another shambolic response from EM barely hidden, 'Lapsa's just had a go at her as well. She's at her wits' end – they're not showing it as a live job, but apparently it's not unheard of for assignments to be informally escalated and then synced to the system later. She's got everyone in that department running around trying to work out who sent them so they can work out who they are so they can be contacted. If I ran my division like that, I'd be bloody well sacked!'

'Can't you get Lapsa to—?' He heard the ping of her tablet over the earset just as his own went and felt a faint premonition as he swiped at his screen. 'Oh *fuck*. Sharon—?' He heard her own sudden intake of breath.

'You've got this—' It wasn't a question.

'Yes.' He was already crossing the piazza at close to a run. 'I'll be there in twenty minutes. Do you have more?'

He could hear her moving; she'd be gathering her things with one hand, tapping up more information with the other. 'It's not a drill,' she told him. 'Emergency contact at the scene reports no sign of fire or smoke, but the building's being evacuated and units are en route. Might be a false alarm.'

'Might be.' He was on the riverwalk now, almost back at the channel that led into Sinkat Basin. A small launch was coming out, its engine a low roar, bow waves creaming away on either side as it curved into the river without slowing and headed off downstream at speed. 'Damn. So much for that idea.'

'What?'

'The EM techs just left Sinkat – I'm no boatman, but I'm pretty sure they've just violated all the marine safety regs, the way they tore out of there.'

'I'll add it to the list.'

He heard a door slamming in his earset, followed by hurrying footsteps. He was across the channel himself now, off the foot-bridge and jogging along the quayside towards an alley that would take him away from the basin. Then he would be in the network of streets that led back towards the Squats and the school. His feet itched to move faster, but he knew that if he gave in to his fear and ran flat-out he would be winded before he was even halfway there.

In his ear he could hear Sharon talking, not to him, her voice tightly controlled. 'Danladi, I have to go, there's a fire – a fire alert – at my children's school. No, I don't know if it's serious. Tell Inspector Achebe he needs to get forensics to the bridge without delay. I'll be available on 'set.'

*

311

Zavcka Klist sat in the back of the private cab, watching the city slide by as she had done so many times before – many times, but not for a *very* long time; there had been no windows in the van that brought her home from prison just a few days ago. She knew there was a chance that this expedition would end with her returning there, so she savoured the view and refused to allow herself any trepidation as she listened to the empty hum of the earset she had hastily slaved to her now unrestricted tablet. Flicking it to standby, she ran back through the conversation she had had and the instructions she had been given.

For all his flaws, Patrick Crawford had not been wrong to assume that she had hiding places in the flat about which the authorities knew nothing. From one she had retrieved a debit tab preloaded with enough cash to put the lie to her claim of having no ready spending money. Debit tabs might be a rarity in a stream economy where almost every transaction was linked to a credit account, but they were legal tender nonetheless. The cab driver's surprise at the tall, regal blonde woman in her elegant coat and rich silk scarf, strolling up to his stand instead of waiting to be collected from some luxurious hotel or stylish restaurant, was compounded when she snapped the tab to his meter and authorised it with a finger scan.

'Don't see these too much any more,' he said.

Zavcka smiled thinly and settled herself into the seat. 'I imagine not.'

'Where to?'

'East. You know the area that used to be called the Squats? It has another name now, I believe.'

The man snorted. 'Yes, ma'am, I know the area. Riveredge Village,' he said, and pulled the vehicle out into traffic. 'They rebranded it a few years ago. That's where you're going?' She could not see his face but he sounded doubtful. It was entirely possible, she thought, that he had never before taken a fare from this part of town to that one.

'It'll be somewhere around there, close to the river. I'll have the exact location in a moment. And,' she added, 'I'll double your money if you get me there in twenty minutes.'

'What—?'

'You heard me,' she said, and felt the vehicle pick up speed as she pulled up Crawford's comcode. He was stuttering and frightened, and reluctant to confirm anything until she told him she was less than half an hour away from the Riveredge quayside.

'But . . . But how—? I never said—'

'It was quite obvious,' she replied wearily. 'Am I meeting you there, or somewhere nearby?'

There was a sharp intake of breath, and then the rendezvous point was confirmed in awestruck tones. 'Madam, I've spoken to my associate,' he added hesitantly. 'She's not at all comfortable with this turn of events.'

So his travelling companion was a woman. Zavcka's instinct for schemes and conspiracies told her that this would be the person in charge of the operation, the one running Fischer and Crawford and who knew how many others. And no, the unknown woman would not be at all pleased to discover that a wrench was being thrown into the works at this late and dangerous stage, no matter how she might feel about Zavcka herself.

'But you are intelligent enough to rely on your own better judgement, Mr Crawford,' she said soothingly. 'And I'll address her concerns personally when we meet. What did you say her name was?'

'Oh,' he said, blindsided by the compliment, 'Moira. Moira Charles.'

'I'm sure Ms Charles and I will quickly come to an understanding. Is my daughter with her?'

'Not yet. Eve has been collected by her watcher, he'll bring her to us.'

'Eve,' she said, tasting the name. 'Is she all right?'

'She won't have been harmed, madam – possibly just a mild sedative.'

'Very good, Mr Crawford. I'll see you shortly.'

Eve, she thought. *Her name is Eve.*

I like it.

The fire service had thrown up a cordon to keep the public from straying onto school grounds and the pupils from straying off them, and parents were piling up against the barrier, demanding to be allowed to get to their children. Fire officers tramped in and out through the front door, trailing equipment as they searched for any sign of what had triggered the alarms. Someone killed the screeching noise just as Gaela and Bal arrived, but the clamour of the kids corralled in the playground was almost as loud.

Gaela leaned round the scrum of anxious adults, looked at the schoolhouse and said to Bal, 'Warm air coming out the front door, and it looks like another door's open at the side. Couple of leaks at the windows. No hot spots.'

The patrol officer manning the barricade overheard and gestured the couple forward, looking suspicious. Terissa, standing beside him and checking parents off against children on the tablet she held, put out an elaborately tattooed hand to forestall any challenge. 'They're two more of ours, and believe me, she'd know: hyperspectral vision. So far they can't work out what set off the alarms,' she said to Gaela, 'so we're sending the kids home so they can check the system as well as the building. Let me fetch Eve for you.'

She was gone longer than Gaela and Bal had expected, long enough for a trickle of relieved parents to start departing with their children, and for Mikal to come panting up and be reassured that everything was okay.

But the moment she saw Teri's worried face hurrying back to them Gaela knew that it was not.

'I can't find her,' Teri said, her normally calm demeanour now distinctly ruffled. 'I thought she might have snuck away from her class to go be with Misha, but she's not there, though Sural is.' She looked at Mikal. 'He was scared, but he's fine now they're together. But I can't find Eve, so I thought maybe she'd slipped back here ahead of me, but she hasn't.' She looked round despairingly, as though a small blonde girl might suddenly materialise in front of them.

Gaela felt unable to breathe. Beside her, Bal said, 'Could she still be inside? You know what she's like.'

'She was in Mr Yucel's class and he says she left with everyone else; he's certain she came outside with the others. And the fire-fighters have already checked the building . . .'

Instructions were issued for it to be checked again, and they were all let in to help search through the crowd of children. Sural and Misha hung off Mikal, demanding to know where Eve was while he scanned the crowds from eight feet up. Bal and Gaela had quartered the playground calling her name, and by the time Sharon arrived a couple of minutes later, they knew for certain that the child had gone.

'How,' Gaela heard herself gasping over and over again. 'How? How?' She held on to Bal, who was oblivious to the fact that her nails were digging into his arm.

Sharon rounded on Teri and Mr Yucel, who were both ashen-faced. 'Good question. Could she have left with another child? Are all the teachers accounted for?'

'We're all here,' said Teri, 'and no, she wouldn't have been allowed to go with anyone else – and anyway it was me checking them.' She thought. 'I guess there were a couple of minutes while the kids were being evacuated but before the fire units or the police showed up when she could have slipped away.'

'Did you see her in the playground at all?' Sharon asked Mr Yucel, then looked down and said softly, 'No, Suri, not now. This is serious.'

'I . . . I don't think so. I don't remember seeing her there,' the teacher said desperately. 'But it was bedlam; the children were running around – I wouldn't have thought that Eve was the kind of child who would do that, just wander off.'

'Maybe she went home?' offered the patrol officer.

'Then we would have met her on the way,' Bal told him.

Gaela whispered, 'No, that's not what happened.' She spun away, flicking at her earset to activate it.

Sharon disengaged her children's hands and pushed them gently back to Mikal. She looked over at the chief fire officer, who had come up to stand, grim-faced, at the edge of the group. 'Any chance this alarm was a hack?'

'There's every chance,' he replied. 'There's no heat source in the building.'

Sharon swore under her breath and activated her earset. Gaela ended her own call as Sharon talked steadily for close to a minute: issuing the missing-child alert, calling in search patrols, ordering up override scans of security vidcams. She listened to Sharon as though in a dream, feeling herself moving slow and heavy through a nightmare space.

'We need to search,' she said as Sharon finished. 'We can't stay here.' She started heading for the gate, but Bal grabbed her.

'No one else leaves,' Sharon was telling Teri. 'We need to question the children and the teachers; they may have seen something.' She took hold of the patrol officer, spun him around and pointed him at the crowd beyond the barrier. 'Start with them: anyone who was already here when you arrived. She's blonde, with very dark eyes, eight years old, tall for her age. Wearing?' She looked at Bal and Gaela.

'Blueish jumper, reddish trousers,' said Bal.

'Blue jumper, red trousers. Go.'

As the officer trotted off Sharon's tablet starting pinging acknowledgements. She pulled it out, saying to Gaela, 'Yes, we have to search, but we need a plan and we need to stay in touch. We should each take a direction but stay on 'set so as soon as we get any leads—' She stopped dead, staring at her screen.

Bal was still holding Gaela's arm but his other hand went up to his own earset for an incoming call. 'We need you,' he began urgently. 'Eve's been—' And then he said, 'No, *listen*—' and went quiet for a moment. And then he said, '*What? She what?*' And then, 'No, she couldn't have. Oh no—'

Agwé's reaction was all that Gabriel could have hoped for. He felt the bewilderment and vexation give way to incredulity, then curiosity and now waves of understanding and a staunchness of purpose that left him weak with relief. He'd had to explain it all, of course, fill in the details of what had happened, because she'd been much too young to be following the story herself; but now that she knew, she had instantly, without a moment's hesitation, become one of Eve's guardians and a fierce keeper of her secret: a member of the select, burdened few on whom Gabriel and his family could always rely.

'Bloody hell,' she said. 'If I had something this monumental to worry about every day, I'd be flipped out permanently.'

'We're used to it, you know? We knew it would be this way from before she was even born. Mama and Papa were in the delivery room and I was waiting outside with Aryel and Eli, and I remember everybody being really eager, but also anxious and a bit sad. So many terrible things had happened so that she could exist. Rhys had only just got out of hospital and there was a lot of speculation about what would happen at the trial. The whole Klist story was the biggest thing on the streams. We were all thinking that we had to do right by this baby, that she mustn't ever suffer or be made to feel bad about things she had nothing to do with. She had to be safe, she had to be allowed to live a normal, happy, healthy life. It was part of the commitment from the beginning.'

'And your parents just *volunteered* for that? That's an amazing thing to do.'

'It was Aunt Aryel's idea, because she knew they'd already applied to adopt another child and it was taking a long time. We were in Wales then, up in the mountains. They'd moved to get me away from the city, out of the spotlight, after what had happened when *I* was little. She knew the baby – Eve – couldn't be placed anonymously; whoever took her would have to know what they were getting into, and be people who could be trusted. So she suggested it to Mama and Papa, they said yes, and the authorities were happy – it solved a whole lot of problems for them.'

'What happened to the surrogate mother? Ellyn?'

'Grandpa Reginald became her guardian – she's a batch sibling of Rhys and Gwen and he'd raised them really well. And her injuries didn't scare him. So she's out there running around in the hills, climbing trees and chasing butterflies and being doted on. She's too brain-damaged to understand what was done to her.'

'Maybe that's—' Agwé caught herself and shook her head sharply. She looked at him askance. 'I didn't mean to think that!'

'I know. It's really hard not to.'

'Are you sure that Eve has no idea? I mean, when she saw me with the vidcam at the TideFair she got *so* excited – she was saying no one *ever* takes pictures of her and if they do they *never* put them onstream. I thought she was just being dramatic. Of course I understand now, but I think she knows, Gabe.'

'She doesn't know that it's on purpose, she thinks we just forget or we don't think about it. But I know it makes her cranky; she's really been acting out recently, pushing the boundaries, and it's going to get harder and harder to manage as she gets older. Our parents haven't quite worked out how to deal with that yet. So we were all already a bit worried, and then Zavcka Klist got released last week – and I guess home confinement isn't all *that* different from being locked up in prison, it's not like she can go anywhere, but still.' He let himself sag wearily into the chair. 'Hence my meltdown yesterday. I'm really sorry.'

'If you say that again, I will . . . well, I won't hit you, but I'll do *something*.'

He snickered, then glanced at the comcode flashing on his tablet as his earset buzzed with an incoming call. 'Good,' he said to Agwé, as he flicked the 'set. 'My mum's probably calling to check that you haven't killed me or anything – Mama? Hi, I'm with Agwé, it's all fine . . .'

'No, it isn't,' his mother told him. 'Eve's gone. She's disappeared from school. There was a bogus fire alarm, they evacuated the building and by the time we got here she was gone.'

The world dropped away from under him.

It was the longest, strangest walk there had ever been. Eve felt like she was in a bubble, distantly aware of the endlessly slow pick-up-and-put-down of her feet but unable to tell whether she was actually moving or not. She turned her head, *slowly slowly*, and saw her own small hand grasped by a larger one. She noted with disinterest that the hand holding hers was wrinkled and spotted, and that it emerged from the cuff of a dull brown coat. A question pushed at her, pressing against the balloon-surface of her consciousness, but it couldn't get in and when she tried to focus it just slipped away. The edges of her vision were blurred and indistinct, like peering underwater through a dive-mask placed on the surface of the sea.

She found that if she moved her head, the small window of perception through which she had seen the hands and the coat would show her other things. She looked around, slow as honey, and saw a rough brick wall, a high metal fence, leaves blown into a corner between buildings.

Maybe I'm dreaming, Eve thought. *I guess I'm walking in my sleep. But why would I come this way?*

That question was inside the bubble with her, where she could get hold of it, pin it down, try to force an answer. Something pulled at the puppet that was her, tugging her hand. Someone with a hollow, faraway voice said, 'Hurry up.'

The outside question poked at her again, hard, and again failed to penetrate. The inside question had what there was of her attention.

Home is over there, on the other side of this, what are these called? Can't remember. Bricks, these are bricks. *Alley, behind the brick things, behind everything, why am I dream-walking in the alley?*

This isn't the way. This isn't the way we go. Why would I go to the river this way?

27

Once, a long time ago, before the Temple Act gave gems the same rights as every other citizen, before the Declaration released them from forced indenture, before the retrieval squads sent out to hunt down runaways were banned, Zavcka Klist had assigned one such team to reconnoître the neighbourhood of abandoned buildings, cupped by a southward curve of the river, where escapees were rumoured to be finding refuge. She had watched the resulting surveillance vids with the squad leader, silently repulsed by the dank streets, the dark, menacing alleyways, the broken windows and the weeds that crawled out of cracks and hung from gutters like the tattered pennants of some defiant army. Shadows not cast by their lights had shifted and moved just out of range, disappearing around the corner of a side street, retreating from an empty casement three storeys up; there was the slap of running feet echoing back from one of those narrow, damp passages. The squad leader had frozen and refocused the image a couple of times, identifying head-high glimmers of green and purple and once, a flicker of something that looked like Bel'Natur red.

'They're beginning to congregate,' the squad leader had told her matter-of-factly. 'Ours, Gempro, Recombin, the lot. We do a full sweep, we could hit the competition up for bounty payments as well.'

They had started to put together a plan, a good one, but Zavcka had waited too long, or maybe word had got out, and one judge ruled standard retrieval practices illegal and another extended that ruling instead of overturning it, and suddenly the police were notifying them that they could no longer turn a blind eye but would be obliged to treat any such actions as kidnap.

And just like that, it was over; just like that the war zone Zavcka's one-time retrieval squad had approached with extreme caution became a haven for wave after wave of first the escaped, and then the emancipated. It acquired a name, an identity, a reputation: the Squats, the place where the gems lived, where the institutionalised learned to be free, the engineered discovered the full range of their talents and the crèche-born forged the tightest of tight-knit communities. Zavcka had not believed any of it, not really, not until she crossed swords with Aryel Morningstar. And none of the vids she had seen since, from the earliest days when the area began to be safe enough to live in openly through its transition into an edgy, vibrant district for the artistic and the adventurous to its current status as the most diverse, iconoclastic, liberal and innovative of the city's many villages, had ever quite supplanted in her mind that first impression of a dirty, derelict, dangerous place.

What she found when the cab delivered her into its heart was so at odds with that recollection it almost induced a sense of vertigo: the streets were still narrow and twisty, but clean and in good repair. Those old buildings that remained had been restored, often with quirky applications of materials and technology that hadn't existed when they'd originally been built. Between them, entirely new structures of shimmering aggregate and biopolymer and recycled brick looked neither out of place nor overbearing. She saw galleries and greengrocers and restaurants and nightclubs, theatres and bakeries and offices and workshops, parks and playgrounds

and terraced houses and blocks of flats. Regardless of age or prov-
enance, the structures looked practical, lived in and well used, a
cheek-by-jowl jumble of styles and colours and shapes and textures
that nevertheless looked comfortable together.

The feature she found most striking was a strange organic translucence to some of the modern surfaces, as though a light were
being shone from behind layer upon layer of melted silicate. That
would be the new tech adapted from gillung dwellings: quantum
cells embedded in the walls, constantly being recharged and
releasing their energy in response to demand. Against all odds,
the waterbreathers had found ways to survive and thrive in the
wild, and then had confounded expectations again by adapting
their inventions to work for topsiders too. Seeing it here, panel
after panel on structure after structure, she understood why Bankside, quite possibly in partnership with others, must have felt it
necessary to bring Thames Tidal Power to heel. The outcasts had
gone from being an embarrassment to an inconvenience to a clear
and present threat.

The revolution was here, she thought, in these buildings. It was
here on these streets, in the people with glowing, jewel-coloured
hair or odd anatomies or no gemsign at all who walked and talked
and shopped and laughed and quarrelled and played and ate and
worked together, all lifting their faces to the pale noonday sun as
though nothing whatsoever about them was strange. The refugees
and their allies had become the pioneers of a new landscape, the
citizens of a city remade from its own ruins. She stared through the
window, mesmerised, as the cab slid through these altered streets
and thought again about the course she had embarked upon, and
knew that no other decision had been possible.

The driver got her as close as he could, down a lane that dead-
ended at a line of bollards. Beyond them she could see it continuing

as a pedestrian way lined with small shops and cafés, sloping down until there was just the wide sky above the river, dotted with the soaring, calling shapes of seagulls. She scanned for a larger airborne figure but did not see it.

'Just down there,' said the driver, pointing, and she thanked him and paid double as promised. He asked if he should wait.

'No,' she said, 'I'll have different transportation from here,' and walked away quickly. She had beaten the estimate she'd given to Crawford by a full five minutes, but it would not do to linger.

By the time they had worked their way down a network of narrow passageways and stopped beside the old sailor's hostel that faced the riverwalk, Eve realised that she no longer thought she was dreaming – or maybe she was now waking up? She could see further; directly opposite the mouth of the passage was the narrow jetty where you got the boat upstream to Sinkat or Southbank or Westminster, or down to Limedog, or even all the way down, through the barriers and out into the estuary and to sea – Gabe and her and Mama and Papa had done that one time when the quantum-battery banks were being built on the north and south banks. There had been lots of talk about energy storage and conversion ratios and other things that weren't interesting, but they got to dock at the floating platform and then go down into the airwalk on the seabed. From there they were able to watch all the people swimming outside, their green hair like clouds of shimmering seaweed round their heads, carrying stuff that would have been way too big and heavy for them on land but was light because it was in the water. Gabe said they were working, but it looked like fun to Eve. And there were fishes and crabs and eels and snails, and she had spotted a tiny, delicate seahorse in the weeds at the base of the thick, transparent airwalk membrane, and that was *really* interesting. The memory came back to her clearly, and it suddenly struck her that she could *see* clearly now too, and could hear the gulls screeching as they skirmished above the jetty, and that they no longer sounded echoey or distant. She had walked here in a dream, but now she was here for real – how had that happened?

She turned her head to look up at the man who was holding her hand and the motion no longer felt weirdly slow and disconnected; instead it was like she was moving too fast now and a wave of nausea washed through her. She felt herself grimace and sway a little on her feet, and she closed her eyes to stop everything from spinning. When she opened them again the man was looking down at her.

'Are you feeling sick?'

She nodded.

'Well, don't be. Just take a few deep breaths. We're almost there.'

'Almost where?' she asked, thinking there was something strange about this situation, this man, and that there was another question she should be asking, if only she knew what it was.

He did not answer, but looked out at the jetty and then leaned around the corner of the hostel, peering up the riverwalk to the left as though searching for something in particular. Eve leaned forward too, carefully, so as not to make her head go funny again. The morning's fog had dispersed into a thin haze, but the air above the riverwalk was bitterly cold, far colder than the sheltered alley, and mostly empty. She saw two people in the distance, a man and a woman, wearing the kind of formal business clothes that meant they were probably visitors to the neighbourhood, not residents. They had proper coats on over their suits, and it dawned on her that she was only wearing her jumper and it was way too cold to be out here in just that.

Why am I not in my coat? she wondered, and almost grasped the main question, the *important* one, the one that kept slipping away.

She was so intent on it that when the man said, 'There they are,' in a relieved voice, pulling at her hand as he stepped out from the passage onto the riverwalk, she failed to move with him. The fingers grasping hers tightened and she was dragged out, stumbling. The unexpected jerk, the frigid air, the sight of approaching faces she did not know, combined to shock her all the way back to herself. She tried to yank her arm away, and was suddenly struggling to free herself, and the slippery question was there in her mind and she was shouting, *'Who are you?'*

She dug her heels and tried to wrench herself away from the Brown-Coat man, filled with a sudden terror of him. His hand slipped and she was almost free, but he still had the cuff of her jumper and he grabbed her wrist, gripping it so tight she thought it might break. She turned, her wrist twisting painfully, looking for the two people coming up the riverwalk, about to shout for help; but as her eyes fell on them the woman made an impatient gesture, waving at the jetty towards which she was being dragged, and she knew at once that they were with Brown-Coat. He was trying to drag her towards them. The man walking next to the woman had a worried expression and was looking past where Eve was still thrashing frantically. Was someone coming from the opposite direction, someone who might help? As Eve tried to swing round to look, above the screaming of the gulls and the hammering of her own heart she heard the sputter of a boat's engine starting up.

'Stop struggling,' said Brown-Coat, sounding like he'd lost all patience with her. 'This is for your own good.' Another vicious tug on her wrist made Eve yelp with pain, and then she saw the small, dark thing coming at her in his other hand and remembered the schoolyard and the puff of white mist that had made her go all foggy, and she screamed.

Another hand came down over the dark spray-thing, covering it, and though she heard the hiss of the mist and saw its edges blow out at the side, it was caught and stopped by the long, pale fingers that had slammed down over Brown-Coat's own age-spotted hand. Instinct made Eve close her eyes, hold her breath and duck her head away so she wouldn't get any of the spray in her face. She felt her bruised wrist finally pull free and she fell, sprawling on the cold stone of the quayside.

High above her she heard a woman's voice, haughty and arrogant and very angry, exclaiming, 'What is the meaning of this?'

It wasn't exactly a shout, but it was crackling with authority: the voice of someone who is used to giving orders and being obeyed without question. Eve looked up and then scrambled awkwardly to her feet, her hurt wrist cradled in her other hand. The woman who had spoken, who had blocked the sleep-spray and broken Brown-Coat's grip on her, was tall and blonde and elegant. She wore an ankle-length, golden-brown coat made of some stuff that looked soft and luxurious and even to Eve's inexperienced eyes, very expensive. A richly shimmering green-blue scarf was wrapped around her throat. She looked a bit older than Mama, though Eve couldn't have said how much.

Brown-Coat had staggered away and was staring at the Blonde Lady with a stunned expression on his face. The man and woman in business suits had come up to them; the man looked flustered and the woman looked cross, but both were also staring at Blonde Lady as though awestruck. Eve's wrist was throbbing so badly she could barely think, let alone run, and her head was starting to hurt too, but she shuffled backwards, further away from the other three. She had decided that Blonde Lady was the safest of the four strangers, although the tall woman's next words made her slightly less certain.

'You said that Eve would not be harmed, Crawford. You gave me your word.'

'She . . . she hasn't been, madam,' said Business-Suit Man, then he turned to Brown-Coat. 'Has she?' he added anxiously.

Brown-Coat was still staring at Blonde Lady as though she were a ghost. 'Y-y-you never said,' he began, stuttering, 'you never said *she* would be here – you never *said*!'

'Change of plan,' snapped Business-Suit Woman, who kept looking out towards the river and the sound of the motorboat. It was purring now, and Eve saw it come into view, curving towards the jetty with two more people on board. 'Now we have both.'

'Oh,' said Brown-Coat, staring at her and sounding amazed. 'Well, I had to give the young one a dose to make her come along quietly. It must have worn off. You saw what she was like; it's not my fault if she's stubborn. Just a little more and she'll be fine.'

His hand holding the spray-thing twitched and Eve shrieked, 'No!' and pushed herself backwards, away from him but keeping her distance from Blonde Lady too now. Blonde Lady turned, watching her. There was a small smile playing on her face.

'Going along quietly has never been my way,' she said, which made no sense to Eve. She held out her hand. 'Eve? Come here, dear.'

'No,' said Eve, and then, 'Who are you?'

'You don't know me, my dear, but that doesn't matter. I'm here to help. I won't drug you or hurt you or make you go anywhere you don't want to.' She waggled her fingers encouragingly.

'She can't be left behind now,' said Business-Suit Woman crossly. 'The boat is here and we're wasting time.'

'I have to go,' said Brown-Coat. 'I have to get out of the area – I can't be part of this.'

'Then go. We'll be in touch.' Business-Suit Woman held out her hand and he passed the spray-thing to her and scuttled backwards, still staring at Blonde Lady, aiming for the narrow passage they'd come down. Business-Suit Woman, holding the sprayer thing purposefully, went to go around Business-Suit Man and get to Eve, but she yelped and jumped towards Blonde Lady, grabbing the waiting hand with her own undamaged one. The long fingers squeezed hers reassuringly as Blonde Lady moved to put herself between Business-Suit Woman and Eve.

'Madam, I assure you no harm will come to her,' said Business-Suit Man. 'But we have to hurry, and we can't afford to attract attention.'

Business-Suit Woman had halted her advance and was regarding Blonde Lady with a strange blend of admiration and suspicion. She said, 'What's the status of your tracker?'

Eve wondered what a tracker was, but then Blonde Lady reached up with her free hand and parted the folds of her beautiful scarf. Beneath it she was wearing an ugly polymer-and-metal necklace, not nearly as elegant as her other things. There was an even uglier dull red band clamped round it, just where it rested against her collar bone.

'I didn't have the tools or the time to remove it,' she said. 'But as I am here and unaccompanied, you can safely assume that the blocking device is working.'

'Well,' said Business-Suit Woman, sounding uncertain. 'Well . . . all right. We have to go. We don't have much time before—' She stopped and glanced at the boat, now standing just off the jetty, then up the river towards Sinkat, then back at Blonde Lady. 'I suppose we don't have much choice now: we can't afford to leave you behind at this point either. If she'll come along with you quietly, then fine.' She jerked the sprayer in Eve's direction and turned away towards the jetty. 'If she makes a fuss, I'm sorry, but she'll have to be dosed – it won't do any permanent damage. Let's go.'

Eve tensed to pull away, thinking that, despite the pain in her hand and her head and the nausea once more making everything dip and sway around her, she would have to try to run.

The cool fingers holding hers squeezed again, in a comforting sort of way. 'No,' said Blonde Lady, 'I don't believe Eve or I will be going anywhere with you.'

28

Gabriel ran as he had never run before, slowing only when he passed close enough to read someone, scanning frantically for any thought, any memory, any recent encounter with a small blonde girl, especially one who was protesting or being carried. Few people would remember a stranger glimpsed in passing; unless something had happened to make them actively think about Eve, there would be nothing for him to perceive. But an unwilling child being dragged along was memorable, so he slowed down to check their minds and then sped up again, with Agwé loping alongside, easily keeping pace.

All she'd said in response to his frantic explanation as he'd dashed out of the meeting room, barrelled down the stairs and raced away from Thames Tidal was, 'Let's go.' He knew she felt sick to her stomach at the thought that she might have played some part in this disaster, however inadvertently; but she also understood that saying so now would be of no use. They had neither time nor breath to spare. Instead, they ran by the fastest route: past the UrbanNews vidcam crew outside on the quay, over the bridges across Sinkat Basin and down into the back streets, zigzagging through them until they could get onto the riverwalk and run flat-out. Then they would turn up one of the side streets, weaving through the Squats until they got to the school. He had no better plan. His mother didn't know which way Eve had gone – which way she had been taken – and so the only thing he could do was to get to his parents as fast as possible, looking and scanning for his sister along the way.

He and Agwé were at the mouth of a little lane that dropped down from the heart of the village to the riverwalk via a short pedestrianised promenade of cafés and shops. He was swinging round to run along it when Agwé grabbed him and brought them both to such a skidding halt they almost fell over.

'What?' he gasped, panting. 'This is quicker—'

'Shut up,' said Agwé. 'I thought I heard something.' She turned her head, listening hard, and he bent over, hands on his knees, listening too, and hearing nothing except the rasping of his own breath and the screaming of seagulls, but thinking *Gillung hearing, gillung hearing is so much better than ours . . .*

She clapped him on the arm and was off, heading down the riverwalk. 'Shouting,' she called over her shoulder as he took off after her, 'I heard a child shouting, it sounded like—'

And then he had it from her mind, and they were both running round the corner of a hulking building that pushed out towards the river, charging up half a dozen steps, and then he could see the long curve of the quay and the Riveredge Village jetty with a motorboat nosing up to it, a man in a brown waterproof stumbling away, disappearing up that grotty little alley behind the old hostel, leaving behind three people having some kind of confrontation: two dark-haired figures in sober business black facing a tall blonde woman in a long blonde coat. The woman shifted as though to keep herself square-on to them, and as she turned, he could see, behind her, holding her hand, a small shape in a bright blue jumper and dark red trousers and he knew who the woman was, and who the child was, and he screamed her name.

*

Eve could barely keep track of what was happening. Her wrist was hurting badly, and she was feeling horribly sick. The three grownups were all talking angrily at once, all trying to persuade each other to do things, but nothing they said was making any sense to her. She wanted Mama, because if she was here then everything would be all right and she wouldn't have to try and understand any of it; or Papa, because he was so big and strong there would be no arguing about anything, he would just pick her up and take her home and that would be that; or even Gabe, because he was good at explaining things and cheering her up when she was down, and although this was a lot worse than just feeling grumpy, he would still know how to fix it. Or all of them, she wanted *all* of them, and she wanted to be *home*. She was trying hard not to cry because she knew that would only make her more sick and muddled, but the tears were rising in her throat and she did not know how much longer she could swallow them back. She closed her eyes, squeezing tight, and above the clamour of the adults and the confusion of her name flying back and forth between them, she thought she heard one of the voices she longed for.

It sounded like Gabriel, but not normal Gabriel: this was a *frantic* Gabriel, a *frightened* Gabriel – a Gabriel who was desperately calling her name, and she had to hear it a third time before her eyes snapped open and she looked. A flood of relief, greater than anything she had ever known, washed through her, because it really was her brother and he was running towards them along the river-walk, him and Agwé, and he was shouting at the other people now, shouting at them to get away from her, to leave her alone.

Business-Suit Man and Business-Suit Woman backed off as they raced up, the woman glancing worriedly over at the jetty with the boat and the waiting men.

The blonde lady holding Eve's hand did not move except to turn her head and pass her gaze over them as if they were not that interesting. Gabriel was breathing hard, and he glared at Blonde Lady, a brief, bitter look, as if he knew exactly who she was and didn't like what he knew. Eve moved to go to him, but Blonde Lady's fingers tightened and held her back – not harshly, as Brown-Coat had, but with caution, as though this too might be someone from whom Eve needed protecting. Eve stopped, and Gabriel's eyes widened.

'Eve,' he gasped, 'Evie, what are you doing? Come over here.'

'She's quite all right,' said Blonde Lady in that dismissive, irritated voice, and only looked surprised when Eve tugged at her hand.

'Please,' Eve whispered, the sobs very close to the surface now, 'I want to go to my brother.'

The woman looked down at her in amazement. 'Your brother,' she said in a wondering voice. 'Your *brother*? Who is your brother?'

Eve pointed at Gabriel, standing next to Agwé with a look on his face she didn't think she had ever seen before. It was the look of someone who is terribly, terribly afraid and trying hard not to show it.

'Him – that's my brother,' she told Blonde Lady. 'His name is Gabe. Gabriel.'

The woman's eyes, dark grey like her own, widened when she heard the name and she stared at Gabriel, then at Agwé, as though something she had not yet understood was becoming clear to her.

'Gabriel,' she whispered. 'Gabriel is your brother. Of course.' The fingers on Eve's slipped, loosening, but there was something about the shock in the woman's voice, something sounding close to tears in it, that made Eve not pull away, made her wait to be released. The woman's long, strong fingers slid over her small, cold ones like a caress, gentle and sad, and finally slipped free. 'Go to your brother then, Eve.'

Eve ran, and Gabriel met her in one stride and swept her up, holding her tight, backing away fast from the Blonde Lady and the others, saying, 'Eve – oh, Eve. Oh Evie, thank goodness, thank goodness, we were so scared, we were so scared,' and she could feel that he was shaking and he was hot from running and his heart was hammering as hard as hers was, and she finally felt safe enough to cry a little.

The blonde woman stayed where she was, watching them, and Eve caught a teary glimpse of her face over Gabriel's shoulder as her brother turned towards where Agwé had been. She could never afterwards shake the feeling that, although the woman was standing still as a statue, strong and regal and with a countenance as impenetrable as stone, in that moment an avalanche or a tidal wave or some other cataclysm beyond imagining was crashing down on her.

Business-Suit Woman broke and ran first, skittering across the riverwalk cobbles towards the waiting boat, shouting at Business-Suit Man as she looked back – but she was staring up, above their heads, and now Eve heard other feet too, running hard, coming closer, moving incredibly fast.

'Madam,' Business-Suit Man called to Blonde Lady, beckoning as he ran after the woman, 'madam, come quickly! *Quickly!*'

The expression on the blonde lady's face when she turned to him was one that Eve did not properly have a name for then, although in later years when she remembered the moment she would recognise it as complete, venomous contempt.

'I have no business with you,' said Blonde Lady, and looked up.

There was a huge whoosh of displaced air, a waft of chill breeze on her face, and Aunty Aryel dropped lightly onto the riverwalk between Eve and Gabriel and the Blonde Lady.

'About time,' said Blonde Lady.

Whoever was running blew past them and caught Business-Suit Man just short of the jetty, knocking him off his feet as though he were a toy and sending him crashing to the ground so fast that he spun away across the stone pavement, arms and legs and coat whirling round in the air. The running figure barely paused but swerved to leap onto the jetty where Business-Suit Woman was scrambling desperately towards the boat. But something had gone wrong there, Eve realised, because the men in the boat were shouting curses and trying to do something with the motor and the boat was skewing sideways across the river's surface and then it came slamming into the jetty and knocked Business-Suit Woman over too.

The motor died. The pursuing figure stopped, keeping his own balance easily, and now Eve recognised the dark brown of his skin and the ruby shimmer of his hair.

On the opposite side of the jetty from the crippled boat there was a glimmer of deep green, just as radiant, as Agwé pulled herself up a ladder and out of the water.

Aunt Aryel raised a reproving eyebrow at Blonde Lady and called, 'Rhys? They're not going anywhere.' Then she turned anxiously to where Gabriel was crouching on the riverwalk with Eve in his arms.

'Eve, darling, are you all right?' She knelt quickly and hugged them both before sitting back on her heels to peer at Eve, stroking her tear-stained face while her wings fanned out behind like some great, rich cape. When Eve looked up, she could see Blonde Lady watching silently.

'No,' she wailed, 'my hand hurts and I have a headache and I want to go *home!*' She sniffed hard and batted at her eyes, but the tears kept leaking out.

'Mama and Papa are almost here, sweetheart, and Uncle Eli and Aunty Sharon and everybody else, they're all right behind us, it's just that Uncle Rhys and I were a little quicker. I think we need Dr Rhys now,' she said, glancing back over her shoulder, and then she stood up and stepped aside. Eve didn't understand the look Uncle Rhys threw at Blonde Lady as he passed her, or at Aryel, but then it was him crouching down in front of her and Gabe, looking at each of her eyes and asking how she felt in his doctor voice, gently examining her bruised wrist, then tapping at his earset and requesting medical transport.

And finally, coming up behind them, over the sound of more running feet and the squeal of approaching sirens and Uncle Rhys' doctor questions, finally, *finally*, she could hear her mother's voice.

Gabriel could feel their arrival in the waves of relief that washed over him as Gaela threw her arms around him and Eve, who he was still holding close. Bal followed, bodily picking them both up, and Gabriel scrabbled as he was lifted. He found his feet and turned into their embrace, releasing Eve to them and saying, 'Careful, her wrist is hurt – sprained, maybe. Rhys says she needs to go to hospital.'

Eve was sobbing without restraint now, and his mother was fighting back her own tears so as not to make it worse, and Papa, wrapping his arms around them both, was weak with gratitude that his children were safe. Gabriel had a moment of déjà vu that resolved into a memory: himself, littler then than Eve was now, brought safely to earth in the arms of his winged aunt and being handed back to his frantic mother. Aryel had saved them both that day, but although she had once more swept in with the cavalry, he knew that this time it wasn't she who'd rescued Eve.

Aryel knew it too. Zavcka Klist had finally moved, retreating to stand with her back to the blank wall of the old hostel and after a few swift words to the others, Aryel walked over to her. He had caught enough from Zavcka's mind, coupled with the look Aryel had thrown her way, to suspect they were best left to it – and anyway, he was surrounded by clamour. Sharon and Mikal had arrived with his parents, all racing over from the lane where they'd had to leave the car because of the bollards. Seconds later Callan and Eli came up, puffing and blowing after the run from Maryam House, and all the while more and more police officers were arriving, trotting towards them from both directions along the riverwalk. Out on the water, a patrol boat was cruising towards the jetty where Agwé was still standing, hands on hips, contemplating the boat she had somehow managed to sabotage and its cursing occupants.

Rhys had gone over to check on the man he'd sent flying, who was now sitting up painfully. Aunt Sharon was already there, several loops of toughened biopolymer restraints dangling from one fist. She looked around until she spotted Uncle Mik, who pointed at the injured man and called, 'That's him! That's the one I saw with her!' and nodded grimly.

Gabriel realised that Uncle Mik was talking about the darkhaired woman, the one who'd run out onto the jetty. She must have clambered back to the riverwalk and thus been the first to encounter a severely ticked-off Detective Superintendent Varsi, for she was slumped awkwardly on the stone pavement now, her coat rucked up uncomfortably, back pressed against the rail with her hands behind her in a pose he recognised from a thousand crime dramas. He scanned the scene again, feeling weirdly disconnected, as though he had somehow fallen into one of the more melodramatic productions. Far too much was happening far too quickly; it felt implausible that only a handful of minutes could have passed since he had found his sister.

He felt Eli's mind swim up against his a moment before a comforting hand landed on his shoulder. 'Gabriel. Are you okay?'

'I think so.' He looked over at Zavcka, who stood, arms folded, responding to Aryel in a clipped, peremptory manner, all the while surveying the scenario in which she found herself much as he himself had done a moment before. Her smoke-dark gaze fell on him and he shivered. 'I'm just trying to understand . . . *She* called?'

'She did: she said that Eve had been kidnapped and that she believed the kidnappers were planning to use the river to get away. She was on her way there and was going to try to get the precise location – but Aryel was in a meeting at Bel'Natur, so Zavcka had to leave a message, which Aryel didn't get right away. She took off for here the moment she heard it, but she couldn't get hold of Sharon because *she* was calling in the bulletin on Eve. So Aryel forwarded Zavcka's message to her and tried Gaela – who was on with you, I think – and finally she got through to Bal and connected me and Callan and Rhys, and we all got here as fast as we could. Thank goodness Rhys was home today.'

Eli glanced over at the two women. Aryel was talking in even, firm tones; Zavcka, her jaw set and stubborn, was not looking at her. 'I imagine Aryel is pointing out that she could just have called police emergency and stayed home.'

Gabriel snorted. 'She'd never do that – what if they hadn't believed her, or hadn't prioritised it quickly enough?' He closed his eyes for a moment, concentrating over the distance, then said, 'The way she sees it, once she moved, people would be *forced* to pay attention.'

'So she wouldn't be asking,' Eli mused, 'she'd be *compelling*?'

'That's what I'm getting.'

Eli chuckled and examined Zavcka with a kind of amused disapproval. 'That's so like her.'

She must have felt his gaze because she turned and glared balefully back at him.

Sharon tramped past, heading for Zavcka and Aryel, and as one, Gabriel and Eli turned and followed her. Uncle Mik was still helping his parents, and Eve had now calmed down and was wrapped up in Bal's coat as they waited for the hospital transport. Callan had gone over to Rhys, his handsome face tight with outrage, his blue coat swirling with a glamour not even Zavcka Klist could match. The man on the ground must not be in too bad shape because Rhys had left him there and was standing with his arm around Callan's waist, watching her.

Sharon stopped in front of Zavcka, exchanged a swift glance with Aryel and tapped the remaining restraints meaningfully against her thigh. 'I understand you placed a device on your tracking collar to disable it,' she said conversationally. 'May I see?'

Zavcka silently twitched the scarf to one side to show her the dull red band clamped around the collar.

'What is it, out of interest?'

'I have no idea,' Zavcka drawled, tucking the scarf back into place. 'Something I found in a drawer in my kitchen. My staff had nothing to do with this,' she added sternly. 'The first thing I did was send them away, out of the house. They have no idea.'

'I doubt that, unless they got far enough away not to hear the proximity alarms go off when you left. Those things make quite a racket.'

'Indeed they do.' She smiled wryly. 'I had a good long walk to find a taxi rank that was out of earshot.'

'And no one accosted you?'

'I don't look like an escaping convict.'

The corner of Sharon's mouth twitched, but she did not smile back. 'Just to be clear,' she said, 'since you did not, in fact, attempt to disable the tracker, and you alerted Aryel both to your departure and your concerns for Eve, am I to take it that escape was never your intention?'

'That seems a logical conclusion to me, Detective Superintendent. Are you arresting me or not?'

'I haven't decided yet,' Sharon drawled back, and glanced round at their audience. She cocked her head enquiringly at Gabriel.

'She's not trying anything,' he said, then added, 'At the moment.'

'In that case, I'm not arresting you, Ms Klist. At the moment.'

She turned to Agwé, who had left the jetty at a run and now charged up to them. 'What did you do out there?'

'Fouled the propeller so they couldn't get away,' she said, 'but that wasn't the only reason. I thought I recognised the boat, and I was right – Gabe, that's the boat that was at Sinkat, but the people in it, they aren't EM techs.'

Gabriel felt the fear washing off of her as she said to Sharon, 'They're the men you've been looking for! The toxin suspects. They've grown beards and they kept trying to hide their faces, but I finally got a good look when they had to stand up. I'm *positive* it's them—'

As one, Sharon and Gabriel swung towards the boat, staring, and then Gabriel strode over to the woman, the one in the black business suit, her wrists clamped tightly to the riverwalk's safety rail by one of Sharon's restraints. Another officer was dealing with her, but Gabriel shouldered past him and shouted, 'What did they do?' He pointed at the stalled boat and the two men now standing up with their hands at shoulder-height, palms out in the surrender pose, as the river patrol edged up alongside. 'What did they do at Sinkat? *What did you have them do?*'

He was shrieking at her, spittle flying and a vein throbbing in his temple, and she flinched and tightened her lips. He didn't expect an answer and she didn't offer one, but he guessed that in the face of such an onslaught she wouldn't be able to keep herself from thinking it and he was right; he could feel the shapes form in her mind as she remembered the instructions she had given, her shaky attempt to calculate whether it was better to speak or be silent – all of it blurred by her fear that even this far away they were too close to be safe, what time was it now, how close was too close, was she far enough away to be safe?

He concentrated harder—

—and then he was reeling back as though from a blow and swinging round, desperate with the urgency of what he had discovered. Aunt Sharon was right behind him, along with Agwé and the confused patrol officer.

'Gabriel,' said Sharon, 'what is it?'

'Bombs,' he replied, his voice echoing back at him from a place of such horror that he could barely comprehend it, 'disruptors. The quantum cells—' He turned and ran.

29

Once more Gabriel raced with Agwé at his side, but this time they had covered almost no distance before Rhys was alongside them, slowing his pace to match theirs, and shadowed by Aryel overhead.

'Get them *out*,' Gabriel screamed at the sky, 'go ahead, get them out, *get them out!*'

She rose, flying swift and straight, and Rhys accelerated away as though they were merely jogging, taking corners faster and more surely than they could ever manage. Gabriel's earset buzzed and he flicked it on without slowing.

'Maintain this call,' Sharon said, all Detective Superintendent Varsi now, her voice brusque, not wasting time. 'We need an open channel. I'm linking in Aryel as well. We have police and fire on their way, but you'll get there first.'

By the time they came panting up to the Sinkat quayside a few minutes later, alarms were screeching from several of the buildings that lined the basin and a confused trickle of people had started coming over the first of the bridges – but there were a lot more milling around in front of Thames Tidal Power, where Aryel was standing, her wings splayed wide to make herself bigger than she was, waving people to get out, shouting at them to *move faster*, to *just go!* The UrbanNews crew had their vidcam trained on her; they didn't appear to understand that she meant them too.

'Below,' Gabriel said, 'the residences – the water entries – they can evacuate quicker . . .'

'Got it,' said Agwé, and dived smoothly into the basin. She was wearing her cherry-coloured bodysuit today and he watched the streak of red flashing through the brown depths as he followed topside, shoving past the evacuees on the bridge, sensing with despair that people behind him were slowing and turning, uncertainty morphing into hesitation as they saw him running towards the very place they had been told to run away from. When he got to her, Aryel was simultaneously trying to explain to Pilan, ignore the news team's shouted questions and urge others to hurry.

'Rhys went inside with Lapsa to clear people out; he can move faster,' she said to Gabriel, 'but everyone's stopping to ask questions: is it really a bomb threat, how do we know? A bunch of TTP staff have set off the alarms and gone to evacuate the other buildings, but I don't see them coming out fast enough . . .'

Over their earsets Sharon heard, and swore.

'Yes,' said Pilan, 'that's what I mean: exactly what *kind*—' then he saw the look on Gabriel's face and stopped.

Gabriel swung round, looking for something that would give him height, then clambered up onto one of the recycling units set into the stone quay. The UrbanNews crew trained their equipment on him. *So much for a low profile*, he thought, but he knew that if he didn't make them all understand, *fast*, it wouldn't matter any more.

'Listen to me,' he shouted, turning from side to side so he could see the people streaming out of the Thames Tidal airlocks topside and below, trickling slowly out of neighbouring buildings, mounting the bridges and massing on the quays. *'Listen to me!'*

Finally they heard and saw and stopped, and he screamed, 'Listen! I got this out of the head of the person who ordered it: they're *not* just bombs! They're tapping into the quantum cells –

344

they're designed to release *that* energy! Do you understand me? They're *detonators*; it's the quantum cells that're the explosives. *DO YOU UNDERSTAND?* We've only got minutes, *WE'VE ONLY GOT MINUTES*, so *run*! *RUN!*'

There was a moment like a short, sharp gasp for breath as what he was telling them sank in and then – *at last!* – they started running, properly shifting, shouting at each other, the strong and the quick helping the weak and the slow; children and babies snatched up in their parents' arms as they fled. His words were shouted back to those who had not heard and his plea swept into the buildings around Sinkat like a wave, and by the time he jumped back down onto the quayside, alarms were screeching from *every* building and the stream of people fleeing on foot and underwater had become a flood.

'They're moving now,' he muttered into the earset. 'Your people need to help ferry them away from here, fast.'

'Understood,' his aunt said, and spared a moment to add warmly, 'Well done, Gabe.' He heard her barking orders.

Aryel was shouting at the dumbstruck vidcam crew who looked too stunned by the story they now found themselves on top of to know what to do. 'There!' she cried, pointing towards the exits from the basin, 'go and cover the evacuation – that's where the police will be arriving. We need to clear this area; *go!*'

And at last they went, the reporter talking into her throat mic as she ran.

Pilan grabbed Gabriel's shoulder, his copper-dark face as pale as Gabriel had ever seen it, even when he'd been ill.

'How many minutes?' he said urgently. 'How much time have we got?'

'What time is it now?' Gabriel fumbled for his tablet, but before he'd got it out, Aryel had flicked at her band and told him.

'If they go off at 13.00 hours like they planned we've got fifteen minutes, but that woman – Moira Charles – she wasn't confident it would be exact. She was thinking they knew the devices would work, but could only work out approximately how long they'd take—'

'That's why she was so desperate to get to the boat,' Aryel said, and Gabriel nodded.

Pilan turned, shouting at the Thames Tidal staff who had lingered to listen, and with a few words he organised them into sweeper teams to check the buildings lining the basin, instructing them to herd any stragglers out and away and on no account to return themselves. As the teams went running, he spun back to Gabriel.

'Can we disarm these things? If they're detonators, can't we just detach them?'

'I don't know. She didn't think they could be removed, but maybe—' But he was speaking to the soles of Pilan's webbed feet, disappearing beneath the water; he'd dived in leaving barely a ripple.

'Where's Agwé?' asked Aryel, and he told her. 'Good,' she said, 'but they need to get out of there. *You* need to get out of here.'

'So do you. I'm not leaving until everyone is safe.' He ignored Sharon's imprecation over the earset. Aryel raised an eyebrow at him, but did not bother to try and send him away again.

As another group of people appeared at the Thames Tidal main topside airlock, confused and stumbling in their haste to get to safety, Gabriel recognised some of his colleagues from the secure laboratories deep within.

'Aunt Aryel,' he said, 'the infostream, the data – if we lose the building . . .'

'Herran's already on it.'

Rhys chivvied the final few stragglers and Gabriel ran to help, and with a few more words sent them flying along the quay.

'That's it for this one,' said Rhys, 'at least in the topside spaces. Lapsa went to clear out below.'

'Agwé's doing that too – she should be done, they need to get out. Pilan went to see if he could remove the detonators and he hasn't come back yet either.' Gabriel was hopping in his anxiety; he spun round at a splash behind them.

Pilan was pulling himself up one of the ladders that dropped down into the water, shaking his head in disgust. 'It's like a kind of maglock,' he said. 'They've tapped into the actual cells somehow; I can't just pull it off.'

Rhys threw his coat at Gabriel and kicked off his shoes. 'Show me.'

He and Pilan hit the water together and disappeared, swimming down along the convex lobes of the building. People were still pouring out of the buildings around Sinkat Basin, coming through doors topside and portals below, moving fast underwater and running along the quays and over the bridges, pausing only to gape uncertainly at Gabriel and Aryel standing there and speeding up again when they screamed at them to *move*, to *RUN*!

As Aryel took off to check the upper floors and rear of the buildings, Gabriel could see the uniformed figures of police and fire officers begin to appear at the entrances to the basin, the nearest they would've been able to get their vehicles. He let Sharon know, adding, 'They need to concentrate on getting people away, out of blast range, and to check the buildings at that end too if they can. We're pretty sure the ones down here are clear.' He broke off as Lapsa powered up from below carrying Pilan's utility vest, heavy with his engineering tools. Agwé was right behind her.

'You have to *go*,' she sputtered at her foster-mother as they broke the surface together.

'I thought something in here might help,' Lapsa gasped, holding up the vest and looking around. 'Where is he?'

Gabriel reached down to grab it from her. 'Below, with Rhys. They've been gone a l—' He broke off as two shapes bulleted up from the murky depths of the basin.

Rhys erupted out of the water to at least half his body length, such was the force of his ascent, and splashed back down, breathing in huge gasps.

Pilan's head popped up with far less drama and he shouted, 'He got one! Rhys is strong enough to pull them off!' He spotted the vest in Gabriel's hands, whipped round until he saw Lapsa and Agwé and bellowed at them. 'What the fuck are you still doing here? Get out, go up the canal – *now!*'

'But—'

'It's at an angle to the basin, if there's a blast, you'll have some protection!'

Gabriel could feel Pilan doing the calculations and judging that would be the safest place they could reach in the shortest time; his focus was switching back and forth between the two women and the devices underwater and what he had learned from the way Rhys had twisted one of them loose, wondering whether he could generate the same torque using a lever of some kind, whether the quantum cells embedded in the biopolymer of the walls had already been damaged and rendered unstable.

Gabriel leaned down towards the water and handed Pilan the vest almost before he reached up for it. Their eyes met, and Gabriel felt the thought the other man wanted him to have.

'I will,' he mouthed, and Pilan nodded grimly and turned in the water. Lapsa was still hanging there, staring at him, while Agwé was trying fruitlessly to get her to turn and swim away.

'Lapsa,' said Pilan, dragging on the vest, 'we don't have time. I'll come and find you as soon as it's safe. I love you, and I *really* need you to go. Agwé, get her out of here.'

'We're going. Gabe?'

'I'll be right behind you,' he said, and knew that she knew it was a lie. She gave him a long look, and he felt a very clear, very specific thought form in her mind and felt his own eyes widen at the import of it. Then she caught hold of Lapsa and they turned and swam away at high speed. Pilan had already disappeared beneath the surface.

'It's not easy or fast,' Rhys called up from the water, still gulping air but in a more measured way now, deliberately hyperventilating before he went below again. 'Gabe, how many are there?'

That information had not been in Moira Charles' mind. 'I'll find out,' he said. Rhys nodded and went under again as Gabriel asked, 'Aunt Sharon? We need to know how many of those things there are. Rhys has disarmed one and Pilan thinks maybe he can too, but they don't know how many they're looking for.'

'One moment,' she said in her crisp Detective Superintendent voice. He heard her mute the earset and took a moment to look around. There was hardly anyone exiting the buildings anymore, topside or below. He shouted at the stragglers to hurry up as Aryel appeared above the rooftops, sweeping past windows to peer in. She looked down at him and he gave her a thumbs-up as she curved away, making a final perimeter check of the basin.

Rhys surfaced, gulped air, raised his hand with three fingers splayed to show how many of the bombs had been disabled and was gone below again before Sharon came back on.

'Twelve,' she reported, 'one for each building segment.' There was a world of impotent fury in her voice. 'Gabriel, get out of there.'

'We're getting them,' he said. 'Rhys has done two, Pilan one.'

'There isn't enough time – they could go at any moment, you said so yourself.'

'Or they might take longer than they thought. Aunt Sharon, I'll go as soon as I know there's nothing more I can do.' He hesitated, then said, 'If I don't get out in time, tell my family—'

'Gabriel, don't you dare. Don't you *dare* make me have to do that!' There was a break in his aunt's voice he had never heard before. 'Your mother was frantic when she and Eve left for the hospital. Your father's still here; he's losing his mind, it's all Mikal can do to hold him back. *Don't you dare.*'

Aryel came on, calm and almost amused. 'Suppose there's no point me making the same request, then?'

'You're airborne. You can get away.'

'Not likely. If the whole thing goes, it'll blow whatever's left of me halfway to Hammersmith.' Gabriel saw her hovering above the far end of the basin. 'Damn. Still a bunch of people over here,' she said. She told Sharon where to send support and dropped out of sight.

Rhys came up again and flashed five fingers. Gabriel shouted back, 'Twelve total,' showing his own fingers, ten then two. He checked the time and his insides constricted. 'Six minutes left,' he shouted.

Rhys nodded, and dived.

'Five down,' Gabriel said to Sharon. He didn't need to tell her that Rhys and Pilan were removing the detonators at the rate of roughly two a minute now, but there were still seven to go.

They have time, he thought. *Enough to spare, maybe, if they keep knocking them off at this rate. The countdown isn't precise; you said it yourself, you felt it in her head. They disrupt the cell stasis, but the terrorists weren't able to calibrate exactly how long it would take. They could go off two, maybe even three minutes late.*

Or early.

It was cold beneath the water, and none too bright, but Rhys had night vision to go with his strength and his speed, and although his ability to withstand the chill was nothing compared to a gillung's, it was far superior to any norm's. Besides, he was working too hard, too fast, with too great a sense of impending doom, to notice. There was a metronome in his head counting down the seconds, the minutes, from Gabriel's shouted warning. There was no time for the cold, the burning in his lungs, the ache in his arms and the stinging in his fingers; still less for the thoughts of Callan that kept trying to intrude against the ticking of that clock. It was not until his hands cramped up on the sixth device that he realised he was freezing, becoming distracted and losing dexterity. That, along with the rapidly dwindling oxygen levels in his blood, would slow him, making him lose focus, even start to panic if he was not careful. He let go of the slippery disc and slowly and methodically clenched and unclenched his fingers before trying again. If he didn't get it on the next go, he would have to lose precious seconds surfacing for a breath before he could make another attempt.

There it was: the tiniest movement, the slimmest of gaps. He shoved the tips of his fingers beneath the mechanism, wincing at the pinch to his already sore skin, and twisted. He felt more than saw the water flood in behind the seal and break it; there was a thrum in his hands as the weak circuit that had formed between the device and the cell-thin layers of quantum battery buried deep in the biopolymer shorted out. He'd had a belated presentiment of folly with the first one, imagining himself electrocuted underwater by a massive discharge when the detonator pulled free, but it was only a small spark; whatever the device was doing was internal to the cells, disrupting them and breaking down the subtle tensions that held huge energies in stasis. He knew enough about the physics of quantum storage to have been able to imagine, as he slowly and painfully twisted one after the other off the energy-rich walls of the Thames Tidal Power building, how the devices were doing what they were doing.

He let the thing fall and kicked for the surface, glancing right and left for any glimpse of Pilan, who was working with some great angled tool that Rhys thought must've been used to manoeuvre parts of the estuary turbines into position. Pilan was at heart a *maker*, a man who liked to build things with his own hands; he had started as a field engineer in the Gempro underwater construction business and it had been he who had first seen how to integrate the delicate bioelectrics of quantum-energy storage into the tough layered polymers and resin-stone that could keep them stable, accessible and rechargeable. He had jury-rigged a system to power the first free gillung encampment, and gathered a team of refugee technicians to help refine and perfect it as the years went by. Nothing, not even the demands of a growing company, had ever made him lose sight of the importance of getting down to work with everyone else, of leading by example.

Rhys breached without spotting or sensing Pilan, and gulped air. Gabriel was still on the quay, scanning the water anxiously, and now he ran to lean over the nearest rail.

'I've done six,' Rhys called up to him. 'Pilan?'

'I think he's somewhere there,' Gabriel shouted back, pointing. 'He's not coming up as often as you. Maybe four?'

Rhys stroked for the spot, ignoring the pain in his shoulders, and dived deep. He found Pilan grappling with one of the devices that had been tucked under the curving surface at an awkward angle. His lever kept slipping. Rhys swam up and helped muscle it into position, then braced his back in the angle between the wall and the metal bar. They heaved, and another detonator went skittering down. Pilan showed five webbed fingers and pointed at himself, then at Rhys. Rhys showed him six, and pointed up.

They surfaced together. 'One to go!' Pilan shouted up at Gabriel as Rhys caught his breath and tried to still his shivering. 'Just have to find it.'

Gabriel gave them a thumbs-up and spoke into his earset. The countdown in Rhys' head told him they had a little over two minutes left. *Plenty of time*, he thought, but when they found the last detonator he knew that he was wrong: it was in a cramped corner at the deepest part of the building, stuck to the underside barely a foot above the silty bottom. The diver who'd placed it there must have pulled himself along headfirst and then extended his arm fully. There was no room for them both, and anyway, Rhys' stiffening hands could get no purchase. He kicked free, watched for a few seconds as Pilan squirmed under and tried to snag it with his lever, then tapped him and pointed up.

'We can't,' Rhys gasped as they broke the surface, 'not in the time we have. But it's the last one and it's furthest away from where there are any people.' He swivelled in the water and saw Gabriel, still on the quay, still refusing to leave, leaning over the rail and waiting for the signal that would tell him they were all safe. The timer in his head said less than a hundred seconds. 'Leave it, Pilan. Let's get out of here.' His teeth were chattering now, and he could barely feel his hands or feet.

'I can reach it,' the Thames Tidal boss said, 'and I'll be damned if I'll let them destroy this place. All our work is here, everything we've built. But you need to get out of the water.' He grabbed Rhys and kicked for the ladder. He shoved Rhys up it, and Gabriel reached down and helped drag him onto the quay.

'I need a little more time!' Pilan called up. 'Don't wait for me – you have to get Rhys out of here – he's hypothermic.'

'But—' Gabriel shouted back.

Pilan bellowed, 'Go!' and disappeared.

Rhys dragged himself to his feet, and as Gabriel helped him pull on his discarded coat and shoes, he felt his supercharged circulation start to bring tingling, painful life back into his fingers and toes.

'He's mad,' he said to Gabriel. 'It's in a terrible position; it's going to take too much time—' He broke off, staring along the quay at a figure that had appeared at one of the side passages that led to safety. Instead of heeding the alarms or the shouts of police to come back, he was running *towards* them: a figure with flaming red hair, dressed in a flamboyant, royal-blue coat.

Rhys' heart lurched.

Beside him, Gabriel saw, or maybe just felt the surge of panic, and said, 'What?'

'Callan,' Rhys gasped. 'What the *hell* is he—?' and moved to go to him, then looked back at Gabriel, standing there on the quay, helplessly waiting for Pilan to surface again, and made a decision.

He reached around Gabriel's back and grabbed his upper arm on the far side, clamping both of the young man's arms against his torso so that he could not hit out with them, and began to jog towards Callan, dragging Gabriel along. He tried to pull away, stumbling, but Rhys was many times stronger and he formed the thought clearly so that Gabriel would know it too.

'I am going and I am not leaving you, so either I carry you or

354

you run,' he said aloud, through gritted teeth; they were already rapidly leaving the Thames Tidal quayside behind. Rhys waved Callan back with his free arm: *Go back, go back, don't come any closer.*

'There's nothing we can do to help Pilan, do you understand?'

He's my friend too, and he's not doing this so we can risk our lives just to keep him company, he thought at Gabriel. *He's made his choice: we have to respect that.*

Gabriel cried out, a little gasp of anguish, and then he stopped resisting, got his feet under him and started to move in earnest. Rhys shifted his grip to Gabriel's elbow and ran as fast as he could without pulling him off his feet. He heard him mumbling into his earset as they went.

'Aunt Aryel,' he was saying, almost crying, 'time to go. Get down somewhere safe.'

If there was a reply, Rhys did not hear it. They reached Callan, who had turned but kept looking back over his shoulder as though afraid to let them out of his sight. Rhys grabbed his husband with his other hand and dragged them along on either side as he ran, desperately aware that if he missed his footing, or if anyone tripped, they would spin off at speed and most likely be injured. It was a risk he had to take. The metronome in his head had ticked down to the target point and past it; now it was plus ten seconds, plus fifteen, plus twenty.

They were at the far end of the basin now and swerving off the quay into a side road. At the head of it he could see massed ranks of police and ambulances and fire vehicles, and the news crew with their vidcam pointed towards them; he heard the sounds of a frightened mob and the shouts of officers shepherding them back. It looked as though many of the evacuees were still no more than a hundred yards away from the quayside.

He just had time to think, *Bloody hell, they're way too close – if we hadn't cleared so many they'd have been WAY too close . . .*

Then the explosion slammed into them, lifted them off their feet and threw them towards the retreating crowd.

30

Even though the investigation quickly established that development of the quantum-battery disruptors had begun even before work on the toxin-producing algae – that Moira Charles had, in fact, set out to buy or steal the secrets of quantum storage years before – Mikal Varsi could not shake the suffocating feeling that it was somehow all his fault.

'If I hadn't told Mitford to get stuffed,' he said, over and over again, 'if I'd gone along with his plan – or pretended to . . . If he'd still believed he could win by undermining the company . . .'

'He was never just counting on that,' Sharon and Aryel told him, over and over again. 'He was always going to do this. He started by sowing doubts about TTP's competence and safety record – that's what the turbine sabotage and the toxin attacks were all about. They didn't expect us to uncover the truth, at least not as quickly as we did, and Kaboom was there to keep talking up the lie. Then one day the famous Thames Tidal building would just blow up, taking most of the members and directors with it, and it would look like everything they'd been warning about all along had come to pass. They'd already bought off or figured they could bully whoever was left in control of the company; it would have been a great coup for Bankside, and therefore Standard – and, let's not forget, the Traditional Democrats: Mitford was really multi-tasking here. You didn't start this, Mik, and you couldn't have stopped it.'

'I could have stopped it happening *then*. If I hadn't flipped Mitford off, he wouldn't have moved so soon . . .'

'If it hadn't happened then,' Aryel pointed out, 'we wouldn't have found out about it in time to save as many lives and as much of Sinkat as we did. If Moira Charles hadn't pulled the trigger before she found out that Kaboom was compromised, Mitford's plan would have worked and many, *many* more people would have died.' She'd squeezed Mikal's big, increasingly stiff, double-thumbed hands in her own small strong ones. 'I know that doesn't make the one we lost any easier to bear, Mik. But if Pilan were here, he'd tell you the same thing. You know he would.'

And he did know. He knew, but he could not be convinced.

Of Pilan's body there was no trace. After days of painstaking searches through the wreckage of the iconic headquarters of Thames Tidal Power and the rest of Sinkat Basin, Sharon was forced to tell a grief-stricken Lapsa that there was nothing left to commit to the deep but memories. And so they had done that, this morning; they had gone down to the jetty at Riveredge Village at the head of a parade of mourners and boarded one of a great flotilla of boats heading out into the estuary. It was the first time Eve had been back to the river since her ordeal ten days earlier, and she held tight to Bal's and Gaela's hands as they approached the quayside, peering around for any sign of the Blonde Lady.

'She said I didn't know her, Mama,' she reported to Gaela, 'and that's true, I guess, 'cept I felt like I *did* know her, a little. She kind of reminded me of somebody.'

'Who, sweetheart?'

'I don't *know* who.' She'd pushed away the blonde curls tumbling over her forehead, even more tangled than usual now that she had the excuse of a bandaged wrist. 'At first I thought it was Aunty Aryel, 'cos the bad people had to stop and listen to her; they couldn't just do what they wanted and they were sort of afraid. But then Aunty Aryel actually *came*, and I thought no, she's really different. It's somebody else.' A massive shrug. 'But I don't know *who*.'

'Maybe you'll work it out one day, sweetie. But there's no rush.'

They had worried that the child would find the quayside embarkation too traumatic, until Gabriel, his own bruises still purpling his face and arms and hip, talked to her for a while and then told them she was fine, that she would be fine.

'She was scared, and she's still a bit on edge, but she's not fragile,' he'd said quietly. 'And I think it's important for her to understand that it wasn't just about her. That something really, really terrible did happen.'

The pall of it hung over all of them as the black-bannered boats proceeded down the Thames. It was an unseasonably warm day; the breeze chased small, fluffy clouds across a crystal-blue sky and sent little wavelets skipping merrily as though in defiance of their grief. Aryel flew for most of the way, matching the slow pace of the boats. When the banks fell away on either side as the procession entered the estuary, she dropped down to join Eli on the foredeck of a barge and they stood there with Rhys and Callan. Callan's left arm was in a sling and his right was tightly clasped by Rhys. The young genmed physician was the only one of the trio caught in the explosion's shockwave to appear unscathed, but Mikal suspected he was just as scarred by doubt about whether he could have moved faster, tried harder, whether there were things he might have done differently.

From where he stood in the stern with Sharon and their boys, and Bal, Gaela and Eve, Mikal could once more hear Aryel's mantra for these dreadful days, this time floating back from the bow: 'It wasn't your fault. There was nothing more any of us could have done.' He looked ahead to the lead boat, where Gabriel was travelling with Lapsa, Agwé and most of the surviving Thames Tidal team, and thought it might take the boy longer to believe than any of the rest of them, for the only one of his colleagues not there to mourn Pilan's passing was the source of the purloined secrets of quantum storage that had made the disruptors possible; the turncoat who had traded his people's lives for the wealth and power their deaths would have brought him; the traitor now banged up and awaiting the pleasure of the courts.

Qiyem.

Agwé had guessed it, knowing that the destruction of the facility and its people would profit no one if the knowledge of how to manufacture and manage the quantum batteries died with them, and wondering how the businesspeople they'd foiled on the Riveredge jetty could possibly have got that information. She'd recalled Qiyem's strange insistence that she leave early that day, and as she and Lapsa evacuated the lower storeys she'd confirmed that Qiyem had departed without explanation shortly after talking to her. The traces of his perfidy were now so clear that Gabriel felt a fool for having assumed a more reasonable explanation for why Qiyem was never, *ever* seen without his cranial band, despite never apparently using it.

'People think things they're ashamed of, they have fantasies they don't want anyone else to know about, they remember things they wish they hadn't done,' he'd said miserably from his hospital bed when Mikal had told him that Qiyem had been picked up trying to leave the city. 'I knew he was hiding something, but I thought it was that. I thought it was that.'

'It's not your fault,' Mikal had told him. 'He fooled everyone. You couldn't have known.' He felt like an actor in a bad play, saying his appointed lines in the endless round of useless consolation, aware that Gabriel was no more likely to consider himself blameless than he himself was. 'You couldn't have known,' is what they told each other, and 'I should have known,' is what they told themselves.

The streams were less concerned with the self-recriminations of those who had lost a friend than with unpicking the hard facts of precisely who had known or done precisely what to whom in the dizzying confluence of business and politics. Moira Charles had without doubt been at the heart of it, drawing on her network of contacts to activate various parts of the plan: Conrad Fischer for public relations, Patrick Crawford for the channelling of payments, various others for microflora modification, the engineering of quantum bioelectrics and other technical requirements. The mystery submersible waiting out in the estuary to spirit away the fleeing terrorists, their party belatedly doubled by last-minute instructions to collect Charles and her party from the Riveredge Village jetty, added a nicely retro flavour of drama and derring-do.

But, more serious minds enquired, just how far up did the conspiracy go?

Standard and Bankside denied all knowledge, as did Abraham Mitford. Arguments raged about the likelihood of the former, but the latter's protestations were dismissed out of hand; it beggared belief that so much of Mitford's money could have been siphoned into funding the plot without him being aware of it, and the relationship between Mitford and Charles was well known. On top of that, Councillor Mikal Varsi had made a statement to the police the day before the explosion, detailing threats Mitford had made against Thames Tidal.

The big question, the *huge* question, the question on which it appeared an election might hang, was whether Mitford's strategy had been sanctioned by anyone in his party. They denied it all, of course, and appeared perplexed to find themselves largely disbelieved.

One of the very rare moments of clear-eyed perspective came courtesy of Zavcka Klist, who was profoundly unimpressed with her former corporate bedfellows. 'You don't eliminate the brains behind an operation that you want to maintain,' she observed to Eli, who kept his next appointment with her a few days after the disaster. She was once more ensconced in her luxurious apartment, but her tracker's proximity alarms were now set to trigger alerts at police stations as well as with Offender Management monitoring teams. 'You *induce* them – take the business over, certainly, but in a way that keeps the key people in post and working hard. This appears to have been a strategy to steal a single clutch of golden eggs and slaughter the goose that laid them.' She'd shaken her head in irritation. 'Stupid and wasteful. I thought Abraham Mitford had more sense.'

Eli repeated the story now, several hours after the memorial ceremony out in the estuary, where the boats had clustered in the lee of one of the battery banks Pilan had lived to see built. The words had been said and the tears had been cried and the boats had returned up the river. Gabriel stopped off with Agwé and Lapsa, still settling into their new quarters in Limedog, and Rhys took a weary and aching Callan home; Mikal, Sharon, Aryel and Eli had come back to the flat above the café and sat there now with Gaela and Bal, listening to the sounds of the children playing in the garden below which came drifting in through an open window.

'I do not want to be agreeing with Zavcka Klist,' Mikal declared from his seat deep in an old and frighteningly comfortable arm-chair. 'I've had to do a lot of unpleasant things in my life, but I'm struggling with that one.'

'I'm tempted to say it's not her fault that she's right,' Eli replied. 'I won't,' he added, as they all looked at him.

'It's instructive,' Aryel murmured, 'to know what Zavcka's strategy would have been. We were lucky, in the end, that she wasn't behind this.'

'I suppose,' said Sharon. 'She's cold, that one. Did she even pretend to regret that Pilan lost his life, while she was busy critiquing Mitford's tactics?'

'She's not as cold as she was,' Eli told them. 'She wanted to know if Eve knew the man who died, if he'd been a friend whose death would affect her. I told her that yes, he'd been a friend of the family and her brother's boss, and his death was being felt very keenly. There didn't seem any point pretending otherwise.'

He hesitated for a long time, but Mikal knew his friend well and knew that he wasn't done. He sat up, expectant, as Eli pulled a small, flat package wrapped in delicate, pale gold paper out of the slide-pocket where it must have rested next to his tablet. He held it carefully, as if he was not sure how to continue.

Aryel put an encouraging hand on his knee.

'She said she was sorry, then,' Eli said. 'And she gave me something.'

They had been in her book-lined study once more, sipping the exquisite coffee Marcus had served and talking, although the subject this time was current events rather than history. Eli had hoped for this, despite knowing that questions about Eve would inevitably be part of the price. He was braced for a diatribe that did not come, although he decided later that Zavcka was most likely saving it up for Aryel.

Instead, she had looked at him over the rim of her cup: quiet, reflective. 'So,' she said, 'you're Uncle Eli.'

'I . . .' She would have heard and seen, there on the riverwalk. She had heard and seen Eve with all of them. 'Yes, I'm Uncle Eli.'

She did not look angry, or sad, or happy. She was just waiting, so he added, 'I don't think I'm her favourite, if it makes you feel any better.'

She waved that away as a matter of no moment, put her cup down and said without rancour, 'No, I would guess that's most likely Uncle Mikal, although I think she's very fond of you too. And Rhys of course, and Callan.'

He had said nothing, just watched her.

'And her Aunts Sharon and Aryel,' she had murmured, and there, finally, was a touch of the bitterness he'd been expecting, along with something else: the lingering amazement of someone who has witnessed a marvel and was still coming to terms with it. 'And is it Aunty Gwen as well?'

'When she's around, which isn't that often.'

'I see,' she said, and asked about Pilan, and he told her.

'So he wasn't one of the uncles. A friend, but not . . . one of the family.'

'No. I mean,' Eli said, thinking he had to explain, thinking too that even now he must be careful not to explain too much, 'she knows we're not her biological family.'

'That hardly matters, Dr Walker, as I think you understand very well.' Zavcka got up and walked over to the books, arms folded as they had been the first time he'd seen her stand there, although the attitude was different now: less calculated, less concerned with his presence. Her head was bowed in contemplation of something resting on the shelf. Then she picked it up in a rustle of wheat-coloured tissue paper and came back to stand next to him.

'This is very, very old,' she said. 'When I was born it was already almost as old as I am now.'

She handed the book in its wrapping to him and he gasped. It was a copy of *The Velveteen Rabbit*, with a brightly illustrated cover: the toy abandoned in the garden, bright button eyes peeping out from beneath a riot of pink and blue and yellow flowers and clumps of vivid green grass.

'It's for Eve,' Zavcka said, standing now at the window that overlooked the elegant park with its bare-branched trees. 'Read it first, go through it. Check to make sure I haven't tagged it somehow, or changed the text or anything. I haven't, but you'll want to make sure. Gaela will be able to tell. And Eve . . . She doesn't need to know who it's from. Make up whatever story you want.'

'Ms Klist,' he said, awestruck at the ancient, beautiful thing that he held. 'Zavcka. This is priceless.'

'So is she,' she said, and then, gazing out the window, 'I never understood why I liked it. I love that story, but I never knew why.'

'Because it touches on immortality?'

Her face when she turned from the window to look back at him was like nothing he could describe.

'But that's not what it's about, is it? I read it again last night. That's not what it's about at all.'

'Eve won't understand,' he said. 'She's eight years old. She's not you. Whatever it is you hope she'll grasp from this, she won't.'

'Not now. Not for a long while, and maybe not ever. But time is a funny thing, Dr Walker. It turns everything over in the end.'

Now he reached over and handed the book to Gaela. 'I've checked it,' he told her and Bal. 'I checked the text against archives of the original, I verified the edition with the university library, I had them run a spectrometer over it to make sure there was no hidden text or other tampering. I didn't want you to have to be the one to find it if she'd done anything, hidden anything. It's clean. The library was desperate to keep it.'

'What's she up to?' Bal asked, gently turning the pages. 'Does she really expect us to give this to Eve? What are you thinking?' he asked Gaela.

'I'm thinking that it's beautiful,' she said softly. 'And I'm also wondering what she's trying to do.'

'If I had to guess,' said Eli, 'I'd say she mostly just wants to give Eve a present.' Four pairs of eyes turned to him in disbelief. 'I know,' he went on, 'I know how unlikely that sounds. Maybe I'm wrong, maybe it is some kind of gambit. But I honestly don't think so. It's not subtle enough to be one of her schemes, and there was something about her when she handed it to me—' He stopped, remembering. 'I'd never seen her like that before.'

'Aryel,' asked Gaela, still leafing through the pages of the old storybook, 'do you think we should do it? Give this to Eve?'

'I think you should read it first, and judge it on its own merits,' Aryel replied. 'The book is not at fault for the person who owned it. As for what she's up to, I'll tell you what I think tomorrow.'

The next day Aryel Morningstar flew west, and alighted on the roof of an elegant townhouse situated in an exclusive garden square in the most expensive part of the city. Marcus met her up there in the cold sunshine and conducted her down to the apartment, into the presence of Zavcka Klist.

'Thank you for coming,' Zavcka said, her voice even but brittle.

'I told you,' Aryel replied, 'that I would if you asked.'

'You also told me that Eve was safe.'

Aryel regarded her steadily for a moment. They were in the study that Eli had described, with its walls of books, the low tables and comfortable chairs, Zavcka's work console on which she had been studying something when Aryel entered, the high window looking out onto the street and the square. It was a deeply personal space, neither austere nor intimidatingly lavish, the casual wealth no more calculated for effect than were Aryel's wings. This was, Aryel thought, the place where Zavcka was most purely herself. And the self she was being now was concerned, but not angry; upset, but not defeated; querying, because she was puzzled. There was something Zavcka wanted, but first there was something she wanted to understand.

'We believed she was,' Aryel said. 'The threat didn't come from the direction we thought most likely. But we've always known there was a risk that someone, somewhere, would work out her link with you.'

'They only worked it out because she was visible to them. You could have almost completely eliminated that risk. You could have put her in a private school, or had her home-tutored, like I was. You could have made sure she was never allowed at a public event, let alone on the street. You could have kept her completely out of sight, unreachable.' She waited for a reaction. Aryel did not give her one. 'It's one thing to have kept her kidnapping and my involvement off the streams, but have you changed any of the things that made her vulnerable in the first place?'

'No,' Aryel said. 'Eve's life continues as it was.'

'Why? It's not as though you don't care for her, beyond whatever value you think she might have as an asset. I saw that: all of you charging in, all those aunts and uncles. Gabriel, her brother. Gaela and Bal, her Mama and Papa: they're not just playing those roles. They *adore* her. They were sick with fear – I saw it. The look on Gabriel's face when she went to him, when he picked her up—'

Zavcka blinked and gave her head a tiny shake, as though she still could not quite believe what she'd witnessed. 'You weren't faking, none of you. I've had a hundred and twenty-odd years of dealing with sycophants and believe me, I can tell. So why are you letting her lead the kind of life where something like that can happen?'

Aryel seated herself, uninvited, on one of the low-backed chairs. 'You've just answered your own question, Zavcka,' she said steadily. 'Eve is not an asset, not remotely. If I were ever to think of her in those terms, I'd be more likely to conclude that she's a liability. But I don't, and I never will – none of us ever will. She lives the life she does, with all its risks and exposures, for the simple reason that her parents and her brother – and her aunts and uncles – love her dearly. We care for her far, far too much to let her have the childhood that you did.' She caught Zavcka's eyes and held them. 'That is the risk we will not run, and I think you already knew that. So why are you asking me these questions?'

She was half expecting an explosion, had chosen her words deliberately to provoke. Zavcka remained still and silent for a long moment, dark eyes burning with some emotion that was neither fury nor outrage. She sank into her own chair, the inner turmoil flaring finally into the briefest of outbursts, a note not of anger but of anguish; the cry of one trying to convince herself.

'I *haven't*—' She stopped, and now she looked trapped behind those eyes; hunted. She closed them and breathed deeply. Her hands twitched, but remained steady.

When she spoke again, her voice held just the faintest hint of a tremor. She sounded like someone who has committed herself to a course she knows will be painful, but necessary.

'Because I wanted confirmation,' she said. 'I wanted to see if you would make excuses, or try to convince me she's unimportant to you. I didn't think you would, but I wanted to be certain.'

'And now that you are?'

'Now that I am, I have a proposition for you. A business proposition.' A shadow of Zavcka's usual hauteur drifted back, as though she was moving onto surer ground.

Aryel felt a jolt of surprise, and caution. 'Really? The last one didn't work out that well,' she said acidly.

Zavcka smiled. 'I'd say it worked extremely well, for you and the people who, as you put it, you represent.' She indicated the screen. 'I've been looking into Bel'Natur's finances, and the current corporate structure. That idiot Crawford got me access. It's been enlightening.'

'I'm glad you think so. Is this where you tell me what you've been up to?'

'Nothing as terrible as you probably imagine. Stress-testing, mostly. I wanted to see how this new hierarchy – or non-hierarchy – would stand up.'

'You must be disappointed,' Aryel said evenly. 'There are some very good people there now. They don't get pushed over easily.'

'I can see that, and no, I'm not disappointed, not in the least. I was ready to be annoyed about it a couple of weeks ago, but under the current circumstances it's helped me come to a decision.'

Zavcka looked at Aryel and smiled again: an anticipatory smile, the smile of someone who is about to say something shocking and is looking forward to the reaction. 'I want you to become my business partner, and my executor.'

Aryel stared at her, thinking she could not possibly have heard correctly. Zavcka's knowing smile told her she had.

'That's impossible,' she said, and then, 'Why?'

'Partly because of this.' Zavcka flicked at the tablet screen, scrolling with an elegant finger. 'The way you set up the endowment from Bel'Natur to fund reproductive gemtech.'

The customary disdain in her voice was merely a top note

now to her amusement at Aryel's discomfiture. But there was something deeper in it as well, something that sounded very much like admiration. 'The way the payment schedule maximises income from the compensation we agreed for Herran is one of the cleverest things I've seen. It must give the accountants nightmares, but it's all legal so they can't complain. The governance structure is so transparent, I'll bet hardly anyone's noticed how *completely* sewn up the process is. What you negotiated with me was a contract that would last only for as long as we owed you money. I failed to grasp that you could translate it into an arrangement in perpetuity, especially if Herran continued to work on the development of psionic-interface technology. I also didn't foresee that you could leverage that into an ongoing presence within Bel'Natur, in the name of protecting the assets you hold in trust.'

She pushed the console aside, shaking her head ruefully at the screen as though it was to it that she was speaking. 'You've got no shareholding, no seat on the board, yet you have managed not only to materially affect the direction and structure of the company but to take out a chunk of its profits. Amazing.' She looked Aryel full in the face. 'I couldn't have done any better, not even when I was at the top of my game. Then there's your contribution to the company's overall resilience, which I suspect is considerable. In fact, my guess is that you had a word with the executives after you came to see me in prison. Am I right?'

Aryel nodded silently.

'Thought so. To say nothing of Bel'Natur's new reputation as an upstanding corporate citizen, which appears to be exemplary. That's astonishing, considering the gutter I left it in eight years ago; the recovery should have taken twice as long. That's real talent. It's what I want for my own affairs.'

'You haven't answered me, Zavcka.' Aryel heard the stridency in her own voice now and forced it down. 'Why?'

'For Eve,' Zavcka said. 'I want everything that I have to be placed in trust for her. I want to retain only enough for my own needs. I want to start to structure it now.'

'You want her to have *everything*?' Aryel asked, disbelieving.

'Yes.'

'You know that she's not you, and she's not going to be you. Her mind is her own.'

'I know that. I can see that. I have no designs on her.'

'Why do you need me? You could do this yourself: set it up, name her as the beneficiary.'

'I could, but then how would I convince you – or the world – that I'm not pursuing some strategy of which she is to be the eventual victim? It's one thing to have you working against me when our aims are opposed, Aryel, but it would be ridiculous when we both want the same thing. We both want what's best for Eve.'

'Why do you think having your fortune is what's best for her?'

That knocked her back a bit. For all her years in business, Zavcka had no experience, Aryel thought, when it came to questioning the value of money.

'What am I going to do with it?' she said finally. 'Despite what those idiots in the Klist Club think, I'm not going to live forever. I have no children, nor any other family.' She rubbed her fingers together meditatively, looking at them as she spoke. 'I'm ageing, Aryel. I may not look it, yet, but I feel it. My extended middle age is coming to an end.'

'You once had ambitions of extending it even further,' Aryel said, watching her narrowly.

'Once I did. I no longer do, but how many people are going to believe that?'

371

'Not very many,' Aryel said, beginning to understand. 'Unless I'm involved.'

'Exactly.' Zavcka tilted her head, looking up and to the side. It was a gesture so like Eve's when she was trying to explain something difficult that Aryel's breath caught in her chest.

'You once accused me of a lack of integrity,' Zavcka went on, 'and at the time you were probably right. Times have changed, but it's too late for me. I am tainted, irrevocably, and that is not a legacy I wish to pass on. I do not want Eve subjected to the whispers, the suspicion that I've pulled another fast one, the fear that she's me come again. Let her make her own choices, her own mistakes. I don't want her carrying mine.'

'You don't just want my advice,' said Aryel. Comprehension had settled over her now like a blanket, or a binding. 'You want the public association.'

'More even than that. She's going to be fabulously wealthy, and someone is going to have to teach her how to handle it. We both know it can't be me. But it can be her beloved Aunt Aryel, who is clever enough to train her well and is reputed to be one of the most ethical people on the planet. Even the worst thing you ever did ended up becoming another reason for people to love you, because you told the truth and you made amends. I could try that, of course, but it would probably take me another century to make up for the last one. I don't think I have that much time left. And I don't want Eve to have to wait.'

Aryel sat back in the chair, shaken to her soul, and realised that she was seriously considering Zavcka's proposition, and that Zavcka had known that she would; she had known that Aryel would have no choice.

'You may yet live for many, many years,' she said finally. 'And Eve may grow into someone who does not do things, maybe doesn't do *anything*, the way you would. She may break everything you ever built.'

'I understand that.'

'You're prepared to watch that happen?'

'Yes,' Zavcka said irritably, 'and if you don't believe me, ask Gabriel to sit in on our next conversation. He'll tell you.'

'Why, Zavcka? Why would you be okay with that?'

Zavcka Klist looked sharply at her, and then around at the shelves of books, the lone window, the gilt-framed pictures. Her gaze came back to Aryel, lingering on the gold-tinged bronze of her wings.

'One hundred and twenty years ago,' she said softly, 'there was a child I dreamed of being, but there was no room for that child in that age, no space for her to be. She never existed, and I grew out of the longing for her. I forgot – I forgot until twelve days ago, when I sat here' – she tapped at the tablet – 'and I saw that dead dream-child, alive. You think I may regret what she does when she grows into someone who isn't me? I don't believe I will, Aryel, but so what? So what if I don't approve? What does that matter? I don't want her to need my approval, or yours. She lives in an age that has space for her, and I want to see what she does with it.'

'It might have space for you too, now,' Aryel said. 'Space, and time.'

The older woman shook her head. 'This is a new era, and I do not think I will see it out. Nor, I suspect, will you. But Eve will. Eve will outlast us both, and that's good enough for me.'

THE END

ACKNOWLEDGEMENTS

Regeneration took its time coming into existence, and once again I am greatly indebted to everyone who was willing to talk through aspects of the book with me, and to read and respond to the first, dreadfully rough draft. If she were not already a legend, the inimitable Jo Fletcher would have earned her editorial stripes with this one, and I am deeply grateful for her guidance. Thanks also to Nicola Budd and Andrew Turner at Jo Fletcher Books, and to my agent Ian Drury.

One of the conceits of *Regeneration* is the notion of a disruptive technology that leads to transformation in the energy market; anyone interested in the current state of affairs would do well to read David JC MacKay's comprehensive but easily comprehensible book *Sustainable Energy – Without the Hot Air*, available as an ebook at withouthotair.com. My thanks to Anna Eagar for pointing me to it. I encountered the notion of quantum-energy storage in the essays *A Quantum Leap in Battery Design* by David Talbot (MIT Technology Review, 2009) and *Digital Batteries* by Alfred W. Hubler (Complexity, 2008) and ran with it; any resulting errors, embellishments, wild suppositions and flights of fancy are of course, all mine.

Stephanie Saulter
London, 2015